I0651964

BAD BILLIONAIRES 4

BILLIONAIRE'S CLUB 10-12

ELISE FABER

BAD BILLIONAIRES 4
BY ELISE FABER
Newsletter sign-up

This is a work of fiction. Names, places, characters, and events are fictitious in every regard. Any similarities to actual events and persons, living or dead, are purely coincidental. Any trademarks, service marks, product names, or named features are assumed to be the property of their respective owners, and are used only for reference. There is no implied endorsement if any of these terms are used. Except for review purposes, the reproduction of this book in whole or part, electronically or mechanically, constitutes a copyright violation.

BAD BILLIONAIRES 4
Copyright © 2022 Elise Faber
Print ISBN-13: 978-1-63749-068-6
Ebook ISBN-13: 978-1-63749-067-9
Cover Art by Jena Brignola

Bad Engagement

Billionaire's Club #10

BILLIONAIRE'S CLUB

BILLIONAIRE'S CLUB
CAST OF CHARACTERS

HEROES AND HEROINES:

Abigail Roberts (Bad Night Stand) — founding member of the Sextant, hates wine, loves crocheting

Jordan O'Keith (Bad Night Stand) — Heather's brother, former owner of RoboTech

Cecilia (CeCe) Thiele (Bad Breakup) — former nanny to Hunter, talented artist

Colin McGregor (Bad Breakup) — Scottish duke, owner of McGregor Enterprises

Heather O'Keith (Bad Husband) — CEO of RoboTech, Jordan's sister

Clay Steele (Bad Husband) — Heather's business rival, CEO of Steele Technologies

Kay (Bad Date) — romance writer, hates to be stood up

Garret Williams (Bad Date) — former rugby player

Rachel Morris (Bad Hookup) — Heather's assistant, super-powers include being ultra-organized

Sebastian (Bas) Scott (Bad Hookup) — Devon Scott's brother, Clay's assistant

Rebecca (Bec) Darden (Bad Divorce) — kickass lawyer, New York roots

Luke Pearson (Bad Divorce) — Southern gentleman, CEO Pearson Energies

Seraphina Delgado (Bad Fiancé) — romantic to the core, looks like a bombshell, but even prettier on the inside

Tate Connor (Bad Fiancé) — tech genius, scared to be burned by love

Lorelai (Bad Text) — drunk texts don't make her happy

Logan Smith (Bad Text) — former military, sometimes drunk texts are for the best

Kelsey Scott (Bad Boyfriend) — Bas and Devon's sister, engineer at RoboTech, brilliant

Tanner Pearson (Bad Boyfriend) — Bas and Devon's childhood friend, photographer

Trix Donovan (Bad Blind Date) — Heather's sister, Jordan's half-sister, nurse who worked in war zones, poverty-stricken areas, and abroad for almost a decade

Jet Hansen (Bad Blind Date) — a doctor Trix worked with

Molly Miller (Bad Wedding) — owner of Molly's, a kickass bakery in San Francisco

Jackson Davis (Bad Wedding) — Molly's ex-fiancé

Kate McLeod (Bad Engagement) — Kelsey's college friend, advertiser extraordinaire, loves purple and Hermione Granger

Jaime Huntingon (Bad Engagement) — vet, does excellent man-bun

ADDITIONAL CHARACTERS:

George O'Keith — Jordan's dad

Hunter O'Keith — Jordan's nephew

Bridget McGregor — Colin's mom
Lena McGregor — Colin's sister
Bobby Donovan — Heather's half and Trix's full brother
Frances and Sugar Delgado — Sera's parents
Devon Scott — Kels and Bas's brother
Becca Scott — Kels and Bas's sister in law
Heidi Greene — Kels' friend since college
Cora Hutchins — Kels' friend since childhood

ONE

D isgusted, she walked out of the bakery.

Mostly with herself for being jealous of the clearly happy couple.

Although, partly because they were so *ridiculously* happy. Come *on*. Who looked into each other's eyes with such devotion and joy while getting married in a freaking bakery with mostly strangers looking on?

No white dress or cake—counterintuitive as that sounded, considering they were getting married in a freaking bakery.

No flowers, which would be Kate's weakness because she loved gardening and arranging flowers, having spent most of her extra money on sprucing up her back yard.

The inside might be a bit of a disaster.

But the back yard was a lush, gorgeous retreat.

Not that it mattered because she didn't have anyone to share it with. Least of all, a gorgeous hunk of a man who stared at her with love in his eyes and tenderness in his smile.

Yes, she was bitter.

So, it was the perfect time for her cell to ring, her mother on the line.

Deal with the torture now? Or wait until it frothed to full power later?

She was already cranky and jaded and in a bad mood, so she might as well deal with her loving, but very nosy and interfering mother now. No sense in wasting a good mood later.

Because there *would* be a later.

Her mother loved her, that was never in doubt. What could *possibly* be questioned was the amount of attention she gave to her grown children's lives.

Attention that was now squarely focused on Kate.

On the fact that she was single when her two younger siblings were happily married, and her younger sister had recently popped out a kid.

Impressive. Beautiful—which she knew because she'd been in the delivery room.

But also . . . not *her*.

Hence, the increase in motherly calling.

Sighing, Kate swiped a finger across the screen and put her phone to her ear. "Hey, Mom."

"I've got the perfect man for you to bring to the Christmas party. He's a doctor and . . ."

Her mother continued talking, expounding on all of the wonderfulness that was this doctor. The trouble was that Kate was done with being set up. Her family was great at finding their own soul mates, their own happily ever afters . . . unfortunately, that same ability didn't extend to her.

Either *by* her or *for* her.

It never failed to end in disaster. Both for her *and* for her date.

So, as much as she longed to have a man she could call her

own, one who'd call her his in return . . . she was taking a break from dating, from men, and most definitely from being set up.

"Mom," she began. "I'm not actually—"

"He's a doctor, isn't bald, and can have a conversation about something other than himself, Katie," her mother said. "He is a catch."

Who would turn into the world's worst asshole when he was around her.

Because that was her superpower.

Transforming seemingly *wonderful* men into lying, cheating, arrogant, self-centered, mansplaining, assholes.

And being that lightning didn't tend to strike the same place multiple times, Kate had decided on a hiatus from the opposite sex. Some time to sort out what was happening inside of her to make everyone she dated turn into a jerk.

This wasn't about all men on the planet being the bad guys, or her always picking wrong, or even about her family trying to set her up with a bunch of douche canoes. There was something wrong inside of *her*, something intrinsically wrong with the way she interacted with the men in her life.

So, a break.

Time to figure her shit out.

It was just . . . Christmas.

All of her family in one place. The huge party with the whole neighborhood. Everyone paired off and happy and gathering under the mistletoe her mother hung in each and every doorway.

And her.

Alone.

The pitying gazes plentiful.

Or worse . . . the copious conversations where all the happy people constantly threw every single male with half a brain cell in Kate's direction.

My cousin is in town and fresh out of a relationship . . .

I have a coworker who's new to the area. He's looking for someone . . .

My ex-husband would be perfect for you—no really, he's actually a great guy . . .

And more.

Kate just couldn't take it, couldn't stand the idea of another Christmas party at her parents' house matched with someone who didn't fit her, or worse, spending the entire extravaganza alone and in the corner, playing wallflower.

She wanted excitement.

She wanted someone who could be unequivocally hers.

She wanted someone who saw inside her and didn't run off in a panic.

". . . and Katie, love, he's going to be at dinner this Friday so that you two can get to know each other better—"

Fucking hell.

Family dinner *and* the Christmas Extravaganza?

Please. God. *No.*

"Um, Mom—"

"Remember he's got all his hair—"

"Actually, Mom. I'm kind of seeing—"

"And his stomach doesn't hang over his belt—"

"That's not—I don't really care about that—"

"*And* he's got the loveliest blue—"

"I'm engaged!" she screamed, cutting off her mother's soliloquy of all things doctor, and successfully drawing the attention of random strangers on the sidewalk. Which was a hard thing to do in San Francisco—because it was San Francisco, and these streets had seen a lot of shit—but also could only further confirm that she'd screamed it like a complete and total lunatic.

Shrieking *I'm engaged* on street corners.

What every man wanted.

It was a wonder she was single.

"Katie?" her mom asked. "Did you say you're engaged?"

No. No, she wasn't. Not even close. She was on a break from anyone with a Y chromosome, mostly to save them from herself.

But also . . . there was joy in her mom's tone.

Absolute joy that she had never heard directed at her. She'd heard it leveled toward her siblings. To her brother, when he'd announced he was proposing to Steph, who was really fucking cool and way too good for her brother—something he'd be the first to admit . . . because he was really fucking cool. She'd heard it expounded lavishly again at his wedding this last summer (during which Kate had spent her time fending off the worst setup of all setups, The Can't Take No For An Answer Setup). And obviously, it had rung with crystal clarity in her ears when her sister had announced she was pregnant, and again after her adorable niece had been born.

But her mom had *never* given it to Kate.

Which was probably the reason she let the crazy keep rolling along instead of stopping the joy in its tracks with the truth.

Why instead of saying, "No, Mom. You heard wrong," she said, "Yes, I am, and you'll get to meet him Friday at dinner."

Horror flowed through her as intensely as her mother's excitement poured through the airwaves, expressing her *joy* at meeting him, her *joy* at Kate having finally found a slice of her own happy.

"What's his name, honey?"

Oh fuck.

"What's that?" Kate asked, panic swarming to overtake horror. "You're breaking up."

Oh shit. *Oh shit.* She hadn't thought this through. She needed—

"I asked his name—"

"Hello?" More panic. More horror. More pretending the call was cutting out because she had to end this conversation now.

Hell, she should have never picked up the call in the first place. "Mom? *Hello?*"

"Katie!"

Shit. Shit. *Shit.* "I can't hear you," she said. "If you can hear me, I'll call you later." She hung up.

Call her later.

Ha.

More like never.

As in, she'd *never* call her family again. As in, she was moving to a deserted island and changing her name and living off the grid in a tent with the most technically advanced thing being one of those compostable toilets.

Fuck.

She hated camping.

Which meant . . . she'd be there at the family dinner.

Because despite all of the setups and the pity and the fact that they'd found their happy, she loved her family. So. Damned. Much. And she also loved that stupid fucking Christmas party, even when she was lonely.

"*Ugh.*" Kate groaned, feet sliding to a stop on that dirty San Franciscan sidewalk.

She had a choice here.

She also knew she wasn't going to make the right one.

Because, instead of calling her mother back and telling her that she wasn't engaged, Kate opened Instagram, tapped on the profile of a man she'd been following for a while now, who'd followed her back and commented on a few of her posts, and . . . sent a message.

Later, she'd want to pretend she'd been drinking.

But in *that* moment, the only thing she was consumed with was desperation.

And lust. She couldn't deny lust was also her downfall.

Because surprisingly, shockingly, *insanely* the man from social media, the one whose abs had made her fall just a little in love with him, who had an actual man bun, but not one of those gross, greasy ones that looked like octopus tentacles—a nice one, sleek and shiny and way better than any bun she could wrestle her own locks into. But anyway, that handsome stranger . . .

He said yes.

And suddenly, Kate had a fiancé.

Two

KATE

"What am I doing?" she asked herself two days later. "Oh my God, what am I doing?"

She was going on her first date . . . with her fiancé.

Incongruous.

She couldn't believe that *JaimetheVet*—his Insta handle—and Jaime, her fake fiancé, and Jaime, the man whose last name she didn't know, had agreed to the plan. Moreover, she couldn't believe she was going.

He might be a serial killer.

He might drug her drink, bring her home, and tie her up in his basement.

Except, homes in California didn't usually have basements, so that was probably unlikely. And pretty though he may be, she couldn't imagine that Jaime the Vet was lying in wait for potential victims to DM him and ask him to agree to an elaborate ruse as someone's fiancé.

Which brought her back to . . . why had he agreed to do this in the first place?

Her phone chimed with the alarm she'd set for herself, the one whose label said, "Will You Stay Or Will You Go?" and Kate knew she had to stop thinking herself into knots and start making decisions.

Was she going through with the insanity?

No, she couldn't.

Except . . . she didn't want to stand him up. Jaime the Vet seemed really nice.

On his Instagram page.

Which wasn't real. Which was made up of carefully curated parts of people's lives designed to look their best.

Her phone chimed.

Another alarm she'd set earlier—this one labeled with "No, Kate You Really Need To Decide!"—had gone off.

"Dammit, woman," she whispered. "Come on. Enough waffling."

Sighing, she stared at herself in the mirror. Red hair, but not a pretty red, boring brown eyes, nice lips—even her critical inner voice had to admit her mouth was great, no doubt her best feature. Lush, perfectly formed, and currently outlined in the perfect shade of red lipstick. Having the skin she did, along with the non-pretty shade of red hair, had made finding that perfect shade of red lipstick a monumental task, and one she'd only found recently, thanks to her friend Heidi and an extremely patient makeup atten-dant at one of the wall-to-wall beauty stores in the mall.

Twenty-two testers until the Holy Grail had been located.

Firecrotch.

Crude, but perfect.

Some would say that was the perfect description of *her*.

"Ha," she muttered, eyes drifting down the sleek black wrap dress she was wearing. A simple design. It flattered the good parts—boobs, ass—and hid the bad parts—the little pooch below her belly button that never seemed to go away no matter how much hard work she put in at the gym.

Could be that she liked tacos and wine too much, but for the life of her—and it would be a sad, meaningless one if she had to live without tacos and wine—she couldn't give them up.

Crunchy or soft, red or white, boxed or out of the bottle, from Taco Bell or from the legit hole-in-the-wall restaurant around the corner from her apartment.

Her standards were low.

Fill her belly, give her a buzz, and she was golden.

She was also delaying, because she knew what she was going to do. It was why she'd done her makeup, her hair, why she'd gotten dressed and slipped on her favorite heels.

It was Thursday.

Family dinner was tomorrow.

And she wanted to keep that joy in her Mom's tone. Look, she wasn't a saint, she wasn't going to pretend her actions were purely altruistic, but she just wanted to fit in with her family for once.

Not be the odd man out.

Not be the single lady at the couple's party.

She wanted to just . . . be.

Not to mention that Jaime the Vet was hot—a sexy, brown-haired Viking with a man bun that made her jealous, who took care of puppies and kitties and the occasional bearded dragon, based on his pics.

Puppies and kitties and bearded dragons. Who could resist?

Especially when the last picture of a bearded dragon that she'd seen had been wearing a crocheted purple vest.

"I mean, come on," she muttered, turning away from the mirror and picking up her purse. Because for all her prevaricating, the truth was that she'd always been planning on going.

She headed down the hall, toward the front door.

"Okay, Kate McLeod," she said out loud to herself, pausing with her hand on the knob. "This isn't a big deal. First, suss out he's not going to take me home and bury me in his nonexistent basement. *Then* we go to one family dinner together and one Christmas party. After which I fake an implosive fight and we both go on our separate ways." Purse over her arm, firm nod in agreement already halfway complete. "There. Done."

Straightening her shoulders, she tugged open the door and stepped out onto the porch.

Jaime the Vet.

She hoped he came with animals.

———

He did not, in fact, come with animals.

He did not, in fact, come at all.

And as she sat at the table by herself, having long ago consumed the entire breadbasket, her heart sinking, her inner critic grew exponentially in volume because . . . *of course* he wouldn't come. She was a strange woman who'd asked via freaking direct message to pretend to be her fiancé for a week.

That was a special brand of psycho.

Men like Jaime the Vet did not voluntarily sign up for that particular brand of cray cray.

Would it have just been nicer for him to ignore her message?

Or to just say no?

Fuck yes, it would have been.

But alas, not all on the Instagram was real, and then there was her superpower—the one that turned nice men into assholes.

It was probably some compulsion she'd woven through the airwaves, a subliminal message hidden in between the letters saying, "Turn into a lying, evil bastard upon reading this message."

Or . . . there could be something in the bread.

Or it could be the third glass of wine.

"Did you want to order?" the nice waitress, who'd been patiently refilling the breadbasket all evening, asked.

Kate sighed, part of her wanting to slink home and feel sorry for herself. The rest of her figured she'd done her hair, put on a dress and heels, was wearing her fancy red lipstick, so yes, she should just order a plate of expensive pasta, another glass of wine, and carbo-load away her happiness.

Hell, she might even live extra vicariously and order a slice of that chocolate cake she'd seen float by on a tray earlier.

"Yes," she said decisively. "I'll have the pasta al pomodoro."

"Me, too."

Lightning.

Like that image from the Marvel movie, Thor lifting his hammer up to the sky, a deluge of electricity exploding from the clouds to coalesce on his weapon.

His voice did that to her.

Collided with her nape, exploded out through her limbs, firing her nerve endings, bringing them to rigid awareness as that deep rumble filled her ears.

"Sorry," the waitress said, sounding a little dazed, and Kate couldn't blame her, not when her cells felt like they'd been lit up like glow sticks at a rave. "What was that?" the waitress asked.

"I'll have what she's having," that sexy male voice said, and Kate was still reeling from it when he moved around the table and sat down in the chair opposite her. "Hi," he murmured, as the waitress nodded and slipped away. Kate barely noticed, not when he was beyond fucking sexy with that rueful smile on his lips. "I'm really sorry I'm late."

Heat. Desire.

That fucking man bun.

Then her mind cleared. Because late? *Late?*

Kate glared over at him and grabbed the last roll, tearing a huge bite off with her teeth. "This is mine," she snapped. Or well, tried to anyway, the words came out muffled. "I can't believe you almost stood me up."

Pale brown eyes dimmed. "Damn. You didn't get my message." He ignored her warning and reached across the table, snagged a piece of the roll. "I'm sorry, Red," he murmured, popping it into his mouth.

Anger gave way to confusion. "Um, what?"

He chewed and swallowed then nodded at her purse. "I'm guessing you didn't check your messages."

As a matter of fact . . . she hadn't.

"There was a complication with my last surgery of the day. I had to stay late, make sure he was okay," he said. "I didn't have your number, so I couldn't call, but I sent you a message on Insta. But when I didn't hear back, saw it seemed like you hadn't read it in the app, I worried you'd be here, and . . ."

"You came to check," she whispered. Confusion gave way to melting.

As in, she went melty inside. Shit.

"I didn't want you to be sitting here alone." His eyes drifted to the empty breadbasket, the drained wineglass. "I see I was too late anyway."

Regret in his tone, those brown eyes soft.

"It's okay," she murmured. "It's my fault. I should have thought to check."

The waitress came back then, two glasses of wine in her hand and another basket. See? She was damned good.

"Thank you," he said, smiling that wide gorgeous smile, and the waitress blinked as she left.

Kate was doing some blinking of her own. He was wearing a nice, but slightly wrinkled, blue button-down and jeans, hair-covered ones if the slight glimpse of his leg she'd gotten held true. There was stubble on his jaw, lines of fatigue surrounding his eyes.

He'd had a long day but still came to check on her.

A stranger.

A good guy.

"Were the complications serious?" she asked, heart twisting. Because she was worried about the animal, not the fact that she might fall for the good guy.

"Not great," he said. "Turns out, the little man has an underlying heart condition. It will take some further steps to determine the cause and follow-up treatment."

"Poor guy," she murmured.

"He's a tough one." Jaime smiled. "But he was soaking up all the extra attention like a champ. When I left, he was trying to crawl into my tech's pocket."

She pushed the bread in his direction, placed her own roll on her plate, pretending she had manners for at least a few moments. Then she asked, "Was the little attention mooch a dog or a cat?"

Must be a small one if he was trying to crawl into pockets.

Maybe a teacup poodle?

Or it could be a non-furry critter, another bearded dragon.

Jaime's lips curved further. "Oh, Hank is a guinea pig. We call him Hank the Tank because he eats like crazy but is really small for his variety." He picked up his roll. "His favorite snacks are kale stems and cantaloupe."

A guinea pig named Hank the Tank, who liked kale and cantaloupe.

"Does he wear a vest?" she asked, heart already squee-ing in anticipation.

"No," Jaime said. "But he does have a tiny bowtie collar."

And *boom*, just like that, her ovaries exploded under the power of squeedom.

THREE

JAIME

He stared across the table at a woman he probably should have avoided at all costs.

She'd asked him to participate in a scheme that involved lying to her family. Maybe he could have justified it because who cared, he was lying to people he didn't know, wouldn't know again, but he was a man who preferred honesty.

Had the lying ex once, got the souvenir T-shirt, wasn't going to visit again.

That alone should have been enough ammunition for him to not reply to the message in the first place, let alone agree to the deception.

Except . . . he'd been following *KateMcFunPants* on Instagram for more than a year now.

She was the friend of a friend—apparently worked in the marketing department of Steele Technologies, a large tech company headquartered in San Francisco. His friend, Ben, was friends with Sebastian, a higher-up at the company, and Ben had been photographed with Sebastian and Kate(*McFunPants*) at a few events together. Jaime had been intoxicated first by her mouth, spread wide in a million-dollar smile, then had latched onto her eyes, her curvy body, and he'd followed her. She'd reciprocated, and they'd liked a few of each other's posts—not an obsessive amount going back months and years, but a few here and there.

This was romance in the age of social media, and it was important to use the proper amount of creepage . . . at least publicly.

Because privately?

He'd gone *way* back, far enough to see her feed dotted with more events from Steele Technologies and ex-boyfriends and girls' nights, but he hadn't liked anything from then. He'd been playing the long game—slow and steady, get her comfortable, then boom, swoop in for a date and have her fall for him.

He'd commented on the meme she'd made of fantasy versus reality—in her case a picture of her at goat yoga juxtaposed with one of a model for the company. The half of the meme that featured Kate was an action shot, a goat perched on her head, eating her tank top, as her hands slipped out from beneath her during downward dog. Her expression, along with the goat's, was hilarious, and so far removed from the model's that he'd actually laughed out loud as he'd gotten off BART.

That had earned a few dirty looks in the otherwise quiet train and station, but frankly, the denizens of this city had seen far worse.

She'd liked his comments, and communications had increased.

Date night was in the near future.

At least, that was how it had gone in his head.

But it seemed to be destined to continue that way—remain in his mind and not in real life—unless he got his head out of his ass and pulled the trigger on the whole date thing. The problem was that he was a bit gun shy. Which was the point where his brain circled back to his lying ex and the reason for being gun shy in the first place. They'd originally connected on the 'gram and that had ended . . .

Well, a heat sinking missile had nothing on him and Lori.

Kate was staring up at him with big brown eyes, her long red hair tucked behind one ear, and he was struck again by how pretty she was. And he didn't mean that in a shallow, asshole way, like a woman's worth was only measured in the way she looked. Jaime meant that there was something warm and comforting and just really nice inside her, and it seeped through her smile, shone through those golden-brown eyes, and it felt good to have it directed at him.

Even when she was looking accusingly over her roll at him.

So much so that he found he couldn't resist the urge to tease her. He reached out and snagged another piece of that roll she was so protective of.

"Hey!" she gasped.

He grinned. "I think we missed a few steps."

"Like you eating your *own* roll?" She shoved the basket at him.

"Like me saying, *Hi, Kate, it's nice to meet you,*" he said.

She'd sucked in a breath, no doubt to berate him about the roll, but froze when he spoke. Then made a face. It was fucking cute, that little wrinkle over the bridge of her nose. A heartbeat later, it disappeared, her expression smoothing out, and she sighed. "Damn," she said. "We did miss that part, didn't we?"

Jaime shrugged. "Fiancés don't normally need introductions."

Her cheeks colored, but she kept her eyes on his. "You know, you don't have to do this."

Another shrug. "I know."

"Then why *are* you?"

That was the question of the hour, wasn't it?

He hesitated and then figured the best course was to just tell her the truth, albeit a non-stalking of her Instagram profile version of the truth. "You're gorgeous, and you seem nice, and I'd be lying if I said I wasn't hoping to find a way to ask you on a date."

Her mouth dropped open. "You?" A shake of her head. "Me? A date?"

Shit. He hadn't gotten the non-creepy vibe down. Jaime cleared his throat. "Yeah, and well, my family is . . . complicated, and I figured yours must be the same if you were asking, and also that you wouldn't have asked unless you'd gotten pretty far down your list and were getting really desperate."

The roll fell from her hand to the plate. "Desperate?" she parroted.

"Yeah, I mean—" He shrugged. "I'm not exactly—um—" Double shit. He was fucking this up, making it weird. "It's just we're not exactly friends, and . . . well I—"

Cursing inwardly, knowing he wasn't making any sense, Jaime picked up his own roll, cut it in half so he could lather it with butter. When he risked a glance at Kate, he saw she was studying him closely.

"Insecurity knows no bounds, does it?" she said, and it wasn't pity but rather warmth in her eyes. "You were the only person I asked, Jaime. I've been fantasizing about you for months." A self-deprecating shrug. "Well, about you and your adorable little animals you take care of on a daily basis."

Her admission relaxed him, and lips curving, he admitted something he had only told a few close buddies. "I only take pictures with the cute ones. The ugly and mean ones don't merit a selfie."

She smiled at him, and he felt it right in the pit of his stomach. "That's terrible."

He pulled up the sleeve of his shirt. "The ones who scratch me don't get photo ops either."

"Ouch." She reached across the table, brushed her fingers

lightly over the injury. The scrapes weren't deep, and while the injury had hurt like hell when it had happened—courtesy of claws from a mean old senior cat with a toothache—the scratches hadn't needed much more than a good cleaning. "Why do you do it?" she asked, pulling her hand back.

"The pictures? Or the animals?" he asked.

"The pictures." A shake of her head paired with a sheepish smile. "Both."

"I'll tell you all," he said, deliberately making his tone sound like one of those late-night psychics. "But I need you to tell me something first." He tilted his head to the side. "Well, no, *two* things."

She ran her fingers through the long red strands of her hair, tucked a few pieces that had come lose back behind her ear. "What are they?"

"First, what's your last name?"

A flash of that pretty, generous smile. "McLeod." A beat. "Yours?"

"Huntington."

She tilted her head to the side. "Fits." A nod. "And the second thing?"

"Was I really the first person you asked?"

Gentle golden-brown eyes, a soft curve to her lips. "Yes, Jaime," she murmured. "The first one. The only one." White teeth closing over a plump red bottom lip. "I wasn't lying before. You're not the only one who's done some Insta fantasizing."

"I—"

But whatever he was going to say—and fuck if he knew what he'd been about to force out—was lost when the waitress set down a plate in front of Kate then an identical one in front of him.

"You guys have everything you need?" she asked.

"Yes, thank you," they said at almost the same time.

The waitress left, and Jaime found himself staring at Kate,

the steam from the pasta wafting up and coating his face. But he barely felt it because he couldn't believe she'd asked him first.

They had a connection.

He'd been discounting it because . . . well, social media wasn't real life.

He'd been discounting it because he'd thought that no way could she be into him, not like he was into her.

He'd been discounting it because . . . he'd been off his game for months.

"You didn't answer my question," she said, twining some pasta around her fork.

"Which one?"

"Why you do the whole social media Jaime the Vet thing?"

"Oh." He picked up his own fork. "At first, it was just exciting to have animals to work on, and I wanted to document it. Also"—he grinned, thinking of his mom and her demand for information about his life. She was great, but sometimes needy, and it had been an easy way for her to stay in the loop without having to call her every day—"for my parents. They liked knowing what was up, and it was better than them hounding me about my dating life."

She chuckled as she brought her fork to her mouth, the bite of pasta hitting her tongue, drawing his attention to those plump lips as she chewed and swallowed, a soft moan drifting through the air.

A soft moan that was way too sexy for a first date.

Although . . . not too sexy for a fiancé?

No. Mentally, he smacked himself. Fake fiancé. The keyword being *fake*.

"I know all about families and pushy," she said, pulling him out of all thoughts fake. "I'm the oldest sibling and the only single one. *Oh, the humanity!*" Her lips quirked when she rested the back of her hand on her forehead, *a la* fainting Hollywood starlet of the past. Then she sighed, and a little sad crept into her eyes. "I don't necessarily *want* to be single, but—" She lifted and dropped one shoulder. "Sometimes things don't always work out the way we want."

"I feel that."

A sigh before she set her fork down and then lightly clapped her hands together. "Okay, so here is your last chance to run away or to demand an exorbitant payment in exchange for playing my fake fiancé."

"I thought we covered that already. I'm happy to play your fake fiancé."

Brown eyes narrowed. "Just like that? No ulterior motives, no secret basement with a cabinet full of serial killer tools?"

"Just like that," he said. "And my condo doesn't have a basement."

She began winding pasta around her fork again. "I noticed that you didn't address the ulterior motive piece of my statement."

A snort. "I already told you I wanted a date." He waved a hand at the table, the plates, the glasses of wine. "Thus, my ulterior motive satisfied."

"Hmm."

She put the bite into her mouth, and he took the opportunity to do the same. The pasta was good, great even, but he could barely taste it. Not when his focus was so firmly on the woman across from him. Fascinating. Beautiful. Empathetic. Nice.

And quiet.

Just a little quiet, as though she didn't mind short stretches of silence.

It was nice, that quiet. Peaceful, not oppressive. *She* was nice.

She set her fork down, eyes going wide, and he felt a blip of alarm travel through him. "What?" he asked.

"I just realized that if we're doing this, there is so much I need to brief you on. My family. My parents. My siblings—"

"That's the definition of family, right?" he teased.

"Shush, you," she said, though her smile was teasing the corners of her lips up. "But also, yes, I guess that's what I meant by family."

"Can't we play it by ear?" he asked. "It's only two dinners."

"They're going to interrogate you." She groaned. "They're going to want all the details of how we met and our first date and —oh God!—my friends. You haven't met my friends. They don't know anything about you, and they know *everything*." She picked up her fork, shoved a bite of pasta into her mouth, all while shaking her head fiercely. Once she'd swallowed, she shook her head firmly once more, scattering her hair over her shoulders. "We can't do this. *I* can't do this. It's insanity. I just need to come clean."

He didn't want her to come clean. He *wanted* more time with her. "It's two dinners."

"I—"

He shrugged. "I can manage two dinners, Kate."

"You haven't met my family."

Laughter bubbled up in his chest. "Ditto." He reached across the table, squeezed her hand. "How about you pretend two dinners are my ulterior motive?"

She frowned.

"Two more dates," he explained. "That aren't family dinners. That are just you and me getting to know one another. *That* will be payment for your favor."

"Deception with a side of ulterior?"

His lips twitched. "Seems fitting, yeah?"

"Yeah," she agreed. "Or maybe it's dinner with a side of engagement?"

The laughter didn't just bubble up this time, it burst right out of him. "Yes," he said through it. "That's exactly it."

"Damn." She made a face.

His amusement cut off. "What?"

"You're even nicer than I expected."

"Is that a bad thing?"

"Only that"—she shook her head—"never mind, it's a silly thought."

"No." His hand found hers again. "What is it?"

A forkful of pasta into her mouth, her words muffled. "Really," she said, "it doesn't matter."

"We can't start off a fake engagement on a lie."

Her mouth fell open, a strangled sound emerging. "What? That doesn't even make sense."

"Sure, it does." He snagged her roll again, brought it up to his mouth like he was going to eat it, and her gasp of outrage made it clear that was the best ransom around. "Tell me," he ordered.

She frowned. "So, sexy, smart, funny, nice, rocks a perfect man bun, and also a blackmailer."

"Fiancés should discover these things about each other." He shrugged, forced himself to bite back his smile when she rolled her eyes. "See, Red? We've made progress in our deception."

She snagged the much-abused roll back. "Mine." A bite. "And also, I was thinking that nice never lasts, okay?" She took another bite, chewed and swallowed, deliberately changing the subject. "Okay, so I'm the oldest of three. What about you? How many siblings do you have?"

Jaime knew he had a choice. Push or let it go.

Pushing might destroy the fragile bond they were just beginning to build. Pushing might mean he'd never get to his other plans—that being, how to get more than two dates with this smart, lovely woman sitting across from him. Pushing might mean that he'd never get a chance to turn fake into real.

So, he let it go.

And then he told her about his family.

Four

KATE

H e'd paid the bill, like it was a legitimate date.

He'd talked about his family with equal parts love and exasperation. That was such a familiar feeling and one that made her like him even more.

It made him dangerous, the degree with which she liked him, and yet she also wanted to live in the moment, wanted to grasp on to that floating feeling of a new relationship.

When everything was all puppy dogs and rainbows and fun.

Before it deteriorated and the asshole appeared.

"Can I—?" She blinked out of her woolgathering, saw that Jaime was gesturing at her hand, asking to hold it.

Her ovaries were already dead and gone from one bowtie wearing guinea pig and kind brown eyes, and now her heart spasmed.

Fuck, he was nice.

She nodded, and he laced his fingers with hers. Such a simple touch, but it still took her breath away. His hand engulfed hers, the sensation from the roughness of his palm rubbing against the softness of hers. It raised the hairs on her arm, made heat drift down her spine, slid in—

"Your fingers are cold," he murmured, wrapping his other hand around hers and bringing it up to his mouth, blowing warm air over her skin.

She shivered.

"That's not all that's cold," he said, dropping her hand and shrugging out of his jacket. He dropped it over her shoulders, covering the thin wrap she'd donned but that didn't do much to protect her from the cool evening air. "As much as I hate to cover up that pretty dress," he whispered in her ear, "I can't have you turning into a popsicle." Then slipped an arm around her waist and tugged her against his side.

Being there, pressed against the hard of his muscles, the spicy male scent surrounding her, his arm a hot brand around her middle, meant it took a few moments for her to whisper, "I wasn't actually cold. I just like the way your hand feels against mine."

A soft admission. One she almost couldn't believe she'd spoken aloud.

But then again, nothing about this entire scenario was believable.

He didn't say anything for a moment. "Are you too hot now?"

She shook her head.

"Then it's win-win for both of us."

Smiling, she snuggled closer, and when he asked if she wanted to walk down to the waterfront, she agreed even though her feet were killing her. "Why does it feel like I've known you for more than one date?" she blurted.

His fingers tightened on her waist. "Because we're fake engaged?"

Kate snorted. "Somehow I doubt that's it."

"Because you're really into me?" he teased.

"I'm really into your Instagram profile, that's for sure," she teased back. "All of those animals." A shrug. "And I guess that fact that you're in them too is fine."

He tickled her lightly. "I feel the same."

She tapped her chin, teasing aside, it was a legitimate thought. She never felt this comfortable with men after just a few hours. There was just something about Jaime that made her feel like she'd arrived home. "Maybe it's because we're both part of big families?"

"Big, *nosy* families?"

"Yeah, that, too. Wait. Come this way," she said, pointing to a walkway when he was going to miss the best part of this area. After they'd rounded the building and slid into a little alcove that overlooked the perches where the sea lions liked to rest during the day, but for now was beautifully illuminated by the bright moon overhead, she said, "Well, either way, I'm just really thankful that you agreed to my scheme. I know it's wrong to lie to my parents, but I just want . . ."

Ick. It made her sound like a total wimp to admit that she didn't want to disappoint them. But . . . it was the truth. She'd disappointed them far too often in her life.

"When your family is close, it's hard to feel like you're not meeting their expectations."

A sigh. "Yeah. That."

And also, maybe *that* was the fact that this man had led her over to a bench and was cuddling her close.

Because *that* was incredible.

Big body. Warm hands. Intoxicating smell. Gentle words. Soft hold.

Jaime was a cornucopia of her fantasies come to life.

"What else should a fake fiancé know about his woman?" he asked when they sat in quiet for a couple of minutes.

Kate thought for a few seconds. "Her favorite color is purple. She likes sunflowers and loves Hermione Granger. She can't stand tomatoes but loves all things marinara and ketchup." She nudged his shoulder. "How about you? What should I know about my fake significant other? Besides his amazing blackmail abilities and his abuse of my roll."

A grin that hit her right in the gut, his voice close to her ear and making her shiver all over again. "Well, his favorite color is red. He's partial to dogs over cats and will eat anything as long as he can drown it in ketchup."

She fist-pumped. "Ketchup buddies."

"I can see it now," he said, spreading the hand that wasn't resting on her waist wide as though he were a director painting the scene for his actors. And maybe he was, for all that she'd had fun the last few hours, the crux of what was between them *was* just acting. "We fell in love at first sight when we both reached for the same ketchup bottle at the diner."

"Our hands touched." She reached out, squeezed his fingers, forced herself to keep her tone light. "And sparks flew."

His voice dropped, a silken thread sliding across the back of her neck. "And that was it for me," he murmured, tugging her closer and resting his chin on the top of her head. "I somehow convinced you to give me your number. The rest is history."

A blip of disappointment slid through her. Not because she didn't like the story, but because she liked it too much.

"Exactly," she said, straightening, sliding from his hold, and pushing to her feet. "But we should get going. I have to work at least half a day tomorrow."

"About that," he said. "What time is dinner? Should I pick you up so we can drive together?"

She nodded. "Yes. That sounds good. Dinner is at seven-thirty, but we should try to be there by about six-thirty. Want to pick me up at my place? It's only a half hour drive, even with Friday traffic."

"I can do that." He pushed to his feet, reached for her hand. "I'll be there at six and we can drive over."

"You sure?" Kate asked. "Last chance to run screaming for the hills."

"I'm sure."

"You don't have any temperamental cats on the schedule?"

He grinned and she melted from the inside out, letting him tug her to her feet, reveling in the feel of his warm, rough palm against hers. This might all be pretend, but there was one thing that wasn't fake—the way her body responded. She enjoyed the contact, felt comfortable with him touching her. Okay, so *more* than comfortable. She freaking loved it, wanted to strip off his clothes and see if his abs were as good as his pictures, wanted to feel the strands of his hair brushing across her stomach as he kissed his way down.

A shiver, even with his coat.

"Come on," he murmured. "Let's get you out of the cold."

Not about to confess why she'd shivered this time, Kate leaned close when he wrapped his arm around her waist, walked beside him as they made their way back to her car. "So, no cats?" she asked, after he'd inquired about where she was parked, and had turned them in the direction of it with the confidence of someone who'd lived in the city for a long time.

"Maybe one or two," he said, tracing. "But I definitely have a temperamental chicken."

Her feet skidded to a halt and she tugged him to a stop. When pale brown eyes drifted down to hers, she placed her hand on his chest in a movement that felt natural and yet also far too intimate. But when she made as though to pull back, he placed his palm over her fingers, pressed lightly to keep her hand there.

Her pulse fluttered, but she forced herself to say, "Explain."

The ghost of a smile. "About the chicken?"

She huffed. "Obviously."

"I'll tell you as we walk," he said, urging her forward.

Narrowing her eyes in mock-warning, she started moving

again. "You'd better. What's the temperamental chicken's name?"

"Barry."

Her feet threatened to stop again, but his arm just tightened, hand coaxing her forward. "Tut. Tut. No stopping. My woman is cold."

Another shiver, this one caused not by her brain and its fantasies, but by the notes of heat beneath that phrase *my woman*. In another world. In her dreams. In a fake lie that . . .

"Well, my *man* doesn't give orders," she countered.

He burst out laughing. "Maybe more accurate would be to say that my woman doesn't listen to orders."

She chuckled. "That would be the truth."

"So, you want to hear about Barry the Chicken?"

"That may be my favorite question that anyone has ever asked me."

He snorted. "Is that a yes?"

Her fingers tightened on his chest, pressing against his skin, feeling the steady *thrum-thrum* of his heart beneath. "That's a yes." She grinned up at him, rising on tiptoe, wanting to see his face clearly when he told her the story. Except, she miscalculated and lost her balance, falling against him, her breasts pressed to his chest.

She gasped, nipples hardening, fingers clenching. "Jaime—"

In a move so quick that she could barely process it, she suddenly found her back pressed against the cool stucco of the building they were walking next to. He'd slid an arm behind her back, cushioning her against the hardness of the wall, and his body was pressed to hers, so hot, so hard, surrounding her, overwhelming her, making her head spin, her nipples ache, her thighs quiver.

"I want to kiss you."

It wasn't phrased as a question, but rather a statement. As

thus, it took her a moment to process his words, especially with him all warm and hard against her.

"Okay," she whispered.

His mouth was on hers.

No hesitation. No long, slow descent.

One second she was pushing the assent out of her lips, the next, his tongue was in her mouth, stroking along hers, his free hand on her cheek, angling her head so he could taste her properly.

It was a whirlwind, that kiss.

Not gentle or teasing. Not like a typical first date peck.

This was domination. This surrounded her, took her over, filled her with fire that threatened to incinerate her from the inside out.

Then it was done.

He shifted back minutely, slid the hand on her face down her arm, her side, resting it on her hip. But he kept his body against hers, and the feel of him was enough to take her breath away. "Want to hear about Barry the Chicken?"

Her fingers were in his hair, mussing the neatly organized locks when they clenched at the husky question. "No."

One eyebrow lifted. "No?"

Kate rose onto her tiptoes. "No," she murmured. "*I'd* rather kiss *you*."

And then she put words to action.

Luckily, Jaime didn't seem to mind.

FIVE

JAIME

It had been a spectacular first date.

And he'd been engaged for the entirety of it.

Snorting, he made a few notes in the computer and thought of the snap he'd sent to Kate a few hours earlier, beyond glad he'd managed to finagle her number from her.

Well, in all honesty, it was less finagling and more common sense.

Fiancés had their future wives' numbers.

Simple as that.

Except . . . nothing was simple when it came to this woman and the depth of feeling he had for her after one dinner and a short walk. Maybe it was all the social media stalking, or maybe it was just her, just the realization and fleshing out of that feeling he'd had upon seeing that first picture.

The notion deep inside that this woman was more than just a face in a photograph.

Now he had a chance to prove that to himself . . . or maybe to her . . . or the universe, her parents, her siblings, and friends.

Long ass list, that was.

But the thought of lying to everyone important to her, and the unease it caused, had slipped way to the back of his brain. Because when he was in her presence, the only important thing was getting closer, unearthing all the little—and big, he supposed—things that made Kate, Kate.

Like the GIF and chain of emojis she'd replied with after he'd sent her a picture of him and Barry.

He'd never actually seen that many emojis in a row and had spent a good amount of time going one by one before he'd been able to translate the gist of the message.

And when he'd texted back

Please spare the old man so many emojis. It took me way too long to figure that out.

She'd simply replied with another chain of the tiny pictures. Though at least he'd been able to deduce the meaning of the hearts and kissing face emoji and had replied with

I like kissing you, too.

Long minutes had passed before he'd seen actual words.

You really don't use emojis.

Is this an emoji? :)

A beat

Nope.

Then. Nope, I guess I don't.

Hmm.

Do I need to read up on emoji etiquette?

Only if you want to understand my messages.

He'd laughed out loud at that but then had needed to slip his cell into his pocket and get down to work, otherwise he wouldn't have a hope in hell of getting out of the clinic on time.

Jaime had focused on getting through his patients, on returning calls and following up on lab work, but when he was on lunch break, he'd downloaded an *Emojis for Dummies Guidebook*, screenshotting the cover and sending it to Kate, along with a message.

Prepping for my crash course.

She'd replied almost instantly.

Smart. *thinking emoji*

(see, he'd already learned something)
Then

You said, you're an old man. How old exactly? I may need to rethink my plan.

Snorting, he shoved a bite of salad into his mouth and typed back.

Thirty-two. Birthday is August 2ⁿᵈ. You?

A long, long silence.

Don't you know that's an impolite question?

Don't you know that fiancés know these things? *sad eye emoji*

And okay, now he saw that the tiny and weird little pictures might truly be worthwhile, especially when her reply came through.

Not the sad eyes. Dear God, my heart can't take the sad eyes.

*Noted. *another sad eye emoji* Now, tell me. Please?*

I'm alternating between sighing out loud and giggling in my cube, and my coworkers think I've gone crazy.

He frowned.

Didn't you eat lunch?

*No time today. Not if I want to be on time. I've got a big project that's due. Note the deliberate use of *sad face emoji* in payback to you.*

Turns out, I'm immune. How old, Red? Then I'll let you go.

eye roll emoji Thirty-two, but the painful truth is that my birthday is July 22nd.*

Jaime grinned.

So less old man and more old woman?

Blasphemy! *cursing emoji*

The tech came in as he was laughing and told him his next patient was there, and he quickly shoved the last bite of his salad into his mouth.

I know. It's terrible. *sad eye emoji* That's so you'll forgive me. But I'd better let you work.

Unfortunately, yes.

A beat before another message came through.

I like texting with you, Jaime the Vet.

He could imagine her looking up shyly as she said that, the same way she'd looked up and said *No, I'd rather kiss you* the previous night, right before she tugged him down and kissed him within an inch of his sanity.

I like it, too, Red. See you in a few hours.

A chain of hearts and flowers and strange little yellow faces was his only reply, but it turned out that he quite liked emojis, especially when a gorgeous little redhead with curves for days and pretty whiskey-colored eyes sent them to him.

Sparing another minute before pulling his lab coat back on and heading to the exam room to see one of his temperamental feline patients, he opened the app on his phone and ordered lunch to be delivered to Kate's office.

He knew her favorite meal. Or at least one that had been featured on her Instagram page more than once—a pear and walnut salad and an apple turnover.

See? His social media spying had paid off. He knew where

she worked and what food she liked and her favorite beach and—

Pausing, because that sounded creepy, even in his own head, he forced himself to focus and completed the order for a salad and pastry from Molly's, a city staple that made even the healthiest of meals taste good.

Not that the pastry was healthy, but he figured Kate deserved a treat, especially when paired with the green stuff, and anyone who was anyone got a pastry when they ordered from Molly's. Handmade every day by the owner, plumb full of deliciousness, someone would have to be an idiot to not pick one up, especially given how often Kate waxed poetic about them on her page.

Not that he didn't agree, but the fact that it was another piece of information from her social media was probably semi-creepy. Regardless, he was chalking it up to paying attention to key details about a woman he wanted to win over.

Pastries. Not a bad way to start, he could imagine his sister, Tammy, telling him.

And, considering he'd been well-trained, Jaime knew his instincts on that front were right at least. He might have fucked up with Lori and had his confidence dinged, but he knew after one date with Kate that she was one hundred percent different from his ex.

She teased but in a sweet way. She'd fought him over the bill (though he'd won, Jaime thought with a self-satisfied smirk). She'd leaned into his touch, rather than shying away.

Lori had been beautiful, but with a streak of mean. She'd never offered to pay, had hated if he wanted to hold her hand in public.

Silly, small things. Well, not the mean, but the rest of it hadn't been obvious at first, or at least not enough to have propelled him into ending things. But then again, Lori had been good at manipulating him, good at giving him just enough affection that he clambered after her, wanting more, starved for more contact, more time with her.

Look, he understood her wanting to have her own life. He was independent, himself.

But he wanted more in a relationship.

He wanted a partner, someone he could share funny news stories or memes or inside jokes with. He craved a connection that didn't have him second-guessing every motivation and undercurrent.

Which was why it had been almost refreshing to get the message from Kate.

Will you pretend to be my fiancé for a week?

No subterfuge. No hiding.

Just a request and an in—a way for him to get closer to the fascinating woman he'd been lusting over.

He was mercenary enough to take it, selfish enough to want to tie her to him, smart enough to know that if he had any chance of success that he'd need to utilize a charm offensive the world had never seen before.

One glance, and he'd known that she was special.

One night, and he'd known he was hooked on the drug that was Kate.

So, he had a plan. A plan that involved several errands after he was done with his clients.

Speaking of which, a bark in the room next to him startled Jaime into motion. He shook himself, put away his phone, hurried to clean up his lunch. Because yes, he had a plan to make Kate fall for him, but that plan would only work if he didn't actually fuck up this fake fiancé role.

And the first step in that was being on time.

Six

KATE

I t was 5:56 and she was pacing back and forth along the narrow entryway of her house south of San Francisco.

One side had an opening to a small kitchen.

The other opened up into an equally small living room, packed with her too big but cozy microfiber couch. It was soft. It was fluffy. It was a deep, deep shade of violet, and she loved it most of all her belongings.

In fact, she loved it as much as she loved the back yard.

And that had taken blood, sweat, and tears to get to its current state. Though, she supposed, the couch had also taken blood and sweat to get it in through the narrow hall. But no tears. Plenty of cursing, especially from her brother and dad, who'd helped her move in, but no tears.

She'd smiled at the memory.

Her parents were so damned proud that she'd managed to scrimp and save enough to buy a house in the competitive Bay Area housing market, her mom only making one comment about how she could sell when she met her future husband because *surely, he would want to be part of the house-buying-deci-sion-making process* that Kate had been able to easily ignore.

She loved her mom, but damn, could that woman be a dog to the bone.

Still, she had inherited her green thumb from her mom and grandma, her taste in clothing that had notes of trendy but had given her the skills to build a wardrobe with classic, tasteful pieces that had lasted years.

Like the dress Jaime hadn't been able to tear his eyes off last night.

That was one of her favorites—sexy, flattered her curves, showed just the right amount of tits and ass to make her appetizing but not cross that line into nip slip.

Tits and ass?

Clearly, she'd been watching too much bad reality TV, because that particular vernacular had never been in her vocabulary until she'd begun watching a behind the scenes reality show of strippers and their personal lives.

Most of the time, reality TV was fascinating.

Sometimes her consumption habits reminded her that perhaps she needed to throw in a documentary every once in a while, in order to balance out the brain-melting. Still, it was a guilty pleasure, and one she couldn't feel *too* guilty for, given that Kate was in advertising. She found people and their habits fascinating.

What she *didn't* find fascinating was the amount of nerves currently swirling around her stomach.

She should call it off.

But then she'd miss out on spending the night with Jaime, miss out on his sweet, miss out on the way he'd held her hand, and how he'd kissed her until she thought that her clothes might just melt off into a puddle, not giving one damn that they were on a public street and anyone might see them.

Public indecency charge? Meh.

She'd had Jaime the Vet's lips on hers, his body pressed against hers, his fingers on her jaw, his tongue in her mouth.

Yeah. Indecency charges would have been worth it.

But eventually he'd released her mouth, had cuddled her close to his side, and had walked her to her car. She'd been enshrouded in a haze of desire, one she'd wanted to hold on to tightly because it was so potent, but one she'd been forced to pull herself out of because she needed to identify her car.

He'd made it easier by telling her about Barry the Chicken.

Who was apparently a rooster, but his original owner hadn't known that until she'd ended up with a series of very loud, very abrupt early mornings.

Barry had been rehomed and his current owner lived on a small patch of land with much more understanding neighbors and a love for being up when the sun rose. She'd trained Barry to walk on a leash, and her feisty, feathered companion had become a regular at the clinic.

A rooster named Barry who walked on a leash.

"The man is kryptonite."

Shaking her head, she gave herself one final glance in the mirror she kept inside her hall closet for just this case—a last-minute outfit check—smoothed a nonexistent wrinkle out of her pretty emerald green fit-and-flare dress, slipped on her flats, and then slicked on one more coat of her Firecrotch.

Heh.

Never got old.

Eyes flicking to the clock and seeing it was a minute until six, she grabbed her coat but didn't put it on because she wanted Jaime to see her in the dress. Smiling and hoping he'd like it as much as the black one from the night before, she closed the closet door.

Ding. Dong.

Her pulse skittered, speeding up, butterflies emerging from

their cocoons to fly in circles in her stomach, her lips and finger-tips tingling in anticipation.

"Okay," she murmured. "It'll be okay."

She strode to the door and pulled it open.

Then blinked and felt her jaw drop open.

"Oh my God, your *hair*," she moaned, reaching up before stopping herself. Because the man bun was *gone*.

Why was the man bun gone?

He smiled, and she saw he'd shaved off the stubble, too, revealing a strong, clean line that she wanted to run her lips across. "You don't like it?" he asked, rubbing a hand over the shorn locks on the side of his head.

Oh, she liked it.

She liked it a hell of a lot.

But the man bun was gone, and she hadn't even really gotten to run her fingers through it or learned how he made his messy bun look so much better than hers.

"I figured I'd better clean up for your parents," he said. "They seem a bit traditional, and I was more than tired of it, just had been too lazy to get a haircut." A blip of uncertainty flittered across his face. "Did I mess up?"

Her heart squeezed, and she closed the distance between them, running her fingers lightly through the brown locks, not messing them up, but rather giving in to her urge to touch the silky softness.

"No," she murmured. "You look too handsome by half."

His lips turned up. "You trying to charm me?"

A shrug, her tone bordering on grandiose. "I speak but the truth."

Jaime tucked a strand of her hair behind her ear. "Are you going Shakespeare on me?"

"Well," she said. "You *are* looking at the famous Lady Macbeth from Sierra High School's production of Macbeth in

2004. I'll have you know that I got not one but two standing ovations for my performance."

"I'm thoroughly impressed."

She giggled and started to shrug into her coat, breath catching when he grabbed it from her and helped her slide it on. "I didn't get a chance to thank you," she murmured, heart pounding when he gathered her hair at her nape and freed it from the collar of her coat. "For lunch. That was very sweet of you."

A brush of his lips across the back of her neck before he released her hair. "You have time to eat it?"

"Food from Molly's?" she said. "I made time." Spinning around, she decided that she would spend the night not second-guessing and hoping that things between them were different, but instead she'd just enjoy being with this man who was nice and sweet and seemed to like her.

Rising on tiptoe, she pressed a kiss to his lips.

And just like last night, pleasure exploded through her, shutting off her brain so she wasn't thinking or worrying or riddled with guilt. Rather, for the first time in a long time, Kate was able to just be in the present.

His lips moving on hers, his hand cupping her cheek. The spicy male scent of him surrounding her and going to her head more than a glass of wine.

They kissed until her lungs threatened to explode, and then she dropped back down onto her feet, pulling her mouth from his, her heart beating out of control. Her chest rose and fell rapidly, and her lipstick was all over his mouth.

"Shit," she muttered. "I Firecrotched you."

He'd started to smile, to say something, but then it seemed that her words processed because his mouth dropped open. "*What?*"

Which was the moment she realized that this man wasn't

privy to the color of her lipstick. Because his gaze dropped down, scorching a path to . . . well, her fire—

Yeah, no.

"It's the name of my lipstick," she rushed to say, lifting a hand and rubbing it over his mouth. "I'm sorry. I got it all over you."

A wicked gleam in his eyes, a warm palm on her back, trailing up and down, up and down. "You're apologizing because you Firecrotched me." Laughter bubbling in his chest, his fingers wrapping around her hip.

"Fine," she said, stepping back and mock-frowning. "I won't apologize." She reached for her purse, snagging it from the small table she kept near the door, where she'd set it when she started putting on her coat, and caught a glimpse of the time. "Crap." They'd been making out in her hall for almost ten minutes. "We need to get moving." She made a pitstop to touch up her lipstick, opening the closet door and using the mirror to slick on a fresh coat, then turned and glared. "No more kissing with that non-scruffy mouth of yours. It's too distracting."

He grinned. "So, you like the haircut and the shave?"

She just kept her narrowed gaze on him. "It's unfair that you're so pretty." A sniff. "And that you had better hair than me when it was long."

"I dream about your hair spread over my pillow at night."

Silence.

As in *she* went silent.

"What?"

"You're so fucking beautiful," he murmured, coming up behind her, running his fingers through her hair, which she'd left loose to trail over her shoulders. "Your hair is the color of rubies. I couldn't believe it when I saw it shining in the restaurant. I always thought it was a filter, that it couldn't be real. But I was wrong." He bent his head and inhaled. "Roses. Roses and rubies and silk."

Goose bumps prickled on her skin, and she melted back against him, the line of her spine colliding with the hard planes of his chest, his abs. "Have you ever felt this way with another person?" she asked.

"No." A stroke of those fingers over her collarbones. "Only with you. From the moment I first saw your picture, I knew you were different."

Her breath shuddered out.

She'd felt that way, too, had become almost obsessed with seeing his posts, but she also knew that her personality bordered on obsessive, that she was always falling too far, too fast, too soon.

This was too soon.

So, instead of saying what was in her heart, she pulled back.

Gently, and with a joke, but she still pulled back. "So, the man who knows nothing of emojis, knows about filters?"

He seemed to understand she needed the distance because he let her go, also stepping back, his soft chuckle filling the air, gentle now without a hint of sexual tension, then reached for the doorknob. "I *had* to learn about them, or at least that was what my vet tech told me when I started the page last year. I quote *couldn't look shiny*." He opened the door. "And I shouldn't say I know *nothing* about emojis, I've been known to use one of those ones that's suggested when you type."

She snorted, followed him out onto her porch, and took a few moments to lock up.

"I should have asked," she said when they were on their way to his car, a mid-sized black SUV parked in her driveway, "was I on your way? I could have come and picked you up instead."

"I'm not far," he said and gave her the address of his condo, which was actually just in the next neighborhood over. Then he opened the passenger door and helped her in.

"Wait." She grabbed his hand, finally processing that he lived in a condo. She'd imagined . . . what? A farm or a big house with a back yard filled with animals. He couldn't have that in a condo.

Shit. *Shit.* Why had she spent all that time kissing him instead of peppering him with questions? She didn't know nearly enough to pull off this ruse.

"What, Red?" he asked, turning his hand so he could wrap his fingers around her wrist.

"Do you have any pets?"

He shook his head. "No," he said. "Not since my Honey died last year. I . . . sometimes it's hard to be around animals all day, especially when you see them in pain far too often." Fingers on her cheek. "I know I'll get another dog or cat someday, but I just needed some time."

"I'm sorry," she said, reaching out and running her thumb along his jaw, hating the shadow of pain in his eyes. "That must be hard, seeing all those sick animals. I guess, I just had this image it was all . . . kittens and puppies."

"Those are definitely the fun days," he said, voice still soft. "And I love my job, most of the time. It's like anything else and has it's tough moments."

She shook her head. "Except when *I* mess up on an ad mockup, there isn't anyone's life at risk."

Pale brown eyes on hers, filled with so much warmth that she actually felt her heart expand. "True," he said. "But that pressure is part of the job."

"And what do you do to release that pressure?"

He froze. Then he sighed and admitted, "Not enough recently, that's for sure. When I took over the clinic, I knew the hours would be long, but they've been intense and a little overwhelming."

She wrapped her arms around him, held him tight. "I can only imagine."

"Thank you," he murmured. "For asking. And for giving me my first break from the clinic in months with dinner last night," he added, brushing a kiss to her forehead before straightening and reaching to close the car door. Then, as she was beginning to understand was his M.O., this man turned the topic off himself and back onto her. "You know, we don't have to do this. I could go as your boyfriend or just as your date. You could just say your mom misheard or that you made a mistake."

So tempting.

And yet, then she'd have to see the disappointment on her mom's face.

Plus, "What am I going to say?" she asked honestly. "That I thought you had a ring and I was wrong?"

A flicker of humor on his face. "I—"

"Oh shit."

"What?"

She lifted her left hand. Her ring*less* left hand. *Fuck.* She hadn't thought of a ring. *Why* hadn't she thought of a ring? There was no way her mom would believe she'd gotten engaged without a ring. Which, she got, made her sound like a materialistic prima donna, but engagements and rings went hand in hand. If Kate was planning on getting married, she would have a ring.

Except . . . she *didn't* have a ring.

"What, Red?" he asked again, but not impatiently. Instead, those brown eyes stayed gentle, his fingers on her wrist snug, but not tight. His thumb rubbed patterns on the palm of her right hand.

"I don't have a ring." She shook her head. "I should have thought to get a ring—"

"I have one," he said simply and dropped her hand to reach into his pocket and retrieve a box. It was blue velvet, and when he opened the top, she gasped. "Not a real diamond," he murmured. "I didn't think you'd—" A sharp shake of his head. "Anyway, it's called a moonstone, and I thought it was pretty and unique and . . . you. But you can always just tell them it's a temporary ring because I wanted you to be able to pick out what you wanted."

She ran a finger over the soft white stone. It was diamond-esque, but opaque with translucent streaks of sky blue. She'd never seen anything quite like it.

She also thought it the prettiest ring she'd ever seen.

"You did this all today?" she asked. "The lunch, the ring, the haircut, and shaving. All of it . . . for me?"

Jaime brushed the back of his knuckles over her cheek. "It was nothing," he said. "And even if it were, you're worth it, Red. It took no time at all for me to recognize that fact, honey, and if any man was stupid enough to not recognize that, then it was his loss and my gain." He slipped the ring from the box. "Because I intend to get many more than just my two dates." He snagged her left hand, bringing it toward him, and fitting the ring just over the tip of the proper finger. "Got it?"

Her heart pounded, hope filling her with so much helium that she felt as though she could float. Still, she shook her head. "I think we're insane. This is too much and . . . just idiotic. I know it was my idea, but—"

He kissed her briefly then pulled back.

A wicked smile as he slipped the ring down her finger then lifted his hand and ran his thumb over her bottom lip. "Then let's be idiotic together."

SEVEN

JAIME

She'd given him quiet but clear directions to her parents' house, and even with their slight delay in the hall, at the car, and the Friday evening traffic, they still arrived only just after six-thirty.

An old ranch-style house set into the side of rolling hills, green this time of year after the early winter rains, but not yet dried to brown by the dryness of late spring and the summer's heat, it was a beautiful piece of architecture with a wrap-around porch surrounded by lush flowerbeds. The double front doors were stained a rich brown, and a festive Christmas wreath hung centered over each wooden panel.

"You grew up here?" he asked, the gorgeous home so different, so much grander than his own upbringing had provided.

"No," she said. "We grew up in a much smaller house. We moved because—" A shrug. "My mom invented a product that got patented when I was in high school."

That was unusual enough that he managed to tear his gaze from the perfectly straight Christmas lights framing each window, from the family of light-up deer "grazing" on the perfect green lawn. Then again, everything about this woman was interesting, including this house and what it said about her. "What did your mom invent?"

"She's a scientist," Kate said. "Or was. She invented an anti-aging compound, sold it off to the highest bidder, and that became my parents' retirement." She smiled. "Good thing, too. Since my younger siblings seemed determined to eat them out of house and home."

"Excuse me!" a female voice exclaimed. "I'm not the only one who ate." She held up an infant. "Did you hear that, Lacy? Your aunt called me fat."

Kate grinned. "You look beautiful, and you know it." She slipped past Jaime to hug the woman he presumed was her sister, Ann. "In fact, I should hate you, considering you're one of those formerly pregnant females who bounce right back into shape."

A rueful smile. "Believe me," she said. "All sorts of things are bouncing that shouldn't be bouncing."

"Well," Kate said, scooping the baby out of her arms. "I stand by my statement"—she kissed each of the little girl's tiny, plump cheeks—"your mommy is absolutely beautiful. Are you letting her get any sleep yet?"

"Nope." A twinkling laugh. "So, you going to introduce me to the man who you managed to keep a secret for all these months?"

"Not tough with everything that has been going on."

"True enough." She turned to Jaime, stuck her hand out. "Since this one"—she poked her sister in the shoulder—"isn't going to be polite, I've got to take matters into my own hands. I'm Ann."

"I know," he said, smiling and shaking her hand. "I'm Jaime. Kate has told me a lot about you, including the fact that you're her favorite sister."

"Her only sister is more like it," Ann said with a laugh. "But one she's stuck with." She leaned over and grinned at Kate. "I see you've got yourself a charmer."

Kate grinned back.

"Here." Jaime snagged the diaper bag from her shoulder. "Let me carry that for you."

A raised eyebrow before she laced her arm through his. "Thank you," she said then smiled up at him. "Though I have to say that Kate has been surprisingly tight-lipped about *you*."

He shrugged. "Sometimes it's nice to have something that just belongs to you for a bit."

Ann's smile didn't dim. In fact, it seemed to grow larger, or at least more approving. "Well, I hope you enjoyed that time while it lasted because you'd better believe that an interrogation is coming tonight."

Just as she finished the sentence, the front door opened and an older female waved excitedly, calling, "Come in already!"

Kate groaned.

And it turned out that Ann was right about the interrogation.

———

A hockey game was on TV, the Gold decimating their opponent, thanks to the outstanding play of Liam Williamson, but Jaime couldn't concentrate on the screen, not when he had four eyes boring holes in his profile.

An unexpected consequence of him being "engaged" to Kate was the fact that he hadn't considered that this engagement had happened without meeting her family.

Or more specifically, without meeting her father, who had ice in his brown eyes identical to Kate's, or her brother, who had the red hair but a pair of piercing blue irises that were sharp enough to cut.

His "fiancé" had been swept into the kitchen approximately

thirty seconds after her mother, a thin brunette with pale blue eyes, had barreled down the front walk, introduced herself as Marabelle McLeod. She'd bustled them into the house then waved him in the direction of the family room, telling him to make himself "at home."

He'd hesitated in the entrance, glanced toward the two men seated on the couch, and then had said, "Hi. I'm Jaime."

Grunts in response.

Which was the moment that he'd realized this was going to be slightly more complicated than he'd anticipated.

Considering his options, he'd sat in an armchair, had trained his focus on the television, and tried to put himself in their place. A man they'd never met, a stranger had asked their daughter/sister to marry him without ever meeting her family. Wincing, he knew that wasn't exactly the first impression he'd wanted to make, especially because he really liked Kate, had felt that instant connection click into place over dinner, had been drawn in further by the walk, by the text conversations, even just chatting on the car ride over. It felt . . . right.

As though he'd been doing his whole life wrong until Kate had messaged him.

"We're having a long engagement," he blurted, turning to look at the two men who'd been staring him down for the last ten minutes. Jaime saw the blip of surprise on their faces, kept talking. "Things have moved fast with us," he said. "We both know it. So, we decided to slow down, take our time from here on out."

"And yet my daughter has a ring on her finger," her father, Harry, said. He hadn't introduced himself, but Kate had given Jaime a rundown on all the important details—like names, like her being the oldest, like her dad recently retiring and taking up woodworking and having been given a workshop in the back yard by her mom for his birthday, complete with every tool under the sun.

Which meant there were plenty of sharp instruments in the vicinity.

Jaime held back a shudder and answered truthfully. "When you find someone worth holding on to, you don't let them go."

Silence, but he got the feeling that Kate's father approved.

Of that one thing he said, at least.

"And you didn't think you should meet us first? Didn't think you should ask permission before proposing?"

This question, or rather *questions*, came from Kate's brother, Jake.

He met the hostile blue eyes. "I think Kate is smart and capable enough to make the decision of who she wants to marry," he said, and it wasn't a line. Jaime believed it. He wouldn't have asked for permission from her dad to marry Kate. She was a strong, adult woman who could decide for herself. And *if* something like that was important to her—which he highly doubted based on the whole fake engagement thing —*maybe* then he would have given Harry a heads up that the proposal was coming. But he still wouldn't have asked permission. "As for meeting you guys, I did want to and am happy we finally got here. Between our work schedules—Kate's been working extremely hard, and I recently took over full time at my vet practice—along with wanting to keep this one thing for ourselves for just a little while—I come from a large family, too —time just got away from us."

"Sounds selfish," Jake said.

He shrugged. "Maybe, but I don't think it's selfish to spend time building a strong foundation with the woman who you're going to spend the rest of your life with."

The noise on the TV rose then, the crowd screaming as someone from the Gold scored, but Jaime didn't look away from Kate's brother.

Their gazes clashed—suspicion, irritation, frustration in Jake's, but Jaime held firm. If this fake engagement was going to

EIGHT

KATE

S he was sweating as she arranged the bouquet of sunflowers Jaime had given to her mom—gorgeous, beautiful sunflowers that made her smile and want to steal them home for herself.

But the perspiration wasn't from the flowers.

It was because Jaime was confined in the other room with her brother and father, and based on the glares she'd seen when she'd walked by the space, it wasn't going to be a kumbaya moment.

They were going to rake the man who was doing her a favor, who was bailing her out, over the coals.

Fuck. She hadn't thought that through.

Frankly, she hadn't thought a *lot* of things through.

The ring. Her family—though her mom hadn't cared that she hadn't met Jaime because her oldest and perpetually single daughter was "engaged!!" (and yes, two exclamations were worthy of her mom's excitement). But she hadn't factored in the protectiveness of her brother and father, and how they'd always done the whole "you'd better take care of her, or you'll have me to answer to" thing.

That wasn't her favorite.

She could take care of herself.

But she appreciated that they loved her enough to worry, so while their protection had sometimes chaffed and often annoyed, she'd grown to accept it, oldest sibling who should be the one to be looking after the younger ones, or not.

Men being men.

Barf.

But also, it came from a good place. They wanted her safe and happy, and she couldn't deny that she'd also given Ann's then boyfriend now husband and Jake's wife the same narrow-eyed glare that her brother had been giving Jaime when she'd peeked in.

Ann was protective in a different way than she and Jake.

She'd be watching closely, cataloging, and be ready to step in the moment Jaime treated her the least bit wrong.

Her family might be annoying and nosy, but they also loved each other.

Plus, their nosiness meant that she got to be nosy right back, especially when it came to the dark circles under her sister's eyes.

"Did you talk to Dave?" she asked, forcing her gaze away from the living room and focusing on her sister. Who looked absolutely exhausted, and not just the typical post-baby exhaustion, but something more, something deeper.

Her sister sighed. "I tried. I don't know what's going on with him. He doesn't seem to hear me, and then when he does listen, he promises to do better, to help more."

"Then he doesn't?"

"No," Ann said. "He does, but then he disappears into his own head again a-and—" She broke off, blue eyes swimming with tears.

"Come here," Kate said, wrapping an arm around her sister's waist and leading her from the room.

"The baby—"

"Mom's got her."

And their mom did. She was currently walking baby Lacy around the kitchen, telling her all about the colorful Christmas decorations. There was no way the two-month-old could understand her, let alone even see everything her mom pointed out, but Lacy was enraptured by her mom's musical voice anyway.

Kate smiled, thinking about all the times her mom had just talked to her, used her gentle, lyrical voice to talk her out of a tantrum, or off the edge of an argument with her best friend during her preteen years, or even helping her through a work problem.

She loved talking to her.

Minus the whole she-needed-to-be-in-a-relationship-or-her-womb-was-going-to-dry-up nonsense that had filled so many of their most recent conversations.

But now she had Jaime and hadn't heard about the doctor or so-and-so's cousin or anything about biological clocks.

It was glorious.

A lie.

She bit her lip, pushed the guilt away. So maybe it was a glorious lie, but she also had more to worry about in that moment than herself and the mess she'd made and the longing she felt growing with every minute she spent with Jaime.

For now, she needed to focus on her sister.

Keeping her arm around Ann, she snagged a blanket from the rack her mom kept by the back door and led them out onto the porch.

There were plenty of chairs around for them to sit in, but she didn't bother with that, instead walking Ann over to the top step, sitting her down, plunking down next to her, and then wrapping the blanket around them both. Picking up the thread of conversation, she said, "You say he disappears into his own head. How so?"

Ann's gaze was on the horizon, and it stayed that way for a long moment before she spoke. "It's like I'm talking to him and he's saying all of the right things, but he's not really there." She turned, eyes going to Kate's. "I feel so alone."

"Oh, sissy," Kate murmured, wrapping her other arm around her sister and hugging her tightly. "Have you told him that?"

"Yes." She paused, sniffed. "*No*. I mean, maybe not in those exact words?"

Since Dave had always made it clear that he thought Ann had hung the moon, Kate thought there might be more going on here than her sister could comprehend, especially given that Ann had spent the last months of her pregnancy on bed rest, had a difficult recovery after a challenging birth, and a colicky baby.

That was enough to throw anyone for a loop and most definitely enough to knock a couple off track.

"Why don't I watch Lacy next week, and you two can go out to dinner and really sit and talk it out?" she asked. "You both have been virtual zombies since Little Miss was born, and with him just going back to work, maybe he's having trouble adjusting?"

"What if she cries?"

Kate snorted. "She's a baby. She's *going* to cry."

"What if she's hungry?"

"I know you've been pumping and getting her used to a bottle once a day." She squeezed her sister's shoulder. "Let's plan the time around that."

"What if—?"

"You need to talk to him," she interrupted, starting to understand the problem. "And you need time and space to not be distracted to do so, and"—another squeeze—"you need to remember that I've been babysitting your ass since I was ten and you were three."

"I remember," Ann said dryly. "That's why I'm terrified of leaving my baby with you."

She made a face. "Hey!"

Ann smiled and the mischievous smirk along with the dry rejoinder made Kate relax. *That* was her sister—snark and teasing and an irresistible smile that made you beam at her in return. Not the exhausted female she'd been in her parents' kitchen.

And if Dave didn't get his shit together at this dinner, then Kate knew she'd take matters into her own hands.

If he thought her *mom* was pushy . . . well then he'd better watch out.

No one hurt her baby sister.

"Thanks, Katie," Ann said. "Can you watch her on Tuesday?"

She nodded, rested her head on Ann's shoulder. "Of course."

"You know," Ann murmured after they'd sat in silence for a few more minutes. "I almost understand why you didn't tell us about Jaime."

Oh, she did, did she?

But Kate shoved down the blip of guilt and asked, "Yeah?"

"Yes," Ann said. "I know it comes from a place of love, but Mom is a *lot.*"

"You're just recognizing that?" Kate teased. "But you're right. She's amazing and has always been there for us, but she's also a whirlwind, and it can sometimes be tough to hold your ground." She paused. "Is that what you think is happening?"

"I don't know." Ann made a face. "Maybe? Okay"—a sigh—"yes. At least, I don't think it's helping. I mean, at first, I was so relieved to have her with me every day. But now . . . I think I need a little space. It's like between the wedding and then setting up our house and then Lacy . . . maybe part of what's going on with Dave and me is that we haven't had the space to settle into our own skin, you know?"

"I could see that," Kate murmured. "You two did move pretty fast with everything and then decided to throw a baby into the mix."

"Yeah." A sigh. "Damn."

"What?"

"I think I just gave myself two people to talk to, huh?" Her nose wrinkled. "I need to have heart-to-hearts with Mom and with Dave."

"Mom will take it okay," Kate said. "You know that. She's good at accepting boundaries once they're in place."

Blue eyes on hers. "And Dave?"

"Well, he's your husband," Kate said lightly, "and he loves you. I think you two can figure it out."

"I hope so."

Quiet fell between them. "You remember when Mom showed up at my dorm with homemade casseroles for the entire floor?"

Ann froze then burst out laughing. "Are you comparing my marriage to your tricky roommate situation?"

"Seemed apropos." She shrugged.

"I seem to remember that the boy you liked, who lived down the hall, suddenly asked you out after that."

"Yes, he did."

They'd actually gone on quite a few dates. They'd seen each for months, long enough for her to feel comfortable with him, for her to fall in love. First love, freshman-in-college love, *stupid* love. Because she'd given him her virginity then had overheard him with his friends laughing about how bad she was in bed.

See? Assholes?

Her superpower.

Thankfully, she had been comfortable enough with herself

to understand that it had been him—and his inability to last more than three thrusts, not to mention his lack in being able to please his partner—more than something she'd done.

So, she'd taken one of those casseroles her mom had left and dumped it in his lap.

And then she'd gone out with one of his roommates, who'd been much better in the sack and who'd taught her that she *could* have an orgasm during sex, so long as she was with someone who actually paid attention and had the patience to learn what she enjoyed.

So, asshole had met learning experience.

Thus, the path of her life had been laid.

Ha.

"Come on," she said, pushing to her feet and folding the blanket. "I don't know about you, but I'm starving."

She wasn't really. Not after the pastry and salad Jaime had bought her.

But she needed to do something that wasn't sitting on the back steps thinking about one of her asshole exes and then wondering if and when Jaime would become one of them.

Because as much as she liked him, felt a draw, enjoyed how sweet he was being, she also knew that at some point, the other shoe would fall.

And she didn't want to think about that.

Tucking the blanket under one arm, she extended her other toward her sister, giving her a hand up.

"What if it's because I haven't lost the baby weight? My body isn't the same and—"

A blip of fury flew through Kate.

"Then I'm cutting off his balls and feeding them to him," she growled. "You had a baby two months ago, sissy. If that's his problem, then I will cheerfully make him a eunuch and—"

"It's not."

Kate glanced up, saw that Dave was standing on the porch.

She'd missed him opening the back door, missed him stepping out, but what she didn't miss was the fatigue and dark circles beneath his eyes.

And the concern in the pale brown depths.

Concern that made the fury slip away. Especially when he walked over to Ann and took her into his arms with barely a look at Kate.

As it should be.

"What the hell are you thinking, baby? I love you," he said, tone fierce. "Just the way you are. You're the most beautiful woman I have ever laid eyes on."

"I don't know what I'm thinking," Ann said. "I just feel so alone and . . ."

Heart squeezing, but glad that this conversation was taking place, even though it wasn't exactly how she and Ann had planned it out, Kate slipped through the back door, closed it, and hung up the blanket.

Then she walked down the hall, intending to help her mom with dinner.

Instead, when she strode into the kitchen and saw what was happening inside, every cell went to rigid attention, her breath caught, and her feet slid to a stop.

Because Jaime was in the kitchen.

Holding Lacy.

Swaying side to side as he rocked her gently, his big hand cradled over the back her head, his palm on her back, rubbing circles.

She'd felt those circles, had that palm on her back.

Which was why this time it wasn't just her ovaries that exploded, but her heart as well.

NINE

JAIME

"You're good with her," Kate's mom said as she bustled around the kitchen.

"I'm the oldest of four," he told her, patting little Lacy's back when she began fussing again. "I did my fair share of babysitting."

Marabelle crossed by him, pulling out a carton of herbs from the fridge and pausing to pat his cheek. "You're a good boy."

"I don't know about that," he said, "but I do my best."

She smiled and shook her head but didn't argue with him.

"Can I do anything to help?"

"Besides hold the baby?" She slanted a look over at him. "No, honey, you just keep working your Lacy magic. I swear, she hasn't been this content since she was born."

He lifted Lacy up, smiling at the adorable little munchkin. Chubby cheeks, big eyes, a rosebud mouth, she was a beautiful baby. "Have you been giving your parents the run around?" Her face screwed up, and he wasn't sure if it was his question or because he'd dared switched positions. Quickly, he put her back against his shoulder, began rubbing circles on her back. Glancing up, he met Marabelle's amused eyes. "I guess that answers my question."

She laughed then turned her focus back to the sauce she was stirring.

"Where are your parents now?" she asked as he kept walking and rocking, gaze periodically going to the hall. He'd been able to catch a glimpse of Kate's bright red hair through the glass door on the back of the house. She and her sister had appeared to be in serious conversation.

So serious, in fact, that Dave, her sister's husband, had taken one glance at the sisters, wrapped in a blanket with their arms around each other, and had hustled down the hall, with hardly a look at the strange man who held his daughter.

"They're in Utah," he answered. "Most of my siblings are there, too. I came out for vet school at Davis, fell in love with the Bay Area, and never went home." Lacy cooed, drooling against his shoulder, and he smiled down at the tiny infant. Feisty, but also needing lots of love and care.

Kind of like her aunt.

But the good thing was that Jaime had plenty of love and care to give.

"Well, for my Katie's sake, I'm glad you stayed—oh, hi, honey. Everything okay with your sister?"

Jaime turned, saw that Kate had come back inside.

Her expression was soft, a swathe of pink across her cheeks, but it was her eyes that struck in him right in the heart.

Longing.

He was holding a baby, and she had longing in her eyes.

Their stares locked, held, and suddenly he was in the future.

In the same kitchen, with the same women, but holding a child that belonged to him, to them.

Lacy squawked, breaking the moment, knocking the vision

from his mind even as he shifted her. But this time no amount of rocking or circles would calm her.

Kate moved over to a brightly printed diaper bag. "I'll just see if there's a bottle in here."

"It's in the fridge, honey," her mom said. "Bottle warmer is on the counter and set to go."

Kate nodded. "Got it."

Thirty seconds later, she'd retrieved the bottle, had it in and out of the warmer, and was testing the milk's temperature. "Gosh," she murmured, coming toward him. "I haven't done this since my babysitting days."

He grinned. "Me neither. None of my siblings have kids yet, much to my mom's chagrin." He bounced Lacy gently. "Though, as far as babysitting goes, I guess that's not *entirely* true—I spent a few days last spring bottle-feeding a litter of kittens." A shrug. "I guess that's a form of babysitting."

"Please, tell me you're kidding me," she said.

"No," he said. "Is this going to bring about more of your animal obsession?"

"They're *kittens*."

Jake came into the kitchen, headed for the fridge. "That's a yes, in case you were wondering."

"Kittens," Kate repeated, eyes bright. Then she smiled, that big grin that he felt like an actual caress across his skin, the one that made his heart swell and feel more than it had in years, and screwed the cap on the bottle, handing it to him. "Unless, you need a break?" she asked as he accepted it.

"I'm good," he said. "This involves significantly less of a need for octopus arms."

She laughed, Marabelle's chuckle following. "How many kittens were there?"

"Eight." A beat. "And they all wanted to eat at once."

"Naturally." Eyes dancing as she tapped a finger tapped against her bottom lip. "So, a true need for octopus arms."

He started giving Lacy the bottle, glad when she stopped fussing and began chugging the milk down like a champ. "Yup." A sly look. "Or an assistant with an obsession with all things furry. Know anyone who might be interested if the opportunity presents itself?"

She kissed his cheek. "No wedding unless you pick me."

Jaime turned his head, whispered in her ear. "Sold."

She blinked, lips parting, but then Jake laughed and punched his sister on the shoulder. "You might need to get a bigger yard, sis. If Jaime is in close proximity to animals at regular intervals, I think you're going to run out of space in that little garden of yours."

Kate swallowed, her gaze hot, but when she spoke, her tone was light. "He takes care of a rooster named Barry, who walks on a leash." As if that was the only evidence she needed to win any argument.

Jake glanced over at him, smirked. "I stand by my statement. You need a bigger yard."

Jaime smiled. "If Kate wants a rooster, she can have a rooster."

Marabelle beamed.

Jake sighed. "Dude, you've got to set the expectations low. You can't give them *everything* they want, or you'll never have negotiating power."

"I'm telling Steph you said that."

A narrowed look. "You wouldn't."

Kate danced away. "Why wouldn't I? It's my womanly duty to inform her of the underhanded tactics her husband uses."

"Plus," Marabelle said, "all she has to do is blink those pretty blue eyes and—"

A female voice intruded. "Are we talking about *my* pretty blue eyes?"

Jaime turned, saw a petite brunette had strode in, a laptop bag on her shoulder. She wore a black business suit and a tired

expression. And for all his talk of negotiating power, Jake immediately crossed over to her and took her bag, cupping the side of
her neck.

"Hi, baby," he murmured, kissing her lightly. "Work go
okay?"

She nodded. "Fine. Now what's this about my eyes?"

"Jake said—"

Jake picked up a dish towel and chucked it at Kate, the floral-
patterned cotton landing on her face with a quiet *swoosh*.

"Hey!" she exclaimed, yanking it off. "You—"

"Dinner time!" Marabelle called, interrupting the argument
before it could really get going, in one of those quintessential
Mom ways that told him all he needed to know about her
parenting style.

She'd been there, been involved.

As thus, the kids—or well, adults—stopped arguing and got
into gear, grabbing plates and napkins, side dishes, and a platter
from the counter and carrying them into the dining room.

Ann appeared at his elbow, eyes slightly reddened, but a
determined expression on her face, and he gently transferred
Lacy into her arms. "She took the bottle?" she asked, surprise
flitting across her face.

"Like a champ," he murmured.

She glanced up at her husband, and they shared a look that
said more than words. Then he nodded and glanced over at
Jaime. "Hi," he said. "Dave. Nice to meet you."

"You, too," Jaime said and nodded at Lacy. "She's adorable."

Ann smiled and ran a finger down her daughter's nose.
"Thanks for feeding her."

"It was my pleasure," he said. "Babies are exhausting, and I
figured you two could use a break. Thankfully, Kate got me set
up with the bottle."

Kate came up to him, getting close, and instinct had him
wrapping his arm around her, tugging her to his side. "Jaime

bottle-fed kittens last spring," she said then added in a stage-whispered, "and he promised me a rooster."

Two pairs of wide eyes on him and all he could do was chuckle.

"I don't know if it was quite a promise," he prevaricated.

"Told you," Jake said with a sigh. "You've lost that negotiating power and—"

This time, Steph was the one who tossed the dish towel. And with perfect accuracy, he might add. It landed across Jake's face, muffling anything further he might have said, and then as though it were something she'd done a hundred times before, she turned to Jaime, stuck her hand out, and said, "Hi, I'm Steph. Welcome to the crazy."

He grinned as he shook it. "Jaime. And I have to say, the crazy is more than welcome."

Marabelle snagged his elbow, lacing her arm through his. "I'm glad you say that because—"

"Mom," Kate said.

"I was wondering—"

"*Mom,*" Kate repeated.

"—if you'd like to see Kate's baby pictures," Marabelle finished, not acknowledging Kate's groan, continuing to talk as though her daughter hadn't said a word. "I have this great shot of her naked in the tub and—"

"Mom!"

She winked, released his arm, and began shepherding them into the dining room.

"I'm kidding about the naked tub picture," Marabelle added.

Kate sighed, and he stifled a smile.

"Because I have a naked spaghetti picture that's so much better."

Jaime couldn't help it. He burst out laughing. Kate smacked

him, grabbed his arm, dragging him to a halt in the hall, and gasping in outrage.

"Don't you dare laugh!"

Then there was another thing he couldn't help, and that was turning and brushing his fingers over Kate's cheek, bending down to drop a kiss to her lips that was semi-chaste. Chaste because there was no tongue, but semi because it probably went on longer than it should have, considering they were in her parents' house and he'd met them all of an hour before.

But she was like a drug.

One touch, and he wanted more. One kiss, and he wanted to run his lips over every inch of her body.

One night, and he wanted an eternity.

The sound of a throat clearing had Jaime slowing the kiss. He dropped his forehead against hers, his breath coming in short bursts and whispered, "Sorry."

Warm whiskey eyes on his. "For what?"

"That wasn't exactly what I planned."

A heated smile. "Feel free to kiss me like that any time you want."

He lifted his head, brushed back some of the red silken tresses that had crept forward to tangle on her cheek. "I'm going to take you up on that."

Lacing his fingers with hers, he stepped away, saw that her dad was studying them closely, his expression fierce, though it gentled when it shifted over to his daughter.

"Come on, Katie girl," he murmured. "Let's eat before it gets cold."

Those eyes, so like Kate's, flicked to him, and instead of the rebuke Jaime had expected to see, Harry nodded at him approvingly.

Kate squeezed his hand, whispered, "Ready for more of my family?"

He nodded, having more fun than he'd had in ages. "Yeah, Red, bring it on."

They followed Harry into the dining room, and he was hardly one step over the threshold when Ann said, "Jaime?"

He glanced her way, noted the mischief on her face, and braced himself.

And found out approximately half a second later that it had been the wisest course of action because her next question was, "What does Kate have to do to get you to buy her a real diamond?"

TEN

KATE

I t had been the best night ever.

Jaime reached across her after she'd sat down in the passenger's seat and buckled her seat belt. She didn't protest the action, nor the kiss he brushed to her forehead, too exhausted after the workday, after the emotional conversation with Ann, after the dinner filled with laughing and teasing and so much love, after . . . spending the evening living a lie that didn't actually feel like a lie.

She wanted it to be real.

So fucking much.

"You okay?" he murmured.

Kate nodded, forced a smile. "Just tired."

Pale brown eyes holding hers. "Sure?"

She nodded again, heart thumping when he ran his thumb over her bottom lip. But then he was stepping back, hand going to the door. "Well, then, let's get you home."

"I—"

The door closed, cutting off her sentence.

Which was just as well because she was probably going to say something stupid like, "I don't want to go home yet."

But she *needed* to go home.

She needed to remind herself that Jaime wasn't hers, not really. He wasn't *her* man, the one whose gaze had connected with hers over Lacy's head, the longing in his eyes no doubt matching hers. He wasn't her man who'd charmed her mom and sister, who'd calmed the overprotectiveness of her brother and father.

He wasn't even her man who'd fallen for her over a ketchup bottle.

But he *was* the man who'd thought to bring her a ring, who'd bought her lunch and looked at her with open desire, who laughed and smiled freely, who touched her gently and frequently, who buckled her seat belt and showed up at a restaurant after a long and complicated procedure because he was worried that she hadn't gotten his message.

He was a good man.

And that probably should have been enough to slap her fantasy-addled mind into reality.

Because good men didn't want her.

Her door opened again, and suddenly Jaime was there, his mouth inches away from hers, hot breath on her lips, hands holding her face.

"Don't be sad, Red," he murmured.

Embarrassed, she started to turn away, not liking that he could read her so easily, abruptly hating that he'd been able to insert himself into her life so effortlessly. That was dangerous because she was going to miss him when he was gone.

"I'm fine," she said, deliberately not meeting his eyes, not when he saw so much.

His stare she was avoiding felt heavy on her face, but she still didn't turn to meet it, didn't offer up any more words, and after a moment, Jaime brushed his thumb over her cheek. "I like you,

Kate," he said. "A lot. Your family, too. And that has not one fucking bit to do with the fact that the ring you're wearing isn't real."

Her lungs had frozen at the first statement.

By the time he'd made it to the end of his words and had dropped his hands, stepping back and closing the door for a second time, they burned from an utter lack of oxygen.

He paused as he rounded the hood, eyes locking onto hers, and she found that she could breathe again. Sucking in much-needed oxygen, she watched him continue on, heard the slight *pop* from his door opening, felt the car move as he sat down and buckled in, heard the rumble of the engine as he pressed the button to start the ignition.

What she *didn't* hear?

More words.

The man, the good man, was giving her time to process.

He pulled out of the driveway, the path slightly more difficult to maneuver as Ann and Dave had ridden home together, leaving Dave's car parked behind them and bundling a sleeping Lacy into the back seat of Ann's SUV.

Whatever was going on with them had been somewhat tempered by the conversation on the back porch. Ann's eyes were slightly reddened from tears, Dave's lined in exhaustion, but they'd held hands throughout dinner, and Kate had approved of the fact that Dave hadn't left her sister's side.

Ann didn't have Kate's asshole superpower.

It needed to stay that way.

Only one McLeod should have that particular ability, and it definitely shouldn't be her sweet, lovely sister.

Nope, the burden alone was Kate's.

You know what they say, she thought snarkily, *with great power comes great responsibility.*

Ha.

"My ex messed me up."

She had let her eyes slide closed, her brain sinking in a soft haze, full of reality, but also full of pleasure. Because she'd seen joy in her mom's face, approval in her dad's. Because Jaime fit.

His words, however, had her eyes flying open, had her shifting in her seat to look at him.

So fucking handsome.

A strong jaw, a straight nose, plump, kissable lips, short —*frown*—hair.

And gorgeous.

As though her brain had conjured every action star fantasy in her brain and had mashed them all together into her living, breathing dream man.

Who was nice. Who was sweet.

Who was *sharing*.

"What happened?" she asked softly. "What did she do?"

His fingers shifting on the steering wheel, gripping tightly as he maneuvered the car around a turn. "It's been long enough that I know that it's what we *both* did," he said, the half of his mouth she could see curved up into a smile. "She was really good at getting under my skin and could be mean as a snake, but I was also really good at letting her manipulate me and didn't cut ties and run at those first red flags." His gaze shifted to hers then back to the road. "And those first red flags were plentiful."

"I'm sorry," she said, reaching over and squeezing his leg, before adding lightly, "What's her name so I can hate her properly?"

He chuckled. "See?"

Her brows drew together. "See what?"

"You're nothing like her," he said. "I knew that from two minutes into dinner, knew that even though I wanted to paint you with the same brushstrokes—because even though I wanted to know you better, it was safer for my heart if I didn't—that I couldn't." He took one hand off the wheel, covered hers where it was resting on her thigh. "You're lovely and sweet and funny, and have that quintessential human feeling called empathy."

Wow.

"Was she that bad?"

Another glance. "Take what you're imagining and make it a hundred times worse." His fingers tightened on the steering wheel again. "But I still stayed for too long. So fucking stupid."

"No," she whispered. "That's called human."

"Po-tay-to, po-tah-to," he muttered.

She giggled then sobered. "I am sorry, you know? I've dated some men who—" She shuddered.

"What are their names, so I can hate them properly?"

Her heart fluttered.

"Scratch that, what are their names, so I can kill them properly?"

She touched his cheek. "You're sweet."

He turned his head, pressed a kiss to her palm. "You're used to giving a lot of yourself, aren't you?"

"What do you mean?"

"Your heart is generous," he said. "You see someone hurting and you jump in, you make it better."

Kate shrugged. "I have a weak spot for people, I guess. I like to see them happy."

Silence.

"But who makes sure *you're* happy?" he asked. "If you only give of yourself and never take, who cares for you, Red?"

Her breath caught, that question hitting way too close to the vulnerable center of her. Giving meant she controlled the interactions, controlled how much of herself she gave, and meant she could always keep a piece back.

She'd learned long ago she always needed to keep a piece of herself protected and safe.

Because sometimes it was only that single piece that

remained, that single piece she had to hold tightly on to as she rebuilt herself brick by brick.

But she couldn't tell him that.

She could barely accept it herself, preferred to pretend everything was light and easy.

"Empathy is an important life skill," she said, her tone teasing as she added, "So your ex had an inhuman lack of it?"

They slid to a stop at a signal, and Jaime turned his gaze on hers.

Then studied her for a long moment.

Panic bubbled up because, damn, he wasn't going to let her go.

"Alien, maybe," he muttered. "Because I've seen more empathy in animals than my ex had."

Kate squeezed his leg again. "Her name, please, good sir," she said, relieved he hadn't pushed enough to joke. "Hate will be commencing shortly."

He snorted. "Lori."

"Ugh," she muttered. "I knew a Lori in high school. She was the worst sort of bully."

He laughed. "Must be the name."

"Maybe." She bit her lip, a tendril of guilt weaving through her. She actually had a Lori on her design team, and design-team-Lori was really lovely.

"That." Fingers lifting from her hand, drifting over her cheek. "That's how I knew you weren't like Lori." A chuckle. "You were feeling guilty for lumping the whole of the Lori populace into one group, weren't you?"

"I work with a nice Lori and—"

He burst out laughing. "Fuck, but I like you, Kate."

Her heart somehow managed to swell with pleasure and also curl in on itself protectively. God, she liked him, too. But—

"Don't say that," she murmured. "You *can't*. You can't like me, can't make me like you because then when it's over, when you're done with me, it'll hurt too much." She pulled her hand back, sat up straight in her own seat. "I can't like you, not like that, not enough to want a future."

Silence.

Long, drawn-out silence.

Then the car shuddered to a stop on the shoulder, and he turned to face her. "Why can't you want a future, Kate?"

"Why do you care?" she snapped. "This is a fake relationship. It doesn't mean *anything.*"

A deadly calm. "Doesn't it?"

"No!" She tossed her hands up. "We've gone on one date—"

"Two."

Frowning, she stopped. "What?"

"Technically tonight was the second."

That threw her for a loop, and she froze. "Okay," she said, unfreezing after a couple of seconds. "So, two dates. That doesn't mean anything."

"Doesn't it?"

She crossed her arms, sighed heavily. "You already asked that."

"And you're sticking with the answer *no?*" More calm, his voice so smooth, so even, but below the surface she could sense a fury boiling, and she knew, *just knew*, that the asshole was going to rear its head.

Still, she might like this man too much, but she wasn't a fucking weakling. She held his gaze, straightened her spine, and braced herself for the impact that was sure to be lobbed her way.

And stayed braced.

And stayed a little longer.

Then longer still, waiting, knowing he was going to blow up at her.

Eventually, he shifted in his seat, and she jumped, not wanting to, knowing it gave away too much, revealed how brittle and on edge she was.

But she hadn't been able to help it.

Jaime ran the back of his fingers over her throat, making her shiver, and his words when he spoke after that long moment of silence were gentle, were light. "Then I guess I'll just have to prove it to you."

She swallowed hard, missing his hand when he brought it back to the steering wheel. "Prove what?"

Eyes locked onto hers for a searing moment. "That you mean something."

Those words, said in that gentle, light tone, wafted across the console to her ears, but when her brain processed them, their impact might as well have been a bullet to her gut.

They seared into her, branded themselves on her heart.

He leaned over and slanted his mouth against hers.

It was a quick, hot touch of his lips to hers . . . and it still scorched her down to the bone.

"You mean something to me, Kate," he murmured before pulling back onto the road and driving her home, as though he hadn't just rocked her to the core.

ELEVEN

JAIME

He woke up the next morning to a text that made his heart—the one that was thinking he'd pushed Kate too hard the night before—swell with hope.

The truth was that he was all in for her, and seeing her stare at him, wariness written in the lines of her pretty face, made him feel like shit. He got that it was less to do with him and more to do with her past, but part of him was worried that he wouldn't be able to break through the barrier she'd placed between them.

Maybe not a deliberate barrier. Perhaps she'd been hurt often enough that the barrier was a permanent fixture.

"Patience," he murmured to himself, rolling onto his back and sitting up.

Because . . . the text.

Sent at two in the morning, even though she'd been exhausted on the drive home, even after he'd deliberately turned the conversation to something light—movies and favorite restaurants.

The dark circles had seemed to get darker as he'd driven.

Dark enough that he'd eventually stopped talking, stopped trying to think of easy conversational topics that wouldn't put her on the defensive, and he'd thought there was a real possibility that she might fall asleep on the drive.

She hadn't.

In fact, *he'd* fallen. Fallen further, deeper, more entrenched in that woman.

Because then she'd asked about his family—had laughed when he'd described the group text chain he had with his siblings and parents, and how his younger brother, Brad, had left his phone on a table at a restaurant recently and they'd all been treated to a series of emoji-filled texts that took up the entire screen of his cell, courtesy of a rambunctious toddler from the next booth over.

"You need to take lessons from him on emoji-etiquette."

"From the toddler?"

She nodded.

He laughed. "Is this a lesson of more is better?"

A snort. "I take it back." She smiled at him, the barrier still there, but hidden beneath brown eyes sparkling with amusement. "Stick with your book."

Fun. Teasing. Sweet. Smile that fucking took his breath

Actually listening to him when he talked. Touching him when she forgot she was supposed to be keeping her distance—a squeeze on his leg, a brush of fingers on his arm, his jaw.

And now she'd sent him a text in the middle of the night.

I'm sorry about Lori. You deserve someone who sees the wonderful man you are inside.

Absently, he rubbed a hand over his chest, his heart aching. Sweet. See?

But also, completely blind to the fact that she was wonderful on the inside as well, blind to the notion that a man wanted to wrap himself in the warmth of her, to capture the light in her soul and hold it captive.

Because someone had made her believe she wasn't worthy of that.

Which circled back to his notion of Jaime being all in for this woman.

First, he wanted to get her some fucking glasses so that when she looked at herself in the mirror, she saw how wonderful she was. Second, he wanted to hunt down the asshole or assholes that made her believe differently.

But in reality, he couldn't do either of those things until he managed to get through her shields.

Well, luckily, he wasn't an idiot.

He recognized a good thing when he saw it, knew that she was worth the effort to gain her trust.

Which was why he didn't text her back.

Instead, he got up and showered.

Instead, he went down to the Farmer's Market and picked up a bouquet of sunflowers, a half dozen pastries, and two coffees—a mocha for her, just black for him—then drove to her house, glad that they lived close enough that the early Saturday morning drive to her place made the drinks' temperature drop to drinkable rather than cold and unappetizing.

He parked in front of her house and felt the bottom drop out of his plan. Or hell, maybe it was the bottom dropping out of his world, him plummeting through the hole, falling and falling further.

He'd been thinking he would text, and if that didn't work, then he'd call her, and then if *that* didn't work, he'd go up to her front door and knock or ring the bell.

He'd even gone so far as to convince himself that she'd open the door and would be standing sleepily on the other side wearing fluffy pajamas, her hair askew, cozy sheep-shaped slippers on her feet.

Yes, he had an overactive imagination.

But even his overactive imagination had not imagined short-shorts and a hoodie. He hadn't been able to picture Kate bending over a flowerpot on her front porch, her luscious ass and long, *long* legs on display. He certainly wouldn't have been able to conjure up the unzipped hoodie, the thin and worn tank top beneath.

Thankfully, he was already parked at the curb. Otherwise, the gorgeous flowers she had lining the walkway that led up to her house might have ended up under his tires.

Straightening, she turned, that gorgeous ass disappearing. But he wasn't disappointed, not when he got to meet those beautiful eyes through the windshield.

He grabbed the sunflowers, the bag of pastries, and the coffees then popped open the driver's side door.

"Jaime?"

The soft question greeted him before he closed the door behind him, and the sound of his name on her tongue sent heat arrowing toward his cock.

But he wasn't here to be led around by his cock.

He was here with a plan to win over this smart, sweet, beautiful on the inside and out woman. To chip a hole through the concrete and make a place for himself in her heart.

So, he kept his tone even and walked over to her, handing her the flowers. "Morning, Red."

Her voice was husky. "Morning, Jaime." She bit at that bottom lip. "Thank you," she murmured. "They're beautiful."

"You're welcome." His eyes dipped down, lingered on all that exposed skin. He was thanking whatever God had created short shorts when he let his gaze come back up, connect with hers. "Morning, my *sexy* Red."

Okay, so maybe not being led around by his cock by this woman was an impossible task, especially when all she had to do was breathe and he was hard.

Pink painted itself across her cheeks, and her lips parted as she inhaled a shaky breath. "What are you doing here?" she asked.

He held up the bag, the coffees. "Bringing you breakfast." A beat. "Though, I didn't expect to find you out of bed yet."

"Oh."

At the question in her eyes, he added. "You texted pretty late last night."

This time her cheeks didn't go pink. Rather, they paled, and her eyes shifted to the side. "Oh, yeah. I-I—" She stammered for a moment then murmured, "I hope I didn't wake you up."

"My cell is always on Do Not Disturb at night," he said. "I learned my lesson after getting way too many calls from the clinic when it wasn't my turn to be on call."

"Oh . . . good," she murmured.

"Is that your favorite word in the mornings?"

Red brows drew together. "What?"

"*Oh*," he said, setting the coffees down on the porch railing. "Is it your favorite word in the mornings?"

Those brows stayed drawn. "No."

"Okay." He shrugged, sat down on the top step. "So, you couldn't sleep last night?"

"I—well—"

He pulled out an apple turnover, offered it to her. "Hungry?"

She glanced down at her hands, and he saw they were covered in dirt. Then she bit her lip again. Fuck, but he thought that was sexy as hell, even as he recognized it was because she was unsure.

Shoving the turnover back into the bag, he stood and set it alongside the coffees on the railing. Then he snagged her hand, drew her over to the hose spigot he'd spied on his walk up the house, and rinsed off her hands. The dirt disappeared, and he used the bottom of his shirt to dry her fingers, her palms.

Maybe not the most sanitary, but it had given him an excuse to touch her, to bring her close.

And now they could eat.

"Come on." He nudged her over to the porch and down onto the front step. Then he grabbed her coffee. "Mocha," he said and handed it to her.

Her brows lifted. "How'd—?"

"I pay attention." When those brows stayed lifted, he added, "I've seen you express your undying love for them on many an Insta post."

She smiled, shook her head. "Thank God I keep my profile private for everyone except for sexy vets."

Mock-glowering, he asked, "How *many* sexy vets?"

"Hmm." She tapped a finger to her chin. "That is an excellent question."

"Okay, *questionee*"—he plunked the bag of pastries on her lap—"the next question you must answer is which sweet treat do you want?"

Her mouth curved. "I think the question is what sweet treat do *you* want?"

And Jaime found he couldn't resist the invitation.

He leaned over and kissed her.

Soft lips parted immediately, and he slipped his tongue inside her mouth, tangled it against hers. She tasted of mint and coffee, making his senses come alive, heat spreading out over his skin. Never had a simple kiss aroused him more, but then again, this woman was *more*.

She had the potential to be everything.

So, when she set the coffee and the bag aside then wrapped her arms around his neck and leaned back, tried to pull him on top of her, Jaime forced himself to stop.

To gentle the kiss, coaxing her down from the edge, pulling them back millimeter by millimeter until their lips separated. He stayed close, fingers in her ponytail, rapid breaths mixing. "You are so fucking beautiful."

A sharp inhale, her eyes closing for a heartbeat.

Hope. Fear. Pain. Desire. They swirled in those whiskey-colored depths, and he wanted to magnify the first and last, needed to make the middle two disappear.

He released her hair, had to physically force himself to straighten up, to not kiss that slightly swollen mouth and fill her with so much need and pleasure that she forgot all about the fear of the future, the pain of the past. She would be enveloped in desire, smothered in it, coating every inch as he gave her orgasm after orgasm.

And maybe that was ego talking, but also . . . he didn't think it was *all* ego.

They had chemistry, and it was combustible. Dry tinder in the forest, just needing the slightest spark in order to burst into flames.

Need coiled in his gut, fingers clenching, wanting to explore more.

Patience, remember?

Stifling a sigh, he nodded inwardly. That was the plan. Patience and winning her over.

He picked up the bag. "Breakfast."

Kate clasped a hand to her chest and the sight of her parted lips, breaths coming in rapid inhalations and exhalations had Jaime locking his spine, clenching one hand into such a tight fist that his bones ached.

"Breakfast," he said again, starting to hand her the bag.

She wrapped her fingers around his, halted the bag in mid-air. "What if I said I wasn't interested in breakfast?" she asked quietly. "What if I said that I wanted to kiss you again instead?"

His dick twitched. His fingers tightened on the brown paper, making it crinkle loudly in the quiet of the morning. His jaw clenched.

She stretched up, kissed the ticking muscle. "So tense."

"Such a tease," he murmured, covered her hand with his free one. "Wearing those sexy shorts." He dropped his palm to her bare thigh, slid it up an inch, fingers tracing light circles when her breath caught. "Kissing me until I can't think, can't remember all the reasons I'd been promising myself to give you romance."

Her mouth curved. Her eyes went soft. "Were there a lot of reasons?"

"I made a list."

She giggled, the tinkling sound sliding over his skin, helping him wrench himself back under control.

Then she bit her lip again, her eyes taking on a slightly guilty expression.

"What?" he rasped out.

That gorgeous mouth parting, the shuddering exhale drifting over his skin. "I made a list, too," she said, all soft. And close. She was close enough that the floral smell of her shampoo drifted over him, mixed with the damp earth scent of the garden, the humid perfume of the morning air.

His hand clenched on her thigh, and she jumped.

"Sorry," he murmured, relaxing his hold, not wanting to ever hurt her.

"No." She placed her palm over his, squeezed lightly. "It felt good."

More heat. More dick twitching. More of his control fading. More of his plan disappearing into so much smoke.

Jaime traced patterns on her silken skin, feeling goose bumps rise from the contact.

"Aren't you going to ask about my list?" she eventually asked.

Her pupils were dilated, that tempting fucking mouth too close, but there was also mischief in her gaze, warming the brown of her irises, and he wanted her to feel comfortable enough to tease, to play, even if it meant tormenting him with all her sexy skin and lip-biting and a list he thought was going to put his control to the test.

"Yes."

Her brows rose expectantly.

He grinned. "What's on your list, Red?"

Pink on her cheeks, even though she was the one who'd pressed the issue, but the mischief was also still there as she glanced up at him with dancing eyes and put it right out there. "It's a list of all the places I've imagined you kissing me."

There was no tempering his reaction, no holding on to his control.

Her soft mix of shy and not had obliterated any hope he had of pulling back.

He dropped the much-abused bag, knew the pastries inside were probably already reduced to crumbs and not giving one damn. Her thigh that was under his palm tightened, and he groaned, continued massaging the strong muscle that was covered in silk. His other hand went to her cheek, thumb shifting to rub against her bottom lip.

"Did you imagine me kissing you here?" he asked, voice filled with gravel.

She nodded, eyes hot, huskiness invading her words. "Yes."

He dipped his head and slanted his lips across hers, taking her mouth in a kiss that was pure desire, fanning the flames of his need until he was almost surprised to not find himself reduced to ash.

Only when he felt like his lungs would explode did he release Kate's mouth.

Her chest rose and fell in rapid succession, her fingers clenching the fabric of his T-shirt. Her body so close and so fucking tempting.

He ran his knuckles along the column of her throat. "What about here?"

She nodded.

Jaime bent and pressed his lips to the side of her neck, nipping lightly then soothing the slight sting with his tongue.

She gasped, threaded her fingers into his hair and tugged. "*Oh!*"

"Fuck, I love the way you say that," he murmured, stealing a quick hard kiss from her mouth just because he could, but also because he couldn't resist those lips. He stroked a finger lower, dipped it into the front of her tank top. "What about here?"

"No." She grabbed his hand, brought it to her breast. "I imagined you kissing me here."

The edges of his vision went hazy.

"Kate—"

Her fingers twitched, which meant that *his* fingers twitched, and holy hell the feel of her beneath his hand, soft and squeezable and damned near overfilling his hold was. So. Freaking. Glorious.

"Will you?" she murmured, shifting slightly, and he felt the hard bud of her nipple brush against his palm. "Will you kiss me here, Jaime?"

Fuck the pastries.

Fuck the coffee.

Fuck the plan.

He swept her up into his arms and carried her into the house.

TWELVE

KATE

That was perhaps the boldest request she had ever made.
But damn, had it paid off.

Because now she was in Jaime's arms, pressed against the chest she'd admired in so many of his pictures, held close as he stood and pushed through the front door of her house.

A moment of her weight shifting, but before she could do more than grip his shoulders a little tighter, the lock *clicked,* and she was pulled even closer.

She expected him to ask her where her bedroom was, to dump her down onto the mattress, to cover her body with his own and strip her naked. She expected him to take advantage of the opening she gave him, to take everything she had freely offered to him.

And that would have been fine.

Because it *had* been freely offered.

Because she wanted that, too.

Had dreamed about it, had fantasized and imagined and

hoped and prayed it would come about, and in this moment, she couldn't think of anything she wanted more.

But then he spun and pressed her to the door, pinning her against the hard wood.

His lips curved up at the corners. His eyes went hot.

And then he said, "Where else can I kiss you, Red?"

She wrapped her legs around his hips, lurched up so her mouth was a hairsbreadth from his. "*Everywhere*."

Lips curving further. Fingers sliding into her hair, knocking the ponytail askew, his hips holding her in place against the wood, and his free hand slipping under the hem of her tank top, his palm scalding where it met her bare skin. "Yeah?"

Kate nodded. "Yeah."

He dropped to his knees so fast that she shrieked.

But he only stayed there for a moment, long enough to unhook her legs, to help her find her feet, and then he was rising up, and his lips were on hers.

Long and slow and deep, he kissed her as though she were the tastiest dessert on the planet, and he intended to savor every bite. His tongue licked across her lips, slipped inside, and caressed hers, coaxing her into a rhythm that made her thighs clench, her knees tremble.

And all the while, his hands were moving, combing through her unbound hair, stroking up and down her side, over her stomach in delicate circles. A gentle pattern with slightly roughened skin that threatened to melt her into a puddle of goo.

His hand slid up, stopping an inch beneath her bra, and her breasts swelled, her nipples hard little points that ached for his mouth.

"Jaime," she breathed.

"Red." He touched her cheek and crouched again, hunkering down in front of her. He was so much taller than her and when he went down to his knees for a second time, his mouth was positioned exactly where she wanted.

He leaned in, sucked the hard bud of her nipple into his mouth.

She still wore her tank top, her bra. Together they made up several layers of fabric. So, him touching her that way shouldn't have felt good, shouldn't have sent desire spiraling through her body like his touch was a live wire directly to her pussy. But this was Jaime.

And the fact that he held such a power over her wasn't scary.

Because she knew deep down in the depths of her soul that he wouldn't take advantage of that power, that he wouldn't hold it over her, that she would be safe with him.

Because she also knew that somehow, she held the same power over him.

Flick.

She jumped.

Glanced down to see he'd tugged open the button on her shorts.

Her breath caught at the sight of his hands just below her navel, broad fingers tugging the pull of her zipper down. He spread the fabric, denim worn so often over the years that it had grown soft, that it was thin and fraying.

"Unicorns."

He smiled, pressed his lips against the fabric of her underwear, bright purple and dotted with dancing unicorns.

It wasn't sexy or skimpy. But then again, she hadn't expected to have a man between her thighs that morning.

Her hands slid between them, self-consciousness bubbling up, wanting to cover up the ridiculous fabric, but then Jaime took her hands, pressed them, palms flat, against the door.

"I like it," he murmured, the words coming against her skin, hot and damp and making her need spiral up and out of control. She barely felt when he lifted one of her feet then the other, tugging off her shoes and chucking them aside because his lips were moving in time with his hands, sliding up, nudging her tank top out of his way. He gripped the arms of her hoodie and that too disappeared, then her shirt was tugged over her head. "Unicorns," he said, still speaking against her skin, still moving up, only this time he pushed her bra out of the way. "*You're* the unicorn, my beautiful, sweet Kate."

"I'm not—"

The sentence didn't get a chance to form because then his mouth closed over her nipple.

Her words devolved into a moan. Her hands went to his hair, gripped tight.

Thankfully, Jaime didn't stop. Instead, he continued drawing on her nipple, shifting so he could take the other between thumb and forefinger, rolling gently at first, then harder until she was moaning, her hips bucking, her pussy clenching because she needed . . . more.

She needed him.

As though she'd spoken aloud, he began sliding his hand down her side, insinuated it between them, between the fabric of her underwear and her shorts, and cupped her.

"No," she gasped, fingers still tight in his hair.

He growled, nipped the underside of her breast. "No," he agreed. "Skin."

"Yes," she moaned. "Please, Jaime."

One shove had her panties and shorts around her ankles, another abrupt movement had them tugged off her legs. One more had her thighs spread wide.

His eyes met hers, fire in those pale brown depths, and held for a long moment. Then he dropped his gaze, and she felt the slow slide of his heated stare drift down her neck, caress over her breasts, trace over her stomach, dip lower, and hold.

"So pretty and pink and glistening."

She choked but didn't have time to say anything because Jaime was already moving, shifting forward and lifting one of her legs so it was over his shoulder.

And then his mouth was on her.

Or rather, his tongue.

He traced it through her damp folds, sliding over her sensitive labia, until he pressed the flat part to her clit, firm and sure and making sparks flash behind her eyes. Not rushing, but moving slow and steady, his caresses designed to discover exactly what she liked and then using the knowledge ruthlessly.

She'd been turned on from the moment he opened his car door and she saw it was him. She'd been wet from the second his palm had touched her thigh. She'd been on razor's edge from the instant her nipple was drawn deep into his mouth.

So, it was no surprise that his tongue on her clit, its rhythm perfect, and his finger circling the entrance to her body before pushing slowly inside would catapult her over the edge in mere seconds.

She exploded, pleasure coating her skin from head to toe in wave after wave after wave of pure, unadulterated bliss.

Thus was the power of Jaime.

Thirteen

Jaime

She was asleep in his arms.

Which was so not his plan.

It was also so much better.

She'd come on his fingers, his tongue, crying out his name. He'd never thought he would be the type of guy who would crave a woman saying his name, but Jaime couldn't deny that hearing it roll off Kate's tongue was music to his ears.

Then again, anything she seemed to say was music to his ears.

To his soul.

Sappy.

But finding a good woman would do that to a man, especially one as beautiful and wonderful and lovely as Kate.

He'd carried her to the couch, had wrapped them both in a blanket, though he hadn't needed anything more than her naked body pressed to his in order to be warm, to be scorched through down to the bone.

Her eyes had stayed closed, and she'd cuddled close and . . . he'd lost another piece of himself.

Fingers sliding through her hair, gliding down her arm, taking full advantage of the fact that she was asleep, that she trusted him enough already to have let exhaustion and pleasure take her over while in his arms, to study her closely. She appeared unguarded, and just so damned young.

They were the same age, and when she was conscious, that similarity was obvious, made clear by the shadows present in her eyes, the tension in her frame.

But like this, expression gentled, sleep making the rosebud of her lips shape into a tiny O every time she exhaled, and Jaime thought that she could be much, much younger.

Maybe not in age but in spirit.

Smiling when he thought of what her response would be to that —she'd tease him and his poetry skills, of that he had no doubt—he stayed in place, stroking her hair, watching the sun get a little higher, the sky a bit brighter before she stirred, nuzzling at his throat, her breathing changing from to slow and steady to slightly faster.

Then she froze, ramrod stiff in his arms.

She was awake.

And naked.

Conscious that she might be feeling uncomfortable, he slipped out from beneath the blanket, careful to leave it covering her, then made his way into the hall.

Panties tangled with her shorts, both shoved in the corner.

Bra one way. Her tank top the other.

He gathered them all up and snagged her hoodie, which had somehow ended up on the coatrack, then headed back to her, setting them on the couch next to her.

She was staring out the front windows when he walked in, gaze on the lush greenery that was dotted with purple flowers, jumped when he placed the pile on the cushion beside her thigh.

Her eyes flew to his, a blush crept into her cheeks. "Jaime—"

He ran his knuckles over her cheek. "I'll go make some coffee."

"I—" Teeth digging into her bottom lip.

"Coffee first," he murmured, running his thumb lightly over her skin.

More hesitation then she nodded.

He went back into the hallway, moved to the opening he'd spied on his limited travels, and moved to the Keurig. Opening a couple of cabinets led him to a set of purple glasses lined up neatly next to a stack of purple plates.

Her favorite color is purple.

Remembering her quick recital from the other night had him smiling.

It seemed that her favorite extended to plates and cups. His eyes flicked to the right.

And coffee mugs, he realized, reaching past the tidy rows of purple drinkware to retrieve a pair of lilac ceramic cups, plunked them on the counter, and stuck a mocha pod in the coffee maker, then set the machine to run. Once it was working, he slipped out the front door and retrieved the bag of pastries, pleased to find out there were more than crumbs inside.

By the time he made his way back to the kitchen and was placing a slightly squished pumpkin muffin, an apple turnover with one end broken off, and a peppermint scone on the plate, Kate came in, fully dressed.

Now that was a disappointment.

The color was still high in her cheeks, but her eyes when they met his were soft. "Sorry, I fell asleep on you," she murmured. "I ... um ... didn't get much rest last night."

He set down the bag, crossed over to her.

"My fault," he said, tracing a hand down her arm, relieved when she didn't back away, when she let him lace his fingers through hers and hold tight.

"No."

He lifted a brow.

"Mine," she explained. "I keep waffling between guilt at lying to my family, thinking that I should just stop this madness and confess the truth."

"By *stop this madness* do you mean stopping . . . us?"

"Jaime," she said and sighed. "I like you. I really do. But I don't lie to my family." A shake of her head. "I never have, and to lie about something this big." She dropped her gaze to the floor. "I wanted the setups to stop, that's it."

The back of his throat burned, and he wanted to shout at her, to demand she acknowledge this, that *they* were more than just a lie.

But he needed to stay calm.

So, he gritted his teeth, sucked in a long, slow breath through his nose. One. Two. Three. Holding it in his lungs before releasing it just as slowly. Out. Two. Three.

Then he asked, "And the other thing?"

Her gaze came up, eyes sliding to his, questions in those whiskey depths.

He took solace in the fact that their hands were still laced together, squeezed her fingers lightly. "You said you were waffling," he murmured. "What was the other thing you were waffling with?"

Bright white teeth pressed into a lush, rosy bottom lip.

"Kate," he warned, using his thumb to free it, unable to stop himself from stroking his finger across the plump, lickable surface.

She shuddered. "God, I like it when you touch my lips like that."

He grinned. "Then keep biting them, and I won't be able to resist."

Her throat worked as she swallowed hard.

"*Kate.*" Another warning, one that had her eyes flashing with fire, annoyance entering her tone.

"You haven't earned the right to give me orders," she snapped.

He dropped his hands to her waist. "Well, then tell me what you're waffling with, Red. The lying to your family and what?"

A mulish expression on her face.

His fingers tightened.

Just slightly, but enough that he felt her shiver. So, his Red liked it when he gripped her hips. Not that he *didn't* like it. Hell, just putting his hands on her made his cock hard. Still, it was another piece of the Kate puzzle and as thus, he filed it away.

Along with the image of gripping those hips and thrusting deep.

"What, Red?" he asked again, forcing himself to focus.

"I'm torn between the lie and wanting what's between us to be real!"

It was a burst of noise, of words, and combined with her yanking out of his hold, of moving away from him, it took Jaime a second to process.

By the time he did, she was at the counter, shoving another pod into the Keurig.

"I—" *Slam.* The top went down. "Kate—" She kept her back to him and hit the button, the coffee popping and hissing. "I'm—" *Scrape.* The plate slid back onto the counter.

And that was about all of the interruptions he could handle.

He closed the distance between them, coming close just as she spun around, just as she began to speak. "I—"

He sealed his mouth over hers.

Stiff. She was stiff against him for a single heartbeat. Then she melted, hands coming around his neck, and kissed him back, her tongue a scalding brand, her luscious curves pressed close. He'd been dipped into a vat of molten steel, his body burning up from the inside out, boiling with need, his nerves firing, his cock hard and aching.

She pulled back, chest heaving.

"I want us to be real," she said. "I want it so fucking bad." Her fingers tightened. "I want it because you're nice and funny and kind and gorgeous. I want it because you seem to like me. I want it because you're sexy and kiss me like you think I'm the same." Her eyes drifted away. "But at the same time, I know I *can't* want it because it won't last."

Desire blazing through his mind, eliminating his brain cells, but he still managed to ask, "Why, honey? Why do you think we won't work out?"

She pulled back, and though it was difficult, Jaime made his hands release her.

A stumbling step away, a shaking hand pushing her hair off her face. But then her gaze was back on his, and the bleakness in it stole his breath. Because she'd already written their ending, even as they'd just barely begun.

Her words confirmed the sentiment.

"Because anytime someone says they want me, they never mean it."

That was a fucking punch to the gut.

"Red," he murmured.

Her eyes closed and he watched her shoulders lift and fall on a long, slow exhale. Then she spoke, and it was like her tone had taken a one-eighty. "Anyway," she chirped. "That's just reality in dating in this world of Tinder and technology. Everyone has a short attention span and is always thinking of the next great thing." A shrug, her hair whipping as she spun back to the coffee maker. "How do you take your coffee?" She giggled, and it wasn't gentle or sweet or anything like her normal husky laugh. The rough sound cut through him like a dull blade. "I'm guessing black because I've seen the hair on your chest in your pictures."

Since she was doing a damned good job at having her conversation by herself, Jaime just leaned against the island counter and crossed his arms.

Then waited.

"Or maybe one sugar." Another false giggle. "Because you're so sweet." She nudged the plate holding the pastries. "Or at least have a sweet tooth based on the sheer volume of sugar on this plate."

Kate picked up the plate, brought it to the island. She didn't look at him as she set it on the island, nor before she turned and went back for the mugs.

Nor when she then set those on the counter.

"Do you want the turnover or the scone?" she asked. "Because this pumpkin muffin is mi . . . *ne?*"

Her statement ended on a halting question.

No doubt because her eyes finally made it to his.

"Who hurt you?"

"Wh-what?"

"Who hurt you?" he repeated. "You keep talking about our end before we've even begun. I've told you, I'm not interested in ending anything, that you already mean something to me"—he uncrossed his arms, ran his knuckles over her cheek—"I want to prove that to you, but I won't be able to do it if you keep pushing me away before I can."

"Jaime," she breathed.

"I know," he said and took her hands in his, pressed them to his chest. "I know we're new. I know trust takes time to build. But I also can't prove that you mean something important and big and wonderful to me if you won't let me in." He slipped one arm around her waist. "Just crack the door, Red. Just the tiniest bit. Ride this wave with me. Let me in so I can show you."

She dropped her forehead to his collarbone. "I'm scared."

"I'm here," he murmured. "I've got you."

"But for how long?"

Forever.

That was what he wanted to say, to declare, to force her to believe.

But how could he say that? How could he possibly make her understand that when they were so new, when she'd clearly been so hurt?

When pushing her to open herself wide may expose those wounds to the air?

He couldn't.

He just needed to keep practicing patience, to keep showing her that he was there, that he wasn't like whoever had injured her heart, and hope that someday she would see that he was different and recognize he was worth the risk of dropping all of her barriers.

"Okay," he said on a long slow breath. "I get it. I understand and I'm not going to keep pushing you to tell me something you're not comfortable sharing." He touched her cheek. "You don't have to tell me who hurt you, but Red, can you just give me a chance? Can you just let us have some time to learn each other before you end us? We haven't we even had a chance to begin."

"Jaime," she breathed.

"Please," he said, aware that he was pushing, even though he promised he wouldn't, that he was making his own crack in her barriers and shoving himself through.

Less patience than persistence.

But he couldn't make himself stop.

The reason for that made itself clear when Kate and her kind soul gave generously again. The woman who'd cared about his pain in the car. The one who'd worried and texted in the night. The one who looked up at him gently and nodded, lifting her hand and pressing it against his cheek before she leaned close, brought her lips to his, and whispered, "okay."

Then she kissed him.

Sweetly. Gently. Kindly.

Even when she was scared, she gave. Even terrified, she'd cracked the door to her heart.

She'd thrown a lifeline to a begging man.

There was no fucking way he was going to waste that.

He was going to make damn sure he gave back.

FOURTEEN

KATE

She lay in bed that night, hours after Jaime had left, hours after she'd eaten a delicious pumpkin muffin and he'd had an apple turnover.

Hours after she'd made a promise to herself to stop thinking about the inevitable end of her and Jaime and how she knew it would be more devastating to lose him than it had been to lose any other relationship. Hours after she'd decided to focus on enjoying the time they had left.

"Fuck," she muttered, punching her pillow and tossing and turning in her bed.

Her very expensive, supposedly the world's most comfortable pillow. Her pricey mattress. Her ridiculously overpriced linens that were cozy and fluffy and normally had her sleeping like a baby.

Well, like a baby that wasn't little Lacy, up at all hours.

But instead she was awake, the fucking broken record of fear and end cycling through her mind.

Jaime had gone into his clinic about an hour after they'd

eaten together, after cleaning the dishes and mugs, after putting his muscles to excellent work by digging a series of holes for the new plants she'd planned on purchasing later that day.

As a result, she continued to think of him the entire time she worked in the garden.

Hell, he never left her mind.

Not on the drive to the nursery, nor as she picked out plants and she wondered what type would be his favorite and if she got that extra flat of marigolds if she would be able to convince him to dig a few more holes.

She thought of him as she loosened the flowers from their pots, as she broke apart their roots and sprinkled in some plant food before tucking them carefully into the soil. She thought of his capable hands as she used her own hand to pat the dirt down, remembering how his had felt as they touched and stroked and caressed.

But when he'd called that night, she hadn't picked up.

She'd let it go to voicemail then had listened to the short and sweet message he'd left, telling her he was thinking of her, that he missed her and for her to call him back anytime, and if not that he'd try her the next day.

But she hadn't returned the call.

Hadn't texted.

Instead, she spent the day in worry.

No matter all the grandiose promises she'd made to herself and him.

"Ugh!" she groaned, hating this, hating she was so insecure when it came to her love life. She was a confident and capable woman in every other part of her life. Self-assured at work. Self-reliant when it came to her house, her car, her life. She could change a tire, fix a leaking pipe. She could pay her own bills. Hell, she had learned how to patch her own roof last year when a big storm had ripped off a few shingles and she couldn't get a roofing contractor out for a few days and hadn't wanted her dad on the roof.

She could troubleshoot her WiFi and set up her cable box.

So, why couldn't she be in a healthy fucking relationship?

Why did she need to lie to her family or feel inadequate?

Why couldn't she open her heart to a man who was so clearly wonderful?

Knock. Knock. Knock.

She jumped, panic swelling in her despite all of her home-ownership self-reliance. Because it was nearly ten at night, and someone was pounding on her front door.

Kate grabbed her cell from her nightstand, her baseball bat from the side of her bed—it added to her capable because she could swing that sucker like a big-leaguer—and started to make her way out of her bedroom.

She'd hide in a closet or slip out the back door and she'd call the police.

There. Plan. Done.

Knock. Knock. Knock.

It came again just as she stepped out of her bedroom, and she jumped, nearly fell down the stairs.

"Katie!"

She jumped again, but this time it was less fear and more startle.

Because she recognized that voice.

"Katie!"

Heidi.

One of her closest friends. They'd met in college. They'd bonded first over drinking too much and christening the porce-lain goddess, and forever over nerding out about *all* the things—Hermione Granger and unicorns and board games and even gardening, though that was really more of Kate's wheelhouse.

The point was that her very best friend was at her house, and it didn't take a genius to know why.

She'd heard about Jaime.

Knock. Knock. Knock.

"Don't try to hide, my Katie girl," Heidi called. "I've brought wine and ice cream, and we *are* going to talk about it."

And because Kate knew there was no point in trying to ignore Heidi—her friend put persistence to shame—she headed down the stairs, flicked on the light in the hall, and opened the front door.

Heidi strolled in as though they were mid-conversation.

"You've been keeping secrets, college roomie," Heidi said with a tsk.

Kate groaned. "I don't want to talk about it."

"Good," Heidi said, flicking on the lights in the kitchen and making herself at home. It wasn't a surprise. They'd been in each other's lives for more than a decade, had lived together on more than one occasion—four years in college, four more until Kate had bought this house. Heidi had long ago moved beyond guest status and was firmly in the category of family.

Which is why she had little compunction opening up the cabinet that held Kate's wine glasses and pulling out two. Another quick movement had her locating the bottle opener, and in the next few seconds, she had two glasses poured and had set one in front of Kate.

"I need your advice."

Suspicion slid through her. "You're not going to ask—"

"You about your fake engagement?" Heidi finished for her. "Fuck, yes, I am, because clearly you've got something big going on, but as much I want to squeeze every last bit of information out of you"—she lifted her hands and demonstrated her apparently very capable squeezing ability—"I also know your stubborn face."

Kate frowned. "Stubborn face?"

"Yup." A nod. A wave of her hand at Kate's face. "Locked and loaded, front and center, insert other similar clichés here," she said. "Which is why I'm going to wear you down with my life drama, and then you'll dish on yours."

Kate sniffed. "You wouldn't make much of an evil genius, you know that, right?"

"Because I'm telling you my nefarious plan?" Heidi shrugged when Kate nodded then pointed at the wine glass. "You're already halfway through that one. Another and you'll tell me everything I want to know. Muahaha!"

Kate pushed the glass away.

Heidi snorted. "Yeah, right. It's your favorite. I know you won't be able to resist."

Kate made a face. One, because her friend was right—it was her favorite. An ice wine from a small winery in Utah of all places. Two, because it was expensive, and she would feel too damned guilty if she didn't drink it. Heidi wasn't hurting for money, but she worked really hard and had pulled way too many hours re-stocking shelves at the college bookstore to afford to make her way through school, way too many hours doing double shifts in order to pay off her loans for Kate to waste some of her best friend's hard-earned wages.

Kate's mom getting the beauty deal just before college was the only reason Kate hadn't been in the same boat.

She would have had the loans, the extra hours, the struggle.

Growing up without a lot of frills had taught her to appreciate the little things right along with the big—and no bills upon leaving school definitely qualified as big, same as the wine was a small luxury.

One that should be appreciated just as much.

One that had her scowling at her friend and taking another large sip.

Tart and sweet, with notes of berry, it was freaking delicious.

Probably why her friend was looking at her all smug and self-important. "If I have a hangover tomorrow," she muttered. "I'm blaming you."

"You know we're finishing this bottle, right?" Heidi brushed her fingers over Kate's forehead. "It's small, so just three glasses each."

"Three!"

A bop to Kate's nose. "Release the lines. We'll both be pleasantly drunk. I'll spill, you'll spill, we'll all spill."

Kate wrinkled her nose. "That sounds like a terrible childhood song."

Heidi grinned, picked up her own glass, and took a sip. "I quit my job today."

Since Kate had followed her friend's example by drinking some of her own wine, she nearly spit all that glorious, tasty deliciousness out.

Let it be noted that spit takes were not sexy.

She repeated, *they were not sexy*. Sighing, she mopped up what had dribbled down her chin with a kitchen towel, while managing to swallow the rest, and glaring over at her friend. Heidi shrugged, not an ounce of remorse in sight. Kate set her glass down. "Why would you quit?" she asked. "You loved working at Carbon."

Heidi was a molecular physicist whose field of study was the space between atoms.

Her friend had explained the significance of that to her on more than one occasion but had never been able to dumb it down enough for a layman, such as Kate. Heidi could talk about work to only one person in their group, and that was Kelsey, who was a brilliant engineer, had earned multiple degrees—some just for "fun"—but even she couldn't begin to match her friend's expertise.

"It's not sexy enough for you and your advertising brain," Heidi had declared on more than one occasion, which was possibly true.

Okay, it was *mostly* true.

Once Heidi began down a tangent of how atoms were

mostly empty space and the speed of the electrons orbiting them, Kate's brain shut down.

So, Kate might not understand the nitty-gritty of Heidi's job, but she understood her friend.

And her friend loved working for Carbon Industries.

Loved it so much that she'd turned down several lucrative offers for other biotech companies over the years.

Kate reached across and snagged her friend's free hand, held it tightly with both of hers. "Why, Heid?" she asked. "I thought you were really happy there, and I think it was only a week ago that you mentioned your grant money came through."

Hazel eyes lock on hers, and it was impossible to miss the sadness in their depths. "It did."

"So, what happened?"

Heidi made a face. "The climate has just been deteriorating over the last few months," she said. "You know we got bought out"—a pause, her gaze alighting on Kate's for a moment before she nodded—"well, all of a sudden every step of our lab process has to be run through our corporate liaison. The product side of the company wants to make sure R&D"—research and development—and the department in which Heidi worked—"isn't wasting resources and money."

"Okay." Kate squeezed lightly. "That doesn't seem all bad."

"I didn't think so either." Heidi pulled her hand back and pushed to her feet, pacing through the kitchen. "The problem is that our liaison is never available. And when she is, she clearly doesn't understand science. It's only numbers and appearances, and it's so infuriating." She tossed up her hands. "I don't have the supplies I need because the grant money is all tied up in corporate, waiting for my freaking liaison to approve the orders. Beyond that, I can't get approval for my interns to get overtime so they can come in on the weekends or after hours to check our experiments because those are resources that HR refuses to approve because it's too expensive." She paced back, scooped up her glass, and took a large sip. "Never mind that all of that was built into my request when I wrote the grant and the funds are there—"

A sigh.

"I'm boring you."

Kate jumped to her feet and rushed over to her friend, hugging her close. "Absolutely not," she said. "I was just thinking that this is the first conversation I've had with you about your work where I could understand everything." She pulled back on Heidi's snort. "And I empathize. I know you worked hard on the grant, know that you were so excited to get it."

"Yeah," she said. "I was."

"I'm sorry."

"I know." Heidi made a face. "I'm really going to miss my lab."

"Are you . . ." Kate stopped, nibbling at her bottom lip, then figured she might as well just ask. She and Heidi had never hidden anything and if she didn't ask, she'd worry. "Are you going to be okay for a while without a job? Money wise?"

A nod. "I'm good, Katie girl."

Relief slid through her. "That changes, you let me know."

"Will do," Heidi said, "but I've already begun applying other places. Luckily, there aren't too many people who can do what I do. I know it won't take long to find something."

"Smarty-pants."

"*Liar* pants," Heidi countered with a lifted brow that seemed to say, "your turn."

"I haven't even finished my first glass of wine yet," Kate muttered, though there was hardly more than one drop left.

"Here." Heidi topped her off then did the same for her own drink. "Second glass commencing."

Kate pouted. "Bully."

"Assertive," Heidi said.

"Pain in my ass," Kate muttered.

Heidi nodded. "Damn right."

Kate sighed. "Annoying."

"You love me," Heidi sing-songed.

Kate *did* love her friend. So freaking much. Which was why she didn't want to admit what she'd done. Heidi would understand, but Heidi would also . . . understand too much.

She knew all about Kate's superpower.

"Can't we just pretend you didn't hear what you heard?"

"You mean, can't I just pretend that you're not fake engaged when your mom calls me and tells me we *have* to plan a surprise engagement party for you and the mysterious Jaime, and we have to do it fast?" Heidi shook her head. "No can do, babe. We can't pretend *that* didn't happen." A nudge of her shoulder against Kate's. "And you're damn lucky she called me first and I could write my shocked-into-silence off as distraction by something in my lab instead of her calling Kels or Cora first. They would have balked and spilled the beans, and you know it," she said, naming their other two closest friends. "I told her I would do a survey of everyone's availability and get back to her, but Katie . . . this is a big lie."

"I know." She tried to swallow down the guilt and asked quietly, "How'd you know it was a fake engagement?"

"Really?" Hazel eyes bored into her. "We all had dinner not even a week ago, and you went on and on about how you were worried you'd be re-virginized because it had been so long." A roll of those eyes. "That convo ring a bell?"

Oh. Yeah. *That.*

"Pretty short courtship for a real fiancé," Heidi said.

"I—"

Heidi cut her off. "Why'd you do it?"

Kate made a face. "My mom was going to set me up again, and I just blurted something out. I didn't even really mean to say I was engaged. It just slipped out and then it was *out,* and she was so thrilled that I didn't know how to take it back and—"

A nod. "Thus, the lie grew."

Kate winced. "Yeah."

"So, who is he?" Heidi asked.

"*JaimeTheVet*," she said.

Heidi blinked. "The Instagram guy with the man bun that you've drooled over for months?"

Kate nodded. "Though he doesn't have the man bun anymore. He cut it off because he didn't think my parents would approve of him having long hair."

"Really?" Heidi exclaimed. "But his hair was so nice—" She stopped herself midsentence with a wave of her hand. "That's not the most important conversational hurdle at this point. Did he teach you how to do that flawless bun?"—her gaze went to Kate's, who shook her head—"Damn. Okay, we'll circle back to that glorious hair later. The more important part of this story is that he doesn't know you, so why would he agree? Are you paying him?"

A shake of her head. "No," she said. "I messaged him after I talked to my mom. I knew it was an insane thing to do. I mean, I totally get that. But then I asked him, and he said yes, and we agreed to go to dinner on Thursday, and he was late because he was doing a procedure on a guinea pig with a heart problem, and then he held my hand, and we walked to the pier, and then he kissed me, and it was hands-down the best kiss of my life." She gulped down more wine. "I like him, Heidi. A lot."

"But does he like you?"

Ouch.

Kate dropped her stare to the granite, taking in the flecks of silver amongst the pale blue, blinking hard.

Does he like you?

That was the crux of all of her fears, wasn't it?

Did he like her, really? And if he did like her genuinely,

would that like last? And if it lasted, would that lasting be days or weeks or months before he betrayed—

Heidi's hand covered hers. "I didn't mean it like that," she murmured.

Kate's throat burned, but she squeezed out. "I know."

"No," Heidi said, "I don't think you do." Her friend tugged the glass out of Kate's hands, gripped her wrists tight. "You are one of the best people I know. You're smart and funny and kind . . . even though you have a weird redheaded connection thing with Hermione Granger." Kate snorted. "You do," Heidi said, lips tipped up at the edges. "But I love you, and you're my fucking best friend, so believe me when I say that there is no person on this planet who deserves to have everything they want more than you."

"A big *but* is coming," Kate muttered.

"Yes," Heidi said. "Except, the but is that I don't want you to get hurt again."

Neither did she. It was why she kept throwing up barriers between herself and Jaime even though she really liked him. It was why her mind kept pulling her back even though her heart continued to encourage her further.

"He says he was drumming up the courage to ask me on a date when I messaged. That he took the opportunity to get to know me. He says he wants more dates and wants to prove that I can trust him." She sighed. "He says he knows that takes time, but that he can be patient. And—" Her gaze flicked to Heidi's. "He brought me breakfast and paid attention enough to know that my favorite breakfast is from Molly's, that I love mochas. And he's the oldest of four and is great with babies—he even managed to get Lacy to not have a meltdown for almost a half hour. Then he handled my mom and dad and brother and sister with aplomb and kindness. *And* he takes care of a rooster named Barry, who walks on a leash."

Chest heaving, she pulled out of Heidi's grip, shoved her hair out of her face.

"And I'm fucking terrified," she said, eyes burning. "Because I like him, too. Because this was just a stupid lie, and I hardly know him. Except, I *do* know him." She thumped a fist against her chest, just over her heart. "I know him here. From the moment I met him, it was like I had this connection to him. And not even all physical, because of course he's beautiful and sexy, anyone could see that. But because he-he's—"

"Different."

She glanced up at Heidi. "Yes. He's different."

"And you don't want to get hurt again."

"I've jumped into things with men too many times in my life, Heidi. I've thought they were all different, that they were all good, and when they didn't work out, I thought that it was just a matter of finding a man who could be the one. That I just needed to keep looking." She closed her eyes. "Then I realized that lightning doesn't strike in the same place over and over again. Then I realized it was me. I was the thing that connected us, and *I'm* the thing that's wrong in every relationship I've had." Another thump of her fist to her chest. "I'm the messed up one that makes everything implode."

"Well, that's bullshit."

Kate was so far down her proverbial mental rabbit hole that it took her a few seconds to realize what Heidi had said.

"*What?*" she exclaimed.

She'd just poured her heart out to her best friend, exposed her vulnerable underbelly, and confessed all of the twisted and sad things she'd been feeling, and Heidi had just called it all bullshit.

"I'm—"

Heidi's hand came up, palm out. "I heard you, Katie," she said. "Believe me. I heard every single fucking word and the absolute bullshit that is lacing them together. Yes, you might have been guilty of falling for people too quickly every once in a while, but who hasn't fallen harder than the person you're seeing and gotten hurt—"

"That's not what I mean—"

"And further that, maybe you've dated some freaking douchebags, but again, who hasn't?" Heidi said, talking over her. "Everyone I know has gone through plenty of assholes before they realized they wanted something more, something different."

"Except—"

"Except, what? You were stupid and didn't understand your worth?" Heidi took a sip of wine. "Welcome to the club. We've all been a little stupid in love now and then."

"I don't think I understand—"

Plink. The cup settled onto the granite. "I do, honey," Heidi murmured. "I do understand. You've done an A-plus job at picking losers, but I've also seen you with good men, but ones who just aren't compatible with you, personality or lifestyle or otherwise. That doesn't mean that there's something wrong with you. That makes you normal at this whole dating thing."

"Heidi."

"Steve Hollen."

"What?"

"He was a good guy. Nice. You saw him for three months. You two broke up because he moved to the East Coast. *Not* an asshole."

"I—"

"Berkeley Anders. Six dates. Good kisser. Fun to hang out with. But you stopped seeing him because he wanted to go out all the time and you wanted to be home more. Also, not an asshole."

"He—"

"Was a little hurt when you broke it off, yes, and didn't want to continue *being friends.*" Heidi rolled her eyes. "That doesn't happen in real life, no matter how sweet you are inside. I know you joke about your asshole superpower, but you don't have one, Kate. What you *do* have is the ability to give glimpses to that big, wonderful heart of yours, but then to shut anyone out who wants to reach for it."

"That's not—"

"Fair? Maybe." Heidi shrugged. "But it's also true. A few months ago, Thompson Arnold. He was boring. Three dates. You never went on a fourth. Not an asshole. And if you want me to keep going, I can circle *all* to college. Keith Black. Senior year. Totally into you. Took you on at least ten dates and bought you roses and wanted to sync up on his post-grad with your internship so he could keep seeing you." Heidi walked over, held her stare. "Also, not an asshole, but you cut him loose."

Kate's pulse thundered, the memories surrounding her, memories she'd suppressed. Heidi and her list were right. She had seen Keith and Thompson and Berkeley and Steve and frankly *more,* but she'd never really let them in. "*I'm* the asshole," she murmured.

"No," Heidi said on a laugh. "You're not. You have that big heart, the one that draws everyone in, but you're really good at giving, at helping, at jumping in if someone has a crisis. You're great at loving everyone else." She tapped the spot over Kate's heart. "Except, yourself. Because as much as you give, you never really open yourself up enough to truly trust or rely on another person."

"I—"

"Trust on your family, your friends?" Heidi nodded. "Yeah, you do. But even then, you make it hard sometimes, babe. You want to take care of us, but if we try to help you in return, you do the capable thing and push us away."

"I'm not—" She broke off, eyes stinging.

"The hole in your roof Cora's brother offered to fix? Walking home when you got a flat instead of calling us? Being sick as a dog and taking care of yourself instead of calling me or your mom or Cora—"

"The baby—"

"I know, Katie," Heidi said gently. "There's always a logical reason for not. But . . . you need to think if it's really logic that's having you do it all yourself, having you help everyone else, but not accepting that same care in return."

Fuck. Kate had the sinking sensation her friend was right.

"I know you're not trying to hurt us," Heidi murmured, reaching for her hand. "I don't know why you think you have to do it all yourself when we have your back, will always have it, but I can get needing to hold things close to your chest." A squeeze. "But consider, I've known you for a decade-plus, and I don't understand why you build the walls, why you keep me out of the inner sanctum of your heart, so how can you expect to be comfortable enough to be in a relationship that deep?" A pause. "Or how do you really know you want that?"

Kate swallowed hard but couldn't find the words.

It didn't matter, because Heidi had them anyway.

"You have this mental block, babe. Always have. For some idiotic reason, you think that what's inside you isn't valuable or important or grand enough for someone to love every single part —the good, the bad, the in-between." She brushed back Kate's hair. "And yet you don't hesitate to love the people around you, warts and all."

Kate's gaze slid away.

Heidi let her get away with that, but that didn't stop her from having the final word.

"It took me a long time to figure it out," she said, gently. "You give, Katie girl. You give so much that you don't have to risk taking." Heidi cradled her jaw, forced Kate to meet her stare. "You give so much because that means you don't have to open up those steel plates around your heart and actually let someone in to care for you in return. Because if you did, then you would be vulnerable."

Then with those words that pierced right through Kate's armor, she pressed a kiss to her cheek, pulled on her coat, and walked right out of Kate's house.

In like a hurricane, gale force winds knocking everything that Kate thought she knew into disarray, and then out just as abruptly, the aftermath she left behind heavy and silent and . . . shattered.

Sinking down to the tile, Kate buried her face in her hands.

And then she cried.

For a long, long time.

FIFTEEN

JAIME

He knew something was wrong.

How he knew, he wasn't going to second guess.

But from the moment his eyes had slid open, the sun barely cresting the hills in the distance, he'd felt a deep pit of unease in his stomach.

Something was wrong with Kate.

Jaime didn't bother to hesitate or think through the instinct or take a moment to pause and remember they'd been fake fiancés, and something more, for less than a week—message to first date to family dinner. He simply got dressed and drove over to Kate's house.

She was sitting on her front porch, hair tumbled around her face, top of her body swallowed by a huge gray hoodie, patterned pajama pants swimming over her legs. But what had his stomach twisting itself into knots was the expression on her face. Bleak and exhausted, despite the mug filled with what he assumed was coffee that she was holding in her hands.

Maybe it would have been more prudent to keep driving, to

move past this woman who was beautiful and lovely and fun and not complicate his life.

But it wasn't even an option that crossed his mind.

He'd decided on this adventure, on this path that would hopefully gain him Kate's heart, her body, her soul linked to his from two minutes into that conversation at dinner. Hell, if he were being honest with himself, he'd decided on her from the moment that message had hit his inbox.

Such a random, odd request.

And also, one he'd never even considered denying.

It was probably stupid to have been infatuated with a woman he'd only known over social media, probably even more so to have fallen for her two minutes into their first date.

But there it was.

And he was riding it through to the end.

He was going to follow through with what he'd promised. He was going to show patience and perseverance and win the heart of the gorgeous, fun, amazing woman who was sitting so sadly on her front porch.

Decision made.

All in.

No waffling required.

Jaime got out, walked up the drive. Kate's gaze had fixed on his the moment he'd opened the driver's side door, and it stayed there as he moved toward her.

But when her lips parted as he approached the bottom step of the porch, he didn't give her a chance to speak, to find some piece inside her to push him away.

Instead, he snagged the mug from her grip, set it on the wood, and sat, picking her up and plunking her into his lap.

"Jaime," she whispered.

"Hush now," he said, stroking the hair off her face, seeing how pale she was, the dark circles under each eye. He brushed his thumb along both. "You didn't sleep last night, Red?"

She shook her head.

"Because of me?"

Another shake.

"Then why, baby?"

Her eyes filled with tears, the tip of her nose went pink, and he had to struggle to contain the urge to want to pulverize whoever had hurt her when a single tear appeared at the corner of her eye and slid down her cheek. "Because of *me*, Jaime. I'm so messed up inside."

The pain in that statement made *his* eyes sting. "No, you're not," he argued. "You're wonderful and perfect and—"

Fingers on his lips, silencing his words.

"I *am* messed up," she said firmly, pressing harder when he sucked in a breath, prepared to disagree with her further. This woman meant more to him after a week than any woman had ever meant, his family aside. And he didn't want to kiss and touch and hold his mom or his sisters. He also certainly didn't want to sleep with them—*shudder*. Her next words took any of the light in his mind and smashed it to bits. "I'm so fucking broken and ruined and—"

She broke off on a sob, and he held her tight, mind spinning.

Her words aside, he'd thought of little else except for Kate for months now. First, imagining how he might get a shot with her, and now thinking of all the ways to keep her now that he finally got that chance.

And he'd be the first to admit that he clearly didn't know everything about her.

But he knew enough.

The biggest and most important piece of that *enough* was the fact that she wasn't messed up or ruined or broken.

Maybe she'd been hurt. Maybe she was scared. But that was normal.

He had his own fair share of old hurts and pain. "If I said I was damaged inside, if I had too much baggage inside to be in a relationship, what would you say?"

She glanced up, those pretty whiskey eyes damp, but her tone was impassioned.

"You are wonderful, Jaime," she said, straightening and gripping his shoulders. "You've been absolutely kind and amazing this week. So understanding. I feel so lucky that you didn't blow me off and—"

He closed the distance between their lips, pressing a short, firm kiss to her mouth.

When he pulled back, he asked, "Can't you see that I feel the same?"

She bit down on her bottom lip then sighed. "My best friend told me last night that I have walls up and that I give a lot in relationships, that I make such an effort to take care of my family and friends so I can control my relationships, so I can keep distance between myself and the people I love." She swallowed hard. "So I don't have to open myself up, don't have to take their kindness and risk letting them in. I stayed up all night, wanting to pretend I had no clue what she was talking about. To be mad and angry that she would even suggest something so asinine." Her eyes, dry now, drifted to his. "Then I realized she was right."

He held her a little closer, slid his hand up and down her back, tracing lightly, not wanting to interrupt, but also wanting her to know that he was there, that he was listening.

"It's safer to be the one that's giving more sometimes because then you don't have to be open to taking. Ugh! I'm doing the worst job of explaining what seemed so clear when Heidi said it." She groaned, pushed against his chest, and he released her, leaning back against the pillar as she got up and paced the porch. "It makes sense in my head, I guess. It's one thing to make yourself a martyr for other people, to give and *give* until there's nothing else and then everyone can say, *oh, that Kate is so wonderful and generous.*" She tucked her hair behind her ear. "But what they don't realize is that the giving has the power. I've spent so many of my relationships being the caretaker, planning all the things, making sure the person I was seeing had everything he needed, that I then didn't have to make room in my life for someone to look beneath the veneer. There was such a flurry of caring, of giving, of being in charge that I didn't ever have to be vulnerable to them." She sighed. "And because I was the one in control, it was easy for me to step back, to cut ties, to say they weren't giving me what I needed." Her eyes came to his. "Even if I never so much as gave them a chance to take care of me."

Jaime shoved to his feet, understanding now. She wouldn't make it easy to care for her, would push away those who tried. But he was good at caring, and he could be damned stubborn when it came down to it.

He touched her cheek. "You expected me to say no to the message," he said, and she nodded. "And more than that, I started caring for *you*, instead of the other way around."

She nodded. "I didn't even have a chance to build my walls because you were just there and inside and you keep doing all these nice things for me—" A sigh, her chin dropping to her chest. "And I don't know *how* to take." She threw her hands up. "I just don't know how and I keep thinking I need to make it up, to care for you instead and . . . I'm so fucking scared because it's been a week and I like it too damned much."

He crossed to her, pulled her against him.

Maybe this was another moment with a should have.

He should have lied. He should have molded the truth, softened the blow in order to make it so she wasn't scared.

But Jaime hadn't lied to Kate, hadn't minimized or reduced anything between them, and he damn sure wasn't about to start now.

"Good," he said, using one hand to cup her cheek, to force her to look at him.

"Good?"

"Yup." He kissed her again, short and fast and hard. "Because I don't care if you're scared, Kate McLeod. I like you and I like taking care of you and I'm not going to stop." He ran his thumb across her bottom lip. "You're stuck with me."

Her breath shuddered out.

"And a good relationship isn't about keeping distance or measuring all the nice things you do for your partner on a scale. It's not a tit for tat, I do something, you do something." He brought his other hand up, cupped her other cheek so that he held her face in his palms and her stare couldn't dart away. "Sometimes the scale tips one way. Sometimes the other. But it's okay if it's not perfectly balanced, or—" He kissed her forehead. "Or if that care is heavier in your direction for a bit. At some point in the future, it'll bounce the other way."

"But what if I can't let it?"

He smiled. "Good thing I'm stubborn and pushy."

A shaky laugh.

He nuzzled her throat. "You're stuck with me, Red," he said again, wanting to make it clear, even while knowing it would take her time to believe him.

"Jaime," she began.

"No, Red." Fingers on her cheeks, brushing away the tears that were falling in earnest. "You're stuck with me until you order me to go—" He paused, considered that. "You know what? Fuck it. Try to order me to leave. Try to run. Try to push me away, but you'll still be stuck with me." A shrug. "Because you're the most incredible woman I've ever met, and now you inched open that door. I'm not stepping back. I'm not backing off. I'm pressing forward." Another kiss, gentler this time, his next words equally so. "I'm going to make my way through the rest of that armor, baby, and once I get to your heart, I'm going to keep it safe because it will be *here*." He took her hand, pressed it to his chest. "Because it's going to be so tightly bound to mine that I'll always be there to protect it."

He kissed her tears from her cheeks, slipped one arm around her waist to hold her tight.

"You know I'll want to protect your heart, too?" she asked, determination on her face.

Love swelled in him, because that was the Kate he was growing to know. Generous and sweet and so fucking incredible that she was absolutely worth fighting for.

"It's already yours to protect, Red."

And then he let his lips drop to hers and kissed her.

He kissed her until the sun rose fully.

He kissed her until her stomach rumbled.

Then he bought her breakfast.

And then . . . well, then he kissed her some more.

Sixteen

KATE

I t was Tuesday night.

She was still feeling vulnerable, and Jaime was still being wonderful.

He'd bought her breakfast on Sunday after she'd turned into a sobbing fool then had spent the day in her garden with her, digging holes, stealing kisses, and then insisted on paying for the dinner they'd had delivered.

He hadn't argued when she'd said she was making him cookies, though—her way of evening the scales. Yes, she knew, or at least was coming to understand that, logically those scales didn't need to be balanced, but she couldn't just take all the time, she needed to give, to care. She just promised herself that she wouldn't use it as a way to keep her distance.

She would care for Jaime because he was lovely and sweet and it made her happy to see the soft way he looked at her when he'd stolen a scoop of raw dough—and the faux wounded expression when she'd smacked his hand, warning him off because the raw eggs and uncooked flour, and then he'd teased her into a "dangerous" kiss.

And she didn't protest when he'd cleaned the bowl and utensils she'd used to prep the dough because he had already stolen way too many hot circles of deliciousness off the baking sheets after they were baked and before they were fully cooled. He'd laughed when she'd teased and said there was no way he was going to keep his abs flat if he kept that up.

"I think you'll still like me even with a keg," he'd said, stealing a kiss that tasted of dark chocolate and brown sugar.

Because that much was true, she'd kissed him back, slow and deep and—

Had stolen the rest of his cookie. Which had gained her another teasing kiss, another bite of the treat, and plenty of laughter, soothing the tears in her heart, but instead of blocking them off with steel or barring the entrance to the door that had cracked, Kate had resisted the urge to retreat.

She'd stayed open.

And had received another yummy mouthful for her trouble.

And *that* was something she couldn't say around Heidi for fear of dirty-mindedness teasing.

Aw, who was she kidding? Just thinking about it two days later still made her giggle.

Anyway. Moving on.

So, after they'd finished with their Cookie Battle Royale, they'd watched a movie, cuddled on the couch, and he'd said goodbye with a sweet kiss that had left her wanting more.

Monday had been crazy for them both.

She had the usual weekend catch up and he had back-to-back clients, but Kate had pushed herself a bit, too. She'd called him after a particularly trying meeting with a client, let him tease her into a lighter mood with promises of more carbs and kissing and a way to work off the "keg."

Not keeping him at a distance.

Plus, there was little fucking hope of that now. He'd seen the blubbering. He'd listened when she'd explained. He'd . . . stayed.

And after the cheer up call, she'd sent *him* lunch.

A salad he'd mentioned he liked from Molly's—which proved that the man had good taste and might keep his abs yet.

She wasn't entirely vain, didn't begin to think that her body was anything close to perfect. She'd just . . . like to trace those lovely squares once.

Okay, once with her fingers.

And once with her tongue. Maybe twice.

"Focus," she murmured, waving to her sister and Dave as she bounced little Lacy on her shoulder. She had been pleasantly surprised that Ann had called and asked if Kate was still up for watching Lacy so she and Dave could go to dinner.

Of course, she'd said yes, but paired with that affirmative was the realization that perhaps the taking care of everyone and everything around them, sometimes to the detriment of themselves, was a McLeod female trait. Their mom had certainly never taken time for herself. Her whole life had been her work and family, and more often than not, her work had bled over into family—interns staying at their crowded house when their air conditioning went out in the middle of a heatwave, a visiting colleague coming for dinner, endless piles of paperwork stacked on her dresser and nightstand to be completed after the kids went to bed.

Kate's dad worked hard and loved them all.

But she didn't think he comprehended the extra burden her mom carried. Or maybe . . . it was part missing the signs and part those barriers that hid that heavy load.

"Damn," she murmured, waving until they were out of sight before slipping inside and closing the door behind her. This being aware of and trying to ferret out understanding of her emotions wasn't for the faint of heart.

Luckily for her sister, it seemed that Dave was beginning to understand that extra weight Ann was shouldering.

And she was beginning to be able to communicate her needs.

Who said McLeods couldn't learn?

Grinning, Kate thought of Ann tugging Dave's hand when he'd lingered, clearly already missing Lacy, and saying they needed to go because she wanted to be able to have an adult conversation with her husband over food that wasn't from a box or stone-cold because it had been interrupted by a little monster who was absolutely adorable but had terrible timing.

She ran her finger down Lacy's nose, giggling softly when she wrinkled it and squirmed slightly. "They'll be okay," she murmured. "I think your Mommy is a lot less stubborn than your Auntie when it comes to matters of the heart."

Lacy squawked. Kate giggled again. And then she went into the kitchen, ready to start her girl's night.

Jaime had offered to bring her dinner when he stopped by her office that afternoon on the way to a house call for one of his elderly clients—and yes, she was grinning when she remembered that she had a man in her life who stopped by her office, one who'd made her coworkers' jaws drop open because he was so handsome—but she'd seen the circles under his eyes, knew he'd been slammed the last two days.

So, she'd kissed him and sent him on his way, told him they could have a sexy conversation when he was tucked snugly in bed.

"Promise you'll tell me what you're wearing?" he'd asked, sliding his hands through her hair and making a shiver skate down her spine.

"Only if you promise to do the same."

A smiling kiss, and then he'd gone.

And now she had a sexy phone call to look forward to. "Maybe," she murmured, walking Lacy around the kitchen as she scrounged some ingredients for dinner, "I'll even get a sexy FaceTime."

Lacy cooed.

Laughing, she held the tiny bundle of cute and threw together a sandwich and some fruit, not feeling capable enough at the whole cradling a fragile infant and cooking at the same time.

As those things went, she managed to eat exactly one bite of her sandwich before Lacy stopped being adorable and sweet and fun and turned into an angry, crying beast.

Just kidding.

Sort of.

She got hungry. And when Lacy got hungry, she got Mad.

Yup. Mad with a capital M.

Kate bustled over to the fridge, grabbed the bottle of milk Ann had left for her. But what Kate didn't have was a fancy bottle warmer like her mom and sister had on their counters.

She had to rely on her old babysitter tricks.

And they were a hell of a lot slower than the fancy warming contraption.

God, who knew it took water an eternity to boil? Or what felt like one anyway, when there was an unhappy baby in her arms. An unhappy baby who wasn't shy about letting her unhappiness be known to the room.

The house.

The universe.

Snorting as she kept moving, trying the pacifier and rocking and singing and talking and bouncing and anything else she could think of in order to distract Lacy—none of which made the least bit of difference—she wasn't exactly pleased to hear the doorbell.

Pulling the pan of boiling water off the heat, she plunked the bottle into it and hurried to the door, turning the handle just as the bell rang again.

She tugged it open, saw Jaime on the other side.

"Sorry," he said over Lacy's crying, lifting a hand and gently tucking a strand of hair behind her ear. "I didn't think you heard over her."

Kate nodded, turned and kissed his palm. "It's okay." She stepped back, inclined her head to the kitchen. "I've got to grab her bottle."

"Here. Let me take her."

They made the switch, and she bustled into the other room, snagging the bottle and quickly testing the temperature, before screwing on the nipple and walking back over to Lacy and Jaime.

Lacy, who'd stopped crying.

Lacy, who was looking up at Jaime adoringly.

For God's sake, the man was good.

"Do you want me to—?" She began.

"I can," he murmured, rubbing slow circles on Lacy's back. "Unless you want to."

Lacy had stopped crying. Kate wasn't messing with that. She passed over the bottle. "It's all yours, baby whisperer." He glanced up and smiled, and for the first time since she'd seen him on the front porch, she realized that there were shadows in his eyes. She touched his jaw. "Jaime," she murmured. "Are you okay?"

All trace of amusement faded, and a flash of pain slid through his pale brown eyes. "I'm fine."

"Hey—"

Lacy began to cry in earnest, and he smiled, repeated, "I'm fine."

But she'd seen that glimpse of hurt.

And this was a moment she could give as well as take. Give care. Take some of his pain, his burden, whatever he was carrying that day that was weighing so heavily on him.

Because the man talked a good talk about getting Kate to take *his* care, about out-stubborning her into it if he had to, but now she saw he needed a taste of his own medicine.

He needed to accept that she was damned well going to do

the same for him.

First, though, Lacy needed to be taken care of.

Then she was going to find some freaking courage—and hold on to it—and she was going to keep the door cracked while she took care of Jaime.

Not put up barriers while helping him.

Not pulling back.

Because one thing had become crystal clear to her over the last week—she wanted a different future. Not so scared that something was going to go wrong at some hereto unknown point coming down the road that she missed out on all the great things in the now.

Lacy quieted, the sound of sucking filling the space, and Kate took the opportunity of free arms to start pulling ingredients out of the fridge. "Have you eaten?" she asked.

Silence.

Frowning, she turned, saw that he was watching Lacy, but he didn't really seem to be all there.

"Jaime?" she asked.

He jerked slightly. "Sorry, what?"

"Are you hungry?"

A slow blink as he processed her question, and that more than anything told her that her instincts were right.

He was as good as her about giving care.

And as bad as her about accepting it.

Give *and* take. They both needed practice at it.

"Yeah, Red," he finally said, "I'm hungry."

"Okay, baby," she murmured, and went back to gathering up supplies to whip up a quick dinner. Her sandwich and fruit wouldn't fill him up, so she wrapped it and stuck it in a lunchbox for the next day. Then she pulled out a Tupperware of pasta sauce she'd swiped from her mom's freezer not long before, some fresh pasta she'd grabbed at a farmer's market near her office earlier that day. More water into the pot before putting it back on the heat. While that was heating, she grabbed a loaf of bread she'd picked up at the same market and sliced it then threw together a quick salad.

By that time the water was boiling, and she tossed the pasta in.

Five minutes later the pasta was cooked, some sauce was slapped on top, and she had two plates with dinner on them.

Nothing fancy, but tasty and she even got some veggies on.

Jaime paced back in, the bottle empty, and she winced when she saw a spot on his shoulder. Ann had mentioned a burb cloth in the diaper bag, but she'd been too frazzled by Lacy being hungry and Jaime arriving.

He met her gaze. "What is it?"

She crossed to him, paper towel in hand, and wiped off the spit-up. "Sorry," she said. "I forgot about the burp cloth."

The bottle hit the counter; his free arm wrapped around her waist. "Do you know the kinds of things I've had on this shirt?" he asked lightly, brushing a kiss to her forehead. "Thank you for cooking. It smells delicious."

She shrugged. "It's nothing."

Hand sliding up her back, fingers running over her jaw. "It's something to me." Eyes locked on hers. "Thank you."

Kate was still for a heartbeat, taking in the warmth, soaking in the way he stared at her. He saw her, saw what was inside her, and he was still there.

The door creaked open a little further.

And she managed to resist the urge to slam it closed, to throw every lock. "You're welcome," she murmured, and took his arm, bringing him to the table so he could eat.

Which proved difficult with one arm.

"Here," she said, snagging his fork and scooping up a bite, holding it to his mouth. "I think Lacy's trying to say you need to go on a diet," she teased.

He chuckled but parted his lips and let her feed him the

pasta.

"Do you want me to take her so you can eat?" she asked after she'd fed him two more bites.

Warm brown eyes. "I like just what you're doing." A beat. "So long as you feed yourself, too."

A flush crept into her cheeks, but she nodded, even though she suddenly felt shy. The moment hadn't felt intimate before, but with him so close, with that hot gaze on her, she took abrupt notice of exactly what she was doing.

Feeding him.

Fingers on her cheek. "I do like it when you blush. Whatcha thinking, Red?"

Since she wasn't a ninny, she lifted her chin and said, "What I'd like to feed you in bed."

Heat flared, his lips parted, and a soft groan filled the air. "Killing me, Red."

Feeling quite pleased with the obvious hunger in his gaze, she smiled and scooped up a bite of pasta, before chewing and swallowing. "I was thinking of chocolate sauce," she said quietly. "But I figure that would be messy, and I really love my sheets."

His jaw fell open then he laughed, startling Lacy into tears. He stood and rocked her, managing to soothe her quickly, and leaned over to kiss her. "Sorry, little one, your Auntie Kate is funny," he murmured, brushing a kiss over her soft, brown hair, and when she settled down, he sat back down next to Kate. "Thank you," he said, warm eyes on her again.

"For what?"

He shook his head.

She reached over, took his hand. "Jaime," she murmured. "I'm trying here, trying to accept your care, but you need to accept mine, too." A squeeze. "If you want to be in my heart, you have to let me into yours, too."

Soft brown eyes on hers. "You saying I'm being stubborn?"

A brush of her fingers on his arm. "I'm just saying it takes a stubborn to know a stubborn." A beat. "But seriously, I need you to let me take care of you, too, okay? I need to tip the scales as often as you do."

He turned his palm over, captured her hand, and brought it up to his mouth. "Okay, Red."

Her heart swelled. "So, what were you thanking me for, baby?"

He didn't deny her this time, just held her hand and said, "For making me laugh when I didn't think that would be possible today."

She set down the fork she'd been using. "What happened?" she asked. "You didn't seem sad earlier at my office."

The warmth fled, cold filling the depths of his eyes. "My last house call didn't go well."

Reaching over, she squeezed his leg. "Tell me what happened."

He covered her hand with his, sighed. "I don't normally make house calls, but this woman has been one of my clients from the very beginning. She has some health problems, and it's been harder for her to come in for appointments. Her dog, Charlie, hasn't been well either."

The quiet and careful way he said that made her stomach clench.

"Turned out Charlie was doing worse than either of us realized," he said, continuing the quiet recital. "He was struggling to breathe, was septic, and his heart was failing." He sighed. "I had to . . . it had to be done today."

"Oh, Jaime," she murmured, hugging him as well as she could with a sleeping baby between them. "Oh, honey, I'm so sorry. I know that has to be so hard."

He nodded, brushed his lips against her temple.

And her heart clenched.

She pulled back. "That's not it, is it?"

"No."

"What, baby?"

"Margaret was so upset she started having chest pains."

Kate gasped.

"She's okay," he said quickly. "But I had to call an ambulance, and they took her in for monitoring while I took care of Charlie. Her grandson is with her now, and she's going to stay the night."

Carefully, she lifted Lacy out of his arms and carried her to the playpen she'd bought when her niece was born.

Of course, this was the first time Ann had left Lacy, so she'd never used it.

Luckily, Lacy didn't stir when Kate set her down, and she was able to walk back over to Jaime and do what she'd wanted from the moment she'd first noticed the shadows in his eyes.

She straddled his thighs, sat down in his lap, and hugged him tight. "I'm sorry."

He was stiff for a long moment then released a shuddering breath and wrapped his arms tight around her in return.

They held on to each other tightly and for a long time.

And . . . give and take.

Yes. *This* was give and take.

Jaime coming in and not hesitating to help her with Lacy, just stepping up and doing what needed to be done. And . . . Kate doing the same, seeing that he was hurting and offering comfort.

It was Jaime holding her when she realized a painful truth about herself.

And Kate making him dinner when he was hungry.

Give.

Take.

Give.

Take.

Love.

Yes, that, too.

SEVENTEEN

JAIME

Ann didn't seem surprised to see him standing in the hall when they knocked and didn't waste any time in bundling Lacy into her car seat.

Dave took the infant seat out to their SUV in the driveway and snapped it in place while Ann got the recap, smiled at Jaime, and then disappeared with a wave and a coy, "You two have fun."

Then she was gone, looking lightyears happier than at the family dinner on Friday.

"They seem to have sorted out their trouble," he said, once the door was closed and their car had driven down the road.

"Yes," Kate murmured. "They'll be okay."

"McLeod intuitiveness?" he asked.

"Maybe stubbornness," she murmured, and brushing a kiss to his cheek. "You okay, baby?"

It had been a shitty afternoon and early evening but hearing her call him *baby* made it better. Same as Kate not getting mad, even though he'd known she'd needed space and patience and that she'd had plans watching Lacy.

He hadn't the strength to stay away.

But she welcomed him in. She'd cooked and fed and held him, and when he'd felt like the events of the afternoon had loosened their stranglehold, he'd managed to set her away from him long enough to do the dishes.

God, the way she looked at him when he washed a couple of plates.

Fuck.

He knew he'd just signed up to do them for the rest of his life, and he somehow didn't give one damn. Because he loved this woman and it made her happy.

Now she cuddled close to his side, tugged him back to the couch.

"Are you ready for your punishment?"

Jaime blinked. "What?" Were there more dishes to be washed?

"Your punishment," she said again and wound her arms around his neck, brought her body flush to his. "You knew I was having a girl's night and intruded anyway." A shake of her head. "Tsk. Tsk. So rude."

He grinned. "I think you need to consider that I saved the day."

One brow arched up. "Oh, really?"

"Yup," he said. "You needed my Lacy calming abilities, otherwise you'd still be heating that bottle and eating an apple for dinner."

"I'll have you know that apples are delicious," she said, lips tipping up at the corners. "And I took an advanced babysitting course in high school. It's how I was able to pay for my first car."

He chuckled. "Impressive."

"Yes," she said. "It is. I was the most sought-after sitter in our neighbor."

Jaime ran a finger down her cheek. "So, what you're saying is that I'm in the presence of greatness?"

She giggled. "Yup. That's *exactly* what I'm saying."

"Mmm." He trailed his fingers down her throat, stroked across one collarbone and then the other. "And what should I do with all that greatness?"

"Take me to bed?"

His jaw dropped open.

Her smile took his breath away. "Is that a yes?"

Fuck yes, it was a yes. Except, what if she was trying to make him feel better because he'd had a terrible day? What if she didn't really want this? What if she felt pushed into—

Her hands rested on his shoulders, kneaded lightly.

"This isn't a pity offer," she said. "You have to take your care medicine, same as me."

"Kate," he began. "I don't want you to feel like you have to—"

"Have more orgasms?" she interrupted, pressing closer. "Because, I mean, I know I don't *have* to have them." She smiled, and it took his breath away. "But I'd really *like* to have some, and I'd especially like to have them courtesy of you and not my vibrator."

He grinned. "Yeah?"

She nibbled at her bottom lip.

He groaned, used his thumb to release it, to soothe over the small hurt. "You know what that does to me, Red."

"Tell me." She ran her hand down his chest, his abs, gripped his waist. "Or better yet, *show* me."

And Jaime forgot about the teasing, the banter, pushed away the tough day, only pausing to mentally tuck the dinner and how she'd held him tight into a safe place in his heart, a place where he would never forget the memory of her arms around him, and then . . . he gave in.

He closed the distance between their mouths and kissed the woman he loved. One touch, and her lips parted. A heartbeat passed, and their tongues tangled. She moaned, fingers clenching on his waist, nails digging into his skin, sharp bites that made heat scald down his spine, whiskey trail down his throat, warming him from the outside in and the inside out in equal measure.

She jumped and he scooped her up, coaxing her to wrap her legs around him, breaking apart only long enough to ask, "Bedroom?"

A slow, sexy smile that turned his cock to granite.

"Up the stairs. Second door on the left. But I can wa—" She broke off on a moan when he nipped at her lip, when he kissed and sucked his way down her throat. Then he got his ass in gear, carrying this wonderful woman upstairs, down the hall, through the door, and dropping her onto the mattress.

He stopped only to step out of his shoes, to tug hers off her feet, but that was long enough to notice the bedspread. A grin stretched his lips. "Purple."

"Told you it's my favorite."

"Guess you weren't lying."

She crooked a finger, beckoning him closer when all he wanted to do was look his fill of this sexy woman before stripping her bare. But . . . he knew he had no hope of denying her anything, and so Jaime closed the distance between them, crawling up the mattress, reveling in how fucking good it felt to have her beneath him.

"What is it, Red?" he asked, pressing a kiss to her throat, her jaw, the space behind her ear.

Turning her head, she pressed a kiss to *his* ear and whispered. "I have purple other places, too."

Desire burned a trail down his spine, made his cock somehow get even harder.

But all he said was, "Yeah?"

A leg around his hip, a gorgeous smile on that kissable mouth. She took his hand, pressed it to her breast. "Yes." Slid it down the soft curves of her stomach, stopped just above the button of her jeans. "And yes."

His vision hazed, his fingers flicked open the button, then paused. "You sure, Red?"

"God, I like you," she said.

"Kate, I like you, too," he said. "In fact, I lo—"

Then she kissed him, cutting off his sentence. Which was probably for the best, because he knew he needed to remember that patience, knew they'd made big steps, and he didn't want to fuck it up.

Breaking away when his lungs screamed for air, he reached for her, but she batted his hand away, grabbed the hem of her sweater and shimmied it up and over her head,

And . . . Jaime had no words.

She was pale skin and amethyst lace. She was lithe, feminine curves. She was his every fantasy come to life. Freckles dotted her abdomen, her chest like a complicated roadmap that he was absolutely desperate to taste, to trace with his tongue. He wanted to chart every mark, to worship every inch.

Then she took his hand and brought it back to the top of her jeans. "Now, baby. Please."

There was no denying her anything.

He undid the zipper.

"Fuck, Red." Because there was more purple lace, the softest abrasion against his fingertips, damp heat radiating through the fabric, coating his skin. His mouth watered, remembering the taste.

They hadn't had dessert.

Well, he wanted it now.

Pushing off of her, he snagged her jeans at her ankles, tugged the fabric off her legs. A quick jerk had her panties going by the wayside, and a heartbeat later, he was between her thighs, that fucking glorious pink pussy an inch away from his tongue.

He didn't wait, didn't tease.

He licked her up and down, suckled on her clit, exactly as she liked. She'd been wet before he touched her, and the caress of his tongue, the pressure on the bundle of nerves had her moaning, moisture pooling. She was sweet with a hint of tart and by far the best dessert of his life. But as good as she tasted, he wanted her coming on his mouth, wanted her limp with pleasure, her eyes heavy and hooded.

So, he got to work.

One finger circling the entrance to her body, dipping inside, his tongue alternating between circling and pressing firmly. He showed no mercy. Instead, he used what he'd learned the other night and put it to pitiless use.

Not that she seemed to mind.

Her fingers wove into his hair, holding his mouth tightly against her as her hips bucked and ground and she rode his face.

It didn't take long for her to throw her head back, for her to cry out his name as she broke apart around him, pussy convulsing on his finger, liquid drenching his tongue, every muscle in her body going absolutely tense for one long moment.

Then she melted.

Fingers releasing his hair, arms falling limply to the mattress, eyes shut, chest heaving.

"Damn," he murmured, pressing a kiss to the inside of her thigh. "I didn't even get to your glorious breasts yet."

Her eyes slit open, warm pools of heated whiskey.

And then she laughed, a hot, breathy sound. "I don't know if I can handle you getting"—she did a limp attempt of one-handed air quotes—"to my breasts."

He kissed her navel, nipped at her hip, her bottom rib, flicked his tongue over the tiny silver charm hanging in the middle of that purple bra. "I think I called them glorious breasts," he said. "And I'd disagree. I think you can handle anything I dish out." He slipped his finger under the elastic band, traced left and right, the barest brush to those luscious curves.

"Wish"—he slid higher, grazed a nipple—"ful thinking."

"Mmm." He sucked one hard point through the lace. "No, Red, it's not." He reached beneath her, flicked open the clasp and peeled the fabric away. "I *know* you can handle anything I throw your way."

Her eyes locked with his, her hand came up, fingers lacing through his hair.

Then she smiled. "I think I can, too."

And Jaime felt like fucking Superman.

He tossed the bra to the side, slanted his lips across hers and poured every ounce of love he had for this woman into the kiss. She was incredible, and he wanted her to know it, to pour her generosity back into her, to touch and hold and *please* her as she deserved.

He slid his hand up her side, cupped the soft globe of her breast, massaging the tissue gently before he tore his lips from hers and moved down her body to suckle her nipple deeply.

Those fingers tightened in his hair, her hips bucked, and she moaned loudly.

A moment later, however, she was pushing him away.

"I'm—"

"Get naked," she demanded. "I want to feel your skin against mine."

Jaime paused, considered that, but since he wanted to feel her, too, since he wasn't opposed to all that silken skin rubbing against him, he obliged, pushing off her, yanking his T-shirt over his head, stepping out of his pants.

But when he would have left on his boxer briefs, she stopped him with a foot to his chest.

"No, baby," she said, reaching over her shoulder and tugging a condom out of the nightstand. "I want *all* your skin."

Sparks of desire prickled down his spine, through his fingertips. He clenched his jaw until it throbbed, grasping for control, but he was desperate to feel some of the molten heat he'd had on his tongue spread out on his cock, coating the skin as he sank deep again and again and *again.*

Slow. Steady.

Her foot dropped. Her fingers wrapped around his cock. She sat up and . . . he felt a different kind of heat. Her lips closed over him, tongue stroking from base to tip.

And he forgot all about slow and steady.

He forgot all about anything except how good it felt to be in her mouth.

She squeezed tight, hand following the path of her tongue. Once. Twice.

His control splintered. He plucked her off him, tossed her back against the pillows, and he kissed her while stroking every inch of her he could reach. Caressing her breasts, rolling her nipples between thumb and forefinger, stroking over her waist, her hips, slipping his hand down into the damp heat, teasing her clit until she writhed against him in feminine complaint.

"Now!" she gasped, pulling her mouth away and grabbing for the condom, all but shoving it against his chest.

One more stroke of that bundle of nerves. One more breathless moan.

And he took the condom, tore it open with his teeth, rolled it down the length of his cock. He shifted, positioned himself over her, and then stopped, met those gorgeous whiskey eyes. "Yes?"

Her face went soft. Her arms wrapped around him and she pulled him closer. "Yes, baby."

Jaime slid home.

Nothing had ever felt more right. He pushed in, bottoming out, feeling her clench tight around him, and he knew there would never be anyone else. That this woman had been built solely for him and he solely for her.

He pulled out slowly and moved back in, finding the rhythm she liked, gauging every moan and movement and flicker in those warm eyes.

He used that knowledge ruthlessly, not stopping until her breathing faltered again, until her fingers clenched, and her hips met his stroke for stroke. And still he moved, disciplined in that rhythm, needing to feel her break apart around him so that he could gather up the pieces and glue them back together.

Her head fell back, her legs convulsed, a moan rent the air.

Jaime lost his discipline. He lost everything except the feelings of the moment, of moving in and out, of tight and hot, of Kate wrapped around every inch of him.

Fire licked over his skin.

Desire pooled in his stomach.

His muscles clenched. His nerves were ablaze.

One thrust. Another. He exploded.

Pieces of him scattered every which way, but she was there. She held them tight as he flew right over the edge and shattered into a million shards.

And she caught every piece.

EIGHTEEN

KATE

Her friends were glaring at her.

But she found she couldn't find the energy to care. Not when she had the gloriousness of last night under her belt . . . or rather *in* her—

"Always the quiet ones," Heidi said with a smirk.

Kate blushed and quickly shoved away all thoughts of how *in* Jaime had been.

Cora nudged Kelsey with her elbow. "Put down your phone and ignore Tanner's lovey-dovey texts. I know he's awesome and you guys are in luuuuv, but give us single girls a break, mm'kay?"

Kels rolled her eyes but shoved her phone into her pocket. "I was actually texting Angie. She was going to come tonight, but apparently her paper writing isn't going well."

Heidi made a face. "You know she likes those hockey girls better than us."

Kelsey chuckled. "She likes us fine," she said about their friend who was married to the professional hockey player Max

Montgomery and who worked with Kels at RoboTech. Angie had gone back to school to get her master's degree and while she didn't hang out as often as the core group of the four of them, hadn't gelled instantly like she and Heidi and Kels and Cora, Angie was fun and likable and popped in often enough that Kate considered her one of hers. "But it *is* probably easier for her to hang with the Gold hockey peeps. They're all on the same schedule *and*"—Kels's eyes narrowed onto Kate's—"there are no fake engagements."

Kate gulped. "It's not like that."

Heidi rolled her eyes. "It's *exactly* like that."

"Fine," she muttered. "It's like that a *little* bit." She held her finger and thumb up just slightly.

"Are you or are you not engaged?" Kelsey pressed.

It was Kate's turn to make a face. "I am not."

"Why is this giving me *Pride and Prejudice* vibes?" Cora asked. "Lady Catherine de Bourgh comes in and demands to know the status of your engagement to the prideful Mr. Darcy." Cora fluttered her eyelashes, pretending to swoon back onto the couch. "And our heroine lifts her chin, says in a firm voice, *I am not.*"

"Dork." Heidi punched her lightly in the shoulder.

"Yup." A shrug. "So, what?"

"Okay," Kelsey said. "I would really like to get back to the whole reason why Kate felt the need to pretend to be engaged to . . ." Her brows drew together. "To who exactly?"

Kate bit her lip, not wanting to say.

Her friends wouldn't judge her. Okay, they *would,* but it was out of love. Copious amounts of teasing and a smidge of judgment. But it came less from her friends' being jerks and more from them wanting the best for her.

Which meant that she understood their reticence with the whole fake engagement thing.

Typically, perpetuating a giant lie to her family with some

fantasy guy she'd been lusting over on Instagram wasn't the most ideal start to a relationship.

But . . . it wasn't like that.

Not that she had the chance to explain how exactly *it wasn't like that* because Heidi took it upon herself to chime in.

"*JaimeTheVet*," she chirped.

Cora gasped. "With the man bun?"

Kate shook her head. "He cut it off because he was worried my parents wouldn't like it." She shrugged, lips twitching when Kels and Cora gasped. "Then he said he'd been meaning to get around for a haircut but was too busy."

Cora moaned. "But that hair." She jokingly swooned again. "So many guys with long hair look gross, like the strands are greasy and tangled and—" She shuddered. "*JaimeTheVet*'s was . . ."

"Glorious," Kels said, "and I hate everything about man buns simply on principle."

Heidi nudged her. "Or maybe it's because you're hopeless at doing hair?"

Kels wrinkled her nose. "Maybe that, too." She turned back, pinned Kate in place with a stern look. "But that doesn't explain why. Why pretend? You're a smart, capable woman who could easily date someone for real and—"

"My mom was going to set me up again." Kate sighed. "And I tried to put her off, but you know about how well that works." She rolled her eyes, shook her head. Her mom was a force unto herself, and while Kate loved her, of course, sometimes doing battle with her felt like standing in front of an oncoming train and trying to deviate it from its tracks.

A.K.A. it wouldn't work, and she was going to get crushed.

"Doesn't explain Mr. *JaimeTheVet*," Cora pointed out.

Kate knew that. "I just . . . panicked and blurted I was engaged. My mom got excited. Like *really* excited and I . . . fuck, I couldn't take it back in that moment," she said. "I wanted her to be happy, and I know it's ridiculous because I'm a grown woman, but I just didn't want her to be disappointed in me."

Like they had been when she'd upended her family's lives.

"I don't think your parents could ever be disappointed in you, Katie," Heidi said, pulling her out of the memory. "They brag to my parents all the time, and I swear if I've heard it once, I've heard it a hundred times, 'why can't you be in a normal career like Kate?'" Her tone mimicked her mother's. "'*She* actually sees her family and doesn't spend all her time in the lab—'"

"A lab from which you just quit working," Kate pointed out.

Silence. Eyes going wide.

Then Cora blinked and said, "Nice try, Katie. But we'll stay on the fake engagement topic for the moment." She pointed at Heidi. "*You,* we'll get to later."

Kels lifted her fist for Cora to bump. "This is why we've been friends since elementary school." Her gaze fixed onto Kate's. "So, how long is this fake engagement going to go on?"

Kate winced. "Um . . ."

Kels groaned. "Oh no. Tell me he isn't a jerk."

"No!" She sat up. "No," she repeated. "He's actually really great. I like him so much. He's sweet and good with my family." A smile curved her lips. "He seems determined to take care of me and—"

"Are you paying him?" Kels asked, cold infiltrating her tone.

"She's not," Heidi said. "And I had a full background check run on him. His vet practice is successful, and his family is loaded—even more so than Kate's after her mom's magical aging serum."

Cora tapped her forehead. "The reason I don't have fine lines."

"Background ch—" Kate began.

"Not the point," Kels said to Cora, ignoring Kate. "So, nothing criminal in his background and he's not looking for money. Why is he pretending to be engaged when most guys would run screaming the other direction?"

Three pairs of eyes turned her way, and Kate felt a rush of defensiveness. She wanted to snap out a response.

But, how could she?

She'd thought the same at first, wondered what possible motivation a man like that would want with a woman like her, especially when it came to something as intense and complicated as an engagement, fake or not.

Still, Kate couldn't lie.

That her friends thought that too stung a bit.

"He"—Cora gasped, and then they all turned to see Jaime standing in the doorway—"was half in love with Kate from the moment he first saw her smiling in a picture on his friend's feed. *He* spent the last months trying to build a slow communication with her so he wouldn't be a fucking creep who slid into her DMs like he just wanted to get into her pants. *He* tumbled the rest of the way into love with her when he saw how much she loved her family, when he got to see how strongly she cared and took care of those around her. *He* plummeted deeper as he got to know her heart, her humor, her strength." Jaime pushed off the frame, crossed over to her, cupped her cheek lightly. "But he fell deeply, irrevocably in love when she cracked the door enough that she let him take care of her in return."

Her heart was pounding a million miles per hour.

Her lungs seemed to have stopped working.

Her skin prickled, her lips tingled, her fingers had gone numb.

Hell, her *whole* body had gone numb with the exception of where he held her face, the slight roughness of his calloused palm against her skin. "I know it's too soon," he said. "But it's how I feel here." He took her hand, placed it against his chest so she could feel his heart thundering beneath. "And it's how I feel here." He let go, tapped his temple, one half of his mouth curving. "Which is why we're going to have a really long fake engage-ment. Long enough for you to decide that you want to be engaged to me for real. And then"—his voice dropped—"then I'll get you that diamond Ann was talking about, okay?"

She was mute.

Stunned and warmed through. Pulse still thundering, but her heart open and full to the brim.

He slanted his lips over hers, not skimping on the tongue, not hesitating to tug her close and send her pulse skittering to even higher rates. Then he stepped back, nudged her onto the couch when she wobbled, and brushed the back of his knuckles down her cheek, over her throat. "Now," he said, straightening, his voice pitched to the whole room. "I apologize for intruding on Girl's Night twice in a row. I left my keys to the clinic here last night, and I won't have any staff there early tomorrow to let me in. Will someone lock up behind me?" He unleashed his sexy *JaimeTheVet* smile before turning for the door. "I knocked earlier, but I think you were having too much fun to hear." A glance back. "Or to realize that the last woman in hadn't locked up."

His eyes cut to Kate's, and he winked.

Then he was gone, the sound of the front door closing gunshot loud in the quiet space.

Quiet until they heard a car engine start up.

Quiet until they heard it pull away.

Kate turned dumbfounded eyes to her friends. "Did he say that he loved me?"

Heidi nodded, mute for perhaps the first time in all of the time that Kate had known her.

Cora's head bobbed. "He *did* say it," she murmured. "And he said it incredibly well." Her stare was glazed, locked on the spot where Jaime had disappeared.

Kels was the first to recover, perhaps because she had her own extremely gorgeous man.

Her own.

Which implied that Kate had *her* own.

And . . . she supposed she did. She'd cracked the door. He'd come in, and he wasn't a jerk or an asshole, hadn't been terrified and run off screaming like his hair was on fire.

He'd stayed.

He'd said . . . God, he'd said so many wonderful things.

"I'm sorry," Kels said, coming over to her. "I made a snap judgment before finding out the facts."

Kate smiled at her friend. "You were just trying to protect me."

"I hurt your feelings." Kels shook her head. "I saw it in your eyes. That wasn't fair of me." She squeezed Kate's knee. "You're my friend, and I love you. I don't want to see you hurt. But that . . ." Another squeeze. "That, honey, is something that only comes around once per life. Don't let it scare you. Grab on to it. Make it yours and hold it tight."

"But it's so soon," she whispered.

"Yeah." Kels stood up and poured Kate another glass of wine. "But sometimes you just know."

"Plus, he seemed inclined on an extended engagement." Cora's lips twitched.

"An extended engagement between the sheets." Heidi grinned, waggled her brows.

They all groaned.

Kels put the drink into Kate's hand, nudged it toward her mouth. "Drink that and keep his words close. You guys have found each other. Now you can take the time to walk the path together."

Heidi frowned. "What path?"

Kels rolled her eyes. "You're hopeless, you know that, right?"

A shrug. "I know that the man just passed his first test."

"True," Cora said when Kels disappeared into the hall, saying she was going to lock the front door. "But also, *I* know that it's now *your* turn on the hot seat. What did Kate mean about you leaving the lab?"

Heidi groaned. "No, I'm not ready. Bug that one"—she nodded at Kate—"some more about the vet. Or what Jaime meant about interrupting a second Girl's Night." Her eyes narrowed. "Are you cheating on us, Katie girl?"

Kate took a sip, smiled sanguinely. "Distractions don't work with us." Another sip. "But because you asked, the first Girl's Night he interrupted was helping me babysit Lacy. He has magical baby skills."

"Hot damn. Walk that path, Katie. Don't deviate," Cora said, clamping her hands over her heart.

Kels came back in and picked up her glass. "Don't get distracted." She turned to Heidi. "Drink that wine and prepare to spill your guts."

Another groan.

But Heidi knew she wasn't going to get off the hook.

She spilled about her job. And after that, Cora complained about her brothers—she had six of them. Yes, six. They were protective and overbearing in a way that almost made Kate's mom seem like a pussy cat. Their dad had died shortly after Cora was born, and they'd made it their personal responsibility to protect Cor from anything and everything that might bring her harm.

And they thought there were a *lot* of things that could bring her harm.

But Cor loved the big lugs, and so the complaining came from a place as much of love as of annoyance.

Sooner or later they needed to realize that Cora was a grown woman with needs, one of which included a need to not be alone for the rest of her life. Oh, and another need, an important one, was hot sex, not that she let her brothers in on *that* sentiment.

Regardless, it was nice to get the heavy out the way then to just sit with her friends and tease and laugh and drink too much as the conversation drifted to reality TV and what they were getting each other for Christmas.

Tradition said they got each other a white elephant gift, along with something they really wanted.

All small things—their budget for both together was forty dollars.

But it made for a fun tradition of getting together on Boxing Day and exchanging gifts.

"Only four more days until presents!" she said with a nod at her tree in the corner of the room several hours later as she shepherded them out the front door.

"Meanie!" Heidi said and stuck her tongue out. "You know I don't have any patience when it comes to surprises."

"Technically, it's only three days since it's after midnight," Kels said, wavering slightly as she made her way into Tanner's arms.

"I stand by my *meanie* statement," Heidi said.

Cora giggled but didn't say anything, just headed down the stairs and for Tanner's car.

Kate smothered a grin and kept walking her friends out. Tanner had knocked on the door after Kelsey had called him not too long before for a ride home—since they were all lightweights and three bottles of wine between them had certainly put them well beyond their limits for operating motor vehicles.

Hell, they could barely operate a doorknob.

A fact that Tanner had busted a gut over after how long it had taken the three of them to figure out the lock and turn the handle.

Three because Kate had eventually nudged her friends to the side and opened the door herself.

She'd always been a little better at holding her alcohol than her friends—something that had been helped even more recently because she and Kelsey had been practicing of late with prickly pear margaritas from their favorite Mexican restaurant.

Anyway, she digressed, but—*shrug*—that was the lovely, pleasant, fuzzy-headed side effect of the booze talking.

Which was probably going to make for a painful morning.

At least for her head.

Her heart, on the other hand, was full. There was champagne in her veins, bubbling and filling her with so much joy that she couldn't wait to see Jaime again.

She'd texted him already, telling him to come back, to come and kiss her goodnight—cough, because she wouldn't mind *more* than a kiss—but it was late, and he hadn't texted back, so he was probably already in bed.

Which made sense. She had the rest of the week off, but he had to work a full day tomorrow—well, later that day—and then another half-day on Christmas Eve. He didn't exactly have the luxury of a midnight-post-Girl's-Night messing around session. Even if she definitely wanted a repeat of the previous evening.

A repeat with the cherry on top. And maybe some chocolate sauce.

And whipped cream.

Mmm.

Just not on her sheets.

Grinning, she checked her cell again, saw that he still hadn't texted back. But that was okay.

He had a life.

Of course, now she wanted that life to be firmly intertwined with hers.

Because, God, what he'd said that night. Unabashedly and without compunction right in front of her friends. Her heart swelled because it meant so freaking much to her and her carefully protected heart. It meant . . . *everything*.

Her eyes burned and she knew she wouldn't be able to resist the urge for one more text before she let sleep take her over.

Just nudging that door open a little wider.

Heidi stumbled, and Kate pushed her sappy thoughts away, focused on getting her goofy ass friends safely into Tanner's car.

"Have fun with the drunk patrol," she said, herding Heidi to his car.

Tanner stopped, glanced from Kelsey to Kate to Cora to Heidi, and though he didn't groan out loud, Kate still saw it cross his face.

"You love me when I'm drunk," Kelsey stage whispered. "It means you're guaranteed to get lucky."

Heidi pretended to gag. "Just drop me off before you start taking his clothes off, okay?"

"No guarantees," Kelsey sing-songed.

Heidi fake gagged again.

At least, Kate *hoped* it was fake.

Tanner was apparently on the same train of thought. "So long as that wasn't a real pretend puke—" He shook his head. "That doesn't make sense. The point is . . . just no puking in the car. Deal?"

"Deal," Cora said and patted his cheek before sitting down and fumbling with her seat belt.

Tanner's eyes rolled to the sky, but he reached over and buckled her in.

"Heidi?" he asked.

"No puking," Heidi said with a nod that made her look like a bobblehead. "Got it."

"I love you, baby!" Kels slurred, leaning heavily against him and throwing her arms around his neck. He stumbled a step, shook his head again, and finished buckling Cora in.

Then he turned to Kelsey and held her close.

Aw.

He rubbed his nose against hers, said, albeit quieter than Kels's blurt, "I love you, too."

Double aw.

Aware she was staring with more than a little jealousy, Kate forced herself to look away.

She snagged Heidi's arm, led her around to the other side of the car, and got her buckled in. "Night, bestie," she said, hugging her quickly. "Thanks for being a good friend."

"Hey!" Cora said, pouting.

Kate sighed then unable to stifle her giggle at the comical appearance of her friend's mock-glower. "Goodnight, other bestie. I love you."

Cora blew her a kiss. "Love you, too."

There was a tap on her shoulder, and Kate sighed again, thinking she was about to declare her third *bestie* of the evening.

Instead, Kels hugged her tight. "Love you."

She squeezed her friend back. "I love *you.*"

A grin and before she could say goodnight, Kelsey gripped her shoulders and stared deeply into her eyes, looking suddenly lucid for all she'd been a slurring, stumbling female just seconds before. "Take the chance, Katie. Leap even though you're terrified."

Kate's heart stuttered. Her throat went tight.

But she found the strength to say, "I think I will, Kels. I think I *have* to."

A confident smile from her friend.

"Yes, babe. You do."

"Not to break up the tender moment," Tanner said gently, though his eyes were soft. "But I'd better get Goofy and Goofier home while my seats are still safe."

Kate snorted and stepped back so he could urge Kels into the seat, buckle the belt. "Good luck with that," she teased. "But I think your race against the clock is going to be getting Kels home before she falls asleep."

"Good thing I like her unconscious," he teased.

Another snort, this time paired with Kelsey's outraged gasp. Of course, her outrage was diminished by the amusement dancing across her eyes. "I promise I won't fall asleep *this* time."

"Yeah, yeah," Tanner grumbled. "I've heard it all before."

But his gaze was warm, and he wrapped his jacket around Kels before carefully shutting the door. Then he turned to Kate, met her stare, and said, "For the record, I second her statement." He brushed his fingers over her jaw and pressed a kiss to her forehead. "Do it, Kate. Leap and trust that he'll catch you."

"You haven't met him," she whispered.

"But Kels has," he said. "And she's the smartest person I've ever met." He stepped back, glanced through the window, and smiled ruefully at his woman who was already passed out asleep in the passenger's seat. "I'd bet on her logic, any day of the week."

Kate just nodded.

Because she agreed with him.

Kelsey's logic. Heidi's fire and spunk. Cora's sweet steadfastness.

And her.

Her giving. Her taking. Her caring. Her . . . love for the man who'd bared his heart, who'd shown up for her when she needed, and who'd lain the groundwork for a trust they could continue to build over time.

She waved as Tanner drove away.

Then she threw the door wide open.

Forget inches.

She was dealing in feet.

NINETEEN

JAIME

This was probably a mistake.

But . . . she'd texted him that her friends had left, that she wanted him to come over, and though he'd already been in bed, Jaime found that sleep wouldn't pull him under.

Not when his woman wanted him.

His. Woman.

The last time he'd thought that had been during his days with Lori the previous year, but even then, the days, the time he'd spent with his ex, had never been like this.

His mom used to tell his sisters, *"You have to date a few bad ones in order to find the right one."* He'd always thought that was ridiculous. Normal people met each other, dated, stayed together, or moved on.

But then he'd dated a bad one.

He'd dated Lori.

And he'd understood exactly what his mom had meant.

Ultimately, it was a good thing. He didn't think he would

have had the strength to say what he had that night, to keep moving forward when he'd overheard the conversation, to declare himself in front of a room of women who were prepared to dislike him.

Except . . . Kate.

She clearly loved her friends. They clearly loved her.

It was a simple as that.

So, it was nothing for him to give her what she needed. Now, he hoped she'd take the words, the sentiment, and hold it close.

Hence, him being on her doorstep.

She'd texted. He'd come.

But now it was almost one in the morning. The house was dark, except for the bright white lights of her Christmas tree in the family room.

And he was looming on her porch like a burglar in the middle of the night.

He'd texted and waited in his car.

Had texted again before going onto the porch and trying the handle, wanting to make sure she'd locked up behind herself, if she was, in fact, sleeping.

She had.

But now he'd driven over here and was finding it very hard to leave.

He wanted to hold her, to kiss her, to make sure she wasn't going to retreat—

The door opened, revealing legs in fuzzy striped pajama pants, her breasts barely contained in a pale blue top with dangerously thin straps, and Kate looking up at him with sleepy eyes and a warm smile.

"I didn't hear my phone," she murmured.

Jaime ran a finger down one of those thin straps. "Want me to go and let you sleep?"

A shake of her head.

Then she stepped forward and into his arms. "I love you."

The impact of her words was visceral. A sheer punch to the gut that had him sucking in a breath and fighting against the urge to drag her closer, to slant his mouth across hers, to kiss her with every ounce of joy those words brought.

But then she kept talking. "It terrifies me, but I do, baby. I do love you. But . . . I don't know if I'm *ready* to." She shook her head, stepped back. "I know that doesn't make the least bit of sense. How can I love you but not be ready? Because I feel it so strongly here"—she thumped a fist on her chest, over her heart—"but I'm terrified that I'm going to get caught in a maelstrom, that I'm going to let it in, and then I'll be lost, blown to the four corners of the world and not able to find my way back."

God, he loved this woman.

If he'd thought it had taken courage to tell her friends what he was feeling, this was so much more.

This was the depth of her vulnerability laid bare.

He threaded his hand in her hair, stepped close enough that her body was pressed to his, front to front. "I can't take away your fear."

She blinked, lips parting. "Wh-what?"

"I can't make you not afraid, Red."

Her breath shuddered out. "I-I—"

"I love you," he said, nudging her inside and closing the door behind them since it was cold. He kept hold of her as he leaned back against the wooden panel. "I've never felt this way for a woman, but I also know it's been a week. I can get a stubborn dog to take a pill. I can calculate the dosage of carprofen for an eighty-pound German Shepherd. I can start an IV on a pissed-off cat, but I can't take away your fear." He rested his forehead against hers. "God, I want to, baby. I want to make everything all right, heal that giant heart of yours, and ride off into the sunset." He pressed his cheek to her temple, held her tight. "But this is real life, so all I can give you is time and my love and the tools for us to ascend that fucking mountain and make it over to the other side together."

She shuddered, and he felt a hot tear leak out of the corner of her eye, drip down her jaw. "Together?"

Fingers in the silk of her hair, mouth next to her ear, bodies close. "Yeah, Red. Together."

Silence.

Her throat working.

Another hot tear.

Then a halting chuckle. "Damn, baby," she said. "It would be so much easier if you could just make all the bad stuff go away." A breath. "I want to make it to the other side of that rainbow."

He leaned back, stared into those pretty whiskey eyes. "I'll pick up some armor. Maybe a white horse."

She sniffed then smiled before rising on tiptoe to press a quick kiss to his lips. "Me, too."

Give. Take.

Fuck, he loved this woman.

———

His alarm came far too soon, but Jaime couldn't complain about waking up with Kate draped all over him.

The world's best blanket, that was for sure.

A grumpy blanket, who groaned when his alarm blared. He quickly shut it off and slipped from the bed, tugging on the clothes that he'd worn the night before. They'd ended up crumpled on the floor after Kate had taken his hand and dragged him to her bedroom.

Then had her wicked way with him.

Not that he was complaining.

Having a sexy, turned-on Kate below him, hips moving,

breasts bare, head thrown back as she came around him was no hardship.

It was a hard *something*.

Snorting, he knelt on the mattress and kissed the base of her spine. She was still naked, neither of them having bothered with pajamas several hours before. He'd just blearily made sure his alarm was good to go then gathered her close and let sleep overtake him.

Now, he tugged the sheets up and over her and disappeared into her bathroom, waiting until the door was closed before turning on the lights. He didn't want to wake her; knew she had the day off. Blinking against the brightness, he remembered she'd drowsily mentioned an extra toothbrush under the sink, and he located it before brushing his teeth and splashing some water on his face.

Feeling slightly more human, he turned out the lights, waited for his eyes to adjust, then cracked the door, tiptoeing quietly into Kate's bedroom.

But she was sitting up, sheet held to her chest, hair a fucking mess that he itched to run his fingers through. He crossed over to her, sat on the bed, and lightly kissed her mouth. "I'm sorry," he said. "Did I wake you?"

Her forehead dropped to his shoulder. "No."

"You okay?"

A nod.

He nudged her down. "Go back to sleep, Red. I'll see you tonight."

"But—" She yawned, started to sit up. "I should make you breakfast."

He nudged her back down. "Another time. Sleep, love."

"I—"

Jaime tucked the covers tightly around her. "There. You're trapped." He brushed her hair back, kissed her forehead. "Raincheck on breakfast."

Her eyes closed.

He smiled. So fucking beautiful.

He pushed to his feet and started for the door.

"Jaime—"

And stubborn. He sighed. "No, breakfast, Red."

Another yawn, a hint of tart in her tone. "I was just going to say, there's a key in the drawer by the oven."

Even a little cranky and tired, she undid him.

"I love you."

"I lo . . ." Sleep pulled her under, the rest of the words a mumble.

But that was okay because he felt them in his heart anyway.

Jaime slipped from the room, headed downstairs, and out to his car. But he damned sure made certain to stop by the kitchen and grab the key from the drawer before he left.

No more closed doors.

He had the key.

TWENTY

KATE

By the time she woke up fully after Jaime left, the sun was bright enough in the sky to rival her high school sleeping in days.

And her head . . . well, it felt a little like high school, too.

Alcohol and sex and not knowing her limits.

Except, she kind of knew her limits when it came to Jaime. That being, she had *no* limits when it came to the lovely, sexy man who'd barreled through the door to her heart and made himself right at home.

Then again, she'd thrown the door wide open.

"That's right," she said, stretching long and slow but keeping her eyes closed because the sun was ouchie.

Technical term, that.

Snorting, but still feeling very satisfied with herself, she rolled over, peeked enough to grab her cell, and slit open one eye to type out a message to Jaime.

You know, I was thinking this whole thing was my fault.

She pulled the covers over her head, checked her emails while she waited, but she'd barely gotten her inbox opened when her phone buzzed.

Oh, it's definitely your fault.

Kate chuckled.

I was referring to the fact that you're stuck with me now, rather than the fake engagement.

A pause.

I was, too.

She laughed outright that time, feeling warm and fuzzy inside and just . . . so much in love.

Barry is here for his check-up, so I need to go. Enjoy your day off.

My heart! Squee! Also, I'll let you go take care of that cock.

Kate (and in case you couldn't tell, that was a warning because I can't get a boner at work).

She giggled.

*See you tonight? *angel emoji**

Wild horses couldn't keep me away.

And you've taken care of wild horses—or regular ones

*anyway, so I know you mean it. *horse emoji, heart eyes
emoji, celebration emoji, heart emoji**

**kissing emoji* Proof that I've kept up my studying. See
you tonight, Red.*

Kate didn't reply, other than with a heart to keep giving *him*
more proof that her emoji skills were as strong as ever before
setting her phone on her nightstand and pulling the covers back
up and over her.

Happy.

She was happy and fulfilled and . . . she didn't have a
Christmas present for him!

How did she not have a Christmas present?

It was two days away. They would be sitting with her family
at her parents' house with presents all around, and she hadn't
bought him anything.

Of course, a week ago she hadn't thought she'd needed to do
any more buying.

But . . . he meant a lot, had done more to transform her life,
her heart in less time than any other person she had ever met.

And he deserved a present.

A *good* present.

Because he'd given her the gift of time, of courage, of
cracking open the door to her heart.

"Well, you can't just get him a door, Kate," she muttered,
throwing back the covers and blinking against the bright before
she got out of bed. Shower. Clothes. Present. Dinner. That was
her plan.

She'd feed him, coax him into staying the night.

And in the morning, she'd make him breakfast then see him
off to work properly.

Perhaps with a blow job.

Talk about presents.

"You're a dork, Kate McLeod," she said to herself as she walked into the bathroom and turned on the shower.

Hot water paired with shampoo and conditioner went a long way to shaking off her hangover. It did not, however, help her figure out what to get Jaime for Christmas. Because what did one get their fake fiancé, their lover, the man they wanted to build something serious and long-term with . . . that they'd only known a week?

A book, maybe, she considered as she blow-dried her hair.

Or perhaps a T-shirt? He looked really good in T-shirts. Except that wasn't really personal now, was it?

She wanted something thoughtful, something perfect for this man she was just starting to know, but this man she also already knew down into the deepest parts of his heart.

Jaime was . . . well, he wasn't perfect, but she thought that he was perfect for her.

She wanted her gift to show that.

To be the beginning of—

"You're making this too big, you dope," she muttered to herself, shutting off the blow dryer and staring at herself in the mirror. Shining red hair, so bright she used to hate the garish color. Over the years she'd grown to appreciate it somewhat, just as she felt deep down that she could grow to appreciate herself.

To not shut people out and blame it on them.

To be strong enough to be open.

No more asshole superpowers. Her new one was going to be . . .

Brown eyes stared back at her, question in the depths.

Then she smiled and picked up her tube of moisturizer.

"Being happy is going to be my superpower," she promised. "To stop being such a weakling and grab on to my happy."

Nodding, she slapped on some makeup, slipped into a festive sweater and boots, a scarf, and her cozy jacket. A cup of coffee and a piece of toast later, and she was prepped to brave the last-minute Christmas shopping crowds.

Confident. Strong. Excited.

Little did she know what awaited her at the mall was going to shatter all of that.

————

She'd gone from searching for the perfect gift for Jaime that would express exactly what she was feeling in her heart to just wanting to find *any* gift.

Everything was cleared out.

Crumbs.

Proverbial, that was. All she had were proverbial crumbs. Oh, and a tabletop ping pong set.

Somehow that didn't scream true love.

Sighing, she set the box down and knew she was back to the drawing board. She was probably being too picky, should just snap up some lingerie and wrap herself up as Jaime's present.

Except, how was he going to open *that* present with her family on Christmas?

They did a small exchange before the neighborhood started traipsing through. Her family would expect her to have gotten Jaime something, and she didn't even want to attempt a conversation with her brother and dad that insinuated Jaime had already gotten his present earlier.

Bow-chicka-bow-wow.

Nope. No, thank you. She liked all of Jaime's body parts exactly where they were.

Of course, she could always get him lingerie *and* something else.

A slow smile curved her lips as she walked out of the entrance to the shop. The kiosk in front of her sold bands for smart watches, but one in particular caught her eye, and she knew it would be perfect for him to open in front of her family.

Then she went to the ridiculously expensive lingerie store and spent far too much money on lace. Red, because it was his favorite color.

It was as she was walking out of the store, carrying an extra bag filled with emerald green lace that she hadn't been able to pass up—she had to stick with the festive season and get outfits in both holiday colors, right?—when she saw it.

Or rather, *him.*

Jaime.

With his arm around a beautiful redhead. She was snuggled close, gazing adoringly up at him.

Her heart turned to ice.

Was he—?

No. He couldn't. He wasn't an asshole. He was kind and patient and . . . she'd only known him a week. And he had his hands on another woman when he'd promised to build something rock-solid between them, a trust that would never falter.

He brushed back a strand of the redhead's hair, tucked it behind her ear.

Bile burned the back of Kate's throat. She knew what it felt like for him to do that, to touch *her* that way . . . and he was doing it to another woman.

Her heart cracked.

She wanted to run to her car, to lock herself away, to slam the door shut.

But she forced herself to take a breath. To think this through.

There must be an explanation. She couldn't have opened her heart and been so wrong about the man. She *couldn't have.*

Shaking legs carrying her over to a bench, she pulled out her phone and called him.

Then watched as he glanced down at his watch and declined the call.

Another crack. Another fissure.

Still, she needed to try once more. She didn't need to be one of those idiot females who made a snap judgment then ran off when there was a perfectly reasonable explanation.

No matter how much that explanation might hurt.

She typed out a text.

Are you free for lunch? I'm finally coherent.

He glanced down at his watch again. Kate nibbled at her lip. But then he said something to the redhead, stepped away, and reached into his pocket. A second later, he had his cell in hand and was typing.

She held her breath, waited for it to ping through onto her phone.

Ten seconds passed then her cell buzzed.

Can't. Sorry. I'm slammed at the clinic.

Reading those words snatched away the breath she'd been holding, had the door in her heart slamming shut as hurt overwhelmed her.

"Fuck," she whispered, rubbing her hand over her chest, over the spot where her heart was breaking into pieces. She shoved her phone into her purse, picked up her bags, and took a step toward the couple, preparing to unleash her fury.

Then . . . she stopped, the crowd of shoppers all around her.

And she couldn't.

God, why *couldn't* she?

Maybe it was the kiss to the top of the woman's hand. Maybe it was the way she pointed and smiled coyly at the lingerie shop that Kate had spent an exorbitant amount of money in just minutes before.

Maybe it was the sinking, oppressive, really *fucking* sad feeling.

Maybe it was just her realization that for all her pretending, she'd been right about her superpower all along.

Assholes.

They cropped up everywhere.

Even when she least suspected.

TWENTY-ONE

JAIME

He stowed the bags in the back of his car and got in, his sister, Tammy, already in the front seat of his car.

She'd come into town unexpectantly and had tagged along on his Christmas shopping expedition for Kate, teasing him relentlessly for his last-minute mission. Until she'd seen the store he wanted to get the big present from.

"I'm going to marry her," he'd announced.

Then her eyes had widened, but she'd quickly shrugged off her shock and helped him make his selection.

Gleefully spending his money.

But that was okay. He was happy to see his favorite sis, even if it was just on a pit stop before she headed to their parents' house.

"Still can't believe you're making me go home alone," she grumbled as he navigated the crazy parking and pedestrian situation at the mall.

"Unfortunately," he said. "The clinic will be open the day after, and I need to make sure I'm there."

It was the truth, but also not.

Because while the clinic *was* open. It hadn't been until a week ago when he'd told the front desk to open up the schedule for a few hours in the afternoon.

He'd kept the staff off, and no one had actually booked the appointments.

But his family didn't need to know that.

The truth was that he didn't want to be away from Kate. Not this soon. Not when they were just starting out. And it wasn't like he could bring her home. His family didn't even know he was fake engaged, let alone seeing a woman.

Though, he knew both of those—minus the fake part— would change as soon as Tammy spilled the beans.

Fine with him.

He wanted to be with Kate, no holds barred.

The sooner everyone on the planet knew that fact, the better.

And so, maybe he was feeling the tiniest bit possessive.

Meh. A man had to do what he had to do, and that included making it clear to the rest of the populace that Kate was his.

"Hmm."

"What?" he asked, playing innocent, even as he turned in the direction of the airport. Tammy needed to get to her flight, and he needed to get back to the clinic. He'd already pushed several appointments when she'd shown up unexpectantly. He didn't want to disappoint his clients, knew their time was just as important.

"And none of this staying here for the holiday has anything to do with this Kate?"

"Not going to say it's not a benefit," he muttered. "Sex with the woman I love versus opening a poop brown sweater from Aunt Janet."

Tammy smacked him. "You're terrible." A beat. "But not wrong." Sighing, she leaned back in her seat. "I miss sex."

He groaned. "No, my ears!"

"What? You can talk about it, but I can't?"

"Yes," he said, flashing her a grin. "Exactly that. You're my baby sister. That means I'm going to go through the rest of my life pretending you've never had sex."

"Newsflash, dumbass," she grumbled. "I've had sex. Loads and loads of really hot, really awesome—"

"La. La. La."

"Don't cover your ears," she said. "You need your hands to drive."

He laughed, shook his head. "Wasn't planning on it." Jaime paused, checking traffic as he merged onto the freeway. "It didn't work out with your guy?"

"No."

"Want to talk about it?"

He saw her make a face out of the corner of his eye, expected the change in conversation that came a second later. "When do I get to meet this Kate?"

"When I can get her to not run screaming from our family," he said dryly.

"Good luck with that." But it was a lighthearted response, one equal to his words. Because Kate would love his family. It was the same reason he'd felt so comfortable stepping into hers. Love and teasing. Jokes and banter around a dinner table. Enjoying each other's company. Not hesitating to drop anything to help, to be there, to show they cared.

Two sides of the same coin.

He just had an extra sibling in the mix.

Which is why he knew he'd be making a trip home soon—as much as he grumbled, he loved his family, would miss seeing them for the holiday. He just hoped that he could convince Kate to keep trusting him enough to hop on a plane with him.

Tammy changed the topic to work, and they spent the

remainder of the ride to the airport talking about her plans for her job.

She was considering a move to the Bay Area but wasn't sure she wanted to get mixed up in tech, not when her skills in Human Resources meant she could work in a variety of fields.

"Well, just remember that your favorite brother is here," he said, hugging her tight.

"My favorite *older* brother," she teased. "My favorite younger brother has decided his role is jet-setting around the world and giving our mother coronaries." They shared a grin, knowing that wasn't hard to do. Their mom wasn't exactly known as being easy-going.

"He's good at that," Jaime said.

"*Damned* good."

"We should take notes."

She laughed and rose on tiptoe, pressing a kiss to his cheek. "Love you, Jaime-Maimy."

He groaned. "Really? Pulling out old nicknames?"

Tammy grabbed her bag. "It's part of my privilege as a younger sister."

"Safe flight, Tammy Two Shoes."

A roll of her eyes. "And yours, too, apparently. I always hated that nickname."

He tugged her ponytail. "At least you've figured out you only need one shoe on each foot now."

"They were slippers!" She tossed up her hands. "I was four. How was I supposed to know that you didn't wear hard shoes over them?"

"I'm not touching that," he said with a smirk.

"Good. Don't. Love you."

"Love you, too."

Then after one more and a wave at the automatic doors, she was inside the terminal and Jaime was back in his car, driving to the clinic.

The rest of the afternoon passed in a blur, an emergency pushing his already messed up schedule into the realm of fucked. He kept his head down, tried to stay focused, but as the hours passed, a knot grew in his stomach.

At first, he thought it was something he was missing with the dog.

It had been hit by a car, had suffered some severe injuries.

But as time went on, as he stabilized the lab mix, he realized it wasn't the case or the clinic, or the devastated owner.

This was about Kate.

She hadn't texted back earlier.

And when he sent her a message, saying he was caught at the clinic, would still be several hours, she didn't respond to that one either.

Nor did she pick up his call when he got out of surgery and washed up, having finished up with his other clients and sent his techs home.

It was just him and Roger, the lab mix, whose prognosis was good, but who was loopy and needed more fluids before his owner could come and take him home. Pushing the sinking feeling away, he called his client, told her the good news.

Then he called Kate again.

And again, she didn't answer.

The knot in his stomach grew, and his fingers flew across the keyboard. He had the distinct notion that the woman he loved was slipping away, and he didn't know why . . . or how to keep her.

Don't close the door, Red.

No response.

"Fuck," he muttered, closing his eyes, and sliding down the wall.

Roger's tail thumped once on the floor.

"Good boy," he said gently.

He sat and waited, and as each minute passed without a reply from Kate, his heart sank further.

He was losing her, and he had no clue how to stop it.

Twenty-Two

KATE

She hadn't cried, knew that would come later.

For now, she wrapped Jaime's presents and shoved them under the tree.

Maybe she'd burn them later.

All that lace would make for a nice flame.

For now, she was digging a giant hole in the back yard. The front was pretty much set, and it wasn't like she could add any more bulbs than she already had. It was December and too cold to plant much else.

Maybe she'd buy a huge tree.

Then bury the ashes of her lingerie in it.

"Fucking asshole men," she muttered, still digging. Her T-shirt soaked with sweat, though it was barely above forty—and that was cold for California, okay? She was in old, baggy jeans, had dirt covering her hands and arms, and she suspected, her cheeks. But she didn't stop digging, not even when the sun went down and it got colder, the impact of the shovel stinging her palms. "Fucking. Asshole. Cheating. Asshole. Fucking. Asshole.

Men," she said, the metal blade reverberating through the ground with each grunted-out word.

"It might take you a while to dig that hole big enough if you're trying to bury my body."

Silken male words.

And she was pissed, but not pissed enough to miss the caution underlying the attempt at a joke.

Well, no. Charming wasn't going to work with her. Nope. No fucking way.

She turned back to her hole and kept digging.

Soft footsteps. "Did you not see my call? My texts?"

Oh, she'd seen them. Meaningless words from a fucking cheating asshole. God, remembering how it felt to see him lie to her from fifty feet away, seeing him dismiss her so easily, it made her already broken heart hurt even more.

But she wasn't a weakling.

She stabbed the shovel into the dirt and spun to face him.

"How was the mall?" she snapped, crossing her arms and glaring up at him.

Clarity on his face, silence falling. But he didn't deny he'd been there, with that woman. "It's not what you think."

Damn. Dammit all to hell.

The idiotic part of her that had been holding on to some random slice of hope—that he had an identical twin who was dating a gorgeous redhead, or something equally ridiculous— shriveled up and died.

She turned, returned to digging her hole.

Maybe she *would* make it big enough to bury him.

"Go home, Jaime."

"No."

Fury tore through her, and she whipped around to face him. "You're just like all the rest of them. I trusted you," she shouted. "I let you in, let you see parts of me that no one else has ever been able to, and y-you—"

Eyes burning, she spun back to the hole.

"Kate."

"No!" She scooped up a pile of dirt and threw it at him.

It landed with a soft smack against his chest, turning his white T-shirt black in the harsh glow of the floodlights she had shining.

"You're a liar!" she screamed.

"Yes," he said.

Fucking asshole. *Fucking* asshole. Kate shook her head and got back to her hole. But just when the tip of the shovel made contact with the dirt, it was pulled from her hand and tossed aside.

"I *was* at the mall," he said, tugging her against his chest. The smell of the damp earth filled her nose.

"I know." She shoved, tried to wriggle out of his hold.

He held fast. "With my sister."

"I kn—"

Her words died on her lips.

"With your sister?" she asked numbly, her fury turning to horror to embarrassment to fear. Because this would make him change his mind.

"Yes, Red."

She'd given him a glimpse of the terrified woman inside and—

A hand on her jaw, tilting her head back, forcing her eyes to his. "Stop."

"I—"

He kissed her.

The soil—okay, it was really mud—squished between their chests, a cold shock sinking into her skin even as his mouth scorched her to the bone.

He pulled back. "I shouldn't have lied." He rested his forehead to hers. "My sister, Tammy, showed up unexpectedly, and I took advantage of her to help me buy your gift."

"Jaime—"

"I lied," he said. "I promised to build trust, and I didn't do that."

"No," she said, gripping his arms. "I was there buying your gift, and I saw you with her, and . . . I didn't trust you." Shame washed over her. "I acted like an idiot, calling and texting instead of just walking up to you and finding out the truth."

"Patience."

"I know." She blinked. "I didn't have any. I'm sorry. I should have—"

"No, Red. I meant you need to have patience with yourself."

She froze. "You're not mad?"

"That you're digging the hole you want to bury my body in?" He rubbed his nose against hers. "No, baby. Fuck, I don't know what I would have done if I was in the same boat as you. Freaked out? Beat the asshole up? Kissed you in front of everyone and make it clear you were mine?"

She bit her lip. "I should have gone for the last."

He nodded. "Yeah, that's what I would have voted for, too."

"I don't want to have a hard time trusting you," she said, voice shaking. "I love you and want to not doubt us together, to not doubt *you*—"

"But we've been fake-engaged for a week," he said. "Cut yourself some slack."

Kate nodded and knew that it was time for her to tell him the last piece of the puzzle, something even Heidi didn't know.

The real reason it was so hard for her to trust anyone.

"I didn't use to be like this."

He stilled, pale brown eyes on hers. She shivered.

"Hold on, honey," he said gently, and then he bent, picked her up into his arms, and carried her into her house, bypassing the kitchen, the family room, moving up the stairs, and passed the bedroom.

He carried her all the way into the bathroom then turned on the shower.

It wasn't until steam filled the space that she realized she was chilled to the bone and trembling.

Her shoes hit the floor. Her clothes joined them.

Jaime's followed suit.

Then he was lifting her into his arms again, stepping into the shower stall, hot water sluicing over her, warming her, combining with his tight hold and stopping her shivers.

Only then did he say, "Tell me."

Her eyes dropped to the tile and she sighed. "It's stupid when I think of what started it."

"I don't care how stupid it is," he said. "I just want to know what hurt you." Fingers on her cheek. "Take away the power. Let the pain be washed away."

"It's not fair that you're so normal and I'm—"

"Wonderful, smart, sexy, loveable Kate."

She sniffed, released a ragged breath. And then she told him the reason her family had to move when she was in high school.

Why she'd gone away to college. Why it had been damned hard for Heidi to break through her tough shell, and her friend had only been successful because Heidi rivaled Kate in her stubbornness.

"I was bullied," she admitted.

Surprise across his eyes and his jaw clenched. "Oh, Red."

She shrugged. "At first, it was just normal kids' stuff. A jerky boy who made fun of my hair, a mean girl who teased me for my freckles. God, this is *so* embarrassing." She covered her face with her hands. "It's so long ago—"

One move had her pressed to the tile.

She gasped at the cold tile on her back, contrasted against the hot body pressed to her front.

"Not stupid." Terse words. "*Tell me.*"

Kate swallowed hard, knew that she would have an argument on her hands if she denied him. And . . . he was right. Wasn't it beyond time for her to stop letting this have power over her?

"Middle school came," she said. "I developed early." And embarrassment gave way to anger, because what was done to her wasn't right. It wasn't stupid kid stuff any longer. It was mean and hurtful and . . . illegal. "I had this crush on a boy. I thought he was the cutest. Long hair"—a smile in his direction—"gorgeous blue eyes, and he was two whole years older. An eighth-grader when I was a lowly sixth-grader."

Her fingers tightened on his shoulders when the memory cropped up, and she went to release them, not wanting to hurt Jaime.

"Don't," he said. "Hold on as tight as you need, Red."

God, she loved this man.

But she wanted to finish this, to be done with the painful chapter, to do that looking forward she'd promised herself earlier.

"His sister was in my grade. We'd been friends for years, but grew apart in middle school, and it went as you might expect." Kate sighed. "She started hanging with a different group, with the popular kids, and when they found out I liked him, they took pictures of me changing."

Now Jaime's grip tightened.

"Not naked," she said. "But close enough. I was in a bra and underwear, changing from P.E., and those pictures were *everywhere*. The sole good thing about this is it was before Facebook and Snapchat and Instagram. But they printed out the pictures and taped them up all over school. I'd tear one down and then I'd open my locker and another copy would be there. Or go to the bathroom and there was one taped to the stall door, and to the mirror, and passed out at football games." She shuddered out a breath. "*Everyone* saw them. It was . . . well, for a girl not comfortable in her own skin, especially for one with boobs and curves that were more developed, it was horrible." A shiver had Jaime turning up the heat on the shower, and she was grateful. "Then they spread the rumor that I'd known about the camera, that I was posing for the pictures, and . . . guys made assumptions. Hell, girls and teachers did, too."

Her chin dropped to her chest.

"Red," he said hoarsely. "I'm sorry."

"That's not all," she whispered then forced herself to lift her head, to strengthen her tone. "The police opened an investigation, and because I was underage and the pictures were shared, it was considered child pornography."

"Shit."

"Yeah." She stroked her hands down his arms. "It was the right thing to do, obviously, but . . ."

"It blew back harder on you."

Kate nodded. "Yeah," she said. "Eventually, we moved. The timing was good in a way. My mom had made the sale, was ready for a new job, and my dad could work remotely. But Ann and Jake were devastated." She leaned her head back against the tile. "They had a hard time adjusting to the new school, to leaving their friends, their sports teams. I think they understood as we got older, but I knew they resented it at the time."

"Your parents did the right thing."

"I know," she said. "I just hate that they had to, hate that even after the move I wasn't even in any shape to go to school in-person. I home-schooled until I left for college."

"You were violated, Kate. People don't just bounce back to normal."

She sighed. "I know."

"Do you?" he asked quietly.

Her normal response would be to say *of course* she knew. But if the last week had taught her anything, it was that her first instinct wasn't necessarily right.

"I'm working on it," she admitted. "I think I spent so long

trying to shove everything down and move forward like nothing was wrong that I didn't realize exactly how much it had affected me, even now. Silly, huh?"

He shook his head, held her tighter. "No, Red. That's normal."

"Oh yeah?" she said, wanting to turn the page on this, to grasp on to something lighter, something not so painful.

Not that she was going to ignore it or pretend it had never happened.

Not any longer.

She was just going to put it behind her. To—in Jaime's words—take away its power, wash it down the drain.

"Yes," he agreed, pressing a kiss to her cheek, to the tip of her nose, to her forehead. "Completely, totally normal."

"Well, what's your quote-unquote normal that still haunts you?"

He didn't hesitate, just offered himself up on a platter. "I wet the bed until I was eight or nine. Sometimes I still wake up in terror, thinking I've done it again, and it's been more than twenty years."

"Oh, baby," she murmured.

"Pathetic, right?"

"No." She kissed him.

"Not gonna tease me about Pull-Ups or a mattress protector?" he asked and though his tone was light, she picked up on the nearly hidden vein of embarrassment of a painful memory.

He'd given.

He'd given so much.

So, it took no effort at all to tell him the truth. "No, baby," she said. "Not that. *Never* that."

His eyes softened, and he held her tight for another long moment.

Then he leaned back, propped her back under the stream of

water. "Should we finish getting cleaned up and then go back to digging your hole?"

Her lips tipped up. "That's an oxymoron if I've ever heard one."

A chuckle, hands pouring soap onto her loofa. "Well, then, we're both wet and naked, whatever shall we do?"

She burst out laughing. He joined in.

Then she snagged the loofa. "I've got some plans."

Oh boy, did she have some plans.

Twenty-Three

Jaime

I t was Christmas Day. Well, Christmas *evening*, and Jaime
was staring in shock at the crowd of people in the hallway
of Kate's parents' house. "What are you guys—" A shake of
his head. "*How* are you guys here?"

Tammy pushed past his parents and walked up to him. "I
called Mom from the airport, told them about the girl, about
your Kate and how you bought"—

This was the point he started making slicing motions with
his hands.

Of course, his sister missed them.

"—her a big, fat diamond—"

More slicing motions. More ignoring.

"—and were going to ask her to marry you—"

For fuck's sake. Half the crowd might already think he'd
popped the question, but Jaime had plans. Plans he should have
enacted that morning, but she'd distracted him with gorgeous
red lace.

Then with green lace.

And . . . time had gotten away from them. So much that they'd barely made it to the party on time.

For Christ's sake, they hadn't even cleared the hallway before the knock had come.

"How did you—?" He blinked. "I mean." He shook his head. "You've never been here before."

Tammy held up her phone. "Find Your Phone family plan works both ways, buckaroo." A grin. "We tailed your car."

"And then barged into a house you didn't know?" he asked.

He loved his family, but . . . for fuck's sake. Were they trying to nuke his personal life?

"Hi," Kate said, extending her hand to his sister.

Jaime sighed. "The wannabe spy is Tammy, my sister. My mom and dad—" He pointed to his parents, but Kate had slipped by him, closed the distance.

"I'm Kate," she said to his mom. "It's so nice to finally meet you, Mr. and Mrs. Huntington."

"Tawny, please. And this is my husband, Andrew."

"So nice to officially meet you both," Kate said. "Jaime talks about you all the time—"

"What's this?"

The crowd turned to see Marabelle in the hall, her hair perfectly coiffed, a reindeer-printed apron wrapped around her slender frame.

Silence then, "Mom! Isn't this great?" Kate said. "Jaime's family came to town and surprised him."

To her credit, Marabelle didn't miss a beat.

She walked over, introduced herself to Jaime's parents, then they completed the introductions with Jaime's other sister, Penny, and his brother, Brad.

"Mom," he said, tugging her a little ways away and sending death glares at his siblings for letting his mom bundle them all into the car and drive out. Not one of them appeared unabashed. Hell, they were all so nosy, they'd probably encouraged her. "Not that I'm not happy to see you," he said quietly, "but . . ."

She lifted her chin. "You were too busy to come home, so we decided to come out and meet this girl," his mother finished for him. "Do you know how expensive last-minute flights are? We ended up driving out."

"From Utah?" Kate's mom exclaimed, tuning into the conversation. "Gosh, you guys must be so tired. Please, come in. Dinner's almost ready."

"Oh, we wouldn't want to intrude," his mom said.

Jaime snorted.

And got a smack on the back of the head for his trouble.

But Marabelle ignored them both. Instead, she took his mom's arm and led her down the hall. "There's always plenty of food. We'll just bring in some more chairs. Harry! Dave! Jake! I need chairs."

"We'll help," Brad said, snagging Penny and Tammy and hauling them down the hall after the moms.

Hell.

The moms.

"Welcome to the family, Kate," his dad said. A shake of his head. "For the record, I tried to stop them."

Kate giggled.

And Jaime? He decided to roll with it. What choice did he have otherwise? "At least we won't get sweaters from Aunt Janet this year," he said hopefully.

"Oh no." His father patted his shoulder. "Your mother packed those."

Kate giggled again, and with another shake of his head, Jaime's dad followed everyone else down the hall.

"They drove out?" she whispered, wide eyes meeting his.

Jaime rubbed his suddenly throbbing temple. "Apparently."

Kate turned, wrapped her arms around him. "They love you."

"I circle back to my original statement," he muttered, "and repeat *apparently*."

Warm whiskey eyes slid up to his. "I think we need to come clean about the engagement."

"Why?"

She frowned. "Jaime, I don't want to lie anymore."

"Neither do I." He stepped back.

"Exactly," she murmured, turning for the kitchen. "So, I'll just go in there and let everyone know—"

He snagged her hand, tugged her back to face him.

"Wh—?" She began, brows drawn together.

Probably because he wasn't on his feet any longer.

Instead, he'd sunk down onto one knee.

"Jaime."

He reached into the jacket he hadn't even had a chance to take off yet and pulled out the ring he'd bought with Tammy. More plans gone askew—he'd thought to sneak Kate out back, to snag a quiet moment and make her truly his.

Instead . . . family.

Instead . . . give and take.

Instead . . . he found he didn't give a shit if it was the perfect moment. He just wanted this woman in his life.

Forever.

"I didn't ask you to marry me properly the first time," he murmured and opened the box. "Will you make me the happiest man on the planet and marry me, Kate McLeod?"

"After a *long* engagement," her dad muttered.

Kate jumped, he blinked, and they both turned, saw that both of their families had crowded into the hall. She sighed and shook her head, a slow smile curving that luscious mouth before she dropped down next to him, leaned close, and whispered in his ear, "If I say, yes, will you grow your hair back and share all your man-bun secrets?"

Jaime burst out laughing.

"What?" his mom said. "What did she say?"

Kate turned, smiled at their respective families gathered around, at the nosy and love-filled hallway, then turned back to Jaime and threw her arms around him. "I said, yes."

A cheer went up as she pulled back, turning away from him again, her gaze going to her father's. "And yes, for the long engagement."

Harry nodded approvingly.

But Jaime wasn't paying attention to any of them. He had Kate in his arms, albeit facing the wrong way.

Spinning her, he tugged off the moonstone ring then slipped the diamond on her finger and used the excuse of mistletoe overhead to kiss her senseless.

He kissed her as the doorbell rang, as voices echoed in the hall behind them, as bodies shuffled by them because they were blocking the path to the rest of the house.

He kissed her as her father cleared his throat, clearly telling him it had been long enough.

He kissed her until his head spun, until she pushed against his chest, and broke away for air.

But he still didn't let her go.

"I love you," she said, cupping his jaw.

"Hey, that's my line." He nuzzled her throat.

Behind her, the sounds of the party intensified, and Jaime knew their moment was almost over, but he still couldn't get his hands to release her. Though, realistically, he wasn't trying very hard, not when it felt so damned good to have her close.

"You sure about this?" she asked as he helped her to her feet, and though she looked up at him with love, with trust, Jaime knew she still needed time and affection and patience and care, knew she'd give him the same back.

"More sure than I've been of anything in my life," he said.

Kate tucked herself into his side. "Good," she said. "Because you're stuck with me."

He laughed.

And then because he could, he kissed her again.

Being stuck with Kate wasn't a bad place to be at all.

EPILOGUE
PART ONE

KATE

"I didn't get a chance to give this to you," she told Jaime two days later, setting the small package she had tossed in the direction of the Christmas tree after that day at the mall on his chest.

They were naked in bed.

A common occurrence around the man.

Giggling to herself, she tugged up the blankets and nudged the package at him when he didn't immediately move to open the present. She'd forgotten about it in her excitement in showing him the lace. Then forgotten again in the rush to get to her parents' house and once more after the excitement of his family showing up.

The McLeod crew had hit the pause on presents, not wanting Jaime's family to be left out.

Then she'd had her time with her friends yesterday, and Jaime had spent Boxing Day with his family doing their own exchange and traditions . . . and she'd forgotten until she'd spied the palm-sized package on the carpet earlier. But his family had headed home earlier that day, her family was planning on a New Year's Eve present exchange, and she didn't want to wait to see his face when he opened it.

A little gift.

But one that was sure to make him smile.

"What's this?"

She rolled her eyes. "Open it."

He waggled his brows. "Is it a ring?"

Another roll of her eyes. A kiss pressed to lips she loved kissing. "Long engagement, remember?"

"Mmm," he said, winding his fingers into her hair and transforming her light kiss into one that had her heart pounding and moisture pooling between her thighs.

And circling back to naked. Mmm.

She pulled away when his fingers slid up, brushing his hand away. "Behave."

He nipped her bottom lip.

She nipped back. "Open it," she demanded. "Then you can get back to kissing me." A beat. "Everywhere.

The wrapping paper disappeared.

The box was open a minute later.

And then Jaime was laughing. That warm, slightly rough chuckle that slid down her spine and made her pussy clench. He glanced from the watchband printed with roosters up to her eyes. "We're going to have a Barry, aren't we?"

She grinned. "Yeah, we are."

A quick, hot kiss. "On that note," he said, pulling back and getting out of bed.

"Hey! Where are you—?" Her question cut off when he disappeared into the hall, and not that she minded seeing his sexy ass striding away from her, but he was naked, *she* was naked, and they were supposed to be getting back to sexy naked time.

Then he was back, a present in *his* hands.

He crossed over to her, plunked it in her lap. "Open it, Red."

Since Kate loved presents, she didn't bother prevaricating. She tore open that paper, pulled the lid off the box, and . . .

Laughed until tears poured from her eyes.

It was a leash and harness. The same type as she'd seen Barry wearing in the picture Jaime had sent to her.

"Think you can teach him to carry our rings down the aisle?" he asked.

"I'm not sure roosters are trainable."

He tugged the box from her lap, dropped it to the floor. "My money's on you."

"No." Kate shook her head. "My money's on *us*."

Then while he was still smiling, she wrapped her arms around him and kissed the man she loved with everything she had.

She tasted that smile in her soul.

Yeah, her money was on them.

Bad Bridesmaid

Billionaires Club #11

ONE

HEIDI

She was wearing a bridesmaid's dress and holding a leash.

Not the strangest sentence ever uttered.

Unless, perhaps, she included what was on the other end of the leash.

Because she'd been escorted down the aisle by a rooster name Sir Fuzzy McFeatherston, or the Fuzz, for short.

He was cute. He was cocky—*ha*—and he was not happy to be on a leash.

Thankfully, though, the ceremony was wrapping up. The bride and groom—her best friend, Kate, and her almost-husband, Jaime—were kissing. Soon, she'd be able to put the rooster in the cage, and she could get to drinking.

Because her best friend was getting married.

After an engagement she had promised Heidi would be extremely long but had ended up sort of average because Kate hadn't been able to wait to make Jaime officially hers.

Barf.

Heidi loved Kate, loved Jaime, and how he treated Kate.

But she was losing her best friend.

So, yeah, maybe she was feeling a little mopey, but she wasn't going to let her funk ruin her friend's night. She was going to be the best rooster-wrangling bridesmaid there was.

Not maid of honor.

Kate hadn't wanted to hurt Kelsey or Cora's feelings, the other half of their quad-sized friend group, so they were all bridesmaids, each with a different job.

But that was Kate.

Kind. Sweet. Inclusive. In a word, the absolute best.

That was two, or *three,* Heidi, supposed, but the point still stood. Kate was awesome and her best friend in the whole world.

And now she was *married.*

God, they were all growing up. Sniff.

She hated it.

Still, her heart was full, and she sniffed again, dashing away a tear as the officiant declared the newlyweds officially married before they strode down the aisle hand-in-hand.

Heidi followed, striding—hand-in-leash?—with the rooster.

And, well, if that wasn't an apt description of her dating life . . . she didn't know what was. She could find a man who wanted to sleep with her—cough, *cock*—but couldn't find one with staying power.

"Not the point," she muttered under her breath, somehow getting herself and Sir Fuzzy McFeatherston safely down the aisle. The rest of the bridal party paired off and followed her.

They snapped some pictures, but eventually the Fuzz got tired of the paparazzi, and Heidi wrestled him into her arms, taking him to the crate Kate had ready for him.

She was just bending to place him inside—while trying to slip off the harness without letting him escape—when she felt someone come up behind her. Assuming it was Kate, she said, "I'm fine, Katie girl. Go enjoyed your husband. I've got your"— she giggled, a twelve-year-old at heart—"cock well in hand."

Silence instead of her friend's cackling.

Shit.

Heat stained her cheeks, and Heidi yanked the leash and harness out before slamming and locking the cage. Then she shored her spine and spun around.

Tall. Dark. A smirk on a gorgeous mouth.

One that grew as his gaze traced her down then up. "Sure you can handle that cock, baby?"

She *had* handled that cock.

Six months ago, Jaime's brother Brad had stopped in the Bay Area for a quick visit, and she'd had a few too many glasses of wine. He'd offered her a ride home . . . and then he'd given her a fucking *ride.*

So yeah, she'd had that cock, and she couldn't lie, it had been *incredible.*

But . . . he'd been gone before she'd woken the next morning.

And she might be tough on the outside, she might be a strong, independent woman who hadn't been expecting a ring and a relationship, but she'd thought she at least warranted a note or a text or a fucking goodbye.

Heidi sniffed. "I've had plenty of cocks in my life," she said, chin lifting, eyes narrowing. "And none are more than I can handle."

She pushed past him.

He snagged her arm.

She yanked it free, stepped back when he went to grab her again. "Don't," she snapped. "Just because I made a mistake once doesn't mean I'm easy prey now."

A cocky—no pun intended *this* time—smile. "Mistake? I happened to think we were—"

"*That* was your mistake," she said, glaring. "*Thinking.*"

Pretty hazel eyes flared. "Baby—"

"Not. Your. Baby."

A sigh. "Heidi."

"Yes, Brad, the groomsman who should be paying attention to his brother's wedding instead of bothering a woman who *isn't interested?*" It wasn't a sweet question, for as sickly saccharine as her tone was.

"I think—"

She rolled her eyes. "Not *that* again."

Heidi didn't mean to. It just . . . it all happened so fast.

Brad grabbed her arm.

She shoved him back at the same time the crate door burst open, and Sir Fuzzy McFeatherston shot out of the pen.

The rooster took off running.

Brad lost his footing, crashed into a waiter, who was carrying a large tray of appetizers.

The food went flying.

Brad went flying . . . into the cake table.

Sir Fuzzy McFeatherston went flying, feathers scattering in all directions.

The tray came down.

And Heidi didn't think she'd ever forget the sound of it colliding with Brad's head.

Nor how much joy it gave her.

At least until she took a step back, promptly tripped over the fucking rooster . . . and ended up sprawled across Brad's chest.

Fuck, she loved that chest.

Two

Heidi

"I am so, so, *so* sorry," she said, wiping cake off her temple. "I—"

Kate giggled and swiped a finger through the frosting currently occupying space on her cheek. "I told you, it's fine. The Fuzz is a naughty rooster, and I should have known better than to think he would behave at a wedding of all places."

Heidi grabbed her friend's hands. "He was the cutest ring bearer ever."

Kate's face softened, and she pulled free to grab another towel from the counter of the tiny bathroom they'd sequestered themselves in after the cake debacle, dampening it and working at the frosting embedded in one of Heidi's curls. "He was, wasn't he?"

Heidi snagged the towel and nudged her friend toward the door. "Go, babe. Enjoy your big party." She forced a smile. "I'll do my best to not ruin anything else."

"Heid—"

She reached for the handle, tugged open the wooden panel,

nudged her friend out into the hall. The music vibrated through the airwaves, punctuated by laughter and conversation. "Go. Dance yourself into sweaty exhaustion. I'll be out once I'm frosting free."

Kate hesitated.

"*Go*. This is your night. I'm fine."

With a nod and a squeeze of Heidi's arm, Kate disappeared down the hall, her dress swishing and sparkling in her wake.

Her friend was a goddess.

Thankfully, Jaime realized how lucky he was and treated Kate right.

Which meant Heidi didn't have to kill him.

Snorting to herself, she closed the door, going back to work on her frosting-filled curls, and eventually just gave up on her half-up, half-down hairdo and started to take bobby pins out, lining them up neatly on the counter.

The door opened as she had her chin tucked to her chest, staring at the line of pins on the white granite while fighting with a pin stuck right at her nape.

"Go party, Katie," she said, fingers trying and failing to grasp the little folded piece of metal. "I'm fine."

Fingers on her nape, tugging the bobby pin out.

"Thank—" She glanced up and saw that it wasn't Kate in the bathroom with her, guilt drawing her back from her own party to help Heidi out.

It was *him*.

Brad.

Brother of the groom, best lay of her life, and a complete and utter player who was . . . looking at her like he wanted them to play all over again.

Look, she couldn't lie. A part of her wanted that—wanted the hot, sweaty sex, wanted him to hoist her up onto the counter, lift her dress, and plunge home, over and over again. But the rest of her still had *some* self-respect left. She was smart and reasonably pretty. She couldn't hold her booze, but she *was* a funny drunk on the odd occasion she got that far. Plus, she could cook a mean meatloaf, bake killer chocolate chip cookies, and she always made coffee for herself and whoever stayed over —whether it be friend or fuck—first thing in the morning.

Heidi was more of a catch than not.

And she was tired of being with people who didn't recognize that.

So there would be no hoisting onto counters or dress-lifting. And the man certainly wouldn't be getting any of her special chocolate chip cookies *or* expensive, caffeine-laden coffee.

He reached up to grab another pin, and she smacked his hand away. "You can go."

A slow, sexy smile. "I made the mess. I don't mind cleaning it up."

"I guess I wasn't clear." She kept her back to him, glaring at him in the mirror. "*Go away.*"

Silence.

But he didn't move. She could feel him at her spine filling up the small bathroom, didn't know how she could have ever thought he was Katie. The man *exuded* pure heat and sexually, and . . . the fucker just standing there had her lady parts all perked and at the ready, his mere presence a temptation all its own—

U.G.H.

No.

Her fingers went back to her hair, plucking out pins left and right, pretending he wasn't there . . . even as she felt him in every cell.

"So, I was thinking—"

She snorted. The man just couldn't *stop* thinking.

"—that I should go out and buy a cake for Jaime and Kate."

Unbidden, she felt her heart give a little squeeze before she shored it back up, before she slapped a heavy chain and padlock around it, protecting the bruised organ. "I already Instacarted one." She picked up her purse, digging past the various items that had made up her bride emergency kit—clear nail polish for runs in stockings, safety pins, Band-Aids, wet wipes, energy bars, and more—for her cell. Feeling like she should cheer when she managed to retrieve her phone from that black hole, she tapped a finger on the screen, checked on the cake's process. "See?" She turned, showing him the screen. "It should be here in fifteen minutes."

His eyes changed, emotions mixing in them that she couldn't read, but then he shifted back slightly. "Ah."

Right.

She gave him her back again, set her cell down, and focused back on her hair, searching for any bobby pins that might be hiding in the heavy, dark locks. Not finding any, she resumed her patting, scrubbing, and picking at the frosting that had hardened into her curls during the time she'd spent trying to save her friend's wedding.

Capturing the freaking rooster—who was far more agile and much quicker than she was—and wrestling him into the cage, double-checking that the lock was properly secured the second time around.

Righting the cake table and managing to salvage one tier, so at least Kate and Jaime would be able to cut *something* that resembled a wedding cake for pictures.

Getting ice for the pain-in-the-ass's head who was still standing behind her.

And finally, with frosting and cake bits coating the gorgeous purple dress Kate had picked out for all the bridesmaids, she'd attempted to salvage her outfit.

And hair.

And makeup.

All of which were proving to be . . . unsalvageable.

Fingers in her hair making her shiver, making her hate herself for that shiver. Brad tugged out a pin she'd missed and set it on the counter. "I—" he began.

"Will you just fuck off?" she snapped, slapping her hands down onto that granite and glaring at him in the mirror again. "I get I was an easy fuck a few months ago, but I'm not going to be one again. I get that it was good, but what I *don't* get is how it's always so fucking *easy* for men to walk away from me." She blinked, wishing she could take that last part back. Unfortunately, since she didn't possess time-traveling abilities, she pressed on. "A note," she said. "That's all it would have taken. Just a simple goodbye, rather than skulking off before the sun rose like I'm some little dirty, shameful secret."

Hazel eyes holding hers in the reflection.

He had a colored streak of frosting on his left cheek, though his white shirt was almost pristine. Probably because his suit jacket had taken the brunt of the purple and cream-colored cake.

Stupid men. Could just strip off their jackets and look perfectly normal.

"You're right," he said after a long, tense moment. "I'm sorry. I should have left a note or said goodbye."

An apology.

Just like that.

Then he smiled—slow and hot and thigh-quiveringly sexy. "But in fairness to me, I've had some . . . unpleasant morning interactions." A shrug. "Sometimes it's better for everyone if I just leave."

And just like that, back to the cocky asshole.

She stifled a sigh. "Goodbye, Brad."

Then she focused all her attention on the towel and the sink and not the man behind her, nor on her nipples that were perky in memory of the horizontal yummy time, nor on her vagina that was feeling empty and neglected because she was ignoring its urges.

"I—"

"Goodbye."

After several moments, he released a breath and she watched him out of the corner of her eye as he left the bathroom, the door *clicking* closed softly behind him.

"Thank God," she whispered, going back to work with the towel and warm water, and by the time her cell buzzed with the alert that the delivery driver was approaching with the cake, she had at least managed to de-frosting her hair. Her dress was hopeless. She'd scraped everything off, but the buttercream had left greasy stains all over the bodice and skirt.

Dry-cleaning might salvage it, but she didn't have a change of clothes at her disposal.

So, she was embracing the stains.

Stashing the dirty towels in the basket next to the sink, she turned to the door, opened it, and—

Froze.

A white dress shirt was hanging on the outside of the knob, a note peeking out of the breast pocket.

Can't change the past, but maybe this note will help.
-B

Her heart did that squeezing thing, but she shoved it down again, ignoring the stutter, pretending she hadn't even had it in the first place. This didn't mean she was going to forgive the man, and she certainly wasn't going to give him a second chance.

No fucking way.

But she *was* going to use the shirt to cover the worst of the stains. She slipped it from the hanger, buttoned it up, not fully appreciating how much bigger Brad was than her until the starched cotton was surrounding her, engulfing her in his spicy, male scent, the fabric soft against her skin and hanging to her knees, the sleeves draping past her fingertips. It was intoxicating to be wrapped up in him, in the shirt that was still warm from his body.

"It's probably not even his," she muttered, rolling up the sleeves.

But something inside her knew it was, and that inclination was confirmed when she walked out into the area where the reception was being held and saw him dancing with Cora, clad in just a skin-tight white T-shirt.

Ignoring the dance floor, she slipped out to the front of the building, meeting the delivery woman, and then thinking perhaps she went overboard with the cake ordering. Still, she managed to heft the three huge sheet cakes—chocolate, lemon, and vanilla, her attempt to recreate the flavors of the delicious-ness she'd toppled—thanked the woman who was her savior, and headed back to the wedding.

Arms slipped around her, Brad deftly—*somehow*—scooping the cakes out of her hold before she could react or protest or dodge away.

The cakes were worth their weight in gold at this point.

But before she could snatch them back or demand . . . he do *something*, there were hot words in her ear.

"You look good in my shirt."

Words that left her gaping.

And shivering with remembered pleasure, dammit.

Brad was a No Fuck Zone. She'd learned her lesson. Or at least she *should* have learned her lesson.

But nonetheless, she shivered again when those hot hazel eyes met hers and he said, voice husky and feeling like roughened velvet brushing over her skin, "For the record, I wish I'd stayed."

THREE

BRAD

He should have stayed.

He'd known he would regret slipping from beneath those soft cotton sheets, out from Heidi's embrace, moving away from her even softer skin.

But he'd also needed to go.

Not even because he'd had a flight to catch—which he *had* because he always had a flight to catch. He traveled every spare day, spent every extra dollar he had to fly around the world, visiting every sight that had ever caught his fancy. And he'd had a great freaking time doing so, never wanted to stop.

But Heidi was the first woman he'd ever spent any time with that made him want to stay.

To stay *forever*.

So, he'd gone.

Had returned to the postage-stamp apartment he kept for the infrequent times he was in town, having decided that if he were going to be paying for a home he was hardly in, it might as well be filled with California sunshine rather than Midwest humidity and snow. Then he'd packed his usual bag, grabbed his passport, and had flown to Croatia. But as he'd walked through gorgeous coastal cities and explored mountain lakes and appreciated the beautiful agriculture, he hadn't been able to stop thinking of the gorgeous brunette with hazel eyes that were more green than brown.

He'd thought of her laugh while eating alone.

He'd thought of her shining brown hair fanning out on the pillowcase when he'd gone to sleep at night.

He'd *dreamed* of her sexy, curvy body night after night, had woken hard and aching every morning for weeks.

Until he'd forced himself to compartmentalize the woman away, not only for his own sanity, but for hers. Because he wasn't the type of man who stayed, not for a little while, not forever, no matter how beautiful or smart or wonderful the woman was.

And Heidi was definitely all of those.

But still, as time had gone on, he'd almost convinced himself that he'd imagined the draw he felt toward her. After all these months, after making sure to avoid any interaction that might bring them together during the lead up to the wedding, he'd begun to think that perhaps she wasn't . . . so freaking perfect in every way that mattered to him.

But he hadn't been able to avoid her forever.

He'd walked into the wedding rehearsal the night before and felt every cell in his body stand up in attention.

She was there.

He wanted her.

Thankfully, the men and women had separated early in the evening, and he'd been able to keep his distance. But today, seeing her in that fucking incredible purple dress and the way it hugged her curves, watching her eyes go damp as her friend spoke her vows, laughing at the way she'd embraced walking that stupid fucking rooster up the aisle with its vest and sparkling leash.

Hell, she'd embraced *all* of it. The tears, the rooster, even the aftermath of the cake fiasco.

And he'd found he liked her even more.

Fucking hell.

"Give them back," she growled.

"They're heavy," he countered. "Let me carry them for you."

One dark brow lifted. "And you're saying that me, with my weak, feminine arms, can't manage to carry them?"

"Yup." He preemptively bit back a grin, already anticipating her reaction.

Which didn't disappoint.

She scowled, plump lips pressing flat, and he had the distinct notion that she wanted to stomp her foot.

Either that, or she wanted to kick him in the balls.

Maybe both.

"Where do you want them?" he asked, instead of giving voice to either of those thoughts—or to give her any ideas.

Her scowl deepened, but she just pointed to the former cake table, the one they'd spent some quality time on top of, not long before. The tablecloth had been replaced. The one tier they'd been able to salvage sitting on a plate atop it, along with half of a groom figurine and the bride's legs.

Heidi growled, plucking the horrific scene from the cake and wrapping the sad pieces in a napkin, which she stashed in the bodice of her dress. He didn't even bother looking away, not when he had the great privilege to witness the action of her spreading his shirt wide and sticking her hand between the luscious set of breasts he'd once been up close and familiar with. Then she patted the table before buttoning the shirt back up. "Set them here."

He placed the boxes down.

"My bouquet is on the head table," she said, opening one lid. "Can you grab mine, Cora's, and Kelsey's?"

"Got it." He turned away.

She snagged his arm, tugged him to face her. "Do *not* touch Kate's bouquet," she ordered, eyes flashing. "She's saving it, and I will not ruin another thing of hers."

Brad reached down and lifted her hand, bringing it to his lips. "I won't. I promise."

"Good." She snatched her hand free. "Don't."

Then she spun away, giving him her back again, probably not realizing how tempting the line of her nape was with curls teasing the creamy length of skin, nor how her curves were highlighted by the way they pressed against the fabric of his shirt.

He wasn't going to tell her.

For one, he appreciated the view. For another, he appreciated his balls right where they currently resided.

Dodging the dancers on the rented floor, he made his way to the head table and scooped up the proper bouquets—and not the big one with ribbons and a floofy—was that a technical term? Probably not, but it was the only way he could think to describe the flouncing greenery, ribbons, and flowers. Regardless, it only took him a few minutes to return to the cake table, bunches in hand.

What he returned to was . . . amazing.

Heidi had managed to stack the rectangular cakes on top of one another, angling them artistically. The boxes were on the floor next to her feet, and she'd commandeered another flower arrangement from somewhere and was currently placing the buds around the cakes.

"Um," he said, setting the bouquets on the table. "Are you a magician or something?"

She stuck a rose into a gap, not looking at him as she continued placing flowers, adding in ones from the bunches he'd brought over. "Nope."

Okay then. Apparently, this woman could hold a grudge and a half.

Not that he could really blame her.

Most women didn't appreciate being used—and even if that wasn't what he'd intended, that was what she'd thought.

So, he knew he deserved the frosty reception.

He just . . . didn't like it.

Stifling a sigh, he bent and picked up the boxes, folding them and stowing them beneath the table. "Maybe a more appropriate question would be, how did you learn to do that?"

"It's a hobby." A beat as she dismantled her bouquet, tucking in tulips and roses at regular intervals.

"What other hobbies do you have?"

Hazel eyes on his, condescension in their depths. "Really?" she asked. "We're really going to have this conversation?"

"Are you always so prickly?"

A sigh was his only response.

He bit back a smile. "Your hair looks nice."

She sniffed.

"Heidi."

She froze, head tilting up to the sky, hair floating behind her like some curly brown cloud, her throat exposed and tempting. His mouth watered, actually watered, remembering how he'd dragged his lips over that gentle slope, how he'd traced his tongue along the silken skin.

"I truly am sorry."

Her head flopped to the side, tilting enough so she could meet his gaze. "And I truly meant what I said." She straightened, eyes serious. "I'm not interested. I want someone who wants me enough to stick around." A shrug. "The truth is that I know you well enough by now to know you're not that kind of man."

That stung.

But he couldn't deny it, couldn't pretend she was wrong.

He *didn't* have staying power.

"I know."

Her expression changed, and he hated that *he* didn't know *her* well enough to discern the undercurrent in it. At any rate, she focused her attention back on the cakes, and he watched in silence as she turned the supermarket confections into something that belonged in a fancy bakery.

"I wish I'd ordered icing, too," she murmured, perching a final gathering of blooms on the salvaged tier, which she hadn't stacked on the others, but had somehow made its separation seem intentional with the way she'd arranged the flowers.

"It looks beautiful."

She froze, almost as though she'd forgotten he was there.

He was so attuned to her that he didn't think it would be possible to *not* be aware of her. Ever since he'd walked into the church the night before—*no*. Since the moment he'd joined in on that dinner all those months ago, tagging along with Jaime and Kate to meet up with Heidi, Cora, and Kelsey, he hadn't been able to get this smart, gorgeous woman out of his brain.

Brad couldn't even say it was because she came in a beautiful package—though he certainly appreciated her curves, her pretty face with those expressive eyes and kissable lips. But his fascination had begun at that dinner and had only grown through the night. When Kelsey had been picked up by her fiancé, Tanner, and Cora had left with Kate and Jaime because they all lived close, he'd offered her a ride ostensibly because his apartment was close to her place, but in truth, because he'd wanted to spend more time with her.

Yes, he was attracted to her.

But that attraction wasn't just sexual. She was witty and more than once, she'd made some offhand comment that had him bursting into laughter. Beyond that, he could tell she was a good person who cared about the people at that table—including him.

Because he was related to Jaime. Because Jaime was smitten, and because he made Kate happy.

So, he'd had an in, and he'd been attracted to her.

And . . . they'd ended up in bed. And the sex had been incredible. And he'd—

"Ruined," she murmured.

Brad blinked for a moment, wondering if she'd picked the thought from his mind or perhaps if he'd spoken aloud. But she wasn't looking at him. She was staring down at the cake, a sour expression on her face.

Then she sighed and rolled her shoulders, exposing her neck as she stretched her head from side to side again. Tempting him. Again.

"Oh well," she said, straightening on another sigh. "I've done what I can." She fussed with one more flower then stepped back. "I should find Fuzzy McFeatherston and make sure he doesn't get within a hundred feet of this."

"I took him home."

Her lips parted, and it took everything in him to not taste her. "What?"

"I figured it was safer to get him back to his coop at Kate and Jaime's." Which had been convenient, considering the venue they'd chosen to hold the reception at was only twenty minutes from their house.

"You left for forty minutes?"

He glanced at his watch. "Fifty-six," he said, "But who's counting? Especially when you're wiping frosting out of your curls."

Her lips tipped up into a smile that he felt all the way to his cock. Then she sobered, "But it's your brother's wedding."

"I snuck out while they were taking their individual pictures, snuck back in when you and Kate were doing your thing." He shrugged. "Also, I couldn't exactly just shove him in the back of my car, could I? And clearly, the cage couldn't be trusted to hold him securely."

That much was true.

"Oh." A beat. "Well, I should—"

The music changed, the heavy beat of a fast-paced dance anthem melting into a slow melody, into an unhurried ballad that coaxed couples to the floor, that made the hot, sweaty atmosphere shift into something intimate and hushed.

"Dance with me," he said.

She shook her head, those curls bouncing. "I shouldn't—"

"We're a bridesmaid and groomsman," he coaxed, nodding toward Kelsey and Cora, both of whom were twirling with other members of the bridal party, and Jaime and Kate, who were in the center of the mix, looking blissfully happy. "We should be out there."

White teeth nibbling into a pink-painted bottom lip.

He took a risk . . . and took her hand.

FOUR

HEIDI

W arm fingers laced with hers, a slightly calloused thumb stroking across her palm.

Back and forth. Back and forth. Back and—

Then she was pressed to Brad's chest, the heat of his body surrounding her, her breasts tingling as they brushed against the hard muscles of his torso. The sneaky man had maneuvered her into the dance on the back patio of the restaurant Kate and Jaime had rented out without her recognizing it, like a mesmerizing hand-ninja who'd stroked her palm and all of a sudden, she was in his arms, his body coaxing hers into sensually unhurried motion. A shiver skating down her spine when he slid his hand down, the heat of him seeping through the layers of his shirt and her dress, imprinting onto her skin.

"I—"

"I love this song," he said softly.

She blinked, surprised that he'd admit to liking the poppy ballad. "Really?"

"What can I say? I'm a Gaga fan." He smiled, slow and sexy. "The woman's got pipes."

Lips parting, she scrambled to say something. Hell, to say *anything*.

But nothing came.

Which seemed to suit him just fine. He just tucked her closer and swayed them to the music.

"Why are you doing this?" she whispered.

Silence as they moved to the music. Silence for long enough that she thought he wouldn't answer. But then as the chorus ramped up, he murmured, "I'd like us to be friends."

Now it was her turn for silence.

Then . . . she burst out laughing.

Probably not the wisest thing to do in the middle of the dance floor, the music soft enough that her outburst garnered attention. But she couldn't help it. The man was going to be an A-list comic if he thought that was even in the realm of possibility.

She glanced up, lifting a palm from his chest—how had that gotten there?—and using her fingers to wipe the tears forming at the corners of her eyes.

His pretty hazel irises were focused on her, the golden and green deepened to a rich brown with the twinkling lights and navy sky above them. "That's a no, then?"

"That's a no."

He nodded, his eyes on hers as the song wound down, as a faster one took its place, the DJ breaking into it with the announcement that the cake cutting would begin in just a couple of minutes.

"I should—" she began.

Another nod, his arms slipping from around her, one hand grasping her elbow as he led them off the floor. Once on the side, he kissed her cheek, making her breath hitch and her heart skip a beat as his heat came close again, as his scent—spicy and earthy and tempting—filled her nose.

"I should have said goodbye," he whispered.

And then he was gone, walking away, his broad shoulders stretching the white cotton to alluring degrees, his stride purposeful as he disappeared into the restaurant that Kate and Jaime had rented out.

The urge to follow him was strong.

Really strong.

But the moment she actually gave in to the temptation to follow him, the moment she took a single step in his direction, Kate came up and grabbed her arm. Saving her from doing something incredibly idiotic. "Did you do that?"

Run off the sexy, gorgeous man who clearly wanted to give her another glorious night of sexy time?

Yes, she had done that.

But out of self-preservation.

Because . . . self-worth and value and . . . some other things that were important for some reason. She blinked, shook her head. No, not for *some* reason. They were important for her to keep hold of her self-respect, not to mention her feminist card.

But it turned out that Kate wasn't staring after the gorgeous Brad.

She was looking at the cake table, the mishmash of flowers and supermarket cakes she'd thrown together.

Heidi winced. "Yeah. I know it's not—"

Kate hugged her tight. "Why the hell did I spend that much money on an expensive cake when you could create *that?*"

"It's not—"

Kate released her. Then promptly gripped Heidi's chin between thumb and forefinger. "You are an amazing friend, and I love you."

Shit.

Now Heidi's eyes stung.

And then they were hugging each other, and yeah, so maybe it was mostly because Kate was deliriously happy—and perhaps had consumed one too many of the signature cocktails—but Heidi was still emotional. "I love you, too, Katie girl," she whispered then nudged her friend back. "Now, go find that sexy husband of yours and let's cut some cake!"

"Holy shit," Kate breathed. "Husband? *Husband*. I'm *married!*"

Heidi grinned. "You are, honey."

Kate did a little dance. "And now I get to eat cake."

"The literal embodiment of having your cake and eating it, too."

"Precisely." A grin. A kiss to her cheek. And one more squeeze that hurt Heidi's heart—in the best way. "I'm going to go find my husband."

Heidi nodded her chin behind Kate's shoulder. "I don't think you have to do much searching."

Not that the happy couple heard her.

They were smiling and staring into each other's eyes in a way that should have been sickening, but she couldn't fault her friend for that type of love, even if Jaime had regrown his man bun solely because Kate demanded it.

The man had nice hair, but—Heidi shuddered—she just couldn't get behind man buns.

And she digressed down the rabbit hole of unnecessary thoughts.

Luckily for her, the DJ called the guests to attention at that moment, directing everyone to the cake table for the cutting ceremony. Heidi caught a glimpse of Brad—because, of course, he wouldn't miss an important part of the wedding. People could say what they wanted about the wayward traveler, but when he was in town, he was a good brother.

He had good qualities, she supposed.

His family, Jaime included, were great.

But she supposed he was also a decent person—the sneaking-out-of-bed-before morning-problem aside. And really, as much as she wanted to be mad at him about that, she *had* invited him into her townhouse, she *had* wanted him, she *had* slept with him. Because she'd made that choice. Had she anticipated something different for the morning after? Fuck yes, she had. Did it hit a little too close to home because she was feeling vulnerable and the sneaking out he'd pulled hadn't been the first time that had happened to her?

Also, yes.

Did she still really want to hold it against him? Yup.

Did she understand that was unreasonable? Sigh. Also, yup.

But was she going to sleep with him again? That was a no.

A big, fat no.

Her gaze drifted from Kate and Jaime, posed with their hands intertwined on the knife, the blade poised above the frosting, to Brad, sexy in a freaking T-shirt and slacks, a slight scruff on his sharp jawline that she'd spent serious time kissing. He was too fucking pretty, and she hated herself for wanting him.

And maybe she hated herself even more for wanting to skirt the crowd, to take his hand, and lead him into that tiny bathroom for some counter-hoisting and skirt-lifting.

But while Heidi might be a lot of things—book smart, successful, a decent person—she wasn't a liar.

Including to herself.

So, when Brad's eyes shifted from the cake cutting to hers and her breath caught, heat curling in her abdomen, need flaring anew, she embraced that she would always feel that want, that the attraction would always be there.

Because she could also be one more thing.

Incredibly stubborn.

There was no freaking way she would ever open her heart— or body—to Brad again.

FIVE

BRAD

He heard the soft curse long after he'd thought everyone had left the wedding.

Frowning, he pushed up from the bench where he'd just met with the restaurant manager to make sure the final bills had been taken care of—they had, because Kate and Jaime had planned this wedding down to a tee—and stared out into the dark parking lot, trying to discern where the noise had originated.

"Shit," came another mutter, though this time, it was accompanied by the *click-clicking* of high heels.

He'd been enjoying a moment of quiet after the events of the evening, a few minutes to regroup and reset before he headed home, but the noise had him turning in time to see Heidi exiting the back of the building, presents stacked so high in her arms that he was surprised she could even see enough to navigate the dark walk.

"Here," he said, hurrying over to her.

"Brad?"

"Yup," he answered, snagging the teetering stack of boxes and opening up her vision. "What are you doing?" He'd seen her drive off earlier.

A shrug. "I couldn't fit all of Jaime and Kate's presents in my car. Had to drop them at their house then come back for another trip," she said, shifting the packages and prompting him to take several more gift bags from her arms. That she didn't fight him came as a surprise "Thanks." A smile. "My arms are killing me."

She led the way to her car, opening the trunk once they'd arrived, and after they'd gone back to the gift table for one more load of presents, they began the real-world game of Tetris, trying to see if the remaining packages would fit amongst the ones she'd already loaded.

"Kate and Jaime made out," he said, shoving a gift bag into the one remaining hole.

Heidi was cramming boxes into the front seat. "No kidding," she muttered. "It looks like a Bed, Bath, and Beyond exploded in here."

He laughed.

Then attempted to close the trunk.

His attempt was unsuccessful.

"This isn't working," he said. "Let's load up my car. I'll follow you over."

Heidi's lips parted, and he thought she'd protest, thought she'd bury herself in the driver's seat with presents before she agreed to more of his help, but she surprised him once again, nodding then wedging the passenger's door closed and coming to the rear of her car. "You're right," she said, pulling several packages out.

He snagged a few more, and then they managed to close the hatch.

This time, he led the way to his small hybrid—because there was no point in him keeping a big, fancy car when he was hardly in town—and he and Heidi squeezed the remainder of the bags and wrapped boxes into his car.

"I am *so* glad I don't have to write thank you notes for these," she said dryly.

He laughed. "Me, too."

Then he walked her to her car, said again, "I'll follow you over."

Her eyes came to his, held, and for a moment, he thought he saw some heat in those depths. But it was dark, the moonlight overhead hardly doing anything to illuminate the lot. Shadows and blurred lines. Fantasy in thinking this woman would be anything more than polite to him.

"Okay," she murmured, opening the driver's door and sitting down.

A moment later, the engine was on and he was heading back to his sedan, starting up his own car's engine, and carefully pulling out of his spot then following Heidi through the quiet roads and up the winding street that led to the small ranch-style house that Jaime and Kate had bought on the outskirts of town.

Mostly because Kate wanted *all* the animals.

Including the freaking rooster, who'd caused no shortage of pandemonium.

Last he'd heard, they had adopted a trio of goats that had been destined for slaughter, Fuzzy McFeatherston, the evil rooster, and his half-dozen harem of hens, two dogs, three cats, and a turtle.

At least his brother was a vet, so they didn't have to worry about bills from that front.

But bills coming from the *human* baby front?

If Brad were a betting man, he'd say those would be coming soon.

Heidi turned into the driveway, and he followed her, making sure to leave enough room between the cars so the doors could open all the way. They'd need all avenues of maneuverability in order to get these presents out of the cars and into the house.

A moment later, Heidi was out of her sedan and ladening herself with packages.

He popped his door.

"Will you use the keypad and open the door?" she asked, gift bags lined up on her arms like oversized bracelets. "The code is—"

"I know it," he said, grabbing a few boxes before high-tailing it up the walk.

He punched in the code, pushed inside, and dropped his burden with the rest of the presents in the living room then went back outside. Along the way, he made sure the latch was open, but not the door—because he didn't want to be responsible for kitty escapes.

Heidi was coming up the steps, so he doubled-back, opened the door for her, did his whole latch but not wide-open procedure, then returned to his car.

They repeated the process, unloading the presents and stacking them inside the house, until that front room appeared to have become the landing ground for every shade of sparkling silver wrapping paper and the entire stockpile from the tissue paper industry.

When they were done, Heidi set the alarm and they closed the front door behind them.

"The pet-sitter will be here in the morning."

"Hopefully the cats don't get into the bags."

She winced. "I didn't think of that."

"How much trouble can they get into?" he asked.

Another wince. "Have you met the Terrible Two?"

"No, why?"

Her lips twitched. "They make the Fuzz look like the most well-behaved rooster you've ever seen."

His brows lifted.

"I'm not joking."

"Shit."

Her shoulders slumped as she turned back to the door. "Maybe I'll lock the cats in Jaime and Kate's room, and tomorrow I can come back to move the presents into the spare bedroom and lock the door."

"I can help you move them now," he offered.

"I'm tired," she said, chin dropping to her chest. "And my feet hurt."

He nudged her toward her car. "Go home," he ordered.

"I—"

"You took care of Cake-Gate," he said. "I can deal with Present-Gate. Plus, there's no telling if we'll be able to find or catch the cats."

Her nose wrinkled. "That's true. But I should really—"

"Go home and rest?" he said, guiding her to her car. "Yes, *that*."

"But—" He opened the driver's door, and still she hesitated.

Another nudge had her sitting in the seat, and he closed the metal panel as soon as her feet were clear, trapping her inside.

"Drive home. Get sleep," he said loud enough so she could hear him.

She made a face but didn't protest further, just turned her car on and backed out of the driveway. Brad watched the tail-lights disappear down the street then went back into the house and got his workout moving those packages from the living room into the guest bedroom, making sure he closed the door securely to prevent any kitty escapades.

Then he drove home.

And when he finally made it into bed, after a long, hot shower that washed the remnants of cake and frosting from his body, he dreamed of silken brown hair fanning out on the pillow beside him.

———

The Monday following the wedding, he pulled into the underground parking garage then made his way up to his apartment.

His lonely, *empty* apartment.

Funny how he'd never much minded the tiny unit with its drab lighting and noisy upstairs neighbors. Usually, it was just a stopover to the next adventure.

Except . . . he didn't have any more adventures planned.

And the itchy feeling, the one that usually crept in after a few weeks home, coaxing him off into the sunset, was noticeably absent.

Instead, he was drawn in a different direction.

Drawn toward one person in particular.

"Which just confirms what you already know," he muttered, fighting with the old lock for a moment before he managed to let himself into his apartment. "Heidi is the best thing you've ever come across."

Small and dark were the apartment's best qualities—aside from kickass internet, that was. The rest of it, he'd done his best with. A cheap couch that was covered in a tapestry he'd picked up in Peru. Several prints from a local artist in Iceland on the far wall—mostly so he could pretend there was another window there. His bed was behind a screen he'd purchased in Japan. His shelves were made by an artist in Indonesia, who'd collected driftwood washed up onshore.

His life in objects, and yet none of them could fill the hole inside him.

None of them told him who he was.

But then again, why did he need to be told?

Now *there* was the itchy feeling, rearing its ugly head, making him think too much, feel too much.

Jaime was the caring one. Tammy was the smart one. Penny was the go-getter. And he was . . .

What?

Driven by fancy? Lacking attention and focus?

He knew neither of the last two were true, and if there was any fancy involved, it was from simply wanting to make the most of every moment, because he undertook a great deal of planning with his trips, ensuring he didn't waste his money or his opportunity to visit.

"Fucking hell," he muttered, going to the one window in the space. It was half-blocked by the refrigerator, but it provided fresh air and sunlight, and most importantly, a way out.

A fire escape that led up to the roof.

Yanking open the panel, he clambered ungracefully out the frame, grasping onto the metal ladder and climbing.

It was late, and he didn't want to be that creeper outside of someone's apartment, freaking them out, so he moved quickly and quietly up the ladder, past the other windows, until he'd ascended the three floors above him and reached the roof. Not too long ago he'd stashed a blanket on the rooftop space that was definitely not approved by management, adding it to the chair and the lamp other people had brought. Tonight, however, he wanted to feel the chill on his skin, so he hauled himself over the ledge, straightened, and looked up at the sky.

God, he'd seen it in so many iterations, the stars in different alignments depending on what side of the globe or which hemisphere he was in, but somehow it still brought him comfort.

There were bigger things out there than him and his small life—no matter how big he tried to make it.

His cell rang.

He answered without bothering to glance at the screen. Only his family and a few old friends had this number.

"Brad," Jaime said, sounding blissfully happy. "I'm surprised that you're not somewhere without an internet connection."

Considering he'd spent a fair amount of the last decade in exactly that scenario, he didn't comment except to say, "I'm here." Of course, it wasn't until after he'd spoken the two words that he realized his tone was all wrong.

Silence.

"What's wrong?"

Shit.

"Nothing," he said, forcing his tone to be his normal cheerful. "I went to Coit Tower today, and it was . . . well, it was a big tower in the middle of the city, and yesterday I went to this beach—"

"Brad."

Double shit.

Now he'd triggered both Jaime's oldest brother side *and* his intuitive he-cares-for-animals-who-can't-talk vet caring side.

Which basically meant, Brad was in for it now.

"How's the honeymoon?" he asked instead, going for diversion. He didn't want to hash through what was in his head. Not when he felt like it might be the key to a lot of the shit that had twisted him up for so long.

"The honeymoon's great," Jaime said. "Except for a certain younger brother, who thinks that he can get that shit of an attempt at distraction past me. "What's going on?"

"Seriously. I'm fine."

"And *that's* horseshit. What's up? Your flight to your future destination get canceled?"

"I'm staying in California."

"For a few more weeks until we get back?" His brother sounded thrilled. "That's great, we can catch up some more before you fly off again."

"No."

"Oh." Disappointed now. "But at least with you living so close, we can hang out during the times you're back."

"No, Jaim." Brad sighed. "I mean, I'm staying in California

permanently. I'm thinking that most of my traveling days are at an end."

A beat then, "Who are you, and what have you done to my brother?"

He sighed. Of course, Jaime wouldn't understand. Brad barely knew what was going through his head himself. All he knew was that he wanted Heidi, he wanted something more permanent and fixed, he wanted a place to live that wasn't a tiny, dark, questionably clean apartment, where he could build something that wasn't fueled by excitement for the next grand thing out there.

He wanted to be happy with who and where and what he was now.

Because . . . he had a feeling he'd spent all these years running.

"Brad?" Jaime asked. "Did I lose you?"

He clenched his jaw, released it. "No, I'm here."

Jaime's voice gentled. "I was just kidding, you know."

Forcing a laugh, he said, "I know. It's fine. How's the resort?"

"The reason I won't ever seriously complain about all your traveling," Jaime told him. "Being sequestered here with Kate is definitely no hardship."

"Is it as good as I remember?"

"Better."

Brad hadn't stayed on site—it was a bit too expensive and catering for his tastes, especially for a single man traveling by himself. But it *was* perfect for a honeymooning couple who'd deserved plenty of pampering, pool-side service, and good restaurants for whenever they decided to emerge from their room.

"But just because I'm getting copious amounts of exercise with my beautiful wife—and I don't mean in the gym—"

"I never thought you did," he muttered.

"Just because I'm having copious amounts of glorious sex with my lovely wife," he corrected, "doesn't mean my brain has rotted. I know something is up with you. So, out with it already. Otherwise we'll both be here all night."

"I can just hang up."

"I'll call back." A pause. "Or I'll sic Mom on you."

Sighing and rubbing the throb that had mysteriously appeared in his temple, he tried something else. "Look, I'm just a little tired tonight. I stayed up late working on a project and . . ."

"And what?" Jaime pressed.

"Did you ever wish you were different?"

That hadn't been the thought he'd been forming in his mind, the words he was trying to pull together were going to be more along the lines of something to put his brother at ease, a way to move on with this conversation. But, as silence greeted him over the airwaves, Brad realized it was the most important question.

The thing that was at the crux of everything.

Why the souvenirs from his travel meant so much, but also made him feel sad by reminding him that he'd missed out on a lot.

He'd had grand adventures, but he'd used them to build his identity, until that identity was more *him* than he was.

He was *that* guy—the one too busy looking to the future to appreciate the now. Hell, he'd been too enamored of that future to be anything but *terrified* of the now.

But the thought that was nagging at him was *why*.

Why was he terrified to be present, to be fully in this moment?

Was it because it might not live up to expectations? Or . . . was it something else?

And why *didn't* he know? Shouldn't he understand what was going on in his own brain?

Seriously. Why the fuck didn't he understand what was going on in his brain?

"Different how?" Jaime asked quietly.

Brad blinked away the thoughts, the questions that, at that time, were frustratingly unnerving and unanswerable.

"I'm not sure," he admitted.

"That's not an answer."

A bolt of anger shot through him, and a retort was actually on the tip of his tongue before he bit it back. This wasn't his brother's fault. It was his own irritation that he couldn't understand the tangle in his mind and heart, when he wanted to be clearheaded in both.

"I *want* to answer you," he said, voice tempered. "But I don't fucking know *how*."

Jaime released a long, slow breath, sending static through the speakers of Brad's cell. "Mom always told me you're the one she worries the most about."

Somehow disappointed by that reply, somehow wanting his big brother to have the proverbial answer to the flurry of thoughts and concerns and questions in his mind, even though it wasn't like *he* was doling out exceptional wisdom in this conversation with all his *I don't knows* and *I don't know hows,* he sank down into the chair on that roof, the coolness that lingered on the plastic seeping in through his jeans, chilling the backs of his thighs, and forced out a cordial response. "Well, that makes sense," he said. "I have traveled to some pretty sketchy places in my time."

A beat of quiet.

Then, "Ask me when she told me that."

Something in his brother's tone had Brad sitting up a little straighter, tearing his eyes from the stars overhead and shifting them to the roof of the opposite building, even though he wasn't really processing the rectangular lines. Instead, he stared at it, almost unseeing, a feeling of foreboding pressing heavily on him, anticipating that he was about to learn something monumental.

"When?" he asked, the question barely audible, even to his own years.

A long pause. "When she was sick."

Brad inhaled sharply.

Their mom had been diagnosed with cancer when Brad was eight. He remembered it being a terrifying time, with her being in and out of the hospital for surgeries and treatments. She was healthy now, had been in remission for a long, long time, but he didn't think he would ever forget the way she'd looked while in that hospital bed or the sound of her retching after she'd received the chemo.

He'd been worried he might hurt her, had been so afraid to touch her, to hug her.

To get close to her.

Jaime began talking again, intruding on those memories, but Brad was happy to let them go, relieved to be able to shove them down into the locked box in his mind. "I had gone to visit her in the hospital one day. It was when she was really sick, and well, you guys were younger, and I don't think you recognized how touch-and-go it was, so I needed that extra time with her, I guess."

"I knew," Brad whispered.

That feeling sitting heavy in his gut, knowing that he was going to lose the single most important thing in his life. His dad had been around, of course, had been great then, just as he was now, but it wasn't the same as it had been with his mom. There was just something special about moms, he supposed.

And though his parents had tried to shield them from the worst of it, he knew from firsthand experience that the type of battle his mom had fought permeated everything.

Colored everything.

"What?" Jaime asked.

Swallowing hard against that recognition, he said, "I knew that she almost died. Not as an adult, but back then as a kid. I *knew*."

His brother was quiet for several moments. "I get that. It was probably hard to try to hide much from any of us, but I guess . . . I'd always assumed that you and Tammy were too young to understand, to truly get how precarious it was." He sighed. "We're lucky she's here."

"Yes, we are."

"I wasn't trying to bring you back there. It's just"—Jaime hesitated—"I swear, I've never forgotten what she told me that day. I just didn't know how it fit in, especially with—" He broke off. "I'd gone after school to see her before soccer practice, and she was white as a fucking ghost, lying there with her eyes closed." His breathing was unsteady for a few heartbeats, and Brad had the sense that his brother was trying to hold on to his typically even-keeled personality in the face of what had to be a really dark memory. "Well, I thought she was dead, and I think I would have run screaming from the room if not for her opening her eyes."

Brad stilled, a chill going through him.

Jaime cleared his throat roughly. "I don't think I'll ever be able to erase that, the way she looked, the horror I felt, and shit, it's been what? Like almost twenty years since she went into remission?"

"About that," he agreed.

"So, she opened her eyes and waved me over, and I sat down next to her, heart pounding, trying to pretend I was totally fine when I was a thirteen-year-old kid pissing his pants and wanting to crawl onto the bed with her, wanting her to just hold me and tell me everything would be okay."

Brad clenched his jaw, eyes stinging.

"Instead, I started pulling out my homework before she even asked—because you *know* she would have asked."

He laughed. "Yes, she definitely would have asked." Their mom had always had her finger on the pulse of their family, somehow recollecting which of the four of them had a project due or a dentist appointment or needed to wear something special for an event at school.

"But she saw right through me. She knew that I was upset, that I was taking it really hard, and she ordered me into bed with her." He released a breath. "I resisted, said I was too big, too old, but she wouldn't let it go. She made it an order until I finally got into bed with her. And then . . . she just wrapped her arms around me and told me everything would be okay."

Brad released a shaky breath.

"We laid like that for a long time, and I remember at some point looking up at the clock and realizing that I had to get to practice, so I packed up my things, got ready to walk my ass over to the field, and then just before I reached the door, she stopped me and said, '*You need to watch out for Brad.*'" Jaime inhaled, released it slowly. "And I remember grabbing onto the door handle and saying something to the effect of '*Why? What do I need to protect myself from?*' Thinking you'd stolen my Legos or were planning some prank, like you were always doing as an eight-year-old little twerp."

That made him smile, enough that he could actually muster a light retort. "You're just saying that because I always got you."

"I'm glaring at you right now." Jaime laughed. "But, yes, *that's* also true. Still, she wasn't talking about the Legos or one of your pranks. Because in response, she told me, '*I worry for your brother because he's the type of person who always seems happy on the surface, and those are the people who are usually hurting the most underneath. That's why you need to watch out for him.*'" Jamie cleared his throat. "You were a kid, a pain in the ass kid, but you weren't ever sad or down or anything other than an annoying kid brother, so I thought she was being ridiculous."

"I probably *was* stealing your Legos or planning something,"

Brad said lightly, even though his throat was tight, and his heart was pounding in his throat. He actually felt a little dizzy, as though the Earth had just suddenly shifted on its axis.

"That's possibly true," Jaime agreed. "But I've also finally gotten old enough to understand what she was saying . . . and to understand *why* she said it. She put on that good front, *wanted* to kick cancer's ass, but it had to have crossed her mind that she might not be here and that she wanted someone to know . . . well, to know that."

"I—" He struggled with words again.

Was that what he was? What his mom had said? Was he unhappy?

He didn't feel unhappy spending time with Heidi or when he was with his family. He *never* felt unhappy when he was traveling—which was probably why he'd clocked so many hours on planes and in other countries.

"I don't think she was thinking you were sad all the time," Jaime said, "but more that you're really good at putting on a mask. You come across as so easy-going that people don't often recognize that you need more from them." He blew out a breath. "And I think Mom needed me to know in case—"

Pulse pounding in his ears, Brad had to joke.

Because otherwise he might cry.

And God, he really didn't want to cry that night.

"Must be all the gray hairs," he said on a laugh, and even *he* could hear that it didn't sound remotely right. "Mom always said my superpower was giving her new ones hourly."

Jaime chuckled. "It wasn't the gray hairs, though I can't deny that I'm now old enough to find a couple of those now and then." His tone went serious. "But, Brad, it's only because I have Kate now that I understand what Mom was saying then. Because my Kate was one of those people—the ones who seem happy on the surface, but who was hurting underneath."

Heart pounding, Brad couldn't bring himself to form a response.

Which was just as well, because Jaime wasn't done talking.

"So, bro, my question to you is . . . what's beneath the veneer? What's that proverbial grain of sand in the oyster, rubbing you raw? Or maybe it's a big spike that's jabbing at you over and over again, something that's hurting you and just won't go away, no matter how hard you try to ignore it."

"I—" He shook his head even though his brother couldn't see him. It was all he could manage, when all he could think was . . .

Happy on the surface.

And what was beneath?

Nothing.

Empty.

Unfulfilled.

Fuck, that was gloomy. Fuck, that didn't make him feel better. Fuck, *why* didn't he know what the hell was in his own brain?

"Just think about it," Jaime said. "Okay?"

"Okay," he whispered after a moment. "I will."

They said their goodbyes and hung up, Brad continuing to sit on the chair with the stars overhead, continuing to berate himself for not knowing his own mind. But the problem was that he didn't feel jabbed or raw or even hurt.

He just felt . . . alone.

For the second time in as many minutes, he went completely ramrod stiff, not breathing, not moving as he realized that, no, he wasn't necessarily unhappy or depressed.

He was empty.

Because he'd filled his life with all the wrong things—or perhaps, *most* of the wrong things, because he did have his family. But he didn't have any close friendships, and he'd used traveling as a tool.

To avoid connection.

To avoid getting too close to anyone . . . because if he did get close then he might care about them and they would leave, or they might get sick and die. But if *he* left first, if *he* was too busy or off doing his own thing, then he wouldn't be as hurt.

That was why the first night with Heidi had freaked him out so much.

That was why he'd run.

Because he'd known she was different, known he couldn't leave her behind.

The only question was whether he had the strength to fill that empty void inside him, whether he had the strength to put that need to keep people at a distance behind him.

Heidi's smile flashed through his mind, the pride on her face when she'd stared up at him with the amazing cake creation to replace the mess he'd made, the tears she'd wiped from her eyes when she'd watched Kate and Jaime kiss at the altar, her joy when she'd caught the bouquet, her arms as she'd walked toward him, the slender limbs laden with presents from the wedding. Hell, even her glares.

None of that had made him feel empty.

None of that had made him feel alone.

"So fuck that," he whispered. "Fuck the void, fuck the distance."

He was done with running.

He was ready to live a life that was so fucking full it was spilling over.

And he wanted to live it with Heidi.

SIX

HEIDI

S ighing, she shut down her computer and stretched her shoulders, knowing that the calculations weren't quite right but also knowing that she was too tired to sort out where exactly she'd gone wrong.

Gathering up dirty coffee cups and muffin wrappers—her guilty pleasure was the banana chocolate chunk ones from the best bakery in town, *Molly's*—she made sure all the equipment was either shut down or properly collecting data they'd retrieve in the days and weeks to come.

Her assistants had left several hours before, but she was playing catch-up after having had a meeting with the board earlier in the day. Which meant she'd spent more time schmoozing than mathing—and had hated every minute of it.

She understood the need for the schmoozing. She just was never more at home than when she was in her lab. A lab that was hers and hers alone. Well, hers alone if she ignored the fact that the funding came from the company and she had to clear her research with the board members. But for the most part, they left her to her electron microscope, her spectrometer, her calculations.

Aside from the schmoozing.

Thankfully, that only happened quarterly, and the rest of the year, she was left to her own devices, in her own lab. That she was in charge of.

Yup.

She was living the female scientist dream.

When she'd quit her previous job just over a year before, she'd been at a loss. She'd worked at universities and big corporations. But the red tape had been astronomical. And not only that, but she'd felt like every single one of her decisions she'd made, every shred of research and evidence she'd conducted and garnered had been questioned. Ostensibly, she'd been running her own lab for one of the best companies in the world.

And she'd been micromanaged within an inch of her life.

She'd been miserable and ready to change positions—or maybe to go *back* to school and make a bid at becoming a career student.

Then she'd found Volton.

And this company was different. It was still a power in the industry, but it was smaller and run by a CEO who was determined to not let it get bogged down with big company problems.

Which made it a joy to work for.

It was the mystical unicorn of careers to actually love getting up in the morning to come to work, and she was riding that magical, horned horse like a champ, *clomp-clomping* into her lab every weekday morning. And some weekends.

So long as there were coffee and muffins.

Smiling to herself, she placed the dirty mugs in the sink, set the coffee pot to be ready to brew for the morning, and locked up.

Her phone buzzed as she walked to her car, and she pulled it out of her pocket, smiling wider when she saw that it was Kate texting her a picture of her purple-painted toes dipping into the white sand of a beach.

Typing on the screen as she walked, she sent,

Why are you wasting time with your precious hubby to text me?

A beat. Then a buzz.

To torment you with all the luxury that's surrounding me.

The words were accompanied by a photo of two massage tables set up on the beach.

Heidi laughed.

You're evil.

Then added.

But you're having a good time?

Kate's reply came in just a few seconds.

The best.

Heidi's heart squeezed.

I'm glad. Now stop texting me and go enjoy your honeymoon.

When no reply came, she smiled, stowed the cell in her pocket, and pushed into the underground garage. Which was the exact moment her phone buzzed again.

"Kate," she muttered, "you just don't learn."

But when she glanced at the screen, the message wasn't from Kate.

It was a call from her mother.

"Good God," she whispered, debating ignoring the call and the ramifications that might bring. Her mom wasn't like Kate's or Jaime's. She wasn't . . . nice, wasn't the type to make cookies or pull up an extra chair at the table for an unexpected guest.

Nope. Her mother was razor sharp.

And fuck did it burn to be on the receiving end of her words.

But she was old enough to understand that a conversation now would save a longer, drawn-out, painful conversation later, so she waved goodbye to the security guard and swiped a finger across the screen as she got into her car.

She didn't drive anywhere though.

Not yet.

Her mother had a way of infuriating her beyond reason, and after one close call too many while trying to ignore exactly how painful her barbs were and the subsequent distraction making Heidi a danger to other drivers, she'd promised herself no vehicular operation under the influence of her mom.

"Hello?" she said.

"Why aren't you at home?"

Her brows drew together. "What do you mean?"

"Your father was at a meeting in the city. We drove by to pick you up for dinner, but you're not home."

"No," she said, not surprised that her mom, Colleen, had shown up without a word, expecting her to drop everything. That was the status quo. "I'm not home. I'm just getting off work."

Saying that was a mistake.

She knew it.

Somehow, she had been dumb enough to say it anyway.

Colleen's sigh was loud. "How are you ever going to get married if you work so much?"

As far as responses went, that was a one on a scale of ten. One meaning the best-case scenario. It wasn't denigrating her career choice, just a simple, almost normal-mom reaction lamenting the fact that she wasn't married.

That was something Kate or Jaime's mom might say.

Or *had* said, since they were married now.

But then the one turned into a . . . six-point-five.

"You know there's a reason female scientists are rare," her mom said. "It's because most of them actually listen to their biological clocks and get out of the field in time before their ovaries dry up."

Ew.

"I love what I do, Mom."

Colleen scoffed.

"And I'm happy being alone."

Another scoff. "No, you're not," she said, and now her voice approached razor blades, approached that ten out of ten on that scale of awful. "You're sad and alone and will always be that way if you don't get your priorities in order."

Slice.

"Goodbye, Mom," Heidi whispered and hung up, resting her head on the steering wheel, hating that these conversations left her feeling like this—flayed open, vulnerable, like a little kid who couldn't find her voice.

She wished she could shoot barbs back, stand up for herself better, but every time she thought she had a handle on the conversation, her mom brought mean.

And she . . . sucked at fighting mean.

At least she'd gotten better at hanging up.

That was progress—so long as her mom didn't call back.

Right on cue, her cell buzzed in her, and she nearly dropped it like it had suddenly caught fire. She would not pick up. She would not even glance at the screen.

Lie.

She looked, and saw,

Can I tempt you with prickly pear margaritas?

Frowning, the conversation with her mom tucking itself back into the box in the back of her heart with the countless others of that same vein, Heidi was trying to puzzle out who had her number and was texting her about margaritas—albeit delicious ones—when her cell vibrated again.

Just realized you're probably wondering who this is. I'll give you one guess. It's your non-friend, who'd like to make up for Cake-Gate, and maybe a few more things.

"Brad," she breathed.

Then immediately shook her head because she shouldn't be breathing dreamily about the man.

Another buzz as she was starting her car. Sighing, she couldn't stop herself from glancing at the screen before she backed out.

I got your number from Kate.

A beat.

So she'll probably question why you'd refuse to see me when we're practically family now.

"Brad," she growled, snatching up her cell from the cradle on her dash, fingers flying over the screen.

So now you're not only good at slipping out unnoticed, but also blackmail?

Another buzz.

I'm exceptionally good at a lot of things.

"Ugh," she muttered, shoving her cell into the bottom of her purse in disgust and then tossing her purse in the back seat for good measure.

Or maybe so she wouldn't be tempted to keep talking to the man.

Unfortunately, that was also true.

Regardless, she ignored the responding buzz and concentrated her attention on navigating her way through Bay Area traffic and home to her townhouse.

Which was the best thing she'd ever spent her money on.

Located in a small two-story building on the edge of town, it backed up to a lightly forested area. But her favorite part—besides the sauna inside the gym that she pretended to use but really it was just an excuse to make it into that sauna, and the fact that she had a quiet corner unit with a balcony looking out on those woods—were the trails crisscrossing through the trees, several of which led to a small creek. She could wander them for a few minutes, pretend that she was being healthy and was totally a nature girl, and when she'd had enough, be back inside her townhouse in fifteen minutes flat.

It was perfect.

But tonight, she wasn't finding that same satisfaction.

Because of her cell phone burning a hole in her purse.

"Self-respect," she murmured. "Self. Respect."

Except, her body didn't want self-respect. It wanted Brad and his yummy cock and for her to have a repeat of their night together—only this time minus the shitty morning-after feeling.

"That's it," she muttered, pulling out some ingredients for dinner and setting them on the counter. She would make pasta and bread and eat ice cream and drink wine. She would consume *all* the carbs, and then Brad would be gone, flitting from her life again as he traveled to some exotic location.

Heading into her bedroom with that thought, she spent the next few minutes changing from her fancy work clothes—fancy because of the meeting, since she normally wore jeans, T-shirts, and the odd blouse to her lab—into her coziest pajamas. She was tugging an oversized sweatshirt down her torso after hanging up her slacks and button-down, stowing away her sparkly flats, when her doorbell rang.

Smiling, she made her way to the door.

In all likelihood, it would be her neighbor, Mrs. Horowitz. The elderly widow usually came bearing delicious baked goods, and coincidentally, Heidi was out of banana chocolate chip muffins. Maybe she'd get enough of a carb stash to tide her over for a few days.

But when she tugged open the wooden panel, Mrs. Horowitz wasn't on the other side.

"Can I bribe my way inside?" Brad asked.

"No," she muttered, starting to slam the door.

"I have tequila," he coaxed.

"It's a school night." This time, she did shut the heavy wood, flicking the lock with a resounding *click*.

Then she heard the sigh.

A resolved one.

Like he'd known what her reaction was going to be, even before she'd opened and shut the door.

And she hesitated, guilt sliding through her to curl in her stomach. She didn't enjoy feeling like a bitch, especially when the man was probably lonely with his brother gone. He probably didn't have a lot of friends in town. She knew he'd only recently moved to California, that he worked from home, and his travels took him away frequently.

He didn't even have his family to hang out with.

They'd all returned home on Sunday.

So if she didn't take pity on the man, he would be all alone.

And lonely.

And sad.

Or maybe that was her?

Either way, she'd reopened the door.

But he wasn't there. The entry was empty, the street beyond quiet. She started to take a step forward, in an attempt to follow him when she couldn't begin to have a clue to know how to track him down or which way he'd left, and stopped.

Then glanced down and smiled despite herself.

There on her welcome mat was a basket, and inside it, a bottle of tequila, a bag of ice, a squirt bottle of prickly pear simple syrup, a shaker, and two glasses.

The man had charm—and balls—she had to give him that.

SEVEN

BRAD

I*'ll cook. You mix. So long as you remember it's a school night.*

He glanced down at his cell and smiled.

Then got back out of his car, which he'd parked just down the block, and made his way to Heidi's door.

She was waiting in the opening, the rattiest sweatshirt he'd ever seen covering her lush curves, the basket he'd left in her arms. Her hair was down, her legs covered in rainbow-printed pajama pants, and her feet were bare, purple-painted toes peeking out from beneath the hem of her PJs.

And she was the most beautiful woman he'd ever seen.

Seeing her was an actual punch to the gut, a physical caress.

Then she spoke, and he'd be lying if he said it didn't take a tiny bit of wind out of his sails.

"I'm only inviting you in because you're alone."

Ouch.

But still, it was a way in. So he simply took the basket from her arms and said, "Well, if I'm here being pathetic, I don't mind being pathetic with you."

Her cheeks went pink. "That's not what I meant."

He knew that, knew despite the sharp words and her attempts at distance, that Heidi wasn't mean at heart. She had a generosity of spirit and a big heart, both of which had recalled him to her place, even after he'd clearly hurt her deeply a few months before.

Shifting the basket, he brushed his fingers over her cheek. "I know."

"No touching," she muttered, stepping back. "If you want my famous spaghetti Bolognese, you'll stop with the seduction and just be Jaime's brother."

He didn't want to be Jaime's brother in that moment.

He wanted to be this woman's lover, her other half, her everything.

But he'd blown it. He'd run scared last time, and now he was paying the consequences. Also yes, maybe he had a plan to sweet-talk this woman into a second chance. He'd fucked up, he panicked and left, but . . . he'd come back.

He'd *seen* her.

The puzzle pieces in his mind had finally rearranged themselves into proper alignment.

And he knew that he couldn't give her up.

Travel had grown dull, his life empty. But now he was seeing in full color for the first time, and that was simply from being in her presence for a few hours. He wanted more. He wanted *everything*.

He wanted . . . well, first he wanted this woman to not look at him with daggers in her eyes.

Baby steps.

Lifting his hands, he said, "No touching." A beat. "Unless you ask me to."

Her eyebrows lifted, and if her glare were a physical thing, he would have been flayed open and bleeding on the ground. As it was, and lucky for him, she didn't have that power, so he was able to follow her into the house, able to surreptitiously take in her surroundings.

To mark if anything had changed.

It hadn't, and he walked through the clean space, everything neatly in its place, from the dust-free photographs to the purple couch with the cheerful turquoise cushions. She strode into the kitchen, and he saw she had food set out on the counter. As he hovered in the doorway, she bent and grabbed a pot from a drawer, slamming more than placing it on the stove.

"Is there a reason you haven't started mixing drinks yet?" she muttered a little while later.

He'd been watching her at work, opening cans of tomato sauce, browning some meat in a pan—which had required her to do an additional bend and had given him an additional glimpse of those curves currently hiding amongst the rainbows on her pajamas—chopping an onion and herbs, and he hadn't realized that he'd spent long minutes standing in that opening.

She was mesmerizing.

Even grouchy and in enough fabric to cover an elephant.

Which was a thought he would not be saying aloud.

Because, once again, he liked his balls where they were, thank him very much.

"I thought it was a school night," he bluffed. "Figured you'd want to save your one drink for mealtime."

"I changed my mind," she muttered, stirring the pot after adding what smelled like garlic—and plenty of the yummy aromatic if his nose was any indication. "I need more than one drink to deal with you creeping out on me like a peeping Tom."

He burst out laughing.

"That wasn't supposed to be funny."

Crossing over to her, he said, "You're like a kitten trying to be terrifying, hissing and swiping out with your claws but not managing anything remotely close to frightening."

Her hazel eyes darkened.

And he had the distinct thought that if he *really* liked his balls where they currently resided, then he was going to have to stop running his freaking mouth.

But instead of taking her frustration out on his junk, instead of smacking him over the head with that pan—as he probably half-deserved—her lips curved into a rueful smile and she said, "Unfortunately, I've never mastered the art of being scary."

"That's not so bad."

"Oh yeah?" she muttered. "You haven't seen me trying to scare off annoying men in the bar. One of my glares and I swear they pull up a chair and start ordering appetizers." She turned back to the sauce and stirred in one of the cans of tomatoes.

"I'm guessing it doesn't work on annoying men in your house, either?"

Her lips tipped up. "No, it doesn't."

He laughed, finally placed the basket on the counter, started pulling together ingredients for the prickly pear margaritas that he'd heard through the grapevine were her favorite.

"I'm not good at seeing things through to the end." Brad froze, shocked that he'd said the words aloud.

He'd thought them often enough, had berated himself for his jumping about, for his lack of staying power, but he couldn't ever remember a time when he'd admitted that failing to someone else.

She didn't say anything for a long moment, the silence punctuated only by the sizzling meat in the pan, the scraping of the wooden spoon as she stirred.

"Why do you think that is?" she asked softly, when he'd nearly given in to the urge to run screaming from the townhouse.

The question was an obvious one.

Just not one he'd expected her to ask.

It was also one he wasn't prepared to answer.

"I don't know." Did it relate to his mom? Was it some other

failing? Some defense mechanism? Maybe they were all tied together . . . or maybe he was just flawed.

Maybe he had more thinking to do.

Sigh.

She turned, gave him that glare again, the one that was supposed to be scary but was really freaking adorable, and said, "You think I'm going to let you off the hook that easily?"

No, of course she wasn't.

But before his discussion with Jaime, he'd never talked to anyone about this, had never done more than laugh off the comments when people—from teachers to family members to friends—teased him about his flights of fancy and his tendency to go off on his own adventures. Even his career had been something he'd fallen into—website design, predominately for travel companies. His first client had reached out to him after finding Brad's now-retired travel blog.

See what he meant about not finishing things?

But truthfully, with the blog at least, he'd gotten too busy with his website business, with all the places he'd traveled, to keep up. It was either turn down clients or travel less or let the blog go.

The decision had been easy.

Buh-bye blog.

But how to explain that to this woman.

"Okay, fine," she said, after a moment. "Maybe I *will* let you off that easily."

He snorted.

"Be prepared for me to circle back after prickly pears."

"Noted."

She smiled at him and turned back to the pan. "What's your favorite place you've visited?"

He measured the alcohol into the metal cup, scooped up some ice, shook the entire mixture together, and then strained it into two glasses. "We're going to be friends now?"

"I've decided to forgive you."

His heart pulsed. "Just that easily?"

"I've punished you for two days straight, not to mention laughed when you got brained by that platter." He touched the top of his head, probing the still painful spot, and she laughed. "See? I'm terrible."

No, she was wonderful.

Especially when her eyes narrowed. "But I am *not* sleeping with you again."

Now, it was his turn to laugh.

She crossed to him, making his breath catch, his laughter cut off. And his cock twitch. Like it did any time she was in the vicinity. "I am," she murmured, her mouth temptingly close, her floral and spice scent wafting up into his nose. "*Not* sleeping with you again," she added, reaching beyond him for the glass he'd just filled then retreating back across the kitchen.

"Why?" he asked. "You know it would be good."

She'd just taken a sip—or maybe, a gulp. Either way, his assertion made her sputter and cough, and then *he* crossed to *her*, rubbing his hand up and down her spine until she stopped choking, until she looked up at him, heat in her eyes.

Her breath shuttered out. "I'm still not sleeping with you," she wheezed.

Their gazes met.

They both burst into laughter.

And Brad thought that was okay. For now, anyway.

Baby steps.

First laughter.

Then, hopefully, other things.

Eight

HEIDI

It was the next evening, and she was having *déjà vu*.

"Glutton for punishment?" she asked, lifting her brows at the tall, dark, and sexy pain in her ass currently sitting on her doorstep.

He lifted his cell. "You didn't text me to stay away, so I figured that I'd slide into the chance."

Snorting, she unlocked her door, moving inside and allowing him to trail her down the hall. "The ignoring was unintentional. My cell had to be off for my work today"—some top-secret shit, as her assistant Stef called it—"and I forgot to turn it on." She plunked the box with the muffins she'd picked up after work and her bag on the kitchen counter, reached inside, and pulled her phone out. "See? It's not all about you."

He smiled that slow and hot quirk of his lips, making her want to ignore her promise to herself.

But she was stubborn.

She wouldn't be burned twice by falling for his humor and charm.

Even if he was humorous . . . and charming.

Friends, and nothing more. That. Was. *It*.

He snagged the cell from her fingers and powered it on. "But seriously, don't forget, next time," he said, tone more serious than she had ever heard it. "You might get into a situation where you need it and can't wait for it to boot up."

She paused. "Have *you* been in one of those situations?"

Humor in his gorgeous green-brown eyes, tempering the serious. "More than one."

"Oh."

"Yeah. *Oh*." He handed her phone back.

Heidi took it and found herself hesitant, all of a sudden remembering that him coming over to hang out, especially unexpectedly, wasn't normal. Yes, they'd eaten together the previous night. Yes, they'd chatted a bit about the places he'd visited. Yes, she'd actually had three prickly pear margaritas. But then she'd yawned, right in the middle of him telling her a story about a pickpocket he'd fended off in Italy, and he hadn't finished his tale, hadn't listened to her when she'd told him she was fine.

Nope. He'd shown himself right to the door.

And she hadn't heard a word from him.

She'd just slept, worked, and expected to go on with their separate lives—his guilt assuaged, her life moving right along. She even had plans tonight to set up an online dating profile for a new app Stef had recommended.

Apparently, all the cool kids were doing it.

Not that *she* was a cool kid, but it wasn't like she had anything to lose. Plus, maybe she'd find someone who stuck around.

"You'll keep it on?" he asked. Or well, it *sounded* like a question, but his gaze suggested it was more of an order.

All order.

And she shivered, heat pooling between her thighs at the memory of his previous commands, of the pleasure they had found together, of the husky voice, the hard cock, the talented fingers driving her to orgasm as he'd spent the night ordering her around.

Legs around my waist.

Give me your mouth.

Come for me. Now, baby.

Sex. Just sex.

And she wanted more. But unfortunately—no, not *unfortunately*. Not having more of Brad was a good thing. Self-respect and loving herself and understanding she needed more were all good things.

Orgasms are good things, her inner devil prodded.

But she wasn't going there. Couldn't—

Me thinks you doth protest too much.

Ugh!

Ignoring her mental quarreling, she straightened her shoulders and lifted a brow. "Not sure why that sounds like an order."

He grinned. "Probably because it is one."

Glaring, though she couldn't deny that part of her was amused, she hung her purse on the hook she'd installed by the door for just that purpose, stepped out of her shoes, and tucked them neatly on the rack in the hall. Organization was her life's blood—well, organization along with *Twilight*, but she wasn't about to admit *that* guilty pleasure to the world.

It was only bearable that Cora, Kate, and Kelsey knew her innermost secret because she knew her friends' own guilty pleasures, too—unicorns, Hermione Granger, and being freakishly smart, so much so that she collected post-graduate degrees for *fun,* respectively. Still, organization was a perfectly acceptable guilty pleasure for a woman of her age (even though she was still Team Edward the whole way), and it was easier to focus on hooks and folders and perfectly dusted shelves than on blood-sucking, teenage love, and immortal life.

Though, just thinking about it, and she was jonesing for a reread.

"Want another order?" he asked. "I'm sure I can rustle one up. Don't walk alone in the dark. Always check the back seat of your car before you get in."

She'd been so focused on her *Twilight* and organizational haze that she'd forgotten they were having a conversation, particularly a conversation about orders.

She rolled her eyes. "First, those are all examples of the patriarchal bullshit in our society. Women should be able to walk safely any time of day or night and not have to worry about a man accosting them. Or lying in wait in their car. Along that vein, men should also be taught to respect women and their autonomy, and it's such horseshit that women are always told to walk in groups and not to leave their drinks unattended and—"

"You're right," he said. "It *is* bullshit."

Her lips parted on an exhale.

"*Of course* it's total bullshit that those are things you have to consider—or are *told* to consider as a woman." A beat, his hazel eyes dimming. "But unfortunately, just because we *think* that things should be different, doesn't mean they are."

He had a point there.

She still didn't have to like it. "Maybe," she muttered. "But I'm still a grown woman, and there's not a chance in hell that I'll obey any orders you give, just because you give them."

His brows pulled together, those hazel eyes flashing, becoming more brown than green. "You'd risk your life to prove a point?"

"Of course not," she said. "But I'm an adult who makes her own choices."

End of story.

He was still, his shoulders stiff, his jaw clenched, but then abruptly that whole demeanor faded, and he relaxed, mouth turned up at the corner. "Are we having our first fight?"

"More like tenth," she muttered, moving to the fridge. "I suppose you're staying for dinner." A beat as she glanced back at him. "As fr—"

"Friends," he finished for her. Then smiled again. "So long as you're good to cook for me again."

She'd already begun pulling out ingredients for a salad. "Is this your strategy when you're home? Bum food off whatever stranger will take you in?"

"When the stranger is a beautiful woman who's not actually a stranger, and who just happens to be an excellent cook, great company, and sexy as hell?" He grinned. "Yup."

"Careful," she warned.

"I'm not lying."

"Just spinning bullshit."

"Not at this moment," he said. "That may affect my ability to get some of your delicious food."

"Maybe I'll use the opportunity to poison you."

He snorted. "I have no allergies."

"Allergies aren't poison."

"Conveniently, I have spent many years building up my resistance to all types of poison."

"*A la Princess Bride?*"

"Exactly."

She grinned, despite herself. "Well, you have good taste because it's my second favorite movie."

"Seriously?"

"Seriously."

"Only *second* favorite?"

Heidi giggled.

"At any rate, I'll take it because you should see *this.*" It was said with such flourish that she glanced up from where she was chopping veggies to watch him pull out a DVD from the bag he carried. It was a copy of *Princess Bride*. "We're soul mates."

She giggled. "You're ridiculous."

"No," he deadpanned. "I'm Brad Huntington. And you've crushed my ego. Prepare to . . ." He screwed up his face. "Dine?"

More giggles bubbled up in her chest. "I stand by my previous statement. Ridiculous."

"What can I say? I nerd out about Rob Reiner films. Well, him and Billy Crystal."

"Hmm."

He crossed over to her, leaned a hip to the counter. "Hmm, what?"

"Hmm as in, okay, maybe we *can* be friends," she said.

He tilted his head to the side, studying her. "Because I'm a nerd?"

"Because the *only* things I respect are nerds. Case in point" —she pointed at her chest—"nerd."

A shrug. "Well, I'll take my victory in any avenue possible."

"Whatever makes you feel better." She turned back to the fridge and grabbed some chicken, belatedly realizing that a man as big as Brad probably wouldn't be filled up by a salad. "What else did you bring?"

"Besides the most glorious movie of all time, you mean?" he asked.

"The *second* most glorious movie," she countered. "And yes."

He reached into the bag and pulled out a pint of ice cream. "I heard somewhere once that women like chocolate . . . and ice cream."

"Except me." She shook her head. "I can't stand sweet things." Never mind that she'd pounded three pieces of the replacement cake at Kate's wedding the weekend before—both because she had missed the dinner portion of festivities with her cake shenanigans and attempts at saving it, and because . . . she had a sweet tooth.

A major sweet tooth.

His face fell, and immediately she felt guilty that her joke didn't land.

"I'm kidding," she quickly said. "Given the chance, I would make love to that ice cream all night long."

Face clearing, he said, "And here I am, friend-zoned, so I can't partake in the festivities." He stashed the ice cream in the freezer. "I'll just go set up the DVD?"

Except . . .

"About that," she began.

"Oh, you don't want to watch it? We don't have to watch anything. I just thought—" A shake of his head. "I just thought that you might want to . . ." He trailed off, reached into his bag. "I brought a game, too. In case—"

Her heart squeezed.

"I do want to watch it," she told him. "I just don't have a DVD player."

He froze. "You don't *have* a DVD player? I travel the world for half the year, and *I* have one in my tiny, postage stamp of an apartment."

"I don't have one," she confirmed. "But unlike the old man currently taking up space in my kitchen, I *do* have the digital copy, which means that I don't need to have a DVD player." She smiled smugly. "I can stream it on *all* my devices."

His incredulity had faded as she spoke, and he drifted closer. *"All* your devices." He waggled his brows. "And yes, the innuendo was intended."

She sniffed. "You're as bad as the girls with your dirty jokes."

"Hmm." He shifted closer. "I like it when you say *dirty.* "

Placing a hand on his chest, she shoved him away so she could grab a pan to cook the chicken. "Ugh. I'm still not—"

"Going to sleep with me." He lightly tugged a lock of her hair. "I've got that."

"And yet, you're still here," she whispered.

He froze.

She froze.

Steady hazel eyes on hers. "Do you want me to go?"

Three days ago at the wedding she would have said yes, and she would have meant it, too. At least with . . . say ninety-five percent of her being. The other five percent was still wrapped up in the yummy hormones and delicious orgasms. But after the night of the wedding, after *last* night, she—and yes, she was fully aware that this was probably exceptionally stupid—but she didn't want him to go.

She wanted to watch the movie with him, to listen to him tell her about his travel adventures.

She wanted to spend more time with this man.

As a friend.

Only as a friend.

Except, that line was getting more difficult for her to convince herself of, especially the more time she spent with Brad.

Luckily for her, she could occasionally manage to ostrich with the best of them. Because tonight was all about avoiding the traitorous and dangerous thoughts in her mind and sticking her head in the proverbial sand. She would continue pretending she only liked his company as a friend and was hanging out with him just because she missed Kate.

Obviously, she had to fill that space with someone. Brad was as good a fit as anyone.

See? Ostrich.

She could be good at it.

Either way, her mental sand-head-sticking worked. She was able to turn to him, to lift her lips in a smile.

"No," she whispered.

His eyes met hers, held. "Okay. I'll stay."

She turned back to the pan, heart pounding, only to whip back around a minute later when he began trying to tempt her away from the movie. "Oh no, you don't," she ordered, interrupting his expounding on the merits of the board game he'd brought. "You don't get to tease by taking away *Princess Bride* after you offered it to me."

He stopped talking, then his eyes darkened, lips quirking. "Teasing?"

She smacked him lightly with a spoon. "No more innuendos." A beat. "Now make yourself useful and cut up that cucumber."

Mischief crept across his face.

She smacked him again.

Then they both gave in and started laughing.

God, she loved laughing with this man.

NINE

BRAD

She'd fallen asleep right around the time Fezzik says, "Anyone want a peanut?"

Slumping back against the cushions, her lips parted on slow and steady breaths.

He watched her through the duel, through the hillside tumble, through the castle storming scene, and then he forced himself to get up, to quietly take care of the dishes, and pack away the leftovers. By then, the movie was over, so he scooped her up and carried her into the bedroom.

Settling her under the covers only took a moment, but the temptation to stay, to crawl in next to her, was strong.

Except, she'd made it clear what her boundaries were.

And he wasn't enough of an asshole to barrel his way past them.

After tucking the blanket around her, he smoothed her hair back from her face, smiling when her eyebrows drew together into a slight frown. Then he stepped back.

He'd save the crawling-in-beside-her for a future date.

Until then, he turned for the door, saw something—well, *two* somethings on the shelf beside it that had him pausing, considering, and then grinning again.

He snagged them both.

One went into his pocket.

The other he paired with a pen and did what he should have done after that first night.

He left Heidi a note.

Then he let himself out of the apartment.

———

Even when he wasn't halfway around the world, he still couldn't stand staying in one place for long.

Luckily, the Bay Area had no shortage of beautiful places to visit.

And he was like a kid in the candy store, trying to visit each and every one of them.

He'd worked until the sky had just begun to lighten, putting the finishing touches on a website for an up-and-coming airline. Then he'd gotten into his car and driven north along the coast.

Over the Golden Gate, spending more time in traffic than he preferred, but once he'd made it away from the commuters, his journey up the winding highway had been quiet.

After parking along one edge of the road, his car tucked onto a narrow strip of gravel, he climbed out from behind the wheel, navigated the rickety wooden stairs that led down to the beach, and sat on a washed-up log to watch the sky grow bright, filtering in through the heavy fog, gilding the area in an almost-otherworldly glow.

He was just standing, ready to find his feet, to drive back to his apartment and sleep when his cell vibrated.

Retrieving it from his pocket, he saw that Heidi was calling him.

Not texting.

But actually calling him.

A call he was going to miss if he didn't actually swipe his finger across the screen and answer it.

"Hello?" he said, getting his shit together and lifting it up to his ear.

"And they say an old dog doesn't learn new tricks," Heidi said on a laugh that sent heat trickling down his spine, his cock twitching in remembrance of what that laugh had felt like on his skin.

She'd gotten his note.

His lips curved up, happiness sliding through him. "You calling me a dog?"

Another laugh. "I most certainly am."

"Well, this one *has* learned new tricks."

"I see that." She paused. "Thanks for last night."

"You did the cooking."

"And you brought the ice cream," she said. "In my book, that's more than half the battle."

"So, the key to your heart is through ice cream."

A husky chuckle that had him wishing all over again he'd stayed that night, that he'd left a note that first time, that he hadn't been a fucking coward when he'd recognized this woman was someone he should be staying for.

"Not exactly," she said. "The key to my heart is . . ." She trailed off, and he could see her smile in his mind. It would be tinged with a smirk, one corner of her mouth curved higher than the other, and her hazel eyes—the mix of gold and green— would be dancing with humor. "No," she said. "I'm going to leave that for you to figure out."

Every cell in his body froze, jumping to absolute, rigid attention.

Was she saying . . .

Was he getting another chance?

"Heidi—"

A sea gull cawed loudly over his head.

"Where are you?"

He waited for the bird to quiet before saying, "The beach."

Silence. Then. "Of course, you are."

"What does that mean?"

"Only that *only* you would be absconding to the beach on a Thursday morning when most people are commuting to work." She laughed. "Are you ever not the wayward traveler?"

Yes.

When he was with *her*.

When he spent time with Heidi, he didn't think about the ever-growing list of places he wanted to visit. And when he was with her, he certainly didn't imagine traveling alone. He pictured her with him, going to all the cliché places, her hair flowing through the breeze as they walked along the canals of Venice, kissing her under the Eiffel Tower, holding her hand as they circled the upright rocks of Stonehenge. And more. He imagined her on a trek in South America, winding through colorful plateaus, on a hike through trees so tall it was nearly impossible to see the tops. He wondered if she'd go cave-diving with him, spelunking through tunnels in New Zealand, searching for glowworms. He'd bet he could convince her to visit a castle on the coast of Northern Ireland.

"Brad?"

He blinked, forced himself to focus on the conversation rather than the fantasies in his brain. "I'm here. And yes, there are times when I want to do nothing more than sleep in my own bed."

"So, why do you travel so much?" she asked, her tone not unkind. Rather, it was laced with curiosity and softness.

Sighing, he stared out at the horizon, now bright with pops of pink and orange and deep blue peeking out through the fog. "I . . ." He stopped himself from giving her the same pat answer he always gave everyone—that he didn't want to settle down, that there was so much world to explore, and he didn't want to miss an inch of it.

All of that was true, of course.

But as he'd come to realize, there was also something more.

"I guess it's just always been expected that I was the one who'd run wild."

A beat of quiet. Then a soft question. "Why was it expected?"

The log was getting uncomfortable under his ass, but this woman was in his head and heart, and he knew he'd answer anything she asked. "Tammy was always the smart sibling, so it's no surprise she's spent most of her adult life in school. Though she has her second master's in business administration now and is looking to take the corporate world by storm."

"I met her at the wedding." Heidi chuckled. "And I'm definitely not surprised to hear that in the least. I have no doubt she'll succeed. What about Jaime and Penny?"

"Jaime has always been the caring one, so it's no surprise he ended up as a vet. And Penny is the second oldest, even though she pretends otherwise." He smiled. "Mostly because she's made an art form out of ordering everyone around."

"Doesn't she run her own business?"

"Yup. One that just went public a couple of weeks ago and is killing it in its valuations."

His siblings would probably be surprised to know that he'd followed each of their lives so closely. He knew they thought of him as being so wrapped up in his own life and his adventures that he didn't have time for anyone else. But he'd always made it home for the important stuff—birthdays, weddings, Christmas, his parents' anniversary. He loved his family, even more than he loved traveling. Which was why he followed his brother's vet practice on Instagram, why he'd made it home for all three of Tammy's college graduations, why he'd been there to watch

Penny ring the bell on Wall Street when her company went public.

Traveling was his life's blood.

But he only left because he knew he had something solid to come home to.

"And what about you?" Heidi asked. "Which one are you?"

That was the trouble, wasn't it?

He didn't really know.

"My mom always called me her little explorer," he said. "From the time I was little, I was climbing trees and trying to run off in parking lots. We took a trip to London once when I was a kid, and she always says that was the one time I actually stayed by her side." He laughed. "Because I was too busy looking around to wander off. I remember the trip, and it's true. I thought it was amazing and so different from the little Midwest town we grew up in. Then I studied abroad my junior year in college and fed the travel bug that had bit me by traveling all over Europe."

"And you haven't stopped?"

"No," he said. "I haven't stopped. I work for two things—well, three things, I suppose. One, retirement. Two, to eat. Three, to travel."

"So, why did you move out here? It's got to be more expensive keeping an apartment in the Bay Area than where you used to live."

That was true.

"When my parents followed Tammy and Jaime out here, I figured it was better to have a place close to everyone." Even though Penny was still in the Midwest, she was thinking of moving to this coast, since increasingly more of her business was keeping her in San Francisco.

It was a Huntington invasion.

"That's sweet."

He shrugged, even though she couldn't see him. "It just

made sense. What about you?" he added. "How long have you been in California?"

"Born and raised." A chuckle. "East Bay all the way."

"And you haven't gone far."

"Nope. Just away to college and then right back here." She laughed. "Hang on a second." There was a blip of noise, almost sounding like she'd rolled her window down, and then he heard her say, "Thanks." He waited another moment, and then her voice was back on the line. "Sorry about that."

"Where are you?"

"Driving into work. I had to show my credentials," she said, tone amused. "As my assistant would say, so I don't put the top-secret shit at risk."

"Top-secret? Wow, color me impressed."

She snorted. "It's a lot less exciting than it sounds. Trust me. I'm just a nerd with lots of computers, running lots of models, who spends her days in muffin-crumb-covered T-shirts and chugs coffee like it's my life's blood."

"What's your favorite type of muffin?"

"Banana chocolate chip. From Molly's." She waited a beat. "What's yours?"

"I don't know, cinnamon and sugar?" *He* waited a beat. "What's Molly's?"

"*What's* Molly's?" She gasped. "Only the best bakery in all of the Bay Area. And as a connoisseur of all things baked goods, *that's* saying something."

"I guess I'll have to check out this Molly's."

"Not without me," Heidi said. "It's sacrilege to go by yourself the first time. You need help navigating the deliciousness."

"Deliciousness?" He couldn't help but tease. "Is that even a word?"

"Don't know," she said, her voice going slightly muffled. "Don't care. Unless that caring gets me to Molly's."

"Is this you asking me on a date?"

"Again," she said. "Don't care, so long as it gets me to Molly's sooner."

He laughed outright. "You'll take me to Molly's as soon as possible."

"Sold." A beat. "You coming over tonight?"

His heart squeezed tight, excitement trickling through him. She was asking him over. She'd *called* him. This was big. This was him making his way back into her good graces. This was him getting his second chance. "Do you *want* me to come over?"

"I . . . well . . ." Now there was hesitation in her words. *Shit.* He should have just said yes.

"Heidi—"

Voices in the background.

"I've got to go." He heard a rustling, as though she'd lifted the phone from her ear.

"Heidi," he said quickly, pulse pounding in his veins.

The rustling stopped. "Yeah?"

"I'll bring pizza."

Silence. Long, interminable silence.

Then a soft sigh. "I'll be home by six."

Relief poured through him as they said goodbye and hung up. God, he was so not smooth, so not a player. He'd already fucked up the best thing he'd ever had with a woman once. Now he needed to be smart, to play this right.

Because Heidi was . . . everything.

TEN

HEIDI

Normally, her work drew her in, made her lose all sense of time, forget every bit of her real life.

Normally, she was reduced to spreadsheets and calculations, the occasional coffee and muffin break. Oh, and her favorite kind of email exchange.

With her dad.

He wasn't like her mom. He was nice, if more than a bit absentminded and wrapped up in whatever project he was currently working on. She remembered that distance used to hurt her feelings. But then he'd seemed to sense her loneliness, or maybe some part of him had finally registered what her mom's sharp words had been doing, because one day he had brought her to his lab.

He hadn't said a word to her mother.

Just packed her up one Saturday morning, loading her backpack with coloring materials, books, her favorite set of paper dolls—she'd had a thing for the American Girl dolls when she was young, okay?—and plenty of snacks, and they had disappeared into the world of science for a day.

She'd fallen out of love with paper dolls.

And into love with mass spectrometry.

Yup, the nerd gene ran deep.

Her mom had been furious—she'd missed some activity that Colleen had deemed *very* important for Heidi's female education, never mind that she'd been all of seven at the time—but that hadn't stopped her dad from taking her back every Saturday.

And sometimes on Sundays, too.

That time had kept her sane.

She still didn't understand how her dad could be married to her mom—it wasn't like she didn't love her mom. She was her mom; *of course* Heidi loved her.

She just . . . didn't like her.

But she loved her dad, and she kept in regular email contact with him, and because of him, she'd held on to her sanity during her childhood. Also, she supposed her mom wasn't *always* completely awful. Occasionally Colleen said something nice, and it wasn't like her entire childhood had been traumatic.

There had been good times.

They just . . . mostly involved her dad.

But regardless of the good or bad times, she loved that she could boot up her computer, get to work, and start the day with an email from her dad,

Remind me of the assay calculation for barrelene we talked about last time?

She loved that she could smile over lunch at the picture he'd sent of him posing in front of his new mass spectrometer.

And then feel her heart squeeze with happiness when he sent mid-afternoon,

I read your paper. It's good, peanut. I'm proud of you.

Silly, huh?

Short little notes in her dad's typical scattershot method. Some days they'd exchange two dozen emails, sometimes a week would go by without a word. But their virtual contact would always pick right back up as though they were in the middle of a conversation. It was never uncomfortable, never strained.

Just . . . connection.

And like it had been when she was a kid, that connection was over science. Luckily, she loved both her dad *and* the theoretical properties of barrelene, even if it was a long ways from the molecular physics she studied and used in her lab.

Signing off on her reply to the final email, an exchange that would normally energize her for several more hours, Heidi found her eyes going back to the clock.

Again.

Counting the minutes down until she could leave. Again.

Because despite the emails from her dad, for the first day ever, she hated her job.

Part of her kept repeating the conversation from that morning back to her, cringing at the desperate way she'd asked Brad to come over. Brad, who she wasn't going to see as a love interest. Brad, who she wasn't going to sleep with. Brad, who she was only going to be friends with.

And Brad . . . who she wanted to be so much more than that.

Sighing, she tapped a few keys across her keyboard, logged off her computer, and pushed back from her desk. "I'm out of here," she told Stef.

"Everything okay?" her assistant asked.

"Fine. Just my brain is fried. I'm going to call it a day."

Stef nodded, and they spent a couple of minutes discussing

the day's outstanding items. Fifteen minutes later, she was signing out of the lab and heading toward her car.

Then she was on her way home, ridiculously early.

But she honestly couldn't hate the ridiculously early, not when it was smooth sailing through traffic, not when she took fifteen minutes upon arriving to her complex to bypass her condo and walk down her little trail. She stood in front of the little creek, trying to get the fist gripping her heart to relax—the same fist that was telling her to run from Brad, that she'd only get hurt again.

Because she *had* been hurt.

Deeply.

After one night.

Which was . . . too much and ridiculous and something that shouldn't have been possible. She'd slept with plenty of people, so Brad being a one-off shouldn't have hurt.

Except, his leaving without a word had.

And now, she worried that she would be opening herself up for a *world* of that hurt if she let him back in, if she *dove* into things with him, like she so desperately wanted. They'd had all of one phone conversation. Had only spent a couple of hours together. He'd left a note. Not poetry. Not undying love. Not . . . *what?*

What was she looking for?

She had no freaking clue.

Aside from the fact that all of those things were combining to draw her more firmly down the rabbit hole that was Brad Huntington.

Could she risk being his friend without falling in deep?

Because he would inevitably leave, and he would leave her behind.

But . . . what if he wanted her to come along?

"This is pointless," she muttered to the tiny babbling creek.

ELISE FABER

"We slept together. We hung out a bit. That's it. It's not life-changing, even if it feels like it."

And it *did* feel like it. She was addicted.

She wanted more.

But he was going to leave.

It was an inevitability.

"So, knowing that," she whispered, "why can't I just enjoy the process? Why can't I just go in and have fun and soak in every bit of the experience?" She tossed a rock into the water. "Because, dumbass, you've been talking a big talk about wanting more, about wanting something more than just a quick fuck." A sigh. "And you'll never have that with Brad."

"I don't want a quick fuck."

Heidi shrieked and spun around, losing her footing at the sound of the voice so very close to her ear. She slid down the embankment, dirt and leaves rolling over her, landing in a heap at the bottom, the all of three inches of water in the creek soaking into her jeans.

"Heidi!"

A second later, Brad was at her side, scooping her up, holding her tightly against him.

"I'm fine," she said, shaking her head to clear it. "You can put me down."

"I didn't mean to scare you," he muttered, definitely *not* putting her down as he carried her up the slope, back onto solid ground.

"I'm all wet. Put me down before you get soaked, too," she said.

Scorching hazel eyes on hers had her replaying her words.

"That wasn't an innuendo," she muttered.

Those eyes narrowed, and she realized that the heat in his gaze wasn't remotely sexual. No, instead, it was fury. Pissed-off, intense anger.

"I never expected it to be," he snapped.

"Why are you mad?" she asked, putting aside her request to be put down.

He bent down and snagged her purse. "I hurt you."

"I'm not hurt," she said. "I'm fine."

His eyes flashed to hers again, and as he started carrying her back down the trail, she placed her hand on his chest.

"I swear, Brad. I'm not hurt." Her groin might be a little tetchy from the slip-slide—she must have been attempting to do the splits while falling down that ridiculously tiny hill—but she was fine.

"You're bleeding."

Her mouth fell. "What?"

"You're bleeding."

"I can't be bl—"

He stopped, spinning them, and in a heartbeat, he had her pinned between his chest and a tree trunk, her purse crammed into her abdomen. One hand lifted, brushed lightly against the top of her cheek. He held it up so she could see the bright red painting his fingertips. "You're bleeding."

Her heart stuttered. "Just a little."

Eyes flashing again. He was fierce, glaring down at her, with the setting sun gathering in the trees, shafts of sunlight highlighting motes of dust in the air, the wind lightly rustling through the leaves. "A. Little?"

The last was said so dangerously that she shivered, heat trickling down her torso, gathering in her stomach, making her thighs tremble.

In a second, his expression shifted. "You're cold." He shifted again, straightening and cradling her against his chest, and starting to walk along the path again. "I need to get you inside and warm."

Heidi found herself without words.

She'd not expected him to be like this, to be so intense, so ferocious in his protection of her.

It was . . . not numbing exactly, but she was suddenly having an out-of-body experience as he carried her along her little trail, his legs eating up the space in hardly any time at all. What had taken her fifteen minutes of meandering, took him just a handful, and when he was walking up the stairs to her door, holding her like she weighed no more than a feather, she still hadn't found her voice.

All she could think was . . . she hadn't expected this.

Probably, that said bad things about her and her intelligence—that being held by this man had fried her brain—but she was still struggling to reconcile the normally easy-going, funny man with this one in front of her.

Though, he *had* gotten all protective about her phone.

"Keys," he said, stopping in front of her door.

She blinked. "What?"

His jaw clenched, a muscle twitching in the hard line, tempting her with a desire to taste that little pulsing spot, to soothe away the tension. But she didn't have a chance. He wedged her against the door, dug her keys out of her purse, then somehow managed to finagle them into the lock to open it.

A moment later, they were inside.

He kicked it shut and carried her down the hall, dumping her onto her bed. "Stay," he growled and then disappeared out of the room.

She stood up, not wanting to get her blankets wet, and moved to her dresser, opening the top drawer to pull out some pajamas.

Which was the moment Brad came back into the bedroom.

His eyes met hers in the mirror. "What part of *stay* don't you understand?"

Fresh pair of underwear in her grip, she dropped her hands to her side. "Are you fucking serious right now?"

His expression turned mulish.

"What part of stay don't I *understand?*" She spun to face

him, crossing the room and prodding him the chest with her finger. "*Stay?* Fucking *stay?*"

He captured her finger. "You're bleeding. You're limping. I reserve the right to go a little crazy."

"You don't have *any* rights. Reserved or not. Bleeding and limping or not." Even *if* her cheek was starting to burn, and her groin, along with her ankle, *were* feeling a bit sore. She whirled around, took a step—

And stumbled.

Brad caught her. "Woman," he muttered.

Then she was in his arms again, pressed against his chest, his heat surrounding her, his scent in her nose. He marched into the bathroom, set her on the counter, and then turned to crank on the shower.

Her breath hitched when she saw the look on his face, fury written into every line, but his fingers were gentle when he reached for the hem of her T-shirt and tugged it over her head, when he unfastened the button on her jeans and slid down the zipper before hefting her again and working the damp material down her legs. He started to set her down then hesitated, reaching for a towel and tucking it beneath her before setting her on the marble surface.

The small act of kindness, the bit of care without a word undid her.

"Brad," she whispered.

His eyes came to hers, filled with an emotion that made her lose her breath all over again. "I can't hurt you again," he whispered. "I did it once. I can't be responsible for doing it again."

Her heart rolled over in her chest. "I'm not hurt."

He didn't answer, instead reaching for a small towel, dampening it in the sink, and bringing it up to her cheek, dabbing lightly at the cut.

She inhaled sharply, the sting taking her by surprise.

"You're hurt," he whispered.

She covered her hand with his. "It's just a little cut."

He set the towel aside, stepped away to check the shower temperature. Then he stripped off his shirt, shoved his pants down, and scooped her up again.

"What are you—?"

He stepped into the shower with her.

Hot water sluiced over her skin, soaking into her bra and underwear, slicking their skin, and suddenly, she didn't feel the cut, or her aching groin, or the slight throb in her ankle. She could only feel Brad. Just the wide breadth of his chest, the strength of his arms, the abrasion of the damp lace of her bra against her nipples, the cotton growing hot and wet between her thighs.

"Better?" he asked.

And she had to remember how to speak again.

Because this was a hell of a lot better. It was fucking incredible and not enough. It was intoxicating, and she was desperate for more. It was—

"Put me down," she whispered.

His gaze met hers, and whatever he saw there must have been intense enough that he actually listened to her, setting her carefully on her feet.

"Why are you doing this?" she asked, voice barely above a murmur.

His eyes slid closed, opened slowly, then his hand came up, cupping her uninjured cheek gently. "I've spent the last months hating myself for leaving that night." His shoulders rose and fell on a breath. "Because it was more."

More. More. *More.*

The word echoed through her mind.

"I didn't know what I felt that night—" A sharp shake of his head. "No, that's a fucking lie, and I promised myself I wouldn't lie to you, not after I'd seen what it did to you when I treated you like that." His fingers convulsed slightly. "You're a fucking keeper, Heidi. You're the real deal—smart, beautiful, funny, kind—and I wanted to keep you from the first moment I laid eyes on you." He slid his hand to her nape. "Then we made love. Then I got to hold and touch you, to be inside you . . . and I knew I'd give up *everything* for a shot with you."

Her heart thudded against her ribs—a rapid *whoosh-whoosh, whoosh-whoosh, whoosh-whoosh*. Water streamed down her skin, warm rivulets that slid down her back, her legs, dripped forward and over her breasts.

"But you knew you couldn't actually give everything up," she whispered.

His face sobered. "No, I couldn't." A moment of quiet as she felt like she'd been stabbed in the gut.

Pretty words.

Nice compliments.

But he still hadn't wanted to stay.

God, here she was wanting him so much that she was almost willing to sacrifice her beliefs, to ignore everything she'd promised to jump into bed with him again. "I need you to go," she whispered.

"Heidi."

"You need to go," she repeated. "You need to *go.*"

"I—"

"*You need to go!*"

He retreated a step then his face clouded. "*No,*" he said. "Not until you understand. Yes, I fucking panicked. Yes, I ran off that night because you made me feel things I have never felt with anyone. Yes, I left because it was too fucking much!" She flinched. "But I've thought about you every fucking day since then. I dreamed about you. I imagined what it would be like to have you with me."

Her chest rose and fell rapidly, her pulse danced a speedy tattoo in her veins. She couldn't summon any words, but it didn't matter.

Because he kept talking.

"Yes, I ran, but I've regretted it every day since." He closed the distance between them. "All I've wanted to do, all I *want* to do is make it up to you."

Her air stuttered out. "Brad."

His hand came up to her uninjured cheek again. "So, maybe I'm fucking this up. Maybe it's all too fast, too much. But I need you to know that I'm not leaving. I'm not running again. I've seen how wonderful you are, and I'm going to prove to you that I'm not some jackass." He pressed a kiss to her forehead. "Because you are special and wonderful, and I'm sorry I ever made you doubt that."

What could she possibly say to that?

How could she possibly respond to something so wonderful?

How could she possibly not panic about something so terrifying?

Because his words were . . .

Everything. Too much. Frightening. Terrifying. *Everything.*

"I know it's a lot to spring on you, a lot for you to believe when I just left you without a word. But . . ." His warm breath skated over her skin. His voice was soft, gentle. "Let me take care of you."

"I—"

"Please, just for tonight. Let me stay. Let me help you. Let me prove to you that I mean everything I said."

Heidi should have told him to go, for self-preservation, to keep her self-respect, to make certain she could keep her heart safe. But . . . she couldn't make herself form the words to tell him to leave.

Instead, she just gave in to the need in her heart, her soul.

"Okay," she whispered.

ELEVEN

One word that made everything inside him settle.

His heart had been thudding in his chest, filling him with terror, thinking again about all the ways he wasn't smooth and charming. God, how was it possible to have bungled this more, to have not explained properly, making her think he'd say all those things but then just toss her aside . . .

Add in scaring her into falling down a fucking hill and making her injure herself and—

She shivered.

Fucking hell.

Still fucking up.

He grabbed a towel from the rack just outside the curtain, turned off the stream of water, and wrapped it around her. Snagging one for himself so he didn't drip on her floor, he wrapped it around his hips then carefully lifted her out of the shower.

"Why didn't you take off my underwear?" she whispered into his chest.

"I didn't want you to think I was trying to get you naked."

She snorted. "You mean, you're *not* trying to get me naked?"

Something inside him relaxed, and he shifted so he could meet her eyes. "I'm *always* trying to get you naked."

A quirk of that luscious mouth as he set her on the counter.

"I'll grab you some pajamas."

"I'm guessing they're somewhere in the middle of my floor, considering I was doing just that when you went all caveman on me."

He lifted a brow but couldn't deny she was right. Instead, he just went into the bedroom, spied the pajamas, along with some underwear that reminded him of the ass-hugging pair she was wearing, made even huggier—was that a word? Probably not—by the water. Regardless, they were plastered to her honey gold skin in a way that had made his cock stand at rigid attention.

Not unusual, since this woman seemed to do that to him just by breathing.

Add in tight fabric and see-through lace, and he was a goner.

She'd slipped off her bra by the time he returned, had spread it on the towel next to her.

"Here," he said, handing her the pajamas and looking away.

Not leaving though, and also not stopping himself from glancing at her out of the corner of his eye, from seeing the pink tip of her nipple, the swaying globe of her breast.

Pervert?

Yup.

But he had to make sure she didn't fall.

That was the only reason he stayed. Simply for safety purposes.

When she went to slip off the counter, after she'd tugged the pajama top over her head, he stepped forward, lifted her down.

Her lips parted, a hot, damp exhale coating his skin.

But she didn't push him away, not even when he reached for the waistband of her underwear and worked the wet material down her thighs, bending further to bring it past her knees, lifting one foot then the other to slip it off.

She released another shaking exhale, but it wasn't like his breathing wasn't steady either.

Still, he backed up a pace, handing her the dry underwear and pajama bottoms, and turning away.

Movement behind him, the soft sound of fabric sliding over naked skin. Then a warm palm on his back. "I have some clothes that should fit you in my closet."

"I'm fine," he told her.

"How are those wet boxer briefs feeling about now?"

Not great.

They weren't feeling great, but she had bigger things to worry about other than his chafing issues.

"Fine."

"Brad," she warned.

"How's your ankle?" He moved to lift her up again, readying to carry her to the bed.

"Fine," she said, brushing past him.

Well, *limping* past him.

"Heidi." It was his turn to warn.

"Not so fun, is it?" she muttered, making her way through a door that was attached to the bathroom.

He did some muttering of his own. "No, it isn't." Following her, he saw it was walk-in-sized, and one look around the space told him that Heidi had a *lot* of clothes—though they seemed to only come in the T-shirts and jeans variety.

"You have an extensive collection of graphic tees," he pointed out as she hobbled toward the far side and stood on tiptoe.

She turned one on a hanger, showing him that it had the words *This T-shirt is the color of my soul.* It was black and had him fighting back a smile. "That's because they express me better than *I* can express me." A shrug. "Plus, I don't have to wear adult clothes very often. I love my tees. *And* my pajamas. Half my dresser is filled with them, and I can honestly say that I've probably spent more on them than anything else in my wardrobe, combined."

He ran a finger over the silk sleeve of her pajama top. It was soft and cut high to expose a large portion of her arm. "I like them."

She glared over her shoulder, wavering to the side so much that he had to catch her shoulder to steady her. "Because you've seen the underwear I have on beneath them?"

"That *is* a plus," he said, finally realizing what she was reaching for, and nudging her to the side so he could snag the large plastic tub before she forgot she was hurt and started scrambling up the shelves.

"Where do you want this?" he asked.

"Open it up, help yourself to the clothes inside." A shrug. "My exes won't care. I promise."

Like it had burned him, he dropped the box on the floor.

Heidi laughed. "I'm kidding," she said, opening the lid. "My dad left these behind when he stayed over a while back. They're clean and free from any ex cooties." She tugged out a pair of sweats, a hoodie, and a T-shirt, handing them over. "No underwear, I'm afraid, but I'm guessing you don't want to wear another man's boxer briefs."

"No."

She snorted. "You look like you swallowed a lemon."

"Maybe just a lime," he muttered, freezing when she snagged the shirt from his hands and tugged it over his head.

A pat to his chest, her lips curved into a smirk, but there were deep lines etched into the space around her mouth.

"You should lie down," he said.

For once, she didn't argue, just nodded. "I think you're right. I'm actually starting to feel a bit dizzy."

He dropped the clothes, snagged her arm when she wavered.

"Did you hit your head when you fell?" He'd seen the cut on her cheek, knew it had looked worse than it was. After he'd cleaned it, he'd realized it was just a scratch. He could also see that her ankle was bothering her, and maybe her hip. But he didn't think she'd hit her head. Still, she'd fallen so fast he couldn't be sure.

"No," she said. "I think it's just the adrenaline coming down." She pulled her arm free. "Well, that and the fact that I didn't eat lunch."

God save him from this woman.

He bit back a snarl, wanting to yell at her for not taking care of herself. Yes, he knew her particular predicament was his fault. But that didn't give her an excuse to not fuel her body. First the cell phone, now skipping lunch.

A pat to his jaw. "More lemon-swallowing." She turned and made her way carefully out of the closet, shuffling across the bedroom to her bed. "Stop hovering," she muttered. "I can make it five feet to the bed. If you really want to make yourself useful, why don't you go get me a bag of ice?"

That was an excellent point.

But he still made sure she'd made it into bed.

A fact that didn't escape her notice. Probably because he was currently tucking the covers up and over her.

"I didn't take you for one of these men."

He'd just straightened, and her words made him frown. "What do you mean?"

"Manly. Caveman. Protective."

Some of the fear that had gripped him since seeing her fall, since he'd thought she was going to kick him out because he kept flubbing things with her, faded. Enough for him to say, "I don't know whether to be insulted or complimented. You think I'm manly?" He fluttered his lashes. "Oh, thank you."

She snorted. "Ice, please, Mr. Caveman."

"For the record," he said, heading for the kitchen. "I'm

always protective." A beat. "Especially, when it comes to a woman who matters."

"Brad—"

But he was just going to let that statement hover in the air.

He took the opportunity to escape into the hall.

TWELVE

HEIDI

She just stared at Brad's retreating back and tried to figure out what in the fuck she was doing.

Getting naked in front of him—or naked in intervals, she supposed.

Showering clothed with him—or more like showering *semi-*clothed with him.

Talking with him—as though it were no big deal to have this man in her bedroom, casually discussing her pajama and T-shirt collection.

It *was* a big deal, and he'd said . . .

A lot.

Too much, probably, but she was good at isolating parts of her brain, at pushing things down. Because part of her *couldn't* believe it—not because she didn't think it was possible for a man to really like her, to want to look after her, and be with her.

But because she didn't believe *this* man could feel that for her.

And back into circles she went.

She liked Brad, sincerely enjoyed spending time with him. She just . . . didn't trust him.

"You're asking too much, Heid," she murmured. "You *want* too much."

Now *that* was her mother talking, always telling Heidi to lower her expectations. *"No one wants to listen to a female scientist."* That was when she'd announced she wanted to be a physicist, like her dad, in kindergarten. *"Girls aren't good at math. You should take Home Economics, learn some real skills."* That had been in high school, when she'd been testing into calculus and applying to colleges. *"You should stop going to school before no man ever wants to marry you."* That had been just before she'd received her PhD. *"You work too much. You'll never have a family if you keep going like this. Men want their women to be home."*

That had been last week.

Good times.

The worst part of it was that she did want to have a family of her own. She wanted to get married and have babies, to bemoan dirty diapers, to get a pet—though definitely not one as unruly as the Fuzz—and to have her washing machine break down and have to go to Lowe's to buy a new one. She wanted to have all of those things.

She just also wanted to have her career.

Why was that so difficult?

These were modern times, with modern women and men. Jason Momoa could wear a pink scrunchie, for God's sake. Harry Styles could pose on the cover of a magazine in a skirt. Transgender and gay rights were expanding—she wasn't so naïve as to consider those rights were already equal to hers as a white, cis person, but strides were being made. People of all genders and color and sexual orientations were living their lives and standing up for equality.

So, why couldn't she just work at a job she loved *and* have a family she loved?

Why did her mom seem to think she had to sacrifice one for the other?

She didn't mind having a man in her life, one who gave her input on her choices, so long as her partner was open to her having the same input on his. She certainly didn't mind Brad's strength, the way he'd swooped down the hill, how he'd clearly been worried for her, but he had to also not mind her swooping in to save the day just as often.

If she cooked, he could do the dishes.

If she worked late, he should figure out dinner.

If she wanted to go somewhere, she didn't need his permission, though she had no problem offering a check-in.

Because wasn't that what partners in life and love were supposed to do?

Support one another. Be there for each other. Love despite flaws and shoulder the burdens of his life on occasion because she knew that he'd shoulder them for her just as often.

That was the kind of man she wanted.

But maybe he didn't exist.

Maybe it was a fantasy. Maybe *that* was why she was single. *Maybe* that was why she would never have a family, like her mother threatened.

She wanted a unicorn.

And, as much as she hated to admit, unicorns did not fucking exist. Well, they definitely didn't exist outside of her glorious unicorn of a job. She supposed that *was* existing, at least in one form, so maybe she should qualify her thought. Men as unicorns didn't exist.

Brad walked back in, the T-shirt she'd given him fitting snugly on a chest she'd been nose-close to not long before, one she'd spent plenty of time kissing months before. He was definitely yummy, but again . . . she didn't trust him.

Didn't trust that he could be what she wanted.

It would be easy, so fucking easy to just invite him to join her in bed and to have her merry way with him—when she wasn't feeling lightheaded or like her groin was a rubber band that had been stretched too far. But wouldn't that discount all of those things she wanted, push aside that unicorn she was searching to find, even if she could somehow compartmentalize that this was a fling and nothing more, and that she could never expect to find a note or receive a goodbye.

Except . . . he'd left a note.

Except . . . she'd told him how his disappearing had made her feel, and last night, when she'd passed out on him during the movie, he'd—sort of sweetly, she might add—tucked her into bed, fully clothed, and then had left her a note.

A man who changed.

Perhaps she'd found her unicorn, after all.

He handed her the ice pack then started to sit on the bed, before hesitating and straightening. "Let me go finish changing first," he said and turned, disappearing into the closet.

She couldn't deny that she watched his yummy ass bounce as he made his way.

Perv.

Yes, she supposed she was.

Well, she'd just chalk it up as another of her unenviable qualities—career-driven, bossy, outspoken, workaholic, and a total perv.

And that was just the short list.

A minute later, Brad reappeared, his arms full of clothes and towels. "I saw your washer's in the hall," he said. "I'll just start a load."

Heidi's mouth dropped open.

But he was already gone, and when he stuck his head in a little later, telling her to make herself comfortable and he was going to call for pizza, her mouth fell open a second time.

Make herself comfortable?

With him puttering his way around her place doing laundry?

And apparently also making a salad as an appetizer, which he filled with corn and shredded chicken and beans, all of which she didn't remember being in her kitchen, but must have been, otherwise the man had mysterious pantry stocking abilities—either that or Instacart, she realized after she'd dopily stared for several minutes at the salad that was more filling than most meals she ate on a regular basis.

He'd set the TV remote on the nightstand, retrieved the book she'd left propped open on her coffee table—much to her chagrin, since she never seemed to be able to organize her books all that well.

She was always pulling down an old favorite and rereading part of it, jumping to her favorite scenes before forgetting to put it back.

Once a week, she forced herself to do a focused walkthrough of her place, gathering those half-read books and stashing them back on the bookcase—in alphabetical order by genre, of course.

But that wasn't important.

Okay, it *was* important, just not important to this exact moment, because what was truly important right then was the fact that Brad was being . . . well, The Unicorn.

Without a word, without being asked.

He was just being . . . Brad.

And by the time he brought a plate of pizza to her, her resolution to stay far away from him was steadily being chipped away. Hell, the truth was that had been gone the evening of the wedding. What she felt chipping away in this moment was her resolve to keep the man firmly in the friend zone. Because it was as though he'd picked the thoughts out of her brain and had manifested himself into that Unicorn.

Pretty man.

Nice man.

Helpful man.

Unicorn.

Heidi was being sucked down in the whirlpool, that resolve dripping to the wayside, her need for him taking its place, and growing, and even worse—what would be even more devastating to her heart, to all of those carefully held dreams she worried about ever coming true—she worried she was falling for him all over again.

"God," she hissed, tossing the remote on the bed next to her with a groan.

She needed to stop living in her head.

She needed to stop circling this dead horse.

Did she want to have a fling with Brad, even knowing that despite the pretty words, it would inevitably end?

Yes.

She . . . just didn't want the broken heart.

This was like one of the calculations she was so good at, only except for detecting the space between electrons or attempting to figure out the top-secret shit (the speed of those electrons and how they moved, so it might be implemented for communication across the globe), this one was more . . . cost-benefit for her heart.

And if one night had dinged her confidence, had her thinking about this man for months, so on edge now, when they were hardly friends, what would a relationship do? What would happen when she grew attached and then he said goodbye?

But what if he didn't?

She groaned again, sitting up and shoving her mouth full of the pizza he'd brought her.

Self-medicating with food.

Because she already knew what her answer was going to be— even despite all the whirling thoughts in her head.

Because whatever anyone might say about Heidi's faults . . .

She wasn't a coward.

Thirteen

Brad

Something had shifted.

He didn't understand exactly what it was, except that it was as though someone had pricked the barrier holding the atmosphere of the room, the air that always seemed to ripple with awareness, with a pin, and the tension was slowly leaking out, a balloon deflating molecule by molecule.

He'd folded Heidi's now clean and dry clothes.

He'd changed back into his original, also clean and dry, had put the temporaries back in her bin, that bin back on the shelf. He'd fed her—once with salad because he was too freaking worried about her having not eaten all day to wait an hour for the second, which was the pizza he'd ordered, laden with meat and veggies to make up for that lack of lunch.

She'd gobbled down three pieces, moaning about how delicious it was, before later groaning and patting her stomach, saying that she'd need to invest in larger pajamas.

Now, he was sitting in a chair next to the bed, she'd turned on some reality TV show, and they were coexisting peacefully.

That tension continued to ebb away, along with his guilt, and he was starting to worry less, to actually enjoy himself.

Then she spoke.

And his heart seized.

"Brad."

She was going to kick him out. Well, fuck *that*. He wasn't going to leave her. He wasn't going to let her go without a fight. He needed to take a page out of his so-called manly book and dig in his heels.

"Brad?" she repeated.

He kept his eyes glued to the screen. "Yeah?"

"Come into bed with me."

Suddenly, the TV was nowhere in the periphery, his gaze flying to hers, locking onto hers. "What?"

She patted the pillow next to her. "That chair's not comfortable, and you're going to get a crick in your neck. Come relax with me."

"Crick—" He shook himself. "Neck—"

Pushing her elbows up beneath her, she reached out and snagged his hand. "Brad. Honey," she murmured. "I'm inviting you into bed with me."

But he hadn't won her over yet. He hadn't shown her that she could trust him.

Hadn't—

Dumb shit. He needed to get his ass in gear.

Shoving out of the seat, he crawled in beneath the blankets next to her, initially leaving a couple of feet between them, then deciding, what the hell, and sliding closer, slipping his arm beneath her, shifting his body so they were pressed together, shoulders to thigh.

"How's your ankle?"

She pointed and flexed it a few times beneath the covers. "Better. The ice helped."

He made a face.

"I saw that."

"How could you see that?" he asked, smoothing a hand up and down her spine. "Your face is in my chest."

"Fine. I *sensed* it."

"Sensed what?" He was playing dumb.

And he was rewarded for his acting skills when she tilted her head back so she could glare up at him. "Sensed *that*," she grumbled, waving a hand in the direction of his face. "More lemon-swallowing."

"I hate that you got hurt because of me."

She sighed. "Yes, you startled me." She pushed up farther. "But no, you're not responsible for my clumsiness. Nope. That all comes from me. Want to ask the room at large who's the girl who once managed to stab her hand and toe with the same knife? Or the one who burned herself because she was in too much of a hurry trying to make breakfast once and managed to catch both her hair and the hem of her T-shirt on fire at the stove. Oh, and that doesn't include the time I broke my wrist skiing, the concussion I received from walking into the open door of a locker, or the torn ACL when I tripped walking up the stairs."

He paused, hand stilling on her back. "*Up* the stairs?"

A grin. "Yup. You heard that right. I tripped going up the stairs, right in front of school my sophomore year." She rolled her eyes. "I actually tore it so badly that I had to have surgery. Don't laugh!" she accused when he attempted to bite back a smile.

Fingers brushing over her cheek, her jaw. God, her skin was like silk. But he also loved the look in her eyes, the teasing expression on her face. "I still can't believe you tripped up the stairs."

"I told you *not* to laugh."

"I'm not." But he was chuckling now, his chest vibrating with the sound, even as he kept taking this opportunity to touch her.

He might not be smooth, but he wasn't dumb.

He'd ended up in bed with the woman he wanted, and he wasn't going to squander this opportunity.

Now, to get her as addicted to his presence as he was to hers. Cue evil laughter, plotting-to-take-over-the-world hand rubbing.

"Like I said," she muttered. "I'm klutzy, and it has nothing to do with you."

"Well, next time, I'll make sure to not frighten you near inclines." Or declines either, he supposed.

"Cora always says I'm likely to kill myself just walking down the street to 7-Eleven to get a slushie."

"Remind me to never let you out of my sight," he said, half-joking.

Only half, because he was half-serious, too. Broken bones and torn ligaments and twisted ankles. Burns and stab wounds. God, he shuddered to think of what might go wrong in that top secret lab of hers.

She could blow up herself and the world right with her.

"The only place I'm somehow not clumsy—" A smile before she relaxed back down on his chest. "No, it's two places. One at work—and mostly because I have computers to do the dirty work, assistants to handle any of the finicky work, and anything *I* have to do is usually stationary, so there is significantly less chance of my klutz skills to factor in."

He smoothed a hand down her hair. "And the other?"

Her chest rose and fell on a long exhale. "The other place is . . . ice skating."

"Ice skating?" he asked incredulously.

"Yup." A laugh. "And I know exactly what you're thinking."

Nope. She couldn't. Because he was wondering how many stab wounds he might end up with if blades were strapped to her feet. He assumed it would be a great many.

"You're thinking that with my amazing clumsy skills, that someone is going to end up bleeding out on the ice."

He bit the inside of his cheek to keep from laughing out loud.

"See?"

"See what?" he asked.

"See, that I am—" A yawn. "Exceptionally smart. Even if I do watch"—another yawn—"horrible TV as you accused."

"Well, I don't understand the appeal of watching people who don't even like each other stumble their way to the altar."

She gasped, sitting up and the fatigue slipping out of her pretty hazel eyes. "They like each other. They love each other. They've moved across the planet to see if they're compatible—"

"Or for a green card."

Heidi paused, considered that. "Yes," she agreed. "I do think that sometimes that's the case."

"I'll add very smart to your list of positive attributes, right along with talented at work, ice skater extraordinaire, and—*oh*, how did you learn how to skate? Didn't you tell me once that you grew up in California?"

A smile. "All of last night," she said. "I did tell you that."

"So, Cali girl somehow learns to do a popular low-temperature activity?"

She shuddered, settled back down on his chest. "Okay, first rule for my new Californian. Don't call it Cali."

"No Cali." He nodded. "Got it."

"The second rule—or I guess less rule and more . . . general knowledge that you can put to good use is that hockey is big in California. It is especially big in Northern California, and because of that, there are plenty of opportunities for skating in the area."

"Noted," he said. "So, does this mean you'll go ice skating with me?"

"Are you asking me on a date?"

"Are you going to say yes?"

"Isn't ice skating a little pedantic of a date for you?"

He smiled. "I don't know." A shrug. "Depends."

"Depends on what?"

"On whether or not you say yes."

She laughed, arms tightening around him. "I'd say yes."

Joy bubbled in him. "Okay then, will you go ice skating with me, Heidi Greene?"

"No."

His jaw dropped open.

"But I *will* go on a date with you." A beat. "Even if it's ice skating."

He blinked, trying to keep up with the circles this woman was spinning around him and understanding that he probably never would be able to. Then he shrugged, began tracing light circles on her back again, and decided he didn't care.

Not when it meant that he'd just scored a date with this woman.

Fourteen

Heidi

He didn't take her ice skating.

But he did take her to prison.

To Alcatraz, that was.

"It's funny," she said as they leaned against the railing of the ferry, wind blowing through their hair, The Rock, coming into view in the distance.

"What's funny?" he asked.

"I grew up here, and I've never done any of the touristy things. No Alcatraz, no cable cars or Lombard Street. Hell, I've only ever done Ghirardelli Square and Pier 39 when relatives visited and wanted to hit the tourist traps."

"Well, there are far more exciting things to see in California besides the stuff that makes it on the postcards."

"That's true." She turned to look at him. "So, why bring me here?"

"You only agreed to one date," he said, eyes twinkling. "This is my backup plan in case you don't agree to a second."

She laughed. "Backup plan because you'll lock me up until I agree to it?"

"Precisely," he said. "Either that, or I hope that you'll be so bored with the history that you'll fall asleep, and then I can have my way with you."

"So romantic," she muttered dryly.

A swathe of pink exploded on his cheeks. "I—shit—I didn't mean it that way. I wouldn't take advantage of you—"

She touched his hand. "I know you wouldn't."

"I just meant in the sense of an evil genius taking over the world, not that I would do something you didn't want." He winced. "Shit. I sound like an asshole."

She rested her palm on his chest. "It was a joke," she assured him. "I got it. So, maybe it's not the best one I've heard"—a smile—"but I'm glad you at least understand consent, and how something like that might not land properly. You're a very evolved man," she added lightly.

He rolled his eyes.

But she was serious.

He was thoughtful and compassionate . . . and protective, while also doing laundry. Capable, a little bossy without minding when she pushed back . . . and he also made coffee.

Maybe he truly *was* the Unicorn.

She felt herself slide a little deeper down the rabbit hole.

Especially when she glanced up into those hazel eyes to see them edged with concern. "Plus," she said. "I *am* interested in the history. I heard a lot about Alcatraz growing up, so I'm excited to expand my knowledge of all things tourist trap."

He relaxed, capturing a strand of her hair that had escaped her ponytail in the gusty winds and tucking it behind her ear. "Should we walk across the Golden Gate next?"

"Yeah, no," she said, shuddering. "That's a step too far for me in my newly-donned tourist hat." Snorting and shaking her head, she watched the ferry slice through the surf, the bay water blue tinged with brown and breaking into whitecaps as it bounced against the hull. It was chilly, fall turning into winter, and yet with Brad next to her, standing close enough that his entire body was surrounding hers and blocking the wind, she was perfectly comfortable.

Silence lapsed between them as they both took in their course across the Bay, and though it was beautiful, the fog curling in ribbons across the sky, Heidi couldn't help but reflect on the week. It had been precisely fourteen days since she, Brad, and Fuzzy McFeatherston had participated in their cake disaster, but it felt like a lifetime ago.

They'd had nine nights together.

Nine nights that ranked up there with the best ones of her life, even though they'd hardly done anything—just eaten together, watched TV, cuddled on the couch . . . and in her bed.

Yes, that fact terrified her.

But . . . she was firmly addicted and had just decided to accept her fate.

She'd ride this ride to the end, and hopefully, knowing that there would be an end meant that her heart wouldn't hurt so much when Brad decided to flit off.

Or—her pulse thrummed with possibility—maybe he'd stay and—

Enough.

So, yes, these last two weeks had been wonderful, filled with easy conversation and warm arms. The evening of her creek shenanigans he'd stayed late, watching bad reality TV and then the various segments from all the late-night shows posted on YouTube that had struck her fancy before finally slipping out around midnight. He'd pressed a kiss to her forehead, leaving her drowsy and snuggly tucked under the covers. And when she'd woken up the following morning, it was to find that he'd prepped her coffee pot to automatically brew and had left a muffin under some plastic wrap on a plate on the counter.

Then that night, he'd coaxed her from work to Molly's for dinner.

Okay, truthfully, it hadn't taken much coaxing . . . because Molly's.

And while dinner wasn't quite as good as breakfast— because they didn't have the normal amount of freshly made baked goods—it was *almost* as good. They'd scarfed down hot sandwiches made on freshly made bread, had slurped up steaming soup laden with veggies and plenty of potatoes, and she'd washed down the huge portion with the best pomegranate iced tea she had ever tasted.

And then they'd gone back to her place to watch more bad reality TV—though this time it was from her couch and not her bed—and he'd left around midnight again.

The following evening, he'd called to say he'd gotten stuck in traffic returning from a beach in Santa Cruz, so they hadn't hung out, hadn't cuddled on the couch. And . . . she'd missed it.

Which had made her stomach squeeze, her pulse flutter.

Because she'd known then that she was already hooked on Brad.

Hooked on the dangerous, dangerous man.

But he hadn't seemed to notice her disquiet—or maybe he *had*, she realized, remembering the conversation and how he'd drawn her back in with a funny anecdote, how he'd continued to talk with her until she'd relaxed again.

Then he'd finagled an invite to her condo the next night.

He still hadn't stayed over, and she hadn't asked him to, even though she'd wanted to.

He'd just kissed her on the forehead again then slipped out the front door.

And wash, rinse, and repeat.

He'd coaxed her to Molly's for breakfast one day before work —saying he just *had* to try the freshly baked pastries. Another evening they'd walked hand-in-hand on the trails behind her house. Two nights ago, he'd shown up with a big bag of takeout without a word, not long after she'd mentioned that work that day had been exhausting. And on the couple of days he was off doing Brad things and not cuddled up with her on her couch, he'd called just to chat, and they'd ended up talking for hours.

More light, fun times. More warm conversations. More forehead kisses.

And now it was Saturday, and she was here with him. On a date.

And somehow, she knew there would be no more forehead kissing.

Or maybe, more accurately, it would be replaced with a *different* kind of kissing. Her body liked that thought. Her heart was hopeful. Her brain . . . well, it had already decided it was going to take a back seat to the rest of her.

"Wow," he murmured.

Heidi blinked, reorienting herself as she realized they'd arrived at the dock on the edge of the island located in the middle of the Bay, the decommissioned prison sitting atop it. There were more buildings than she'd expected, and it was also taller, with sharp cliffs leading almost straight down to the bay.

"You better not fall down this one," Brad murmured into her ear.

She laughed, startled. "You're joking about it now?"

"I've witnessed several more of your so-called clumsy skills," he said, his hot breath still on her skin and making her shiver. "Do you remember the incident just last night when you somehow managed to get your hair stuck on the knob of the cabinet?"

She remembered all right.

She also remembered the gentle fingers untangling the strands, the way her body had reacted so intensely to his proximity.

"Rude," she muttered, even though she was definitely

affected by his proximity even now. A woman had to have *some* pride, and if she couldn't muster at least a modicum of sarcasm, where would she be?

"The truth," he said. "And my point is that I think I can afford a small joke."

She wrinkled her nose. "At least this one is better than your prison joke."

He hissed out a breath. "Ouch, that's cold," he said, stepping back and taking her hand. "You're right, but damn, that's cold."

Giggling, she tugged him toward the stairs that would take them to the bottom level of the ferry, where they could disembark. "Come on, I need to get my audio tour and visit the gift shop."

"And here I'd prepared myself to play tour guide," he said dryly as they hit the bottom step. "I even have one of those little flowers so you can easily find me in the crowd."

"Do you really?"

His expression went serious, and he reached into his back pocket.

Her mouth dropped open.

But then he grinned, holding up his empty hand. "Seriously, though, I did do some research before coming. Redoing the visitor's center's website is next on my client list."

"Isn't it run by the government?"

"I have a contract with the government," he said and leaned close. "And now that I've told you that, I have to kill you."

She swatted him. "Stop joking around," she told him. "Because seriously, that's awesome. How long have you had the contract?"

"For a few years. The actual National Parks Service site is run and managed by the government—I would never have the capacity to set up something so vast. But a lot of the visitor's centers and tourist attractions are run by an outside company." He shrugged. "I did that company's main site maybe five years back, and then a higher up in the tech department asked me to do a spread for Crater Lake. Now, I've been slowly working my way through a lot of the national parks' visitor interfaces. They do the actual functionality and building. I just advise on design and useability." He continued to hold her hand as they walked down the gangway. "Next week is Alcatraz, and since it's here, I figured now would be as good a time as any to see The Rock."

"Wow. That's really impressive."

Another shrug. "Not really, and certainly there wasn't any skill involved," he said, "I'm just lucky that this fell into my lap and I could make a career out of it."

"They wouldn't keep you on if you weren't good."

He glanced down at her, eyes dancing. "Don't you know anything about our government? It's a giant pile of incompetence and overspend."

"Ah, *so* optimistic," she teased.

"Realistic is more like it."

"Okay then," she declared. "I will be the barometer of all things talented. You'll show me a portfolio of your work, and I shall decree whether or not you're worthy."

He tugged a lock of her hair, blowing in the breeze. "Should I get you a crown, too?"

She fought back a smile. "Obviously." A beat. "And a scepter."

He mimed making a note. "I've got it on my mental checklist."

"More like your mental *bullshit* meter," she said.

A tap to his nose. "Ding. Ding. Ding."

She glanced up at him, totally losing her fight with the smile, seeing that he wore an answering one in return. "I also feel obligated to point out," she said, "that you've taken me on a date so you can work."

His mouth dropped open.

"Am I right?"

He shook his head, a band of pink appearing on his cheeks. "No, I— That's not what I was doing. I just thought that since you said you hadn't seen a lot of touristy things and I was getting ready to work on this that—"

"Work," she repeated in a sing-song voice.

His lips parted. Closed. Parted again. "Shit. I'm an asshole."

She went on tiptoe, let her mouth drift close to his ear, and felt a thrill weave through her when he shivered, at knowing that he was just as affected by her as she was by him. "But you're *my* asshole," she whispered.

He turned his head, eyes blazing with emotion as they met hers. Then his lips quirked. "Yes, I am."

Heart pounding at the undertones in the conversation, knowing that neither of them was sincere about the asshole part, Heidi forced her gaze away and concentrated on just breathing. They'd reached solid ground. The ferry-load of people were weaving their way up the path to enter the historic site, and they were all but alone under the partly cloudy day, the wind in their air, the faint scent of the Pacific Ocean just beyond the Golden Gate filling her nose.

It was a beautiful day with a beautiful man, and she was having the time of her life just chatting and joking and walking with him.

If that wasn't the Unicorn, she didn't know what was.

And that was when Heidi lost her battle with self-control.

Rising up on tiptoe, she kissed him.

And not on his forehead, either.

Fifteen

Brad

He was stunned into stillness for a heartbeat.

Then he kissed her back.

He'd been thinking how beautiful she was with the sunlight dappling her skin, the wind ruffling her hair, the laughter dancing in her eyes. He'd been *thinking* how much he wanted to kiss her, how hard it was becoming to resist the urge.

And now she'd just tugged him to the side of the path, had pressed her soft, curvy body to his, and kissed him.

His lips parted automatically, his tongue sweeping forward to tangle with hers, tasting the faint hint of coffee and chocolate and banana on her tongue—the woman was obsessed with those muffins, and he was going to do his damndest to keep up with her demand for them. But it wasn't off-putting, even though he wasn't a big fan of either chocolate or banana. Instead . . . it was coming home. It was Heidi.

It was perfect.

So perfect, in fact, that he'd dipped his hands under her

shirt, fingertips brushing the silken skin of her abdomen on the appetizer to heading north when he felt a tap on his shoulder.

"You can't do that here," the female voice said.

He pulled back, blinked dazedly as he turned, trying to get his bearings. "I'm sorry, what?"

His vision cleared enough to remind him where he was, for him to see that it wasn't just a woman standing behind them, but a guard with an official badge and uniform and intense-looking duty belt.

The guard lifted an eyebrow. "I'd suggest you either start your tour, or you end it."

Heidi giggled—one pure burst of sound that had Brad fighting back a smile. "I'm sorry," he said. "We'll go get started."

The guard nodded. "Carry on—" Her eyes narrowed. "Well, not *carry on*"—she waved a hand—"but please, proceed with touring the facility."

Another tiny giggle that did nothing for his self-control, but he managed to stumble out another apology, to tug a chortling Heidi up the path and away from the guard, all without them getting thrown in the brig or finding themselves packed onto the next ferry back to the mainland.

"Your fault," he muttered.

"Yours." A beat. "You need to stop being so charming."

"I can't help it," he said. "It's a gift."

"One the entire world gets to benefit from?" she asked archly.

"Exactly." He stopped just past the turnstile after they'd paid for their tickets and glared down at her. "But as for the point at hand, I seem to remember *you* as the one doing the kissing."

She sidled closer. "I seem to remember *you* kissing me back."

Well, she had him there.

"Come on," he said, instead of conceding the point. They picked up their audio guide—Heidi had wisely opted out of his tour—then put on their headphones as they walked into the first room.

Cavernous. Cold. Gloomy.

He hated it instantly, and the audio of the tour wasn't much better, adding to the oppressiveness of the place, making him regret that he'd even thought to bring her here, especially on a date.

She slipped her headphones off, glancing around the room, eyes dimmed.

"Let's go," he said.

Her brows pulled together. "What? We just got here."

"I hate it," he muttered.

"Well, it certainly isn't sunshine and rainbows," she said, "but don't you have something for work you should be doing?"

Asked so innocently that he nearly missed the teasing in her eyes.

"I'm not going to live that down, am I?"

"I'll pretend to forget about it if you pretend to forget I lost that battle with the cabinet knob."

"Done."

"Pleasure doing business with you," she said, sticking her hand out so he could shake it. "And I'm fine with going. I don't like it here either." A shiver. "Though part of me thinks we should push through and learn what we can."

"I get that." He nodded. "But I don't think we'd be learning much."

"Probably not. And . . . I guess it reminds me too much of what is wrong with the world." She made a face. "I mean, we *should* know, because otherwise how are we going to help fix things? It's just . . ."

He brushed his fingers over her cheek. "Probably not the best place for a date."

"Yes." Her lips tipped up at the corner. "*That.*"

"Then we'll go do something else."

She smiled up at him. "So, how do we get out of here?"

"Same way you do with all these tourist traps." He brushed a finger down her nose. "Through the gift shop."

Laughing, she leaned close, weaving her arm through his. "Then lead on, oh master of all things travel-related."

He snagged her audio device, carrying both as they made their way through the cells, the cafeteria, the workrooms, the isolation room, weaving their path through the other patrons, pausing to take in a few signs with historical information, but for the most part, making their way to the exit as quickly as possible.

Which, unerringly, meant they ended up in the gift shop.

"Of course," she said as they stepped into the bright room, filled with racks of T-shirts and magnets and shot glasses and postcards. One entire wall had candy. Another held books. Heidi stopped by a set of dish towels and held them up. "Just what I always wanted."

"Come on, Trouble," he said, tugging them from her hands and putting them down on the stack. "Let's see if we can catch this ferry before it leaves."

A mock pout. "You owe me more shopping time at a future date."

He towed her toward the door, down the path toward the dock. "I'll remind you of our earlier conversation, in which you expounded on all things that are terrible about shopping."

"Yes, shopping in general," she said. "But not about the only type of acceptable shopping."

"What's that?" he asked as they boarded the ferry.

"Books." She smiled. "And there happens to be some amazing bookstores in San Francisco."

"Well," he said with tacit agreement as they both climbed the stairs. "Since my date idea was a bust, I think it makes sense to try yours. Should we hit up some of those bookstores instead?"

Her lips parted, surprise flitting in her eyes. "You're serious?"

Thumb tracing that plump bottom lip, he couldn't resist pulling her close, the scent of her shampoo tangling with that of the sea air. He couldn't get over how she seemed to fit perfectly against him, as though her body had been made for his, as though *she* had been made for him. "I'm serious," he said, unable to bite back a smile.

Joy lit up her face, and she did a little happy dance, one that had the positive benefit of brushing all those luscious curves against his body and one that made him lose his battle with control.

He dipped his head and kissed her.

And this time, there wasn't any guard around to make them stop.

At least until they arrived back in the city proper.

And *then* they got kicked off the ferry.

But seeing Heidi with swollen lips, her hair doubly messed from his fingers and the wind, her cheeks pink, and her eyes warm, and he decided a permanent ban from that ferry line was totally worth being able to kiss her.

Bar none.

Sixteen

Heidi

She kept glancing over at Brad, expecting to see boredom creep into his face, but every time she stopped browsing to check in, his expression wasn't annoyed or impatient.

Instead, he almost seemed to be studying her, watching and filing away each movement.

He'd disappeared when she'd become engrossed in the historical romance section then had reemerged some quantity of time later—she really wasn't good at keeping track of the movement of the Earth around the sun when there were books in front of her—his hands holding a few novels.

And then she'd expected the impatience to start and so had quickly shifted her bundle, trying to hurry in her selections, even though there . . . were . . . just . . . so . . . many . . . choices!

But instead of telling her to make a pick, he'd just snagged the books she'd tucked under one arm and told her to, "Explore."

She'd fallen in love—just a little bit—with that one word.

Explore.

God, the man was a menace.

Now, she was running her pointer finger over the spine of one more book—this one being one she already owned, only she had the UK version at home and was trying to decide if she liked the US version enough to have two copies.

She started to push it back into place.

No. Her bookshelves were already overflowing as it was. She couldn't justify the second copy, especially with the stack that Brad was already carrying for her.

"Okay," she said, turning to him. "Your torture is over. Hand me my stack so we can go check out."

Except, as the last word slipped off her tongue, her cell phone rang.

"Sorry," she told him, reaching into her purse. "That ringtone is the lab."

"Go ahead and answer it." He nodded toward the exit. "I'll buy these and meet you out there."

She took a step, stopped, her cell in her hand. "I'll pay you—"

"*Go,*" he urged as her phone rang again. "We'll figure it out later."

"Thanks," she said, hustling out onto the street and answering the call. Her weekend lab assistant, Maggie, was on the other end.

"We have a problem . . ." she began.

And that was the moment Heidi realized her day with Brad was over.

Because problem was an understatement. A mere problem would have meant that she might have been able to handle it over the phone, or at worst, email in written instructions to follow. A problem might have meant that she needed to check on the lab tomorrow, just to make sure all was fixed.

This . . . *this* was a disaster.

This had her immediately barking instructions. It also had Brad—who'd come out of the bookstore with two giant bags—take one look at her face and instantly begin directing her to his car.

"Tell me where to go," he said when they'd gotten in and she'd paused in her orders.

She rattled off the address.

Ten seconds to put it into his cell, a quick lift in her direction so she could confirm the location was correct, and then a minute later they were on the road, winding through city streets jammed with pedestrians and Saturday traffic and eventually making their way to the freeway and hightailing it south.

"No," she exclaimed. "Don't shut it down." They'd lose everything. She spared a look at Brad's cell, perched in a cradle connected to the air vent. "We'll be there in ten minutes. Just keep the computers up and running, I'll adjust the machinery when we get there." Maggie said a few more things—mostly listing what she'd do to keep the computers working, but Heidi didn't hang up or get short. She knew that Maggie was panicked, especially since she hadn't been able to reach Stef, who was on call for the lab this weekend for just this type of issue.

Maggie was a new grad. She was smart as a whip and funny, but she was also a bit anxious and a definite perfectionist.

This had thrown her for an absolute loop.

Not to mention, if she hadn't caught the miscalibration, the entire experiment would have been ruined—six months of research would have amounted to absolutely nothing.

"Deep breaths," she said when Maggie had paused for air. "Everything will be fine."

She hoped, but that was beside the point.

"I-I hope so, Heidi."

"It was a good catch," she told her, "and we'll figure out the rest. Now, I'm going to hang up and call Stef again."

"O-okay."

A moment later she was dialing her lead assistant, the call ringing and ringing and ringing until—

"Hello?"

"Stef," she said. "It's Heidi. Why the hell haven't you picked up your phone? The computer's malfunctioned, and the readings are writing over one another, and—"

"I'm in the hospital."

"What?"

"Fred"—her ninety-pound golden retriever—"pulled me over this morning. I didn't think I'd done more than twist my ankle and got a few bruises, but then my foot swelled up like a balloon, and I couldn't walk on it." She released a shaking breath. "I think I'm going to need to have surgery."

"Shit," Heidi whispered.

"I know."

"I'll get the lab sorted and come straight over."

Stef inhaled sharply, her normal no-nonsense tone returning. "Absolutely not, this is supposed to be your weekend off. Damage control and then call in Matteo. He can cover the lab for the rest of the time."

Since she *had* planned on calling Matteo to take over, she didn't argue with Stef, just asked her a few questions about her injury and what hospital she was at. Because she sure as hell wasn't going to allow her assistant to go through that alone. Stef was good people, and she didn't have anyone in the area since she'd broken up with her boyfriend and he'd taken their friends.

Assholes.

Somewhere in the swirling in the back of her head, she made a mental note to make sure she, Cora, Kelsey, and Kate all brought the full-frontal attack into folding Stef into their friend group.

She needed some peeps—and ones that wouldn't disappear just because a boyfriend was a total twat-waffle.

"What room are you in?"

"Five-oh-four," Stef said. "And here I live until at least tomorrow. They don't think the surgeon will be able to see me until then."

"Oh no," Heidi murmured as she jotted the hospital name and the room number on a scrap of paper from her purse. Last thing she needed to do was forget one or the other with everything else going on. "Seriously?"

"Seriously. But don't worry, I'm comfortable and have plenty of bad cable TV to keep me company."

"What about a phone charger? Or a change of clothes? Or snacks? Or a book?" she asked, mind jumping between her friend being in the hospital and the lab.

"It's one night," Stef said. "Trust me, I've roughed it in worse places."

"Hang in there," she said as they approached the gate for the lab.

"Keep me posted on the equipment."

Hell no, she wouldn't, or at least not any more than what was necessary so Stef wouldn't worry and jeopardize her recovery. "I'll call you as soon as I can," she promised then hung up, stashing her cell and pulling out her badge. "I'm afraid they won't let you in without the proper clearance," she told Brad. "You'll have to drop me out here, and I'll grab an Uber home."

"I can wait," he began.

She touched his cheek. "I have no idea how long I'll be."

"I don't mind."

"Well, I do," she murmured. "I won't be able to concentrate in there if you're out here just twiddling your thumbs. Go home. I'll call tonight if it's not too late. Tomorrow, if it is." Dropping her hand, she pulled her purse onto her shoulder. "You can just park over there," she said, pointing to the row of visitor spots before the gate.

He pulled to a stop and looked at her. "You sure you don't want me to wait?" A small smile. "I've got plenty of books to keep me busy."

She nodded. "Thank you for offering. That's sweet. But I'm sure." Pausing with her hand on the handle of the door, she made a face and said, "But I *am* sorry my work ruined our date."

"Don't worry about it," he told her. "Now I've got plenty of ammunition to tease you back."

"I think we're equal, and that's it."

He laughed. "Maybe you're right."

Hand still resting on the pull, she hesitated. "I don't want to go."

"I know, baby," he murmured, pressing a quick kiss to her mouth that had her pulse skyrocketing and her lips tingling before he pulled back. "But your work is important. Our stuff will hold."

She released a trembling breath, her heart squeezing tight, a mental billboard flashing *Unicorn. Unicorn. Unicorn!* across her mind. "Thank you," she whispered.

A sexy smile. "Get out of here before I kiss that look off your face. You've got work to do."

Heart full, she nodded, pulled the lever, and got out. She walked quickly to the gate and showed her pass. When they opened it for her, she glanced back, saw that Brad was still waiting for her, and waved.

He waved back then gestured at her to hurry up.

Laughing, she turned her back on the gate, on the visitor's parking lot, on Brad, and hustled into the lab, thinking that she'd definitely found the Unicorn.

She just wasn't sure how long he'd stick around.

———

Later that night, *many* hours later, after things in the lab had stabilized and she'd managed to save their six months of work, she stumbled into the parking lot, bleary-eyed and exhausted, Maggie staggering alongside her.

Luckily, she didn't have to wait for a pickup, as Maggie had offered to get her home, and so they made their way over to her assistant's tiny hybrid.

A few minutes later, they were on the freeway, heading for Heidi's place.

"Thanks again for driving me home," she said, staring out at the dark sky, at the bright flashes of white and red lights surrounding them.

"Thanks again for not firing me," Maggie said lightly.

"That calculation wasn't your fault, and you know it." Heidi shook her head. "I honestly cannot think of what happened. All the numbers and settings were correct when I left yesterday, and we were the only ones in there."

A beat. "Except, we weren't the only ones in there."

Heidi frowned. "What do you mean?"

"Well, when I came in this afternoon to run the checks, I saw the cleaning crew leaving." She glanced over then back at the road. "I didn't think anything of it at first, and then after I noticed the readings, I was in too much of a panic to make sure the experiment didn't fail that I'd forgotten."

"And now you remembered."

A nervous look toward Heidi. "Yeah. I'm sorry, I didn't remember sooner."

"I'm not irritated with you," she said, digging around her purse and grabbing her cell. There were all sorts of notifications on the screen, but nothing from Stef, who'd texted a few hours before saying they were taking her into surgery after all. "I'm just pissed that the protocol wasn't followed, especially considering everything that could have been jeopardized." She forced her tone to stay even. "In fact, I think you probably deserve a raise for managing to get all of those half-life calculations on the backup hard drive before the data was erased."

"I—well—"

Heidi patted her arm. "You did good," she said. "I promise I'd tell you otherwise."

"Not *so* good," she muttered. "Otherwise I wouldn't have had to call in the boss on her day off."

"Meh. Won't be the first, nor the last. Now," she added, changing the subject before Maggie could go too far down the rabbit hole of feeling sorry for herself and/or feeling guilty for needing to call in backup. "Tell me all about what it's like to be twenty-two and living in the city. What do all the cool kids do for fun?"

She laughed. "What makes you think I'm remotely a cool kid?"

"Because you're twenty-two," Heidi pointed out.

"Trust me," Maggie said dryly. "That's not nearly enough." But she did share a funny story about a bar called Bobby's she'd gone to with girlfriends the previous weekend, and how the front room was super fun with cool décor and fun music, but that the back room was filled with outdated tunes . . . and people.

"I just was looking for the bathroom, and I swear, it was like the middle-aged club had unleashed a party back there. There was dancing and drinking, and the noise was *intense*. I swear, they were having more fun than we were in that front room."

"How old were these middle-aged people?" she asked, well-familiar with Bobby's and definitely knowing that she and her friends were relegated to the back room.

Far away from the cool kids out front.

"God," Maggie said, turning into Heidi's complex. "They must have been like . . . thirty-five, some even forty."

Heidi choked on a laugh.

She was thirty-three, nearing thirty-four.

Apparently, that was almost middle-aged.

Heaven help her.

"Thanks again," she said when Maggie stopped in front of her condo. "I'm so glad I didn't have to wait for an Uber."

Maggie smiled, nodded. "Thanks for being so cool about the lab."

With a quick goodbye, she closed the door and headed up to the front door of her place. Oh, she'd been cool with Maggie— one, because it wasn't her assistant's fault, and two, because even if it *had* been, people made mistakes.

But the cleaning staff going into her lab wasn't a mistake.

Or it wasn't a mistake any longer.

She'd had to have a conversation with occupational health about not allowing the general cleaning company into the room three times already since she began at the company less than a year ago.

This would mark a fourth.

And the fourth broken promise, and one that had nearly jeopardized everything.

So no, she wouldn't be the cool boss. Not any longer. In fact, she and several people were going to have a very stern conversation, and then *if* that didn't work, she was installing a fucking dead bolt herself, with a lock and key only she and her team had copies of.

In fact, she was looking up said locks and keys, just to be preemptively prepared, when her phone buzzed with a text from Stef.

Why the hell did you send tall, dark, and handsome to look after me? Just saying, if he was my man, I'd have him under lock and key.

The mirroring of her own thoughts should have been funny. Except . . . *what?* Sending tall, dark, and who?

But before she could ask that, Stef sent a picture of Brad, a vase of flowers in his hand as he placed snacks on a rolling table.

He says you arranged everything. Surgery is over, obviously. Apparently, it was less complicated than they thought.

Heidi blinked, her fingers starting to type out a reply. But her cell buzzed again before she got there.

Thank you. I know I said I was fine, but even though I didn't want to admit it, I was scared. Knowing that someone was out there in the waiting room, looking after me, even though you'd sent him, made me feel better.

She'd typed out another reply, something that probably barely made sense, because her mind was spinning. But that was okay, because she still didn't get to send it.

Her cell vibrated one last time.

Tell me all about it in the morning. Visiting hours are over, and I'm going to zonk out.

Heidi stared at her phone screen for several moments then shook her head. And . . . then her gaze alighted on something else, something she'd missed when she'd first stumbled her way inside.

Her books were on her bookshelf. On the proper bookshelf —that being her To Be Read shelf. In the proper order—that being separated by genre then alphabetized by author name.

All except the title she'd been waffling about purchasing. The pretty US cover was slotted right next to the UK one on her already read shelves.

The hospital.

Her condo.

The books.

Her friend.

Brad, the *Unicorn* known as Brad, had some explaining to do.

Seventeen

Brad

The knock at his door made him frown.

It was late, and even though his family was pushy, they would definitely call first, especially considering it was nearing midnight.

Someone must be confused, knocking at the wrong apartment.

Maybe a DoorDash had gone wrong.

Sighing when the knock came again, he set aside his book—the thriller he'd picked up earlier that day, and one that also had him wondering whether it was Russian mafia men or a terrifying serial killer on the other side of that wood—and made his way to the door.

He checked the peephole—because Russian mafia men and terrifying serial killers—but when he saw who was on the other side, his mouth dropped open, and he scrambled to release the dead bolt.

"Heidi!" he exclaimed the moment he'd wrenched open the door. "What are you—?"

She poked a finger into his chest. "You," she snapped then slipped by him, striding into his apartment, her shining brown hair fanning out behind her like a cape. "*You!*" she exclaimed, spinning around to face him while he locked up. Her hands were on her hips, her legs were clad in pajamas, and her eyes flashed.

"Me?" he asked when it appeared that was all she was going to say.

Her lips pressed flat. Her chin lifted. "Why?" she asked. "Why did you do it?"

His brows drew together. "The books?" He figured it was time to fess up. "I borrowed your spare key that night when you were hurt. It was there on your little organizer thing, and I didn't want you to be sleeping with an unlocked door, and I know it was probably an invasion of your privacy to keep it, but I've been staying late and didn't want you to have to worry about getting up." He shrugged helplessly. "I probably shouldn't have used it today, but I just figured you might like to read one of the books you bought—"

"*You* bought."

He paused. "What?"

"*You* bought the books," she said. "Not me."

"I . . ." He hesitated, not sure where she was going with this. Her fury seemed to have dimmed somewhat, but she was still standing there, looking fierce and ready to avenge crimes. "I told you, we could figure that out later."

"It's later." She took a step toward him.

"Okaaay." He glanced around. "I probably have the receipt around here somewhere."

She took another step, her expression so intense that he found himself wondering about serial killers again. "But this isn't about the books," she said, coming even closer, until her scent filled his nostrils, until the soft curves of her breasts came into contact with his chest.

Between her smell, her body, the way she kept coming closer, until her front was flush against his, and he wasn't operating on all cylinders. "It isn't?" he asked, confusion battling with desire now.

He pushed the latter down. He didn't want to fuck things up with this woman.

Even though every cell in his body was telling him to yank her close and kiss her senseless, to haul her behind the screen and have a repeat of the night a few months ago.

She shook her head. "No."

"What is it about then?"

A sexy smile curving lips begging to be kissed, but her eyes were serious and sitting heavy on his. "Stef."

Oh. Shit.

She reached up and cupped his jaw. "Why did you do it?"

He could do nothing but tell her the truth. "You were worried about her." A shrug. "I saw her room number and the hospital on the note you wrote. I figured I'd just poke my head in and make sure she didn't need anything."

"And you brought her flowers?"

Shit. Was that what this was about? Did she think that because he brought Stef flowers that he was trying to hit on another woman? That he didn't want Heidi? That couldn't be further from the truth.

"Baby—"

"And snacks."

"I—uh—she's important to you and—"

Heidi rose on tiptoe and kissed him.

Brad felt as though he'd been electrocuted, the sensation was so acute, so absolute. Heat seared into him, arrowing straight for his cock. He froze for one long moment, reveling in the feel of her against him, her lips tangling with his, before he remembered he could touch.

Wrapping his arms around her waist, he pulled her even closer until he couldn't be sure where he ended and she began.

Curves filling his palms, a soft mouth on his, her tongue a sleek dart in his mouth. He gave into his earlier urge, sweeping her up into his arms, groaning when she straddled his hips, thighs clamping around his pelvis and rocking against the hard length of his erection.

And then he carried her behind the screen to his bed.

Heidi tugged her mouth from his when he laid her on the mattress, following her down, sprawling beside her, the haze of desire edging into his vision. "You brought her flowers, you wonderful man." She cupped his cheeks, holding him still when he went to kiss her again. "And her favorite snacks, apparently. How did you know?"

He shrugged. "I didn't. I just made an educated guess based on how much you've been raving about those chocolate-covered pretzels," he admitted. "And then I figured I couldn't go wrong with Molly's." A smile. "Someone really smart might have mentioned that to me once or twice."

Her lips tipped up. "As I said, you wonderful man."

"You're not mad?"

Now her eyes danced with humor. "Does it *seem* like I'm mad?"

"Actually, now that you mention it . . ."

She snorted. "Shut up and kiss me before I forget how wonderful you are."

That was an exceptionally easy order for him to follow.

He lowered his mouth to hers . . .

And sparks.

Her fingers dug into his shoulders, kneading the muscles there, pulling him closer until he was fully on top of her, feeling every glorious curve. He had an immediate sense of belonging, of coming home, of . . .

Heidi.

Her scent, spicy and floral, filling his nose. Her lips parting so he could sweep his tongue inside. Her legs falling open, bringing their hips in perfect alignment. Desire was a rapidly growing tempest, yanking him this way and that, reminding him of how good it had been between them, the memories of all the places she liked to be touched, of *how* she liked to be touched flooding forward.

He wanted to do everything at once, *needed* to stroke and lick, to tear off her clothes and plunge home, to—

His conscience dug its claws sharply into the sides of his brain and shook it fiercely.

Because it had been two weeks since he'd begun his campaign to win her over.

Only two weeks.

And if he really wanted to show her that he was going to stick around, he couldn't just fall into bed with her again. Well, they were *already* in bed, but he couldn't sleep with her until she knew—

A moan slipped past her lips, vibrating into his mouth, her tongue twining with his, those legs that had fallen open lifting to wrap tightly around his waist.

Naked.

He needed her naked.

His conscience gripped tighter, dug those claws in further, shook him even more intensely.

Wrenching his head back, he broke the kiss, though one look at Heidi's face nearly had his conscience's hooks dislodging. Grabbing on to the threads of his control, he rested his forehead on her shoulder, sweat prickling on his nape, breaths coming in rapid intervals.

But being this close to her fabulous set of breasts didn't help his cause either.

Because they were inches away and tempting him and—

He sat up, put the entire length of the mattress between them.

"What's wrong?" she asked.

Brad wasn't able to form words yet. His cock had a fucking heartbeat and was pressing against the zipper of his jeans with a persistent ache that had him very close to forgetting why he'd backed off in the first place.

Which was why his only answer was a shake of his head.

The bed dipped, the consequence of his non-answer being that she came closer. Normally, a perfectly acceptable reaction. Normally, something he would have loved. But right then, right in that moment with him trying to remember all the reasons he could not jump on top of her like a rabid beast and have his merry way with her? Right then, her coming closer wasn't ideal.

She pressed close to his side, and fuck, that was heaven and hell all at the same time. Curves and woman—no, *this* woman. Because Heidi was temptation personified.

But she needed to know that he wasn't back in her life looking for a fantastic night. She had to understand what she meant to him, even if he'd only just discerned the meaning himself. He wanted this woman to comprehend the change she'd jumpstarted, the things she'd made him realize about himself, and she . . .

Fuck, he needed this woman to understand that he loved her.

That he'd fallen that first night and had run because she'd pushed beyond the barriers surrounding his heart, even if he hadn't quite understood the panicked reaction until two weeks before, until that conversation with Jaime.

Because she also needed to know what she was getting into, what baggage he was carrying and how it might bleed over.

Hell, most sane people would say that his life for the past decade was a giant red flag, littered as it was with lost friendships and relationships that had never gotten off the ground because half of their party—him—had quite literally flown away whenever he got the whim.

But Heidi needed to know that he didn't have the whim

now, and that when he did travel, he wanted it to be with her by his side.

And how was she going to believe that, huh, genius?

He'd been back for all of a month, had spent even less time than that with her. Why would she think that anything about him had changed or *would* change or—

She placed her hand on his thigh, making him jump and lurch away from the contact. Because he wanted to move closer. *Fuck.* His breath sawed in and out. His—

"D-do—"

The word was tentative enough that his eyes flew from the ground, from where he'd been counting the grains in the piece of hardwood floor at his feet, up to hers, up to collide with tentative hazel eyes that socked him in the gut.

"Do what?" he asked.

Pink on her cheeks, her eyes darting away. "Do you not . . ." A sigh before her chin rose. "Do you not want me that way?"

EIGHTEEN

"W hat?" he roared, closing the distance between them and all but hauling her into his lap. He grabbed her hand, brought it toward his hips, pressing it firmly against the hard length of his erection.

Her fingers convulsed instinctively, wrapping around his cock as much as they were able through the fabric of his jeans.

He groaned, dropped his forehead to hers. "*That's* how much I want you. You breathe, and I'm hard. You smile, and I'm aching. You laugh and I'm ready to tear your clothes off."

"But . . ." she whispered.

"But what?"

Embarrassment flooded through her, but she had to know, had to make sure that she hadn't imagined . . . well, hadn't made things bigger in her head than they were in real life. "But . . . things were just getting good, and then you stopped."

Brad froze.

Then he grinned, a hot, slow smile that she felt trickle along every nerve ending.

"What?" she asked.

The pale lighting brought out the golden hues hidden in his deep brown hair, made the stubble on his cheeks seem even darker. But it was his eyes that held her in place, that made her heart skip a beat.

He stood, bringing her with him, then walked toward the headboard, positioning them both so they were resting with their backs against it.

Or rather, *he* had his back against it.

She was able to relax in the enviable circle of his arms, sitting on his lap, her shoulder against his chest, but best of all was the way his arms wrapped around her, drawing her close to his body, holding her tightly. She was protected, cared for, held as though she were important.

"Okay," he said. "I'm only going to say this once." He paused, waited until her gaze came to his. "You are quite literally the woman that I want most in this world. And I've been to a shit-ton of places," he added, tucking a strand of hair behind her ear. "So you can know that I'm not spouting bullshit. Also, by want, I mean sexually. Refer back to all that breathing, smiling, laughing, and my cock feeling like it's going to break in half stuff I mentioned previously."

His fingers brushed the shell of her ear, making her shiver and drift closer, until she could feel his next words glaze her lips. "But, also, more importantly, by want, I mean I can honestly say that you are the first woman I've ever spent time with who's made me look inside and recognize that I have some shitty characteristics that I need to change."

She frowned, but he dropped a finger to her lips before she could protest.

"I hurt you," he whispered, his tone making her lungs seize, her heart convulse because there was so much pain in those words, "and I will regret doing that for the rest of my life."

"I'm okay," she whispered.

He smiled gently. "Of course, you are. Because you're smart and capable and beautiful, and you don't let dumbasses like me ruin your groove."

Laughter bubbled up in her chest, but she held it back. "That's true," she said instead, keeping her tone light.

"But," he said. "I *did* hurt you, and I hate that I did, and"— a sharp sigh—"well, the truth is that I didn't even understand *why* I'd done it, why I'd panicked and run until two weeks ago."

She rested her hand on his shoulder, kneaded the tight muscles there. "Why did you panic and run?"

"Because you were different."

Maybe the words should have hurt her feelings—being different wasn't typically good in these scenarios—but instead, she understood at least part of what he was saying.

Because he'd been different, too.

"Baby," she whispered.

"No," he said. "Just let me get this out, okay? And then you can decide if you're going to walk out that door, like I probably deserve, or . . ."

"Or what?" she asked after a few moments when he hadn't finished the thought.

"Or"—his hands came to her jaw, cupping it gently—"if you'll let me keep you forever."

Her pulse had slowed from the frenzied tattoo of their kissing, a steady and calm *thrum-thrum, thrum-thrum, thrum-thrum* that was pumping blood evenly through her veins. But his words sent it into warp speed, carousing through her body, vibrating in her fingertips, galloping through her legs, whirling through her brain.

"For-forever?"

Gentle, still so gentle, but his eyes, they held a touch of

humor. "Yes," he said. "Forever. That's what people do when they find the one person on this planet who's destinated for them above all others."

That almost poetry sang to a part of her—the piece that had been devastated when she'd woken alone that day only a few months before, the same piece that understood what he was saying, that felt the same, that wanted that *forever*.

The rest of her . . . was overwhelmed.

She hardly knew this man.

But . . . was that really accurate?

True, they hadn't logged a lot of hours together yet, but she had seen so many of the important things. His time with Stef, the books, the date, the dinners and ice cream and movies and bad reality TV. The way he made her laugh and was quick to do so at himself. He was a good man—she knew that in her bones, knew it with as much certainty as she understood how many electrons orbited an atom of helium (that being two).

She'd already decided she wasn't a coward.

She'd already decided she was going to see where things went with this man.

So, why couldn't it be forever?

Why not her? Why not this wonderful man?

With the sun long set, with neighbors overhead clomping noisily across the ceiling, with a lovely, funny, sexy man in front of her, saying he wanted her . . . why couldn't that be?

There wasn't any reason.

It *could* be.

Heart still tripping along, her pulse still skittering in her veins, she peeled his hands from her cheeks, lacing their fingers together. "Okay," she murmured. "What do you need to tell me?"

What could this man possibly tell her that he thought might have her bolting for the door?

His eyes were equal parts wary and concerned.

"I keep people at a distance, so they can't leave me." He swallowed hard. "So they can't hurt me."

She waited.

Because clearly, there must be more to this.

"I've done it since I was a kid," he said. "I didn't really realize it until recently, but I think it started when my mom got sick. It was easier to pretend everything was fine, that *I* was fine." He sighed. "But the truth is that I continued doing it, and I used traveling as an excuse to keep my distance even more."

She squeezed his hands. "Hard to have a serious relationship when you're out of the country all the time."

"Yes. That."

"I'm sorry your mom was sick," she said.

His eyes softened. "It was a long time ago."

"She's a big presence in your guys' lives, though." Heidi slipped one hand free so she could push back her hair that seemed determined to get into her eyes. "I can tell that just from the couple of times I've met her."

"She is," he told her. "She's the glue that holds everything together."

"I can see how the fear of losing that might affect you."

Brad stilled. "Why am I hearing a but?"

She winced. "Well, it's not so much a but—"

He cursed. "I get it," he said, interrupting her and taking off down a tangent that had nothing to do with anything that she'd been thinking. "I understand why you wouldn't want to trust your heart with someone who's just going to flit off and leave you alone—someone who's *already* done that. I totally get it if you want me to just keep my distance, to not keep pursuing you. Hell, if I was in your position, I wouldn't have been nearly as nice or understanding as you've been. I would have kicked my ass to the curb and—"

"Are you?" she interrupted, having the feeling that if she *didn't* interrupt, then she might never get another word in edgewise. He was too far along the road of self-chastisement, determined to flagellate himself until he was sufficiently punished for his transgressions.

She saw now.

She understood now. What was in her heart . . . and what was in his.

Beyond the courage she'd summoned to take a chance with him, beyond her own hang-ups with self-worth, she saw that this man would take every opportunity to carry more than his fair share of burdens. He'd continue taking them on, one after another, piling them across his shoulders until he couldn't take a step, couldn't move forward at all.

Unless she stopped him.

His words had faltered at her question, but he didn't answer it.

So, she prompted him again. "Are you?"

He blinked. "Am I what?"

"Are you going to flit off and leave me to wake up in my bed all alone again?"

His expression clouded. "Fuck, no," he said. "I've spent the last months imagining all the places I want to take you, everything I want you to see. If I travel, I want you right by my side."

"So, that's it?"

Brows drawing together, he cocked his head to the side. "What do you mean?"

"Is that all of your baggage? Everything that would have me kicking you to the proverbial curb?"

"I—um—I—" His mouth opened and closed a few times, sounds rumbling up from his throat but not coalescing into actual words.

She took pity on him. "I get keeping people at a distance, honey. I have a fucking PhD in the subject myself. My parents . . . well, my dad is great, if sometimes a bit distant, and my mom . . . she's not so great, even though I keep telling myself that she always means well. It's just . . . she's not like your mom, and she's given me some wounds that run deep. So trusting people doesn't come easily for me. So *I* might push you away to stay safe." She trailed the fingers of her free hand along his jaw. "The thing is you say you've used avoiding connections like a shield. And I get that. I *feel* that sentiment in my bones. I've had my heart broken, have that baggage with my mom, and those hurts, they fucking suck." She swallowed. "But when I saw how happy Kate was with Jaime, when I saw the relationship Kels has with Tanner, I knew that I wanted that."

She rested her palm on his chest, feeling the steady beat of his heart beneath. "I was fucking terrified to take that first step, to even *admit* that what I had in my life wasn't enough, but I did it. I promised myself that I would try, would hold tight to the truth that I was worth finding something as special as they had, and I *did* find it." Smiling up at him, she said, "Also news-flash, what I found was you."

He inhaled sharply.

She pressed a kiss to his lips. "Because you're good and smart and caring and so much more than I could have hoped for, even with that armor on. But you know what's better?"

He shook his head.

"I think we've both come to the conclusion that whatever this is between us is different, is *more*. That it has the potential to be what Kate and Jaime have, what Kels and Tanner do, too."

She released a breath, laid the resolution she'd come to just before calling Kate and waking her friend up in the middle of the night on her honeymoon, who'd then had to wake up Jaime to get Brad's address, on the table (also, yes, she knew that she'd rung the alarm at the gossip committee and that her friends and all their nosiness would be descending shortly . . . but also, she didn't care, because Brad was important. Maybe it was some-thing in the Huntington gene pool, maybe it was just the power of Brad himself . . . or maybe she was digressing when she really should be focusing on telling this man what was in her heart).

"So what I'm trying to tell you is to bring that armor, carry that big ass shield, try to keep me at a distance because I won't stay away. Because . . . my armor is gone," she said. "Or maybe when it came to you, honey, I never had any."

He was still as a statue, hardly breathing, his eyes locked on hers.

Meanwhile, she was breathing heavily, her heart pounding, her lungs working hard after that long-ass speech.

And he was frozen, shock written into every line of his face.

"Did I break you?" she asked, jostling his chest lightly.

Her question seemed to snap him out of whatever trance he'd stumbled into, because he blinked, his hand slipped from hers, his arms banded around her, and he drew her flush against him. "No," he whispered. "You didn't break me. You turned the key, made me see exactly what I was missing."

Her heart pulsed, happiness welling within her. "Great," she said, wrapping her arms around him in turn, bringing their mouths close so the barest millimeter separated them. "So now, will you get back to kissing me?"

She had one quick glimpse of that slow, sexy smile of his, the one that always melted her from the inside out.

Then his mouth was on hers.

NINETEEN

BRAD

Kissing.

It was all back to kissing.

Only this time, it was without the cloud hanging over him, the tendrils of dread in his gut. He was able to just be in this moment with the woman he loved and really fucking enjoy kissing the hell out of her.

There was no hesitation in their touches, in the strokes of their tongues.

They'd gotten that all out of their systems months ago. Tonight was about leaning into those caresses, holding tight to the passion, embracing the need that made his hands shake and sweat break out on his back. It was about remembering every single thing that had made this woman moan, her breathing hitch, her eyes glaze over in desire.

And then he was doing them all on repeat.

One quick movement had their positions reversed and moved down on the bed, her head hitting the pillow, her back on the mattress, her body sprawled out beneath him.

Then he was kissing her again, stroking his tongue along the seam of her lips, tasting the mix of sweet and tart that was only Heidi. She opened, and their tongues collided, waltzing around each other, a frenzy of movements that had him groaning into her mouth.

But his hands weren't stationary. They were busy, remembering every curve, slipping beneath the fabric of her sweatshirt and finding the hot skin beneath. Her breathing hitched when he traced up and over her rib cage, before that hiccup of air turned into a soft, low moan that had his blood going molten. He traced higher, slipping beneath the band of her bra, fingers grazing the underside of one breast before moving to the other in a steady back and forth that had her head falling back on the pillows, their lips pulling apart.

He didn't want to stop kissing her, didn't want to lose that taste on his tongue.

But he supposed there were plenty of other places demanding to be kissed, beginning with the hardened tip of her nipple that was beading against the fabric of her bra, poking through the lace to press against his palm when he cupped one breast lightly.

Dragging his mouth down her neck, he tasted the salt mixing with sweet and spice and tart, soaking it in as he made his way to the zipper at the top of her hoodie, tugging it down, the *zip* loud in the quiet of the room only punctuated by rapid breaths and the occasional *thunk* from his loud ass neighbors overhead. Knowing he'd never get to kiss and touch like he wanted without removing it, he coaxed the sweatshirt down her arms, tossed it to the side, and then stared down at this woman, at his beautiful Heidi—

Who was wearing a T-shirt that said, *I Make Bad Science Puns . . . Periodically.*

And he laughed.

Because she was different. Because she was funny. Because she was just so . . . Heidi.

"What is it?" she asked, reaching for his shoulders.

He smoothed his hand over her cheek, down her arm, along her torso, and stopped, slipping it under the hem of her shirt to rest on the warm heat of her abdomen.

"You're just so fucking perfect for me."

Her eyes widened, lips parting, and he couldn't resist one more taste of that mouth, enticing her into a heated kiss that had them both gasping, and at least for him, his vision edged in black by the time he managed to tear himself away. But though he left her to draw in a breath, he didn't remove his mouth from her body. Instead, he dragged it over her throat, dipped his tongue into the small hollow at the base of her neck, nipped lightly at her collarbones. Still, the fucking fabric of her shirt impeded him, so he managed to pull himself away from her long enough to tug the cotton over her head, to toss it somewhere in the vicinity of her hoodie.

But when he went to return his mouth to her skin, bent on kissing every inch, she placed her hand on his chest, stilling him.

His eyes met hers.

"Naked first," she said.

Well, now. He could work with that.

His fingers went to work on her pajamas, tugging them off her legs and dragging her underwear down along with them. Those two went by the wayside, and a heartbeat later, he'd slipped a hand beneath her, undoing her bra and peeling the pale pink lace away.

Naked.

Yes. So much better.

But when he went to crawl back on top of her, she stopped him again with her hand on his chest.

He glanced down, realized he'd forgotten her socks, and tugged those off as well.

But she halted him again before he could sink between her thighs.

"What?" he asked, mouth watering with the need to taste, fingers itching to touch.

Her color was high, her lips reddened and swollen from his kisses, but still her voice was steady when she ordered, "You need to be naked, too."

That was what he wanted.

That was also a big problem.

Because he wanted this woman quite desperately, and if *he* was naked, too, he might embarrass them both. Well, embarrass himself, and make her quite unhappy.

"Heidi," he began.

She shook her head, arms crossing beneath her breasts, plumping the mounds into a nearly irresistible temptation. "No, Brad. No dice. You get naked right now, or else this isn't happening."

"I—"

"I don't care if you're nearly at the end of your control, or if you want to enjoy me first, or whatever other bullshit man stuff you have flitting through that brain of yours." Her eyes flashed with irritation. "I need to be able to touch you, to feel your skin on my palms, to hold your body to mine without any barriers. Another time you can tease me until your heart's content." Her gaze softened. "But tonight, I need you to be right here with me."

He would have agreed, just because she asked.

But her giving him the words, telling him what was in her heart and mind . . . well, that absolutely slayed him.

And he knew in that moment, that he would never be able to deny this woman anything. He'd been written into existence for her, just as she'd been made to fit him perfectly.

They had the potential to be like his brother and Kate.

No, they *would* be like his brother and Kate.

Minus the rooster and gaggle of animals.

Though, as he stood and methodically stripped off his clothes, letting them drop to the floor, he knew that just as he couldn't deny Heidi what she wanted, if she asked for a rooster, he'd buy the bird the fucking tuxedo himself.

A moment later, Fuzzy McFeatherston wasn't the cock he was thinking of. All his focus was diverted to the woman grabbing onto the cock swinging between his legs. The cock that was harder than he'd ever believed possible and throbbing with the need to spread Heidi's thighs and plunge deep.

Seemingly reading his mind, or at least the mind of the body part south of the border, she kept her grip tight, sliding it up and down the hard length of him. "Please say you have a condom," she murmured.

He was in the middle of biting back a groan, his hips thrusting forward, pleasure rolling down his spine in waves, when he realized what she'd asked.

What she'd asked.

And what he didn't have.

Fuck. *Fuck.*

The groan he'd bit back burst forth, startling her into opening her eyes, the hazel depths cloudy with need . . . and then sharpening as horror dawned. "You don't have a condom?"

He shook his head. "I've been meaning to pick some up, but I've been too busy with . . ."

She was shoving him off her, and for a moment, he thought he'd revealed the straw that had broken the camel's back. But then she was striding across the room, glorious ass bouncing as she stalked to her purse, which apparently had fallen near the couch, and scooping it up.

She strode back, and he was torn where to look—those bouncing breasts, lower to the neatly trimmed dark hair hiding the pussy he wanted to get his mouth on and his tongue inside, or to any of the tempting places in between. The trio of freckles beneath her right nipple, the star-shaped tattoo on her rib cage, the dainty dip of her belly button, the faint birthmark on her hip.

Hell, he would even be thrilled to put in quality time with her feet, with those cute little toes, their nails now painted in a bright pink, all except for the big toe, which had a tiny rendering of a palm tree.

A palm tree that was tapping just beneath his line of vision, Heidi having made her way back to stand by the bed.

She cleared her throat, and he forced his gaze to rise to hers, albeit taking a slow, meandering path up those strong and sensual legs, past the thighs he needed to lick his way up, beyond her stomach and ribs and even her breasts, though it lingered there long enough for her to clear her throat for a second time.

But then his eyes were on hers.

"Do women have to do *everything?*" she snapped, but her stare gave her away, warmth turning the grays and browns and greens of her eyes into a deep russet with streaks of gold, any anger having been edged out by amusement.

Out of the corner of his vision, he saw her wave her hand, and what she was holding finally captured his focus.

He reached for the plastic square—or probably, he lunged for it, so desperate he was to be inside her at this point—but she danced back, holding it out of reach. "Uh-uh," she said, wickedness creeping into her expression. She stepped forward again, pushed him back onto the mattress. "She who brings the condom gets to ride the prize."

"Heidi."

"No arguments."

He snagged a hand around her waist, yanked the condom out of her grip, and tore it open with his teeth. A second later, it was on his cock and he was lying back, tugging her over him, coaxing her down onto the hard length of him.

"I don't care if you're on top," he said, breaths coming in

short, staccato bursts. "So long as I'm inside—*ah . . .*" Holy fuck, that was good, the hot, tight sheath of her slipping down over him. ". . . you."

She bottomed out, and they both groaned in satisfaction, in relief, in . . . coming home.

Then she began to move. With slow, deliberate strokes that told him she hadn't forgotten their night together, that she'd remembered everything that had sent his blood boiling, his pleasure skyrocketing. His eyes rolled back, hips jerking up to meet her movements, and the tiny semblance of control he managed to keep hold of poofed away.

Gone. Disappeared to God knew where.

He forgot his own name.

He forgot to breathe.

He forgot to do anything but catapult toward the edge of oblivion, doing everything in his power to bring this woman along with him as she rode him hard and fast, bringing his release forward far too quickly. He knew he wouldn't last long, knew he needed to get her there. She bucked against his thumb when he circled her clit, her thighs clenching tightly around him, her moans faltering and then breaking long and loud when he lurched up to suck a nipple deep.

But then her moans changed.

And she got close.

And then she was over.

Thank fuck.

Because then he was there, too.

And just like before, he knew he'd never be the same.

But *unlike* before, this time he didn't run.

He slept like a baby, holding the woman he loved in his arms, knowing that everything in his life would finally work out.

Only when he woke in the morning, it was to find that he might not have run.

But Heidi had.

TWENTY

HEIDI

S he'd closed her car door and rolled her shoulders, her brain absolute mush, but her heart completely full.

A night in Brad's arms.

A delicious orgasm, followed by a pair when he'd woken her in the middle of the night with fingers between her thighs and an urgent whisper of, "Please, tell me you have another condom."

In fact, she'd *had* another.

And the results had been . . . explosive.

So, when she'd gotten the call from Stef, asking if she might possibly have time to bring her computer to the hospital, she'd gone to her friend's apartment, gathered anything and everything Stef might need, including the laptop. She'd also inquired about Fred, the misbehaving pooch—who it turned out was safe in the care of Stef's dog sitter—and tried unsuccessfully to avoid the topic of Brad.

Not because she wanted to hide things.

Quite the opposite, actually. She was practically bubbling with joy and excitement and affection for the man.

But she wanted Brad to be *just* hers for a little while longer.

Then she'd do the adult thing and share.

Luckily, Stef's doctor had come in before the interrogation had gotten too intense, but Heidi knew it wouldn't be long before she got the fifth degree from multiple angles. Hell, Stef would probably join forces with Cora, Kate, and Kelsey and then it would be four against one.

And if she were being completely truthful, she *couldn't* wait to share her happiness with her friends.

She'd hoped to go back to Brad's afterward, to knock on his door—since he hadn't had a set of hooks in his apartment with a labeled spare for her to pilfer, like she had at her place—but then she'd gotten pulled into the lab to double-check the calibrations so the assistant staff could be confident running everything.

That was supposed to have been a short visit—her goal of getting back to Brad still within reach.

But after she'd checked the equipment, made sure everything was ready to roll without her, she had run into the head of operations.

And then she'd become mean boss.

Or mean underling, she supposed, since she didn't outrank him, though her lab was run outside of the normal management channels. Either way, she'd read him the riot act—professionally, of course—and by then the CEO had gotten word of what had nearly happened, and she ended up on a call with those two and the heads of the Health and Human Services and Occupational Health . . . and well, she didn't want to get the cleaning staff in trouble, per se. They worked hard, but the team needed to find out if it was a lack of training that had caused the crew to be where they shouldn't, or if it was because they were disregarding the protocols.

The details of how they sorted that out weren't important—and not part of her job, suffice to say—but Heidi was very confident there wouldn't be another issue.

Especially because as she'd left, she'd seen the keypad lock being installed on the door.

It would go into operation tomorrow, and *she* would be setting the codes.

Not quite a lock and key, but she'd take this version.

But now it was late in the afternoon, and she was back at her place after having stopped by to make sure Stef was good, but Heidi hadn't stayed long at the hospital. She was tired from her early morning and from lack of sleep the night before—though she couldn't complain about the cause of the latter—and all she wanted to do was change into some jammies and then call Brad.

Maybe she could convince him to bring pizza again.

"You just going to stand there all day?"

She jumped, whirled around, her elbow colliding with the car window, making her wince and rub the abused joint.

"Stop doing *that*," she hissed at Brad, who was closing the distance between them with a decidedly stormy expression, one that tempered the burst of excitement she'd felt at hearing his voice, at seeing him.

"At least you weren't near a hill you could fall down this time."

He stopped in front of her, crossed his arms.

"What?" she asked.

He just lifted a brow.

"*What?*" she asked again.

"You pulled a runner?" he asked. "Really?" He shifted closer, placing his hands on either side of her, boxing her in against her car, the spicy maleness of him wafting over her, the hard, hot lines of his body pressed to hers, causing her to need a minute to process his words. Which is probably why he continued talking. "You can run, Heidi. You can run from us, from me. You can put that armor back on, but I'm not letting you go. I'm not giving you up—not when what we have is so fucking—"

She was confused and tired, and her feet hurt from being on them for most of the day.

She wanted those jammies and that pizza . . . and this man.

Which was why she placed her fingers over his mouth and asked, "What the fuck are you talking about?" Of course, then she didn't give him a chance to answer, not when the first part of his words processed, and she'd finally comprehended what he'd said. "What the hell do you mean, I pulled a runner?" she snapped. "I came here and put on adult clothes, visited Stef in the hospital, was pulled into work, and then went back to see Stef, and now I came home to shower." She glared. "After which I was going to put on pajamas and see if I could convince you to bring me *pizza!*" She jabbed a finger into his chest. "How is that pulling a runner? How is that—"

"You left," he said, eyes hot with anger, body still pressed to hers, a growing situation against her abdomen, making her lose the threads on her outburst. "And you didn't pick up your phone." His fingers tangled in her hair. "And you weren't here. Weren't on the trail. I even called Jaime to see if Kate had heard from you because . . ."

"You'd thought I'd left," she finished.

He nodded, brows drawn together.

Any irritation she'd been feeling from his demeanor faded. Because she knew what that felt like, and further that, she knew what he'd revealed last night might not have seemed like a giant bombshell to her, but that it had been big to him, something that had eaten at him for a while.

Then to wake up and find her not there.

"Did you not see the note I left you?"

She'd tacked it right to the center of his mirror, thinking he wouldn't miss it, would stumble upon it first thing when he got up and . . . well, used the facilities.

His lips parted on an exhale.

"You didn't," she confirmed.

He shook his head, his expression drawn, his eyes downcast.

"Oh honey," she murmured, pushing lightly at his chest, coaxing him back a step, heart squeezing. "I told you last night, I'm not going anywhere." She took his hand, straightened her purse on her shoulder. "Come on. Let's go inside." Once they'd made it through the door, she asked, "Why didn't you call me?"

He turned and shut the wooden panel, flipping the lock. "I told you earlier," he said, though his tone was without rancor. "I did, but you didn't pick up."

Frowning, she slipped off her shoes, tucked them neatly on the rack, then hung her purse on its hook, reaching inside for her phone. "Oh." She winced. She'd turned it off when she went into the lab . . .

And hadn't turned it on.

Warm fingers covered hers, snagging her cell, and then Brad glanced down at the screen.

His eyes rose to hers, hazel irises darkened with frustration. "Seriously?"

She winced again. "It's not like I *try* to forget . . ."

A sigh lifted his shoulders, sending them south on the exhale, his chin tipping back, gaze going up to the ceiling.

"Plus, no one besides my mom ever really calls me. They always text, and then when I get a moment to check, I catch up." Her own shoulders were inching up toward her ears, defensiveness and guilt warring within her. It really was a bad habit—not to have it off at work—but to be unavailable because she'd forgotten to turn her cell on at other times. This wasn't even the first time that she'd heard this same complaint.

But her friends got it, and she normally wasn't sad to miss a call from her mother, listing all of her inadequacies when it came to being a proper woman who could provide her grandchildren.

Plus, her friends all had the direct line to her lab, so they could get her that way if it was an emergency. Or sometimes they emailed, reminding her to check her messages. But Brad hadn't had any of those options . . . because she hadn't given them to him.

Shit.

"I'm sorry," she said, turning and taking the phone from him—which he'd powered up—and setting it on the cradle she had on the table to charge. Already the screen was filling with missed calls, voicemails, and text banners. Yet another wince. "Really, I'll get better, and . . ."

She gave him her other info—her work email and number, even the information for the front desk, in case it was an emergency and he couldn't get her the other ways.

Dutifully, he typed in the numbers and saved her email to his contacts.

But though the edginess in his expression had eased . . . he still wasn't his normal smiling self, and another bolt of guilt shot through her. She'd dampened the comfortable rapport they'd built, made him worry while she'd spent the day in peaceful happiness.

And now her normally sweet, teasing, lovely man was . . . diminished, shadows beneath his eyes, lines edging his lush, kissable mouth.

"I really am sorry," she whispered.

He closed his eyes, inhaled and exhaled slowly. "It's not—" He shook his head. "It's not your fault, sweetheart. I just . . . it—"

She did what she would have wanted.

She stepped into his arms and hugged him tightly.

He wrapped his arms around her in return, burying his face in her hair and breathed in deeply, just holding her for a long, long time. Eventually, he loosened his hold, stepping back and cupping her cheek. "I'm okay now," he murmured. "Sorry, I freaked out."

"Don't apologize. I'm the one who's—"

"Don't apologize," he said, taking a page out of her book, smiling down at her.

"Did we just have our first real fight?" she asked.

"No," he said, cupping her jaw. "That was when you told me I wasn't washing the dishes correctly."

She frowned, felt her brows draw together. "When was that?"

"One night, last week."

"*Which* night?"

Now she caught a glimmer of humor in his eyes, felt that last little bit of guilt settle and drift away.

"Not telling you, if you don't remember." A smirk that made her want to kiss him.

Well, she could do that.

So she did, lifting up on tiptoe and pressing her mouth to his. His lips parted immediately, and she dipped inside, loving that she could hold and touch and kiss this man. That he'd somehow become hers, that she'd likewise become his.

"You're impossible, you know that?" she asked when they pulled apart for air.

"I'm *something*," he said, wrapping his hands around her hips and tugging her against him, against his hard cock, his lips finding hers.

"Did you buy condoms?" she asked, tearing her lips from his to suck in air.

He gave her that slow, wicked smirk. "What do you think?"

"I *think* that you're a man who's always prepared."

Hoisting her up, his mouth dropping to her neck, his tongue flicking out to taste the sensitive spot, he spoke against her skin. "That's the correct answer."

She laughed, tugged his head back up, and stole his lips in a searing kiss that left her heart pounding, her lungs burning for air. Then she nodded toward the bedroom. "Turns out I'm a little tired," she said. "Maybe you can show me the proper way to use my mattress?"

"Is that a thing?" he asked, already moving in that direction.

She dug her nails into his shoulders when he nipped at her earlobe, sending heat scorching through her body. Rotating her head, she did some nipping of her own. "If it gets you inside me sooner, then, yes, it is."

His eyes seared into hers, and she found herself on the bed a heartbeat later.

And it turned out, he *could* show her the proper way to use her mattress.

Twice.

Twenty-One

BRAD

He stared at the woman who'd stolen his heart and smiled.

She was too fucking cute, her hair pulled back into a high ponytail, tight jeans encasing the sexy legs he'd spent a copious amount of time in between this last month. Her color was high from her exertion on the trail, but she hadn't once complained that he'd hauled her out of bed on a Saturday morning before sunrise and had driven her out to this regional park.

That had probably been helped by the hot coffee and two huge banana chocolate chip muffins he'd used to coax her out from beneath the covers.

Luckily for him, she was a morning person, and though she'd grumbled and groaned a little bit, she'd quickly gotten into the spirit of the adventure.

Now, they'd reached the precipice of that sharp incline and could see the view he'd known would be spectacular, but that was made even more so by Heidi being next to him.

She sank down onto a bench, and he plunked down next to her, warning, "I'm all sweaty," when she cuddled up next to him.

"Well, I am, too," she said, wrapping an arm around his waist and snuggling her head into his chest. "Two sweaties make a right."

He laughed, but then the sun made it fully over the horizon behind them, its rays flying forward to glimmer over the ocean in front of them, making the moisture in the air sparkle like golden smoke, or maybe like some sort of otherworldly magical power. Lifting his camera, he took several shots of the gorgeous display. But then his focus—and the camera lens—drew back down, and he took pictures of Heidi.

Who, once she realized what he was doing, blushed and hid her face in his chest. "Close-up, much?" she said against his T-shirt.

He laughed but set the camera aside, cupping the side of her face and turning it up so he could kiss her. "Only way to capture those beautiful eyes of yours."

She made a face.

He kissed her.

But eventually, they needed air and broke apart, sitting on that bench, on a precipice high above civilization, looking out at the Pacific Ocean, and watching the sky brighten as the sun rose behind them.

He'd traveled the globe, visited all seven continents, stayed in tiny villages and big cities, and never had he felt more certain that he was in the right place.

Because the right person was next to him.

————

Later that day, after they'd taken a much-deserved nap, they made plans to binge another of Heidi's bad reality TV shows—and he wouldn't admit this to anyone, but he'd actually begun to like them . . . okay, *some* of them. But what he really liked was her reactions to them.

The gasps of outrage.

The anger for one of the cast being wronged—which usually came in the form of a broken heart.

The occasional tear when something sweet happened.

But just as they had pulled out their phones to figure out what to order in for dinner, there was a knock at the door.

Heidi frowned.

"I've got it," he told her, shifting her feet from his lap and standing up.

"It's probably someone trying to sell me solar panels," she grumbled.

"Well, I'll tell them to take a hike," he said, opening the door.

"That hike isn't happening, bro," his brother said, towering over a trio of women. He laughed, probably at the confusion on Brad's face when that trio pushed the door open, barreled past him with nary a look, and sandwiched themselves around Heidi on the couch.

"I haven't seen this episode," Kate said, grabbing the bowl of popcorn he'd made—and for the record, had only gotten to eat one handful of. "Start it over."

"Come on."

Brad blinked at Jaime's voice, blinked again when a jacket was shoved into his chest, followed by his wallet, keys, and phone —all of which had been given a proper home on Heidi's organization station by the door.

"Let's go."

"Go where?" he asked as Jaime threw his arm around his shoulders.

"Whatever you were planning with Heidi ain't happening." He coaxed Brad out the door. "So, let's go grab a beer and some wings."

"I—" He shook his head. "What?"

Jaime sighed and started hauling Brad down the porch.

"Wait—" He ducked out from beneath his brother's arm, hopped up the stairs, and locked the door. Then turned back around to see Jaime studying him. "What?"

His brother just smiled and shook his head. "Let's go get that beer."

———

"Okay," Jaime said when they were seated at a bar with a scarred wooden top, their stools slanted so they could watch the latest Gold Hockey game.

"Okay, what?"

"Tell me *all* about it."

He took a sip of his beer. "About what?" he asked, playing dumb.

Jaime rolled his eyes. "Nice try. But we've been back a week, and Kate has been beside herself with curiosity. You need to give me the goods or my new wife will leave me."

Brad snorted. "Then she'd have to find someone to take care of the cock."

His brother froze, slowly set down his beer. "Dude."

"Heidi would have laughed," he muttered, glugging down his own, since Jaime had driven them to the bar.

"Heidi is actually why we're in this mess."

He glared. "Don't say anything bad about her. She's great."

Jaime raised his hands in surrender. "I would never do that. She *is* great, and she's one of Kate's best friends, but . . ." He trailed off, like Brad would fill in the blanks.

And he supposed he would.

Because he knew exactly what his brother was thinking.

When would he be leaving again?

Reaching across, he grabbed Jaime's forearm, squeezing it

tightly—not because he wanted to hurt his brother, but because he needed him to understand. "She's it."

Jaime nodded, but concern was still laced throughout his expression, and Brad knew he didn't get it.

"She's my Kate," he said. "You know all that shit with Mom, with that grain of sand itching beneath the surface, the prickle of irritation that never seemed to go away?"

Jaime nodded when he paused.

"To keep with the metaphor, Heidi is that pearl."

Brad waited . . . and then waited some more for his brother to say something, to congratulate him on finding the other half of his soul, but Jaime just quietly stared at him.

"You're wondering if I'm just going to fucking disappear again, aren't you?" He pulled his hand back, clenched his jaw tight. "Well, I'm not. I've been all over this fucking world, and I can say with absolute certainty that none of that means anything without a person to share it with."

"So, does that mean you're done traveling, that you're just going to live here permanently?"

"Yes." He sighed when he saw his brother still didn't get it. And who could blame him?

Brad had taken a sharp right turn.

Hesitation in his brother's gaze, and fuck that stung. "I don't think you would hurt her intentionally," Jaime began. "But I wonder . . . if you're not moving kind of quickly. You're used to being free and moving to your own beat all the time." He lifted his hands, palms out in surrender. "I'm not saying that's a bad thing, not at all. I just . . . I know that Heidi is married to her job here, and she has deep roots in this area. She grew up here. Cora, Kelsey, and Kate are here. I'm sure she'd be happy to travel—I've never seen that woman back down from an adventure or a challenge, but I don't think that she'd be happy to uproot her life all the time." He winced. "And frankly, I don't think her job will allow for it."

None of these were things Brad didn't know.

But none of these things made that old prickling to run, to leave, to hide beneath the prospect of leaving, come back.

Instead, he just felt certain.

That he'd be putting down his roots where Heidi was.

"Look, Jaim, I know what you're saying." He sighed. "But the truth is that for the first time in my life, I don't have another trip planned. Usually, when I'm still in the middle of one set of travels, I'm already searching for the next place to visit, chasing that high of something new, something that could mute the itch that tells me to keep moving, to keep searching, to never stop looking." He clenched his hand into a fist, rested it on his thigh. "This is different. I *feel* different."

"How?"

"When I first met Heidi, it was like everything inside me both stood up at attention and settled down. I knew that she was special, but I was fucking terrified after spending time with her. I knew that given the chance, she'd burrow herself deep inside my soul, and not because she was trying to, but because she *didn't have to*." A shake of his head. "She was just herself, and I knew that she was more than anyone I had ever met. She's fucking incredible, and she was in me deep in an instant . . . and I was so unnerved that I ran in the other direction."

Jaime was quiet for a moment then asked, "What changed now?"

He stopped, considered how he could possibly encapsulate how *much* had changed.

Because *everything* had changed.

"Jaime," he began. "There's . . ." Then stalled out.

"Hey." His brother grabbed his shoulder, squeezing it lightly until Brad looked up from counting the bubbles in the froth of his beer. "The girls are together and watching reality TV. They've got a bottle of tequila for margaritas, books to discuss, and two members of their Un-Wine Club to interrogate—

Heidi, because of you, and Kate, about our honeymoon." He picked up Brad's beer and handed it to him before snagging his own and *clinking* the glasses together. "What I'm trying to say is that we have plenty of time to hash out all this shit." He took a sip. "It'll be a good four hours before I get the call to go play designated driver."

Brad traced a pattern in the condensation on the outside of his glass.

"I know it seems like I'm being an asshole," Jaime said, "and it's not that I don't believe what you're saying. I'm just—I don't want either of you hurt, and I don't want you to have gotten things straight in your head and then limit yourself and—*fuck*, now I sound like an extra-large asshole." He thumped his hand on the bar. "Ignore me. I'm playing the role of the worried older brother. You're great. Heidi is great. You both deserve to be happy, regardless of my big brother vibes."

"Jaim," he said and stopped, not sure what to say, not when his mind was spinning.

"Fuck," Jaime said, probably catching a glimpse of that whirlwind. He shoved a hand into his hair. "*For real.* Ignore me. I don't have any right to question you or Heidi's decisions. You know that my relationship with Kate all began with a lie. We pretended to be engaged, for fuck's sake, so how could I possibly think that I can give anyone any advice on relationships?"

Brad's shoulders relaxed, the tension in his gut brought on by his brother's questions easing with the sincerity in his tone.

"If Heidi is *your* Kate, then I'm so fucking happy for you." Jaime laughed. "Because God knows these women give us a hell of a ride. But it's absolutely worth it, and I thank *fuck* every single day that I answered that DM, that I somehow managed to get Kate in my life."

"And now she's tied to you permanently," he said.

Jaime nodded, happiness etched into the lines of his face. "Yup. She's mine forever."

A fact that made Brad very jealous.

He wanted Heidi in his life always. He wanted her to wear his ring, to carry his babies, to be tied to him forever.

Jaime chuckled. "Until she realizes that I did a shit job of collecting her gossip."

That made him smile and shake his head. "We'd do anything for them, wouldn't we?"

Jaime clinked their glasses again. "Yes, we would."

And with that, he took another sip, then a deep breath, and he told his brother everything—how his last trip had opened that lid and made him understand he wasn't happy, how coming back and realizing he'd hurt Heidi had made him feel like the lowest piece of shit on the planet, how Jaime telling him what their mom had said had made everything clear, how Heidi deciding to give him a chance had made everything seem possible, and how this last month had been the absolute best of his life.

He confessed every last thing in his heart and mind.

Because his brother *was* that older, constantly worrying sibling.

Because he wanted to tell someone who would understand, someone who got just how important this all was.

And because . . . he didn't want his brother to get in trouble with his wife.

Heh.

TWENTY-TWO

"I'm inviting my friend, Stef, to join us on our next girl's night," she declared, the moment the door had shut behind the boys.

There was a strategy with these . . . playdates, she supposed was the correct word. But the point was, the person with all the gossip couldn't just give it up right away, she had to make the others work for it—

No. That wasn't true.

She wanted to share every detail with them.

Just first, she had the more pressing business of making sure Stef was included.

Cora sat back, snagging the bowl of popcorn from Kate's hands and scarfing down a huge handful. "Isn't she your assistant at work?"

"She's my lab assistant," Heidi told her. "Not answering my emails and taking notes during meetings. She runs the lab when I'm not there, and she just broke up with her boyfriend—who got her friends in the divorce, by the way, the fucking assholes—and she doesn't have any family close."

They all made sympathetic noises, lamenting about fair-weather friends, and she knew that Stef would be welcomed into the fold of the Un-Wine Club.

Kelsey grabbed Heidi's cell from the table, held it out to her. "Why don't you call her and invite her over?"

"Well, because her relationship isn't the only thing broken." Then she related the tale of Stef's dog and the broken ankle and the surgery. "She's been home for a bit now, but she's not up for traveling much yet."

"Oh my God," Kelsey said. "Poor thing."

Kate lifted her glass, already filled with a slushie margarita, courtesy of Cora having commandeered Heidi's blender and getting busy with the tequila, and took a huge sip. "Next time, we bring the party to her."

Cora nodded. "Totally agree. She won't know what hit her."

Kels grinned. "Exactly. We're like the mafia. Once you're in, there's no getting out."

Heidi relaxed, knowing that Stef would be right at home with her crew.

"What does she nerd out about?"

"You know," she said slowly. "I don't actually know."

Kate rubbed her hands together, evil-genius style. "We'll ply her with tequila and find out all of the deep and dirty secrets. Muahaha!"

"You're still high from your honeymoon," Cora said, shoving Kate's shoulder.

"Maybe." Kate shrugged, a smug smile on her lips. "Maybe not."

They laughed, and then Kelsey asked about the resort, and Kate was off and running, talking about all the fun things she and Jaime had done—from parasailing to massages on the beach, they seemed to have hit all that the hotel had to offer.

"But mostly," Kate said. "Mostly we had lots and lots of hot, monkey sex"—she reclined back on the couch—"and it was *glorious.*"

They all made the appropriate sounds of retching and, "Oh God, my ears!"

But they were happy for Kate, happy that their friend had found the person she was supposed to spend the rest of her life with.

And then their eyes turned to her.

"What?" she asked innocently, taking a long sip of her drink.

Which Cora promptly snatched from her, making her nearly choke on the slush she'd managed to get in her mouth.

"Details." Kate bounced on the cushions next to her, cheeks highlighted pink from the power of tequila. "Now."

Heidi thought about drawing it out, about torturing her friends, getting them to beg for details. But in the end, she couldn't, and she didn't want to, and hell, she was fighting back the urge to yell from the rooftops that she loved one Brad Huntington.

Loved?

She froze, words screeching to a halt inside her throat.

Because loved?

A blip as her heart began beating again, as surety slid through her.

Yes. *Loved.*

She loved Brad.

And she was so fucking excited about it.

So she told her friends about falling in the creek, and the dinners and the dates, she told them about coffee and muffins and pre-dawn hikes. She told them about books and keys and a man who cared where she was.

But the *only* thing she didn't tell them was about the whole loving thing.

Because she was going to tell that to Brad first.

———

"Margaritas are the best," she said, curling up on the couch and resting her head on Kate's shoulder.

Kate tapped her glass against Heidi's. "I totally agree."

"Shh!" Cora hissed. "This is the best part!"

Dutifully, they both turned their gazes toward the TV, toward the knockdown, drag-out fight happening on the screen, then to their friend who was riveted by the action.

"You wouldn't be shushing us if you hadn't cheated and watched ahead," Heidi muttered grumpily.

"If I hadn't cheated and watched ahead, you would be missing this gloriousness right now," Cora pointed out.

Rightly so.

Which was why Heidi didn't argue, just put her glass to her lips and enjoyed the rest of her fourth margarita . . . or maybe it was her fifth? Lightweight that she was, she couldn't remember anything after the second. Mentally shrugging, she decided she didn't care. She could kick her friends to the curb, collapse into bed, and sleep until noon tomorrow if she wanted.

A table overturned on screen, sending an arrangement of cupcakes flying in all directions—and making her wince in memory of Kate's ruined wedding cake—but then she couldn't help but giggle.

Because the show's stars had decided to attempt to save the remaining stack that was teetering this way and that. Unfortunately for them, that teetering ended up turning into splatting when two of the cast slipped on fluorescent blue frosting and managed to knock the remainder of the sweet confections to the ground.

"You should take lessons from them," Kelsey said, her color high, the words carefully enunciated in a way that told Heidi she'd had more than three margaritas, too.

"Why?" she asked innocently. "It's not like there are any weddings coming up for me to ruin."

Kelsey took a sip. "Well, actually. Tanner and I did a thing."

She held up her hand.

Heidi squinted through blurry vision, blinking until it focused . . . on the sparkling diamond band sitting next to the engagement ring on Kelsey's finger.

Kate, the only one of them who had any skill in holding her alcohol, lurched up from the couch, nearly spilling the remnants of her margarita as she plunked the glass on the table and clambered over Cora's legs to grab Kels's hand.

"Are you fucking serious?" Cora asked, but it wasn't directed at Kate and her clambering.

Rather, it was said to Kels.

Who they all waited with baited breath to answer.

Who . . . nodded, her lips curving into a huge smile. "We eloped," she said. "We just . . . wanted to be married without all the hoopla." She nibbled on her bottom lip. "I was hoping you guys might be able to help us plan a big party to celebrate."

Heidi looked at Kate, who looked at Cora.

Then they all moved at once.

"Oh my God!" They all jumped up, throwing their arms around each other, a tequila-scented hug surrounding them all, their voices overlapping, the chatter indecipherable except that it was filled with excitement.

"When did you guys do it?" Kate asked once they'd managed to calm themselves enough to conduct actual adult conversation again.

"Last weekend. We just woke up on Saturday morning and decided to fly to Vegas," Kels said, dutifully holding out her hand so they could admire the ring and then told them the rest of the story—how her family was pressuring her for a wedding (preferably a big one since Kels was the only daughter), how the wedding planning was stressing them out, and how they'd ultimately just decided to fly to Vegas and become husband and wife in truth. "I did promise my mom a big party," she said. "After we got home."

"Kels," Heidi whispered, hugging her tight. "I'm so happy for you."

Cora nudged her out of the way. "I need to hug the bride."

"Or the former one anyway. Now I'm just the wife," Kels said, her smile huge as she wrapped her arms about the petite brunette for a few moments before they all circled up, drinks in hand, and toasted Kels.

"Thank you, guys, but actually I feel terrible," she told them, setting her glass down then lifting her hands to her cheeks and pressing them against the flushed skin. "I think my mom is really disappointed."

Cora grinned. "She'll have a big party to plan. She'll be fine."

"You deserve to have what you want," Kate reminded her. "You didn't want a huge wedding with you at the center of it. You wanted your special moment with Tanner."

"You're not mad I didn't invite you guys?"

Heidi smoothed back her hair. "No, babe. We're happy that you're happy."

"You sure?"

Cora snorted and refilled her glass. "We're sure." A beat. "Just keep the cake far away from Heidi."

"Hey!"

Kels sank back down onto the couch, picking up her glass again and drinking deeply, her eyes still tinged with chagrin. "Even my mom and you guys aside, and the requisite guilt, it was still the happiest moment of my life." A sigh. "I love him so much, guys."

"Why am I sensing a but?"

Kels made a face. "Well, he had somehow taken the time to write these beautiful, touching vows, words that made my heart squeeze and my tears coming into my eyes and he'd probably been planning them for months, and I didn't even have anything besides the normal ones, and I kept thinking I should have done more."

Cora snorted. "Kels. Seriously?"

"What?" She tossed up her hands, nearly spilling her drink.

"He was just probably relieved he didn't have to keep waiting forever to marry you," Kate said. "Jaime told me that was the worst part of getting engaged . . . well, our real engagement anyway. That there was so much waiting until our real lives could start—not that we didn't have something real together before the wedding. It was just like there was a hidden hurdle ahead that we needed to leap over, and it didn't matter what flowers we had or the cake or the vows, we were just ready to start our happily ever after." She squeezed Kels's hand. "This is the important part. The rest of it is just . . . calorie-adding condiments to the happy sandwich of your lives."

Cora burst out laughing.

"What?" Kate asked on a scowl.

"Condiments?" Cora asked. "Really? What's the wedding? Mayonnaise?"

"Ew," Kate said. "No, it's fig jelly on a yummy toasted sourdough."

"What about apricot . . ."

Ignoring them waxing poetic about jam, Heidi gave Kels a squeeze. "I promise the vows aren't even registering in Tanner's brain at all."

"Even though mine were really freaking lame?"

"Even though."

Except . . . it wasn't Heidi replying.

They jumped, their gazes all shot to the door, noticing the three men standing in the hall, Brad closing the door behind them. Tanner, who'd been on a night shoot earlier and who also looked gorgeously rumpled, moved forward, closing the distance between him and Kels and pulling her into his arms. His lips went to her ear, and Heidi deliberately looked away after she heard, "I don't care, sweetheart. I just am so happy to be married to you, and I want to make babies and—"

Cora glared at Kate's hubby, talking over the lovey-dovey couple. "How long have you been there?"

"Since the squeeing," Jaime said dryly, slipping past her to kiss Kate soundly on her lips. "Thank God, Heidi has thick walls," he added when they'd broken apart for air. "Or else the neighbors would be complaining."

"I'll have you know," Heidi told him, though her eyes were on Brad, her gaze invariably drawn to his. "That I had the sheetrock sound-proofed for precisely that reason." She nibbled the inside of her mouth, stare dipping down to trace the yummi-ness that was the man who'd stolen her heart.

He was slender and muscled, the scruff on his jaw making her shiver in memory of how it had felt against her skin, her breasts, her thighs. But it was his eyes that truly drew her in. Because he looked at her just like Jaime looked at Kate, Tanner at Kels. With warmth and love and affection, and his own special brand of lighthearted Brad teasing.

One that made her smile, even now.

"Hi," he mouthed.

"Hi," she mouthed back.

His lips twitched.

Her heart thudded. The man was just wearing jeans, a T-shirt, socks, but he was still the most beautiful thing she had ever laid eyes on. Or maybe that was the way he made her feel.

Her gaze dropped down to his feet. To the socked feet.

Socked because he'd put his shoes on the rack.

Without a word from her, he'd noticed that she'd cleared a spot for him on the holder, and she hadn't even needed to mention it before he put his shoes there. He'd just paid attention and accepted that she liked things to be put in their proper spot. And he'd done it without comment.

And that, combined with the excitement of Kelsey, of her early morning with him, of the last few weeks and all his wonderfulness . . . and also maybe the margaritas—five, it was definitely *five*—had her blurting, "I love you!"

His eyes widened.

But she was more aware of the room going silent.

It *had* been filled with chatter, Cora, Kate, and Kels talking with Jaime and Tanner, but her blurt—okay, her yelled-out declaration—had the room going quiet, had five pairs of eyes coming to her. Well, six if she counted Brad, whose pretty hazel eyes were heavy with an emotion she couldn't read from this far away.

Then he was moving toward her.

More than moving toward her. One moment he was across the room, and the next he was *there*, one arm wrapping tightly around her hips and tugging her against his chest, the other moving higher, until his fingers slid in her hair, weaving into the strands and gently tilting her head back. "What did you say?" he whispered.

Kate's voice penetrated the Brad-fog descending around her. "We'll just go—"

"No," Cora said. "We're staying and—*ouch! Kels, let go!*"

And that was the last she heard of her friends—at least of any words being spoken, because obliquely, she processed them gathering their things, of footsteps moving toward the door, of that panel *clicking* closed behind them.

Then her condo was empty of everyone except her and Brad.

Who was stroking tiny circles on her scalp, making prickles of sensation trail down her spine, her arms.

"You love me?" he asked.

Her cheeks went hot—and not from the margaritas this time. The tequila was wearing off, and she was feeling exceptionally vulnerable, especially since. He. Hadn't. Said. It. Back.

"Brad," she whispered. "You . . . um—" She shook her head, dislodging his fingers, starting to pull away.

His arm around her waist tightened. "You love me?" he repeated.

"I—"

Not. A. Coward.

She lifted her chin. "Yes."

Joy in those hazel eyes, and then his mouth was on hers. He kissed her with an intensity that immediately had her pulse skittering, her heart squeezing tight.

Then just as abruptly pulled back.

"Wait," he said, breath coming in rapid gusts. "Are you too drunk to consent to this?"

"Too"—she blinked—"um . . . what?"

"Baby." He smoothed back her hair. "Jaime said you were drinking. Are you too drunk to—"

Her heart exploded.

Well, not literally, of course, but for a moment she was frozen in place, unable to believe that she could feel this much for another person. The only caveat, the single thing that crept into that joy, that weighed down her happiness, was that he hadn't said it back. Maybe it was too soon . . . or maybe it was too much.

Her gut clenched. That bliss was tempered by old insecurities.

Maybe she was destined to be a woman—like her mother had always said—who would end up alone without a person to love her for who she was inside. Maybe she worked too much, was too difficult.

Hell, maybe he'd come across her *Twilight* collection and had decided that was just a step too far.

Which would certainly put a damper on her feelings for this man.

"I'm not too drunk," she whispered, tugging at his arm, now feeling sick instead of joyful.

"You sure?"

She nodded, her gaze fixed on a spot over his shoulder when he didn't release her.

"What's the matter?"

He was honestly asking her what was the matter? She'd blurted out a huge freaking revelation in front of almost everyone who was important to her, and he had hardly acknowledged she'd told him she loved him, aside from confirming she'd said it in the first place.

Her eyes narrowed, and she opened her mouth.

Then froze when she realized he was slowly and inexorably leading her toward—

"Will you *stop* pushing me around?" she muttered, yanking at his arm.

"No," he said.

And then he spun her around.

"What—"

He pointed to a piece of paper in the middle of her command center, neatly written and held in place by four purple magnets, one on each corner.

Her jaw fell open.

"Is *that* what's the matter?" he whispered into her ear, making her shiver, making her melt back against him.

Because that note, written in sure, firm strokes, said, "I love you."

"How long has that been there?" she asked.

He turned her in his arms, cupped her cheek. "Since last night."

A shuddering breath. "Really?"

He nodded.

"You love me?"

Another nod.

"Really?"

His lips quirked up. "Really, really."

"Are you sure?"

Annoyance had those lips pressing flat, his eyes going serious. "Heidi," he warned.

She nibbled at the corner of her mouth. "It's just that you haven't said it." She nodded at the note. "I mean, writing it isn't the same as saying it, is it?"

He growled, swept her up in his arms. "I love you, Heidi Greene. I love you so much that it feels like my heart will explode with happiness when I'm with you." He kissed her briefly, but intensely enough to have her pulse ratcheting up. Then he broke away, his expression gentle. "I love you with every bit of my soul, and I'll love you until that soul is no longer in my body." His forehead dropped to hers. "I never thought it was possible to feel this way for another person—"

She laughed.

He frowned. "What is it?"

Lifting her arms, she wrapped them around his neck. "It's only that I was just thinking the same. I don't know how you did it, honey, but somehow what I feel for you is more than I ever could have imagined." She slid a hand to his chest, placed it over his pounding heart. "And this . . . *mine* . . . it beats for you."

He went still. "Heidi."

"What?"

"Fuck, I love you."

She smiled, lifted up so her lips were just a hairsbreadth from his. "Guess what?"

Affection—no, love—so much fucking *love* in his eyes. "What?" he asked gently.

"I love you."

He grinned.

"Also"—closer now, so her lips brushed his with every word

she spoke—"the answer to your previous question of whether or not I'm sober enough to consent is . . . yes, baby, I am."

"Yeah?"

A nod. "What about you?"

He frowned.

"Are you sober enough to consent to *my* attentions?"

"What do you think?"

She blinked, realized he'd brought her to the bedroom, and then she smiled. "I think—*oof!*" He dropped her onto the mattress. "I think," she said again, gasping as he came on top of her, all of those glorious muscles pressing into her, "you'll do fine."

A wicked gleam in his eyes, his mouth coming down on top of hers.

And then he showed her just how fine he could be.

TWENTY-THREE

BRAD

He was just finishing up the last bit of design for the latest website when there was a knock on his apartment door.

His eyes flicked to the clock on his computer screen, saw it was past seven.

And blinked.

Because *shit*, it was past *seven*.

After quickly saving his work—a habit that had taken just one time of losing copious amounts of data to become engrained in him—he stood and hurried to the door.

Heidi was on the other side.

"Shit, Heid," he said. "Why didn't you call?"

"I *did* call." She smiled, lightly poked his chest. "But I think you pulled a me and turned off your phone."

Closing the door behind her after she'd come in, he went to the counter and picked up his cell. It was on. He'd just been so engrossed in what he was doing that he hadn't heard it go off. Grimacing, he set it back down. "I'm sorry, baby. I lost track of time." He snagged her hand, brought her close. "Let me grab my shoes, and then we can go meet your friends."

"*Our* friends."

He smiled at that then dropped a kiss to her forehead. "Not sure if my brother can be considered a friend when he tries to order me around all the time."

A well-placed nudge with her elbow. "That ordering gene must be engrained in the Huntington DNA because you're sure good at it."

He affected innocence. "I don't know what you're talking about."

She laughed, and just like every other time he saw her happy, he felt the jagged pieces settle inside him. He lived for that sound, for her joy, more than he'd ever thought possible. It had been a month since that night at her place, since she'd told him she loved him, and it had all been . . . bliss.

More hikes—though not predawn, per her request. They'd gone to dinner, to the movies. He'd convinced her to do another touristy thing and take a ride on a cable car—which they'd both enjoyed much more than Alcatraz, him especially so, since she'd gotten cold on that foggy morning and had cuddled close to him as the rattling streetcar went up and down the hilly streets of San Francisco. Last week, they'd driven down to Santa Cruz and visited some absolutely huge redwoods in the morning then had taken a very bumpy ride on an old wooden roller coaster in the afternoon. And just yesterday, Heidi had taken the day off from the lab, and they'd driven a few hours north to a tiny lighthouse perched above a beach filled with sea glass.

And in between, they'd spent almost every night together, with the odd girl's night thrown in. On those evenings, he'd hung with Jaime, with Tanner, and occasionally, with a few of Tanner's friends, Sebastian and Devon Scott. The brothers were cool guys, and the tech worker and former hockey player, respectively, had nicely rounded out the group when they'd brought

Max Montgomery along one night. The current skater for the Gold was married to another one of Heidi's friends, Angie.

It probably should have been overwhelming—that he'd gone from spending so much time by himself to constantly being with people. But instead of too much, every time he opened up, every time he accepted another person into his life, he felt . . . bigger.

No. More complete. Fulfilled.

Like he was finally fully part of the land of the living instead of alone.

And *that* was fucking incredible.

Even more incredible was that Heidi was just as happy as him. They'd gotten into the habit of mostly staying at her place —frankly, it was nicer, but beyond that, it was also closer to her lab *and* both highways on which they often began their journeys. He didn't mind. He loved her place, loved seeing how proud she was of the life she'd built for herself. So on the weekdays, he'd work until she got off then meet her there, and they'd cook dinner or order in. They'd spend the evening together, watching TV—yes, plenty of her reality shows, but he'd also managed to convince her to watch *Vikings*.

Which she liked for a completely different reason than he did, of course.

He was in for the battles, the politics, the suspense.

She liked all that . . . *and* the male lead.

Though, if he were being completely truthful, when she'd woven "Viking braids" into her hair a few days ago, he'd certainly been able to see the appeal. So much so that they'd spent a very pleasurable evening on the faux fur rug she had in front of her fireplace.

But more than just spending time together, no matter how pleasurable it was, he enjoyed finding all the different ways to take care of her. They could be small, from setting her coffee pot to brew so she'd have it first thing in the morning to taking her trash out, to filling up her car with gas when she'd mentioned it was getting low. Or they could be larger, more time-intensive, like when he'd spent the better part of an afternoon under her kitchen sink because the garbage disposal had gone out.

He understood now that these were all things he'd avoided like the plague when he'd spent the majority of his time traveling —the strings that would tie him more closely to another person, would make him vulnerable, would put him at risk of being hurt if they left or got sick or, God forbid, died.

But he didn't feel scared with Heidi.

Because she was in just as deep.

And because she took care of him in her own way.

He'd found throw pillows on his couch the other day. They were in a "manly" (her words, not his) shade of burgundy that went perfectly with the fuzzy blanket she'd gotten for the foot of his bed. She'd had lunch delivered to his place when she'd known he'd been working on a particularly large project with a deadline looming, had texted him a link for hidden places to visit in California with, "Maybe we can go together?" Then there were all the meals she'd cooked, finding out his favorite foods and incorporating them into the menu, stocking up on a certain brand of popcorn since it was his preferred variety, and how she'd cleared a drawer for him so he could leave some clothes at her place.

In two months' time, he'd gone from feeling unfulfilled and a little lost, to being . . . happy.

Such an inadequate word for all that was in his heart, but it was also the only one that mattered.

Because he was here and *happy*, and not searching for the next adventure that would bring him a slender thread of that elusive fulfillment for just a moment, before that buzz faded and then he was off again, searching for the next thing . . . and the next . . . and the next.

So, yeah, he'd take happy.

Hands down.

"I am sorry about not meeting you," he said, yanking himself out of his head and focusing on the important thing—that being this woman whom he loved to the edge of reason, who loved him back just as completely.

She kissed him lightly on the mouth. "Don't apologize." A wink. "I've been known to get lost in my work every once in a while. You'll just have to owe me." Another wink.

"Is there something in your eye?" he asked innocently.

But she was old hat at his humor by now, so she just reached up and squeezed his cheeks, affecting a baby voice. "Oh, cute little Braddie just thinks he's *so* funny."

"I *know* I'm funny."

"You know what'll be *really* funny?" she asked, dropping her arms and stepping out of the circle of his.

"What?"

"Me leaving you here in your apartment with a rumbling tummy while I go devour the most delicious Mexican food around."

Right on cue, his stomach growled.

"See?" she said, lifting a brow. "Hilarious."

"Not so much." He kissed her, long and sweet and with every bit of affection he possessed for her. "I love you," he murmured when they'd pulled back.

She blinked slightly glazed eyes, the hazel irises deepened to swirls of emerald and russet. Then her lips curved further. "I love you, too. But seriously, I will leave your ass here unless you get it in gear." She pointed toward his closet. "Shoes and jacket on, because it is Friday night, and it's past time for prickly pear margaritas."

"It's going to be a tequila night?"

He'd really enjoyed the last one.

Really enjoyed it.

In fact, he'd enjoyed it so much that his legs had been sore enough the following few days to make navigating curbs difficult. And steps. And lifting his foot enough to pull on his pants. And—

Well, it had been damned good.

"Yes, it's going to be a tequila night for me. For you"—she waggled her eyebrows—"only *if* you play your cards right." A beat. "Which means *go get your shoes on.*"

It was amazing how quickly people could get dressed when they were motivated.

———

Thankfully, the restaurant wasn't far from his apartment, and they managed to sneak into the table just as appetizers were being served.

He pilfered some chips from his brother's plate and hadn't bothered perusing the menu. Instead, he ordered what Heidi did when the server came around to get their meals put in.

Then he stole some more chips from Jaime.

"Hey!"

"Little brother perks," he said chipperly.

Jaime sighed but slid the nachos a little closer. "You're lucky this plate is huge."

"Is that what you said to get Kate to marry you?" he deadpanned.

Heidi giggled, attempting to cover said giggle with her napkin, then gave in, laughing loud enough for everyone at the table to look at her.

"Don't mind me," she said, waving a hand in front of her face, still laughing.

And fuck if that noise didn't fill him up, didn't make him feel like the biggest, baddest motherfucker on the planet. He should be swaggering around this restaurant, showing off his prowess—

Or maybe that should have happened after the last tequila night. Or maybe the Viking one. Or last night. Or—

Suffice to say, he didn't think he'd ever get tired of making love to this woman who'd so easily captured his heart.

"Stop smirking." Jaime socked him in the arm.

Hard.

"Ouch," he muttered, rubbing the injured limb. "What would Mom say?"

Jaime snagged his plate back, smacking Brad's hand when he went to take another chip. "Probably that you deserved it."

He shrugged since that was probably true.

"Speaking of Mom," Jaime said, still guarding his nachos. "They're driving up early. They'll actually be here tomorrow and want to do a family dinner with Kate's family." His eyes flicked past Brad, alighting on Heidi. "That includes you, too," he said, "just in case you'd try to get out of the power of the Moms."

Brad shuddered. His mom and Kate's mom together were a formidable force.

In contrast, Heidi smiled. "I love the Moms."

He groaned. "Pretty soon your mom will join the force, and then there will be *three* Moms."

"Heaven help us," Jaime said.

"My mom would be a scary thought."

He glanced at her, something in the undercurrent of her tone making alarm bells blare. "Why?"

Her eyes did a thing.

Precisely *what* thing was hard to decipher in the low light of the restaurant. He would have said she looked pained, but then it was gone so fast he chalked it up to a shadow, especially because when she spoke again, there was no undercurrent. Just normal Heidi.

"Only that she makes Kate's mom look like a kitten in comparison." She patted his arm. "You'd run away in fear."

"I have to meet her at some point."

Her finger, the nails short and unpolished yet no less feminine, came to her lip, tapped the bottom one. Twice. "But *do* you?"

"I do."

"Damn"—a smile that was completely normal without a weird eye shadow thing and with absolutely no trace of an undercurrent—"and here I was thinking of trying to keep you all to myself."

He glanced around the table, the other occupants unabashedly watching him and Heidi make gooey eyes at each other, then back to his woman. "And that's worked so well."

Another tinkling laugh and she leaned closer, waving a hand in their direction. "Ignore them," she said, pitched loud enough for the table to hear. "They mean nothing."

"I resent that comment." From Cora.

"Meh. I don't need your romance. I've got my own." Courtesy of Kate.

"Well, I, for one, am enjoying the banter. How do those two keep it up?" Via Kels.

"No idea. It's kind of sickening." Added by Stef, who had her casted ankle propped up on a chair.

"*Actually*," Heidi said on a shrug, "it's a gift."

He leaned closer, whispered in her ear. "I thought we were supposed to be ignoring them."

She wrinkled her nose. "Oh. Right."

Except, she didn't say anything.

Probably because, same as him, she'd been having so much fun bantering with him that she couldn't remember what they were supposed to be talking about.

"What were we talking about?" he asked.

Her eyes twinkled, voice dropping to a whisper. "I don't remember."

Chuckling, he thought back, remembered. "Dinner tomorrow," he said. "With the frightening supervillains known as the *Moms*."

Heidi linked her hand with his, stretched up, pressed a kiss to his cheek. "You're just still upset with them because you got in trouble about the wedding cake."

"A man ruins one stupidly expensive cake, and he never hears the end of it," he muttered.

"Rightfully so," Kate chimed in from across the table, drawing them out from each other. "I never even got to eat my lemon layer." She pressed the back of her hand to her forehead, adopted a mournful expression. "Oh, the humanity."

"I *did* say I was sorry," he said, knowing she was joking but still feeling guilty about the entire scenario.

"I'm just teasing." Her face immediately gentled. "It wasn't your fault."

"It was your cock's fault," Heidi said.

And by *said*, he meant practically shouting it across the table . . . right when the restaurant had one of those periodic lulls in conversation . . . which meant that she shouted it across not just the table, but the entire restaurant, too.

Her cheeks flamed as conversations paused, stares turned to her, and then she just shrugged helplessly, setting down the margarita. "Whoops," she whispered. "I guess one margarita goes to your head when you don't eat all day."

"You say that like there's *ever* been a time that one margarita hasn't gone to your head," Kate teased.

"Fair point," she replied.

Brad was more concerned about the fact that, "You haven't eaten all day?"

Heidi winced, patted his shoulder. "Don't get all scowly." Her fingers brushed over his lips. "I was out of muffins, and Molly's was closed by the time we got back yesterday." A shrug. "I meant to stop for lunch, but I forgot. And then I drove to your place when you didn't meet me . . ." Another lift and drop of her shoulders. "The day just ran away from me."

He snagged Jaime's nachos, shoved them in front of her, ignoring his brother's, "Hey!" and ordering her to, "Eat. Now."

She lifted a brow. "Remember what I said about orders?"

He leaned in, whispered into her ear, his cock twitching when she shivered and shifted closer, "You said you only like my orders in bed."

Her head turned, those green-brown eyes coming to his. "I do like them in bed."

Bringing his lips to her ear again, he murmured. "Well, consider that off the table *unless you eat the fucking nachos.*"

For a moment, she melted against him, her shoulder resting against his chest.

Then his words seemed to process, because she straightened, eyes narrowing into a glare. "I ought to kick you out of my bed altogether."

He leaned in, nipped at her bottom lip. "You'd miss me."

"Ouch," she muttered, rubbing the lush curve of her mouth.

"You like it," he countered.

She made a face. "So, what if I do? I still don't have to put up with your—"

He lifted a chip crammed with meat and beans, salsa and sour cream, cheese and guacamole and shoved it into her mouth.

Her glare was back.

But then it softened.

She chewed, swallowed. "I fucking love you, even when you drive me insane."

"I—"

"Love you," Cora interrupted, drawing the focus of the table. "And yadda, yadda, yadda. It's so predictable and lovely, and I'm insanely jealous." She threw her hands up. "Look, I'm happy for you fuckers, but I'm surrounded by gushiness on all sides here! Is it too much for me to ask you to give a single girl some relief around here and not to rub all your HEAs in my face?"

Stef, the only other single girl at the table, nodded. "I second this motion."

Kate opened her mouth, an apology in her expression, but Cora shushed her with a finger in her direction.

"As I said, I am happy for you all. So, no freaking apologies." A beat. "But can we just cool it with the soul-deep declarations? Just through the main course?"

Silence.

Three couples' gazes meeting, guilt drifting between them.

"I said *no guilt!*"

"Well, technically, you said no apologies," Kelsey pointed out.

"Ugh," Cora said.

"Can the soul-deep declarations resume over dessert?" Kate asked innocently.

More silence.

Then "*Ugh!*" Cora and Stef said at the same time.

But then the waiter came and began delivering entrees, and pretty soon the group was overtaken by the latest drama on the episode of *90 Day Fiancé*, and Brad had such a good time hanging out with his woman and her friends—now *his* friends, too—that he forgot all about the thing with Heidi's eyes, the undercurrent in her voice.

Later, he wished he'd remembered.

Wished he'd pushed to get to the bottom of it.

If only he had . . . because so much would have turned out differently.

Twenty-Four

Heidi

She woke deliciously sore but in the best possible way.

Last night had been the tequila night to end all tequila nights.

She, Kels, Cora, Stef, and Kate had decided to share a pitcher, and thus, it put all other tequila nights to shame.

And it made her look forward to finding other ways to top it, to make *future* tequila nights even better.

She was going to need to start reading erotica in order to up her game.

Brad had given her that hot, sleek smile of his when she'd told him that, kissing her in that long and slow way of his before he'd gotten up to bring her a coffee, and she knew he was looking forward to future tequila nights as much as she was.

He'd brought her a steaming mug—two sugars and a heavy splash of cream—before ordering her to stay in bed.

Probably, she should have protested, should have gotten up and helped him . . . but she was being lazy, and she was tired and cozied up with her back propped up by pillows, her coffee in hand, and he'd offered to cook for her.

So, she was lounging in bed and enjoying his care.

But she was also making a mental note to return that care.

Because he deserved to have this same warm, fuzzy feeling.

In the meantime, she thought, setting her coffee down and burrowing deeper into the blankets, she was going to enjoy the break. Now, if only she didn't need to have her arms out from beneath the comforter to hold her book.

Tough life, she knew.

Sometime later—well, four chapters later—Brad appeared in the doorway, shirtless, with a streak of flour across his chest, a plate laden with goodies in his hands.

"Where's yours?" she asked.

He smiled, crawled into bed next to her, balancing the plate of pancakes, eggs, and bacon in one hand. "Here."

She pressed her lips together.

"So, where's mine?"

Another smile, his body pressing against hers. "Here."

Ah, now she saw how this was going to work.

He settled the plate on his lap, scooped up a bite of pancake onto the fork, and lifted it up to her lips.

Right as a knock came on the door.

They both paused.

Then he shrugged. "Ignore it."

Dutifully, she parted her lips, ate the bite he'd offered her.

The knock came again. Trailed by the buzz of her phone.

"This is the continue ignoring part," he said.

Another knock. More buzzing.

He sighed, set the plate on the nightstand. "You get the phone, I'll get the door."

She made a face but dutifully reached for her cell, snagging it from the charging cradle, at the same time her glorious—and still shirtless man—headed to the door.

"Hello?" she asked.

"It's me," Kate's voice came on the line, and it was impossible to miss the panic. "Please, tell me you're staying at Brad's place."

She frowned. "No, we're at mine."

"Shit. Listen, you need to know that your—"

There was a movement in the doorway, drawing her gaze up, and . . . horror dawned.

"—mom is in town."

Her cell dropped to the mattress.

———

Fifteen minutes later, she and Brad were both fully dressed, her phone was back in the charging stand, and she was seated at the kitchen table while Brad redistributed the contents of the two-for-one plate into . . . well, two plates, and then made up one more.

For her mother.

Who was wiping a finger across the wooden surface of Heidi's table.

Colleen grimaced and reached into the handbag she hadn't yet put down, extracting a package of wet wipes then cleaning the area in front of her.

Then the back of the chair, and the seat, *and* the fork and knife Brad had placed on a napkin for her before serving up breakfast.

Brad, who'd turned from the counter, two plates in hand, was watching the exercise with raised brows. Brows he then turned onto her.

And all she could do was shrug helplessly.

This was her mother.

The *lite* version of her mother.

Because more . . . of her mother's motherness would come.

"I believe I bought you placemats, dear," she said.

Ugly ass ones with puke green flowers and red trim—like the most unattractive version of Christmas someone could imagine.

"Ah, yes." She cleared her throat. "I only use them for very special occasions." Brad set a plate in front of her mom, rounded the table to set one in front of Heidi, pressing a kiss to the side of her neck.

She smiled up at him. "Thanks," she murmured.

He brushed his fingers over her cheek. "You're welcome."

Then he returned for his own and sat down next to her.

Heidi didn't bother saying anything. Her mother wouldn't trouble herself to listen to anything she had to say that wasn't what she wanted to hear, so the best tactic was to wait for her to start the conversation.

"Breakfast this late in the day?"

Ah.

Cool.

She was going to start off with a bang.

"Yup," Heidi said, feeling Brad's gaze on her face. She glanced at him out of the corner of her eye, saw his features drawn in confusion.

He cleared his throat. "Heidi and I had a late night."

"Hmm."

"And I have to say I'm a big fan of breakfast, no matter the time of day," he added.

"I see."

Except, she answered it like she always said something that wasn't what she wanted to hear. Like someone was suggesting they go out and slaughter unicorns.

Heidi continued to ignore her, glancing at Brad as she shoveled in food. "Thank you," she said between bites. "This is delicious."

He rested his palm on her thigh. "You're welcome."

"*You* cooked?"

His gaze went from Heidi to her mother. "Heidi has been working really hard," he said. "I figured she could use a break."

A sniff. "Working."

More unicorn slaughtering.

And she knew that she had to take this in hand. "Yes, Mom, working. I'm still at the lab, and I love it."

"And does *Brad* love it?"

Her throat seized, but before she could summon a reply, he answered, "I enjoy spending whatever time with her I can, and yes, I love that she has a job that fulfills her."

Stink face.

That was the only way she could think to describe her mother's expression.

"Mom—" she began.

"What do you do?"

Brad was nonplussed by the sharp question. "I'm a web designer."

"And can you make a living at that?"

He chuckled. "I've been making a living at it for close to ten years now."

"Ah."

Cue silence.

"Why'd you decide to come into town, Mom?" she asked into that tense quiet.

"Your father had a conference."

And neither of them had decided to tell her. Right. Her dad, she could understand. Keeping track of a schedule wasn't his strong suit. But her mother . . . she was organized, she knew what was coming.

She just expected Heidi to always drop everything and be available.

"Oh, that's great," Brad said. "I'd love to meet him. Are you two free later? My family is in town, and we're having a big dinner with my brother's wife's family. Actually, I'm sure you guys probably already know Kate's parents, huh?" He glanced at Heidi. "Since you guys have known each other since college."

Heidi shrugged. Yes, her parents *had* met Kate's. And it had gone . . . well, about as well as a nuclear explosion. Kate's parents were . . . nice. Which wasn't a fair assessment to her dad, she knew. He was a decent person, if not a bit detached from anything that wasn't the science in his brain.

It was just that her mom was . . . her mom.

"Actually," she began.

Meanwhile, Brad was still talking. "It's always a good time, and I'm sure they'd love to have you—"

Her mother daintily picked up a fork, cut off a truly miniscule bite of pancake, and ate it. Then shuddered.

For fuck's sake.

"—if you're available and—"

"I'm sure they're busy," Heidi blurted. "My father's conference schedule is always hectic, and he's usually tired after—"

"Kate McLeod?"

Brad smiled. "She's a Huntington, now, but yes, she was a McLeod."

Her mom's eyes widened, hunger inside them. The very same hangers-on hunger she'd had the first time she'd met Kate's parents. The same hunger that had Heidi promising herself she would never, ever bring their two families into contact again.

"They're busy," she said quickly.

"Actually," her mom said. "No, we're not. We'd love to come."

She tried another way. "It's impolite to add guests—"

"It's fine, sweetheart," he said. "My mom is always happy to welcome more, and I know Kate's mom feels the same."

Because, of course, they did.

Because the Moms were both wonderful.

Unlike hers.

"Great," her mother said. "Then it's settled. Your father and I will join in on the dinner."

TWENTY-FIVE

BRAD

He'd fucked up.

He'd realized that after Heidi's mom, Colleen, had left to "go get ready" and he'd finally seen Heidi's face.

He'd known it when her parents had shown up in the rental car, her dad in jeans and a polo that would fit right in with the Huntingtons and McLeods, and her mother in a cocktail dress.

With pearls.

She looked beautiful.

She just didn't look like she was ready to go to a casual family-style dinner.

Fancy eight-course meal? Yes.

BBQ chicken on paper plates? No.

But he hadn't realized *exactly* how much he'd fucked up until dinner.

When Colleen had latched onto Kate's mom, Marabelle, like a limpet, asking her all about her cosmetic business and how much money she'd made and then approaching practically every item in the large ranch-style house and expounding on how expensive the built-in cabinet must be, and—oh look—that TV was huge, it must be super pricey, and what about the outdoor kitchen? That surely must have cost an arm and leg, especially with that glass tile backsplash.

It wasn't so much that she was complimenting Marabelle's style choices . . . it was just . . . all so insincere.

Over the top.

Disingenuous.

But that still wasn't the moment when he'd realized the extent of his fucked-up-ness.

Nope.

That came from the way she'd treated Heidi.

The way she was *still* treating Heidi. And look, his own mom had taught him to treat people with kindness and respect, but she'd also taught him to stand up to bullies.

Colleen was a bully.

He didn't know *why* she was a bully, but he just knew that she must have been that way for a long time, long enough that Frank, her scientist husband, and Heidi hardly seemed to notice the barely veiled barbs, the disapproving looks.

But as the wine flowed and the dinner went on, the barbs became more obvious.

And the hold on his temper grew decidedly tenuous.

"Tell me what you're working on in your lab," Marabelle said. Then chuckled. "Well, tell me whatever you can that's not top secret, that is." She glanced over at Colleen. "Isn't it amazing that your daughter runs her own lab? I heard her last paper was peer reviewed in *The Journal*."

For the first time, he saw Frank perk up, lifting his head from his plate of chocolate cake and reaching across the table to pat his daughter's hand. "It was a fantastic article."

"But she's still over thirty and unmarried."

All eyes at the table turned to Colleen.

Then went back to Heidi—who was gorgeous in an emerald blouse, loose-fitting jeans, and minimal makeup that didn't hide the red stain on her cheeks. "Lucky for me, there's more to life than wedding bells." She smiled at Kate. "No offense to my newly-married friends."

Kate smiled sympathetically. "None taken. God knows, I spent plenty of time being over thirty and unmarried."

"Except—"

"Enough, Mom," Heidi said.

Colleen's jaw tightened. "Well, even if you don't care enough to give me grandchildren, the least you could do is go easy on the sugar and carbs so you can fit into a nice wedding dress." She sniffed. "That is, if you can even get Brad down the aisle."

Kate gasped.

Heidi's eyes slid closed.

And he lost it.

He slammed his hands on the table as he shot to his feet, his chair tipping over backward and hitting the floor with a loud *thwack*. "Where in the hell do you get off treating your daughter that way?"

Primly, she turned in his direction. "Ex*cuse* me?" she asked archly.

"No, you're not excused," he snapped. "Your behavior is atrocious. Your daughter is the most wonderful woman I have ever met, and I'm lucky enough to love her. And yet you treat her like she's not worthy." He slammed his hands on the table again, making several people jump. "You don't fucking deserve to breathe her air."

"How dare—"

"How dare *I*?" He stepped back from the table, straightened his chair. "Is that what you were going to say? How dare I stick up for your daughter? How dare I love her? How dare I be so fucking proud of her for doing something she is incredible at, something she enjoys?"

"I don't care if she plays at the lab," Collen said with a sniff. "She still doesn't have the important things. Plus, she hardly ever sees us."

"I wonder why," he growled. "With a mother like you, it's a wonder she even let you walk through her door this morning. Oh wait, *I* was the one who let you in." A beat as gasps surrounded the table. "Your daughter likely would have used that big juicy brain of hers to slam the door in your face—"

"That's enough."

His own mother's voice was probably the only thing that could have stopped him in that instance.

He glanced over at her, vision tinged red with fury.

She cupped his cheek. "Honey, that's enough."

Forcing himself to take a deep breath, he nodded, sat back down.

"What manners," Colleen huffed.

"Colleen—" Frank warned.

She ignored him, her chin lifting somewhere in the level of the atmosphere. "I've never had anyone speak to me in such a way," she said. "Maybe I don't want such a man to date my daughter."

"Enough, Mom," Heidi said. "That's—"

"The rudeness is just . . . inexplicable. I've never said a cross word to anyone and—"

A muscle in his mom's jaw twitched, but she merely glanced over at Marabelle.

Who nodded.

"I think it's time to leave," his mom said.

"Yes"—Colleen placed her napkin on the table—"it's getting late. This dinner should have ended long ago—"

"No," Marabelle said, standing up and striding into the hall, where she opened the front door. "What I mean is that *you* should go, and the rest of us will enjoy our evening."

Colleen froze in the middle of collecting her purse. "Excuse me?"

"You heard me fine," Marabelle said. "I won't tell you not to come back because I'm not the kind of person who closes doors on other people. Hence, the reason you're back here in my house, despite the rudeness you showed the last time you visited." She crossed her arms. "However, I will tell you that as of this moment, you certainly will not be welcomed back in this house unless you're prepared to treat everyone with respect and understanding, including your lovely, wonderful daughter."

Heidi blinked rapidly, her gaze falling to the table. "Mom," she said. "Please, just go." Brad took her hand. She pulled away, held them tightly in her lap.

"Well, I never—"

Frank seemed to finally grow a pair. "Colleen," he snapped. "That is *more* than enough."

She whirled on him, glaring darkly. "Don't you dare—"

He stood abruptly, his chair screeching against the floor. "Don't you see that you're embarrassing yourself? That you're embarrassing your daughter?" His shoulders straightened. "And me. You're embarrassing me." A beat, his eyes, so similar to Heidi's skimmed the table. "You need to apologize. To everyone."

Colleen crossed her arms and glared at the ceiling.

Frank sighed, pushed in the chair, and kissed Heidi—whose expression had turned bleak, her eyes reddened, her skin dull and pale—on the cheek. "*My* apologies for my wife's inexcusable rudeness," he said to the table and grabbed their two jackets from the hook, draping them over one arm, before his eyes went to Marabelle's. "I hope that if we are ever given the honor of an invitation to your wonderful home again that my wife will find her manners. Either that, or you can feel free to leave her off the invite."

Colleen bristled. "How—"

"I," he said, speaking loud enough to drown out Colleen, "on the other hand, cannot thank you enough for the care you've shown my daughter." His gaze went to Heidi, who had dropped her eyes to her folded hands. "Thank you for giving that to her." His voice dropped. "She deserves it and so much more. She deserves all the happiness in the world." A squeeze to her shoulder before he cleared his throat, his volume increasing, forced cheerfulness in his tone. "We'll let you folks get on with your night. I'm sure you'll have a much better time without us."

With that, he snagged Colleen's arm and dragged the still-sputtering woman out the front door.

A heartbeat later, Marabelle slammed it behind them.

Then locked it, rubbing her hands together.

"I meant it when I said I don't normally close doors on people." She rolled her head from side to side. "But damn, did that feel good."

She laughed, and the room joined in.

But not the *whole* room. Because his ears prickled, realizing that someone's laugh had been missing.

Not someone's.

Heidi's.

Because she was gone.

TWENTY-SIX

HEIDI

She was hiding in the darkened shadows of Kate's parent's back yard and wondering if she could dig a hole deep enough to hide in when Brad found her.

Hands around her waist, a firm chest at her spine.

Just holding her silently for long moments.

"I'm sorry," she whispered when she could speak without sobbing.

"For what?"

A startled laugh as she spun in his arms. "For what?" she asked. "For *what?*" She shook her head. "She was being awful, doing the same stuff she always does, and I couldn't break that fucking cycle. I just sat there like a fucking lump, taking it." She pushed away from him then stalked away. "I just let her treat me like shit."

"First," he said, coming up behind her and snagging her hand. "It was damned hard trying to get a word in edgewise with the woman." He tugged her toward him. "Second, sometimes it's not the easiest telling people you love that they're out of line." He smoothed back her hair. "Third, I repeat, there was not a lot of room in that conversation for more words, even though I do seem to remember you telling her to stop."

"She didn't listen, though, did she?"

"Does she listen to anyone?"

He had a point there.

"No." But . . . *God* she was so fucking embarrassed. That scene was just one of those special moments her mother excelled at creating and then adding in the rest of her behavior. It was right up there with the nuclear explosion of her parents' first meeting with Kate's mom and dad.

Only this time, she'd managed to squeeze out a few more words.

Barely.

"Baby," he whispered. "No one is upset at you."

She knew that—well, she *supposed* she knew that, but . . . how could they *not* be mad at her? It was her mom that had ruined the fun night, her mom who'd said all the rude things. It was absolutely despicable, the way her mother had acted.

"I had to battle Kate and both of our mothers for the privilege to make sure you're okay."

She winced. "They should just get on with their meal."

"*We* should get on with our dessert before my dad gorges himself on the rest of the chocolate cake." She smiled, thinking it had definitely been gorge-worthy, or at least the one bite of it she'd managed to eat had been absolutely delicious before her mom had gone on her tear. "Plus, when everyone is done, we're going to play *Ticket to Ride*." He laughed. "And I should warn you, *my* mom has been practicing since Marabelle destroyed her so incredibly badly last time."

Somehow, despite the scene in the dining room, this man still made her laugh.

"There it is," he whispered.

"There's what?"

"The laugh that makes my heart fill with joy." He cupped the side of her neck, drew her against him once again. "Baby, no one cares that your mom is the worst, and certainly not *the* Moms. They've decided to make you an official Huntington-McLeod adopted daughter, and their pledge is to ensure that you understand you're, quote 'beautiful, smart, and beyond wonderful'—all of which are true, by the way." His thumb brushed across her cheek, and she realized she was crying. "I'd also add strong, sexy as shit with Viking braids, and so fucking funny that you give my banter skills a run for the money."

"Brad," she whispered.

"So, good luck dealing with the pair of them," he said. "In fact, I heard Marabelle plotting with my mom that they were going to wrap you up in so much love you would never be able to escape."

She sighed. "They really are quite wonderful."

"You say that now," he teased, then loosened his hold, lacing their fingers together and drawing her toward the house. "Come on, let's go cheat by working together so neither of our moms can get the most successful railroad."

"Wait."

He stopped. "What, baby?"

"Are you sure no one is mad?" Her teeth found her bottom lip, nibbled lightly. "I ruined their night and—"

He kissed her gently and filled with so much love and tender affection that she felt her heart melt. "I can absolutely promise you that no one is mad." He paused. "Well, no one currently allowed in Marabelle's house. *Your* mom on the other hand . . ."

She tugged her hand free, covered her face, groaning. "I hate that I didn't stand up for myself."

He came close again, rubbed his hand up and down her back. "You know what the great part about being in a relationship is?"

Her shoulders relaxed the slightest bit. "Besides the copious amount of orgasms?"

A smile. "Yes, besides those."

"I don't know," she said. "What?"

"That you don't have to fight all of your battles alone."

"Look at you, sounding all logical." She wrinkled her nose. "Of course, I know you're right, and I do thank you for standing up for me. Knowing that you'd go to bat for me, even in an uncomfortable situation . . . it makes me feel all warm and fuzzy inside."

"Does that mean you love me even more?"

She made a face. "Not that your ego needs it, but yes. You saying those things, sticking up for me . . . yes, I love you even more."

The breeze picked up, rustling through her hair, making her shiver.

"You're cold." He bundled her against his warm chest, wrapping his arms tightly around her. "Let's go inside."

She let him lead her toward the house. "I just wish I could have said . . ." She trailed off, realization finally dawning on her, making her go still in his arms, her brain putting the puzzle pieces together.

"What, baby?" he prompted.

"It wouldn't have mattered what I said, would it?"

He just stroked a hand down her spine, let her continue to think about that. After a moment, she shook her head. "No," she murmured. "I don't think it would have."

Brad loved her. He had her back. And further that, her dad, who normally was so deep in his own head had recognized she needed that, too, needed someone to build her up rather than tear her down. She supposed that her mom also loved her, at least in some unhealthy way, a way that made it so she would never turn down an opportunity to make Heidi feel small.

But that didn't have anything to do with her.

Did that suck?

Hell yeah.

Did that make a part of her feel like shit?

Hell fucking yeah.

But could she truly do anything to change her mother's behavior? No.

Nothing she did would ever make her mom change. So, she could only alter *her* reaction, adjust *her* expectations. Heidi could work on extracting herself from the situations, make sure she didn't allow herself to be waylaid into scenarios she didn't want to participate in. She could keep her distance from her mom, only allow the interactions *she* was comfortable with.

And . . . she could continue surrounding herself with people who loved her for who she was.

Who didn't see her as a failure.

Who instead saw her flaws and loved her all the more for them.

"Heidi."

She stopped and stared up at him. "I love you."

His face softened. "I love you." Fingers on her cheek. "I'll love you until—"

"Come on already!" Jaime shouted from the door. "Just kiss her until she gets all dopey and forgets what happened. Then we'll convince her we don't care what happened—"

"Unless, of course, she beats me in *Ticket to Ride*," Marabelle called. "Then all bets are off!"

Heidi had frozen at the sound of Jaime's voice.

The addition of Marabelle's made her smile.

Brad smoothed back her hair. "I guess I'd better listen to him."

"Wh—?"

But she didn't get to finish the question because his lips were on hers, and then he was kissing her until she was loopy, until her heart pounded and her pulse was skittering through her veins.

Then he took her inside to play a board game.

As though it were a normal night and not one where her heart had seemed to grow three sizes.

"Hey," Jaime said as they started to walk past him.

She glanced up, but he was looking at Brad, smiling in that paternalistic, older brother way he just exuded.

"For the record, Mom just told me she's not going to worry about you anymore."

Brad went still, *so* still.

Then his body relaxed, a long sigh escaping him, and he clapped Jaime on the shoulder. "Love you, bro."

"Love you, too." Jaime nodded, and after Kate popped her head into the hall, he hustled into the dining room.

"What was that about?" Heidi whispered as they followed him.

He slowed down, tugging her to a halt with him. "That—"

"Ticket to *Ride!*" Marabelle called from the dining room.

His lips curved up into that special, slow, sexy smile that he reserved only for her.

"I'll tell you—"

"Now!"

Lips on hers for the briefest moment. "Some other time."

Heidi's heart grew another size. "Sometime in our long, happy future together?"

Another smile—this one hot, tinged with sweet. "Yes."

Marabelle's head poked in through the opening. "Ticket—"

"To ride!" they finished in unison.

And then they went into the kitchen. To finally play that board game.

On a night that felt extraordinary, but would become commonplace as the years went by, her heart growing and growing until it seemed to take up all the space in her body.

But that wasn't scary any longer. All the love she felt for them made her stronger, instead of weaker, built her up instead of tore her down.

Because she had her family—the one she'd made, the one she'd chosen.

And she had this man.

Who'd turned normal into extraordinary.

EPILOGUE

Pink-painted nails digging into pale white sand.

A lusciously curved body curled up next to his.

A paperback propped on his chest as she read her latest historical romance.

It was funny, but in all his travels, he had never been one for sitting on a beach all day, having cocktails delivered at his elbow, the hot sun shining down through an umbrella overhead.

But with Heidi at his side like this, he was hard-pressed to picture another type of vacation.

Of course, it might also be the sex.

He could now say with complete authority that he didn't mind getting sand into all sorts of crevices when it meant that he could be with this woman.

Tomorrow they would be going back home to the Bay Area, to Heidi's condo with his newly finished—and exceptionally organized thanks to his woman—office, and they'd be heading back to reality.

Except, reality was . . . heaven.

So they might be leaving the gorgeous beach and warm sand. They wouldn't have cocktails delivered to their cabana, left at their sides by friendly attendants. They'd be back in the fog, in the traffic, in the long hours at the lab and long hours behind a computer.

But they'd also be going back to movie nights and popcorn, to coffee while cuddled up in bed, and blustery trips to the beach.

They'd be going back to the life they'd built.

The huge, wonderful, amazing life they'd built.

Only . . . Heidi didn't know it, but she would be going back with one additional souvenir.

The diamond ring currently taking up space in his pocket because he hadn't been able to let it out of his sight.

He had it planned for dinner. He'd made all the arrangements, a moonlight stroll on the beach, a private dinner at a table perched just above the waves. They'd have the stars and the moon, and then he'd get down on one knee and—

"I was thinking."

Blinking, he glanced down at her, at the woman who held his heart in the palm of her hand, who was so fucking strong and smart and beautiful, and smiled. "About what?"

She set her book down, shifted so she could rest her chin on her folded arms that sat on his chest. Then she smiled.

And damn if his heart still didn't skip a beat.

"Uh-oh," he teased. "That's a very calculating look. What am I about to get myself into?"

A splash of pink on her cheeks. "I was thinking."

He smirked. "You said that already. Thinking about what?"

"Well, our flight home connects through Vegas," she said. "So, I thought we could extend our trip for one more day and . . "

"Go gambling?"

She sighed, narrowed her eyes at him. "Brad," she warned.

"What?" he asked innocently.

She huffed. "We could do the most Vegas-y thing ever and take a page out of Kels and Tanner's book—"

And then he decided to forget the dinner, forget the moonlight and crashing waves and proposal under the stars. Placing a finger over her lips, he used his other hand to reach into his pocket.

He didn't skip the one knee—which required him to do a fair amount of maneuvering, he had to admit—but then she was sitting up and he was on one knee, and he had the ring box open.

"Heidi, my love, my heart, my everything—"

"Yes!"

Laughter bubbled up in his chest. "I haven't even asked you yet."

"You don't have to." She launched herself into his arms, making him fumble to grab her, hold on to the ring, and not end up on his ass. He was only successful in two of the three, but since they were the most important two, he didn't mind the sand getting up his swim trunks. Especially when she said, "The answer to any question you ask me will always be yes."

"*Any?*" he asked, tugging at a strand of her hair. "Are you sure you want to commit to that?"

A glare. "Stop teasing and kiss me."

"In a minute," he said, then looked deeply into those beautiful hazel eyes and asked her the most important question of his life. "Heidi Greene, will you marry me?"

Her expression gentled. "Yes, baby. I will." A beat, her lips curving. "Now, will you kiss me already?"

He smiled, cupped her cheek. "One more thing first."

A mock-annoyed huff.

Then a smile when he slipped the ring on her finger.

And *then* he kissed her.

"So, Vegas?" she asked when they broke for air, breath coming in rapid bursts. "Want to hit up a chapel with me?"

He wanted nothing more.

But . . . "Don't you want to have a big wedding with the giant dress and the bridesmaids and the hundreds of guests?"

She shuddered. "No. I just want you."

"What about your friends?" he asked, wanting to marry her more than anything but also wanting to make sure she had everything she had ever dreamed of. "Don't you want them to be part of your wedding?"

Fingers on his jaw, her mouth very close to his. "Honey," she said. "I never fantasized about having a big wedding with the white, puffy dress and the bouquet and the multi-tiered wedding cake"—a smile he could practically taste, her lips were so near— "that can be knocked over by an errant groomsman—"

"It was the Fuzz."

A brush of her mouth across his. "Sure, it was." Another. "But cocks aside"—she grinned, and he snorted—"what I'm trying to tell you is that all I've ever dreamed of is finding a person who loves me for who I am, someone who I'm not afraid to let close because they would see my flaws and understand that they are just another piece of me to appreciate." She straightened, her eyes growing damp. "And *you're* that person. You're the one who's made me see that I was worthy of all that . . . and so much more. You're the one who gave me more than I could ever imagine, so"—she cupped his jaw—"know that I love you, honey, and I want to marry you so fucking much. In fact, the only thing I want to do slightly more is to make babies with you."

His heart, fuck, it squeezed tight, so much emotion coiling in his stomach that it took his breath away.

"You want babies?"

She nodded.

Thud-thud.

Thud-thud.

Thud-thud.

He stood, tugging her to her feet.

"What's the matter?" she asked as he started dragging her across the sand. "Brad!"

He turned back, swept her into his arms. "We need to get started."

"Packing?"

A slow shake of his head. "No, sweetheart. On the babies."

She laughed, wrapped her arms around him. "That sounds like the best idea you've ever had."

He waggled his brows. "The best—"

She kissed him.

Then he got to work on that best idea.

BAD SWIPE

BILLIONAIRE'S CLUB #12

ONE

"Marry me, Fred," she murmured, tugging her man close and wrapping her arms around him.

He nuzzled into her throat, his warm breath on her skin—

And then started licking her face.

Full stop.

With completely unattractive, smelly breath.

"Ick," she grumbled, burying her face in her pillow to get away from her eighty-five-pound golden retriever.

The only man in her life.

He was hairy, had the aforementioned smelly, doggy breath, but he was loyal and didn't cheat. So, although he would go home with anyone who offered him the smallest morsel of food, his tail always went propellor when he saw her, and he always nuzzled close, especially when she was feeling down.

Yeah, she picked up his shit and waited on him hand and foot.

But how was that different from anyone she'd ever dated?

Spoiler alert . . . it wasn't.

Fred continued licking, thinking her burying herself into her pillows was now the best game ever and attacking her in earnest.

"Okay," she said, pushing him off and sitting up. "Do you want breakfast?"

Breakfast being the magic word, since it sent Fred sprinting from the bed and skidding toward the kitchen, his claws clicking on the tile loudly enough that she could mentally track his path the entire way.

Sighing, she tossed the covers back. She needed to get up anyway, to take Fred on his walk, and then get him off to doggy day care before she headed into work.

Carefully, she shifted out of bed, wincing a bit when she put weight on her ankle.

She'd broken her ankle a few months before—well, Fred and his obsession with a squirrel had been the cause of her injury—and it was still a bit weak and tender. Because of that, she was still going to physical therapy, even though the cast had been off for a while now, and her doc said that she might have to undergo another surgery at some point to remove her "jewelry."

That jewelry being the six screws and two plates currently freeloading their way around town in her body.

And causing her pain when she walked too far or stood too long or, really, just turned in the wrong direction. So truly, it hurt most of the time unless her ass was parked on her plush gray couch or propped up in bed on the special pillow that her friend Heidi had bought for her right after her surgery.

Ah, to be a woman in her thirties.

Sadly single.

Hobbling like a motherfucker.

Pretty soon she'd be bent in half like an old crone, sporting a bedazzled cane. Which—she paused, considered that—might be cool. She could see herself rocking some rainbow sparkles.

They'd go perfectly with her numerous T-shirts and skinny jeans (*and* side part, so take *that*, Gen Z!).

Before she could go too far down her obsession with TikTok, Fred whipped back against the corner, bull in a china shop style.

"Sit!" she ordered, and since he was a good boy, he did just that. Unfortunately because he was eighty-five pounds and had been moving at approximately the speed of light, his sitting didn't mean he actually stopped moving forward.

His ass hit the floor.

His body kept sliding . . . right into the wall.

"Oh, Fred," she murmured as he righted himself just as quickly, sliding some more, his nails clicking on the tile like he was a tapdancing crab until he was finally sitting in front of her.

His tail thumping on the floor.

She stepped by him, careful to not mention the b-word (breakfast), in case he did some more slip and sliding and took her out.

And she did not need *that* on a Monday morning.

"Come on," she said, once she was out of the line of fire, because—like the good boy he was—Fred had waited where she'd told him to sit. And aside from his squirrel obsession, he really *was* a good boy. He was just big and clumsy and all legs and no sense of balance.

Like her.

Ha.

He danced around her legs as she scooped his food, added his vitamins, and then a scoop of supplements that kept his teeth clean and was supposed to battle that doggy breath of his.

Stef wasn't convinced that it helped.

Or it could be a million times worse without it.

Either way, it wasn't something she was going to find out.

Then she sprinkled some shredded chicken because Fred was her boy and yes, he was spoiled as hell.

Once his bowl was in front of him and he was scarfing it down, she got the coffee going, and the moment the bitter, smokey fumes hit her nose, she started feeling less like a Monday Monster and more like an actual human being.

Bagel in the toaster.

Cinnamon cream cheese on the counter.

Plate from the cupboard beside it.

To-go mug open and ready to be filled.

Other mug put in place of the pot and filled with the steaming brew. She took a large sip as her bagel toasted, enough to further chase the Mondays away, and then when it was done, she set about slathering on the cream cheese and doing her level best to replace her blood with the spicy, tangy spread.

It was her absolute favorite.

She bought it by the tub at the local bakery—now bakery chain—Molly's.

And by *the tub*, she meant by the *double* tub, because she always (always!) had a spare container in her fridge.

A girl never knew when she might need a spoonful to chase away the reality of being thirty-five and her longest relationship being with a furry, non-human male who liked to pee on fire hydrants.

Sufficiently caffeinated, she went to pull on a pair of sweats and her tennis shoes then tugged her hair back into a ponytail.

The moment she pulled out the leash, Fred stopped licking his bowl. A walk was the only thing that would convince him to get up because he lived his life alternating between thinking he hadn't gotten every last drop from his dish and worrying that he would never ever eat again.

"Come on, buddy," she said as he trotted over, clipping on his leash and reaching for her oversized hoodie.

They'd do a quick turn around the block and then she'd come back and shower, bundle him into the car for doggy day care, take herself to work, and it would be another glorious Monday.

"Joy of joys," she muttered.

But truthfully, she didn't mind the walk, didn't mind the cool morning air on her face, the quiet of the neighborhood. There weren't many cars on the road at this hour, not with the sun still mostly below the horizon, and it was a peaceful way to start her morning.

Just her and her man.

Smiling when Fred did a little butt wiggle as they moved down the front steps of her condo, she set them on a quick pace as they turned right, looped down through the dew-covered grass in the small park at the end of the street, then back up a block over, before turning onto her street and completing their loop.

His tongue hanging out, Fred sprinted back over to his bowl the moment she opened the door and took off the leash, returning to the business of licking up every last crumb.

Stef flicked the lock and headed into the bathroom to shower.

Was *mid*-shower with shampoo suds dripping down her spine when the doorbell rang.

She ignored it.

Continued washing her hair.

It rang again.

Sighing, since she'd just slathered conditioner on, she kept the water running—yeah, yeah, she knew about the drought, but also, she knew it would take even more water to warm up her shower since her water heater sucked ass—snagged a towel, wrapped it around her head, grabbed her robe, and made her way to the front door . . . just as the bell rang for a third time.

A glance through the peephole made her want to spin around and head right back into the shower.

But she also knew that the knocking wouldn't stop.

Not with Jeremy.

Girding her loins, she unlocked and opened the door. "Yes?" she asked, purposefully blocking the opening so he couldn't just stroll his way into her place. He'd lost that privilege when he'd unceremoniously dumped her months before.

"Where is it?" he snapped, shoving at the door so roughly that she stumbled back a step.

Fred spun around the corner, nails clicking, excitement at seeing a new person—any new person, and especially one who'd occasionally fed him in the past—fueling his barreling. "Wait," she ordered before he could burst out the front door and take her on a sprint through the neighborhood.

He waited, skidding to a stop.

She grabbed the door, pushed the panel back, returning it to its previous position of only being open a crack. "What are you talking about, Jeremy?"

"I'm asking where it is," he growled. "And I'm asking where it is *right now.*"

Water was dripping down her spine. The cool air that had felt good on her face earlier now felt like shit because she was wet from the shower and fucking freezing. "What the hell are you talking about?"

A sharp sigh. "You know."

Why had she been forced onto this particular merry-go-round so fucking early on a Monday morning?

Did the universe hate her?

Was the god of evil ex-boyfriends determined to make her life miserable?

"No, Jeremy," she said, grasping at the straws of her calm. "I *don't* know. However, if you'd clue me into what you're looking for, I'm happy to tell you."

Silence.

Narrowed eyes and a clenched jaw. God, once she'd thought he was the handsomest man she'd ever laid eyes on. But now as she was looking at him, she could only see an angry, sad man and wonder how in the hell had she wasted so much time being upset about the breakup.

"Vase. Blue with white flowers."

She frowned, searching her brain, before remembering that she did, in fact, have the vase. It was sitting on top of her book-case and was actually quite pretty. One of the few things that Jeremy had bought her that she'd actually liked. But, "You gave me that for our anniversary."

His lips pressed flat. "My mom gave it to me. She's flying in today."

Stef read between the lines. He needed it back or his mom would freak the fuck out, and . . . here her petty streak came out because it was so tempting to refuse, knowing that Jeremy would get an earful from his uber-controlling, feelings-hurt-at-the-drop-of-a-hat mother.

It would be glorious.

But . . . *here* her rational streak came out. If she fought Jeremy over this, he would stay, and he wouldn't give up. He'd browbeat her into giving it back, or at the very least, he would annoy the shit out of her until she was so fed up that she chucked it at him.

And then she'd have glass in her entryway, and she'd be further contributing to the drought because she would have another delay returning to her shower.

Namely having to clean up the glass.

Still, it was tempting . . .

Fred whined.

Reminding her that her pupper would eventually lose all self-control and really burst out the front door, equaling more shower delays.

Lastly, now that she remembered the vase and knew that it hadn't been a gift from Jeremy but rather a regift from his mother, the pretty blue container had lost most of its appeal.

"Wait here," she said.

He narrowed his eyes.

She repeated, more firmly this time, "*Wait* here."

Then she closed the door, threw the lock, and moved to the bookcase. It wasn't far, thus, it didn't take her very long to retrieve it, but Jeremy was already knocking again by the time she made it back to the entryway.

God, why did she have such horrible taste in men?

Sigh.

She flicked open the lock, turned the handle, and thrust the vase at Jeremy. "Anything else?"

He scrambled to hold on to it. "Um . . . no."

"Good." She narrowed her eyes. "If you show up on my porch again, banging on my door, I *will* call the police."

Jeremy's lips parted, anger flooding his blue eyes.

"You remember I have another vase or something else, you text, and I'll get it to you when it's convenient for me." Her voice was harder than it had ever been, and she saw the surprise trailing over his expression. Good. The only positive from this morning's call was that Stef was now certain there wasn't a speck of longing inside her for this man. "Now, go home."

"Stef," he began, and she would have to have been an idiot to not miss the sudden interest in his face.

Nor the way his eyes went to her breasts.

As though the first sign of her temper—which she could truthfully admit wasn't something she'd ever shown him, even in their two years together—was a turn-on.

But seriously, yeah. No.

Maybe she'd been so invested in making the relationship work that she'd hidden parts of herself. Okay, no *maybe* about it. That was the truth. She'd definitely hidden whole facets of herself in order to keep things smooth sailing with Jeremy.

Pathetic. It really was.

Well, no more.

She slammed the door, not caring that it was close to his face, not caring if it *hit* his face.

Then she threw the lock and went back to her shower.

Shutting the door on Jeremy, on the person she'd been with him. Forever.

And good riddance.

For the record, her shower was absolutely divine.

Two

BEN

He was half-delirious from jet lag, but he had a full day in the office.

This was the week his company was going public.

And no matter how many times everyone had assured him that all the pieces were in place, shit kept hitting the fan. He was tired of putting out fires. He was tired. Period.

Ben Bradford was thirty-six years old and CEO of a company that was valued at eighteen-and-a-half billion dollars.

He'd never even dreamed something that big was possible.

Not ever.

But it was, and he now had more money than he knew what to do with, money that would grow to an even more ridiculous amount with the IPO.

If only his parents could see him now.

Unfortunately, they were both gone. His dad five years before from a fucking carjacking gone wrong, his mom just the previous year. She'd had cancer, and cancer was a fucking asshole.

So now it was him and his dog—or rather, his mother's dog. A fluffy Bichon Frise who had typical big-dog-in-a-little-dog's-body-syndrome and whose name was Sweetheart.

She was not sweet, not in any sense of the name.

She barely tolerated him, and that tolerating meant nipping at his heels if he didn't feed her fast enough or take her outside often enough or just happened to walk by at the wrong time and she felt like chasing his ass down the hallway.

But Sweetheart was part of his mom, so he tolerated her.

Plus, she was old, and her teeth were worn down.

Not much damage was doled out, even with the fiercest of heel-nipping.

However, the pet sitter he had on retainer wasn't as convinced, and though she'd been a trooper, he'd received a text the moment his plane had landed telling him that she was sorry, but she could no longer do it.

The evil beast had been fed and watered *and* pottied that morning.

But she needed a break before she could step back into care mode.

A *long* break.

Which meant he needed to retrieve the little asshole that morning and would be working with Sweetheart under his feet —the pooch in a crate that was specially designed to fit beneath his desk.

Just what he needed.

Sighing, he swung by his place, bundled up the pup while ignoring her snarling then jammed her into her carrier because there was no way he was allowing the beast to run free at the office, no matter how dull her teeth were.

Twenty minutes later, he was pulling into his space on campus and moving through the floors with the grumbling, unhappy Sweetheart in tow.

Luckily, he didn't garner any second looks.

Or not any second looks that weren't the usual ones shot toward the big boss walking past offices. The additional second looks that didn't come were those associated with him lugging the pink carrier.

News traveled fast at Hunt Inc., and everyone knew they didn't want to be within fifteen feet of the fluffy white beast who had flunked out of every doggy day care, boarding facility, behaviorist, and trainer, and who'd actually become even worse while on anti-depressants and CBD oil.

Yes, he'd even tried drugging the damned dog.

So, now his life was about his work and trying to mitigate Sweetheart, and no surprise, that was more than enough to keep him very busy.

Maybe once the IPO went through—

Sweetheart went bananas, and he glanced around, trying to figure out what had set her off. Did she see ghosts of doggy boyfriends and enemies past? Was there a person in a thirty-foot radius who'd dared to look at her? Or was she just feeling like her snarling, evil self?

Probably the last.

Likely all three.

Regardless, he managed to get into the elevator, take it up to his floor, and then make the transfer of carrier to crate that finally meant Sweetheart went quiet.

Until he had to take her out to pee.

"For fuck's sake," he muttered, straightening, before moving to the large bank of plate glass windows that looked out onto the city of San Francisco.

In the distance.

Because San Francisco real estate prices were ridiculous.

So, he and Hunt Inc. were situated south of the city, not that the prices were significantly better. This was California. This was Silicon Valley.

It seemed like it cost a million dollars just to own the parking spot his sedan was sitting in five stories below, let alone the entire campus that housed the thousands of employees who worked for him.

But it had all been to get to this point.

His crowning achievement, to be one of the big players, to see his company's name on the stock exchange. A dream, a fantasy . . . and now a reality.

So, why then did he feel so . . . empty?

Nerves because his life was about to change, and it wasn't a small one, because there would be new responsibilities and more people relying on him.

That was it.

The stocks would go live, and he'd feel normal again.

Simple enough.

A knock on his office door heralded his assistants—yes, plural, yes *three* of them—and then Ben was drawn away from the window, from the thoughts of dreams and fantasies and back into the one thing that had always made sense.

Work.

"Mr. Bradford," Baine said, even though Ben had told him hundreds of times before to just call him Ben. "I've got your schedule for the day."

Ben's eyes drifted to Spence who said, "I have those files you requested."

Now Ben's stare moved to Claire, who grimaced. "And *I*, unfortunately, have a problem for you."

No surprise there.

Baine spoke before Ben could. "Meetings are pushed until one. Should give you enough time to deal with this problem and any others that creep up."

Spence set the files on the desk, jumping when Sweetheart snarled.

"Don't worry," Ben told him. "I'm the only one on Sweetheart duty."

Relief flashed across Spence's face. "O-okay. Well, I mean, if you need help with her then—"

"Don't finish that statement," Ben said, stifling a smile. "I know you don't mean it."

Baine, proving once again that Ben hadn't made a mistake in hiring the ex-felon, wove his arm through Spence's and tugged the younger man toward the door. "He doesn't mean it," Baine confirmed, drawing him from the office.

Spence glanced back. "I—"

The door clicked closed.

Claire smiled, shaking her head. "Should I ask about the dog?"

"You already know the answer to that question."

"Right," she said, tapping at the screen of the tablet she carried. "So, I'll just get right down to the newest crisis?"

Ben plunked down into his desk chair, ignoring the rumble beneath his knees.

"Hit me with it."

She did.

And just as all the ones before, it was fucking brutal.

THREE

Friday evening brought her friends, wine, and a throbbing ankle.

At her house for a change.

Oh, and margaritas. Somewhere along the way, Heidi had thought it was a good idea to bust out Stef's rarely used blender, bring up the Drizly app on her phone, and bring in some tequila.

They were celebrating.

Finally, they'd managed to get a clean picture.

Which, Stef got, probably didn't seem like a big deal. But to them—they were molecular physicists, and right now their research was focused on trying to quantify the space between atoms—it was a huge deal.

Difficult because they were trying to quantify something that couldn't be seen with the naked eye, a bit of matter that was surrounded by other bits of matter, including electrons that were whirling around and generally making nuisances of themselves. Flying off in all directions, crashing into each other, joining other atoms and fucking everything up.

But today had gone well.

They'd gotten their photograph, and it was clear, and it was a big freaking deal!

Hence, wine and margaritas, even though at thirty-five, she knew better than to mix her liquors.

The only thing that would make her hangover not horrendous, she knew, was that it was Friday, which meant that tomorrow was Saturday. She didn't do an early morning walk with Fred. Saturday had become beach day, and they did their walk late in the day because she liked to walk the beach at sunset.

The blender whirred, and Stef glanced down at her glass, finding it empty, unsure how that had happened.

Which was fine because Heidi was refilling it, demanding they clink cups and declare, "Cheers!"

"Brad is going to have to pour her out of here," Cora said, her dark brown eyes sparkling with humor . . . and also a bit glazed because she, too, had been partaking in wine *and* margaritas.

"I thought your brothers were in town," Kels said, draining her own glass then holding it up for Heidi to top it off.

"They left this morning," Cora said, slugging back her margarita.

Cora had six brothers, and they'd descended on her small house ten days ago without warning—though probably she should have known they were coming since she'd mentioned to her mom that she'd gone on three dates with a man.

Her brothers were . . . protective.

And that was an understatement.

They were six feet plus, built, and could be scary as shit if they wanted. Not that they used those scary vibes with Cora, Heidi, Kels, Tammy, Kate, and Stef. With women, they were gentle, were sweet and kind and chivalrous.

And single.

Every one of them.

The humanity.

"Fuckers ate me out of house and home," Cora grumbled. "And left me with a mountain of laundry, footprints on the floor, and a new video game system."

Kate's lips twitched, her red hair tumbling over her shoulders. "And that would be any different from the state of your house normally?"

Cora wrinkled her nose. "Shut it, you." Her gaze drifted to Tammy, Heidi's soon-to-be sister-in-law, who had recently moved to town. "Don't keep your childhood friends around. They know too much about you."

Tammy snorted, though she'd wisely just kept to margaritas —although that was mostly because she'd arrived after when the wine had already been consumed.

Kate, on the other hand, gasped and swatted Cora's arm. "Rude!"

"Children," Heidi warned.

"Make another blender full," Kels called. "We're gonna need it."

Heidi set the blender on the counter, picked up her own glass. "Someone else is on blender duty," she said, sinking down on the couch. "I'm done for the evening." She glanced at her watch. "Plus, the boys are going to be here soon, and we all know that Kels—"

"Don't say it," Kels warned.

Cora grinned, stage-whispered, "Is primed for Pound Town when the booze goes down."

They froze.

"Pound Town?" Kels asked. "Seriously?"

Gazes collided. Lips twitched. Then they all broke into peals of laughter—or maybe it was cackling. Either way, all Stef knew was that by the time she gained control of herself, her face ached from smiling, her stomach hurt from laughing, and she was once again so damned happy to have found these women.

They could talk about absolutely everything and absolutely nothing. They could tease each other until they were sick with laughter, and they would infallibly be there for each other.

No matter what.

Friends. True friends, and not like the ones who'd taken Jeremy's side in the breakup, who'd left her alone in a new state, even though they understood that she'd moved here for him, that her family was back in Florida, and that she knew no one outside of their circle.

Thank God she'd gotten the job with Heidi.

Otherwise she didn't know what she'd have done.

Go back home? Admit that moving to California and quitting her job without a plan, believing in the promise of a man who'd been incapable of fulfilling it, had been a mistake?

Ah. The joy of relationships.

At least her friends had good ones. Heidi's Brad and Kate's Jaime were both amazing. Of course, they were also brothers, so that was probably a big part of it. One family made good men, and it was all the rest of them that—

Tanner was nice, too.

He belonged to Kels.

So, maybe it was that all the good ones were taken?

Or maybe . . . she swore she had a thought there, swirling around her brain, but it flitted away into a fog of alcohol and pleasant sensations as she reclined on her couch listening to her friends babble on about their newest reality show obsession— this one about first dates.

It was sweet and cringy and . . . *just* the thing they loved watching.

"Oh, no," Kate cried, the nicest one of all of them. "He's not going to pick her."

No, the man on the TV didn't appear to be interested in the

sweet, nerdy, cute blond girl he'd been paired with. Instead, his eyes were focused over her shoulder, and when the camera kindly cut in that direction, they could all see exactly what had drawn his attention.

A gorgeous, buxom brunette, who was smiling shyly at him.

And yup, now the man actually got up, crossed over to the woman and began chatting her up instead of his own date.

"What a fucking douche canoe," Cora muttered.

"Seriously," Kels said.

"Jeremy did that to me," Stef whispered.

There might as well have been a record scratch for how quiet it went. In an instant, all eyes were on her, and Heidi grabbed the remote, pausing the show. "Excuse me?" she asked, her tone deadly.

"I—um . . ." Stef shook her head. "It's nothing," she said.

"That doesn't sound like nothing," Tammy murmured.

Stef whirled and glared at her. That was *so* not helpful.

Tammy lifted her hands. "Just saying."

"What she's *just saying* is right," Cora said. "Jeremy is an asshole, and you're lucky to be rid of him."

"I am," Stef agreed.

"It's just . . ." Kate began, seemingly plucking the words out of Stef's brain.

Stef winced, decided to not admit to that aloud, and set about glugging down her latest margarita, embracing the burn, grasping tightly to the swirling feeling of her mind.

"It can be hard to start over," Kate continued, thankfully not plucking the second part of Stef's inner thoughts out of her brain.

Because what Stef had been thinking was that it can be hard to be alone.

She shouldn't be feeling lonely.

She had her friends—real, true friends. She had her job. She had Fred, who was currently snoozing in the corner after having exhausted himself and everyone's arms from the copious belly rubs he'd received.

"Yeah," Cora murmured, "it can be."

"Well," Tammy said. "I didn't know the fucker, but if he did that to you on a date, then he was a dumbass. You're beautiful and smart and a total catch."

Stef winced again. "First date."

Heidi's brows rose. Kelsey scowled.

"What a bastard," Kate snapped. She slammed her fist on the table. "The next time I see him, I'm going to take this glass and shove it up his ass!"

There went that fictional record scratch again, the room falling silent for a second time.

Mostly because Kate didn't get mad at anyone, least of all threaten to shove things up other people's derrières, whether or not any of the rest of them thought her target was a worthwhile one.

"One could say I was an idiot for giving him a second date," Stef said. God knew, she'd certainly said it to herself more than enough times.

"Idiot or not, he is more of a douche canoe than the fucker on TV," Cora muttered.

Which earned her a smack from Heidi.

"What?"

"Stef is *not* an idiot," she snapped.

"I—" Stef began.

Heidi held up a finger. "Not one word from you, missy. You are beautiful and kind and smart as shit, and just because Jeremy didn't see that doesn't mean it's any less true."

"Heidi," Stef said.

"It's true and just because the guy had a little dick and—"

"*Heidi,*" she repeated, more firmly this time.

"And thinks he's got a pretty face—"

"You've never even met him."

"I saw his picture, and that was enough for me . . ." She trailed off, her glass nearly tipping over in her earnestness to set it on the coffee table. "I knew he was one of those frat boy fuckboys."

"I'm not sure that's actually a thing," Cora pointed out.

"It is," Heidi said.

"Technically, I think it's *two* things," Kels added, both helpfully and not.

"And none of this is really pertinent to this situation," Tammy said, her voice as gentle as her hand patting Stef's knee. "As much as I want to see Kate's attempt at glass shoving."

Stef snorted.

Cora's lips twitched.

Heidi lost it altogether.

Kels merely put a finger up and stated with authority, "The governing board has affirmed Jeremy's status as Douche Canoe and Stef's as Much Better Off Without Him. Now, we shall all drink to that before returning to *First Dates* and—"

There was a knock at the door.

"Curfew," Kate groaned.

But Kels was already tipping back her glass and stumbling to her feet. "My Tanner's here!"

He *was* there.

Along with Brad and Jaime. The three boys having gone to catch a hockey game before returning to gather up the girls. Tanner took Kels and Cora home. Brad and Jaime took Heidi, Kate, and Tammy, since the latter was their younger sister and the newest member of their friend group.

She was wonderful.

They all were.

Even with their drunken shenanigans as they were bundled out the door, trying for one last margarita, insisting on cleaning up, pointing out to their new audience how much of a douche canoe Jeremy was (especially when Kate asked what had happened to the pretty vase that had previously sat on the shelf and had thus been claimed by Jeremy the prior Monday), and then waxing poetic about the wine, the moon, and ironically the pretty pink color of the wax of the candle Stef had burning on the kitchen counter.

Not that Stef herself was immune to drunken shenanigans, considering exactly what she'd blurted when she was supposed to be watching a silly reality show.

Still, she'd never had anyone stand up for her without reservation, without knowing if she were a hundred percent right. Not before these women.

So, Stef knew she was lucky, damned lucky to have found them.

Even if they had snared the final three good men on the planet.

The damned lucky bitches.

So, she told them.

Which earned her a round of hugs, more cackling, and then, eventually, a quiet apartment.

A quiet, lonely apartment.

FOUR

BEN

Sweetheart growled at him when he sank down onto one end of his couch.

The end without the tiny set of stairs he'd bought for the damned dog.

So the damned dog could easily get on his expensive couch and make herself at home.

"At home" meant snarling at him if he dared sit down on said expensive couch.

"Shut it," he muttered, sipping on his beer and reaching for the remote. "And I'm not turning on *Dr. Pol*," he added. "No matter how much you like to watch the male animals get castrated, you ball buster." A snort. "Literally."

Smirking at his own joke and ignoring her huff, he kept drinking and turned on the TV, cued up the guide.

His company was public.

The stock price was good, although it was too early to truly tell if his gamble would pay off. Okay, that was a cop-out. He knew it was going to pay off. The company's valuation was solid, investors were pumped, his business was steady and increasing and *steady.*

A good bet.

A great investment.

So, all would be good.

And for the first time in six fucking years, he could take a breath. He could relax. He could . . . do something that would be relaxing. He just needed to figure out what that would be.

Sex.

Yeah, he could do that. He *should* do that.

When was the last time he'd had an orgasm? Okay, and adding to that, when was the last time he'd had an orgasm that wasn't courtesy of his own hand? Months? Years?

Sweetheart huffed again.

He squinted at the guide on the TV, hit something at random, and if that something was *Dr. Pol* then it wasn't because of the ornery dog next to him.

———

Ben jerked up, his beer sloshing over his hand, splashing onto his expensive couch, probably staining it irrevocably.

The marathon of *Dr. Pol* was still going strong, a line of empty beer bottles on his coffee table, and—his eyes flicked down—the devil dog was curled up next to his thigh. Sweetheart had her head on his thigh, and when he glanced down at her tiny white head, her lips tightened.

"Shut it," he muttered, lifting the bottle to his mouth then wincing and reaching forward to plunk it on the table, ignoring the displeased sound that she made.

It was nearly midnight on a Friday, and he was on the couch with his dead mother's dog—*drunk* on the couch with the dog because he was so out of practice relaxing that five . . . he squinted . . . *six?* . . . beers meant that he was gone.

Room spinning.

Veterinarian on the TV screen shuffling around.

Dog who was the worst dog in the history of all dogs on his lap.

Months since his last orgasm. Years since his last pussy.

For all intents and purposes, he should be out celebrating with a model on each arm. That was what all the tech guys who made it big in Silicon Valley did. They lived large and partied hard, somehow managing to shed their nerdy roots and revel in the excess.

Well, he wasn't much of an excess guy.

And frankly, he was a nerd all the way down to the marrow of his bones.

Before Sweetheart had highjacked his viewing habits, he'd been an all Sci-Fi all the time guy. *Stargate, Farscape, The Expanse, Van Helsing,* old movies he'd seen a million times. The more out there, the better.

He liked to escape.

His reality had been more than e-fucking-nough.

But the last few years, he hadn't needed to escape—or at least, he hadn't needed *that* escape. Work had been enough. There hadn't been a necessity for fantasy.

Now . . . he was a CEO with some time on his hands.

His phone buzzed, and he reached into his pocket to extract it—much to Sweetheart's displeasure—and saw a notification on his screen.

For an app he'd never downloaded.

You've got a new match.

Trailed by some fucking emojis.

"What the hell?" he whispered.

And then he *knew.*

His fingers worked on the screen, ignoring the notification

in lieu of calling the one person who would have the balls to download an app like this onto his phone.

It was nearly midnight on a Friday.

He didn't give a shit.

It rang twice, three times, and then Claire picked up. "Hello?"

Music blared in the background, a thumping bass told him his assistant had more of a social life than he did, and maybe he was an asshole for calling her at midnight on a Friday.

But in that moment, he didn't care.

In that moment, he was tempted to fire her.

Which would make his life a fucking nightmare because she was the best person he'd ever hired.

"You downloaded *Tinder?*" he snapped.

Silence.

Well, silence from the woman, not silence from the background. The bass still thumped, and the noise was intense, so much so that even though he kept the phone a few inches from his ear, he could still hear it.

Same as he could hear her shouted out, "You need to get laid!"

Now, it was his turn for a blip of silence, before he snapped, "I'm your boss, for Christ's sake!"

This time, she didn't miss a beat. "You're my boss, who'll be a better boss if you get laid," she said. "So, consider it my civic duty or office duty or . . . whatever, consider it my duty to humanity to get you a woman so that you can fucking relax."

The balls on this one.

"I should fire you right now."

"Except you won't," Claire said. "Because I'm the shit, and you couldn't survive without me."

Unfortunately, she was right.

"So, enjoy the kickass profile I put together and get swiping.

Find some way"—a hint of humor in her tone—"or rather, some*one* to take the edge off."

Then she hung up.

Hung. Up.

On him. Her boss. The CEO of the company that would set her up for life.

If she didn't get her ass fired.

His phone buzzed.

You're not going to fire me.

Ben narrowed his eyes at the text as another came through.

Now unwind a little. God knows you deserve it.

He kept his eyes narrowed. More buzzing commenced.

I know it's inappropriate, but I love you and care about you.

His glare relaxed, and his fingers moved on the screen.

Fine. You're not fired.

A beat. Then, his phone vibrated again—

I love you too, Claire. That's what you're supposed to say.

That wasn't something he was capable of saying. Not any longer. Which, aside from him working nearly every waking moment, was probably why he was single. All the money in the world couldn't overcome the fact that he didn't have it in him to love anymore.

Sighing, he dropped his phone to the couch cushion, thanking God that it didn't buzz again.

Claire would get back to her night.

He would risk Sweetheart's snarling and get another beer.

Then tomorrow, he'd get back to work. Implement phase two of Hunt Inc.

Because work was all he was capable of. That was it, and anyone who thought that he might be able to give anything more than that was just going to be disappointed in him.

But even with knowing all that . . .

For some reason, he picked up his phone.

And he opened the app.

FIVE

STEF

She loved San Francisco.

She loved her friends—well, the ones she'd made in the last six months, not the jerkwads who'd abandoned her after she and Jeremy had broken up.

Heidi and company were the best. Even if they did get her drunk.

Okay, that was part of the reason they were wonderful.

Also, she loved margaritas. Also, she'd finished the remnants of the sweet and sour drink from the blender, and now she had decided she was *really* in love with margaritas. And her friends. And San Francisco.

And especially in love with the squishy, floating feeling that had invaded her limbs.

What she *didn't* love?

The lack of sex in her life.

Sure, she had her drawer of friendly vibrators, but . . . it wasn't the same.

Okay, sometimes it was *better*. Especially compared to Jeremy and his incompetent penis.

But oftentimes her vibrator time was . . . well, a bit lacking. She wanted more than just a cock. She wanted a hot, hard, strong body poised on top of her. She wanted a man to pick her up and pin her to a wall, pounding deep and hard and—

Hard.

The trouble was that there weren't a lot of men who were interested in a frumpy scientist who had an obsession with *Stargate*.

Especially when her friends had taken all the good men.

"Bitches," she muttered.

Which was why she was lying in bed, wearing her favorite cozy pajamas and trying to work up the urge to . . . swipe right.

Because the man on the app was gorgeous.

When she'd first seen him, her vagina had jumped up, doing a happy dance—complete with pasties and sparklers and a skimpy thong. Well, not so much skimpy because skimpy and her body type didn't mix, but she'd at least slip into some high-cut bikini bottoms, and she'd *definitely* shave her legs.

Maybe her armpits, too.

He was so worth an extended shower and using her expensive soap and spending an hour blow-drying her thick-ass hair.

He would be worth Spanx and lace and—

"Just do it," she whispered.

But the problem with swiping right was that this beautiful man with the sexiest smile she'd ever laid eyes on would invariably swipe left on her picture, and she'd still be here, lying in bed, in her pajamas, and reaching for her vibrator instead of the man himself.

And Fred would be locked in his crate, judging her for getting herself off. *Again*.

But she couldn't flick the bean with her dog in bed next to her.

That was just . . .

She shuddered.

It was also . . . not the point. The *point* being that she was single, and she was horny, and she was drunk.

So drunk. *So* horny. *So* alone.

Le sigh.

That picture called to her again, her thumb hovered over the screen, so close to swiping—

"No," she muttered. "*No* men."

Men were untrustworthy fuckers, who brought unnecessary complications.

Despite their hard cocks that could occasionally bring her to orgasm.

"Ugh."

She tossed her phone on the mattress, hit play on her show, and settled in with her glass of wine (thanks to her hidden stash that her friends hadn't found, ha!) and her sexy, just as fictional as the man in the app, Colonel Jack O'Neill.

See?

Her life was full.

She had good friends. She had good vibrators. She had a good job.

She had a *great* dog.

"I don't need anything else, do I, Fred?"

Her fluffy friend, with his adorable golden retriever face and his fuzzy tail, glanced up at her, tail thumping on the mattress. Yeah, no. No orgasm was worth locking him in his kennel. He was exhausted after a long day of doggy day care, the excitement of her friends coming over, and currently curled up in the space where her imaginary man might reside.

Another *see?*

Because she didn't have room for the app man, any more than she had room for that fictional colonel.

It was her and Fred and her bottle of wine.

That was good enough.

Except . . . it *wasn't* good enough when she finished her episode and went to the kitchen for another bottle of wine, letting the show continue to play. It *wasn't* good enough when she finished that wine over another episode, and her mind got thinking again, only this time swirling because she was plumb full of wine, of margaritas.

It wasn't good enough when her reserve disappeared into the wind, and she used her drunk coordination to pick up her cell, her lack of inhibition to . . . swipe right.

Bleary eyes shutting, she let her arm drop to the bed, the phone slipping out of her grip, sleep claiming her fast and heavily.

And in the morning, *SG-1* still rolling on autoplay, when her headache and hangover meant that she'd almost forgotten about the fictional man and her drunk swiping . . .

In the morning, she woke up, peeled back her lids, squinted with bleary eyes, and saw—

He'd swiped right, too.

Oh, fuck.

SIX

BEN

He'd expected an immediate response.

He'd seen the red lips, the shoulder-length brown hair, the brown eyes that on first glance looked open and happy, but on closer inspection, held a slice of sad.

That sad had called to something inside him.

The eight beers he'd consumed, probably.

But still, he'd ignored everything in him telling him to delete the app, to ignore the woman, to ignore the fire that had begun burning in his gut when he'd seen the sad, and he'd swiped right.

And then he'd expected something to happen.

Instead, he'd gotten a screen telling him he had a match and then . . . nothing.

Now, there was still no response, it was morning and for some fucking reason, he was Googling what he should do after a match and realizing that he probably needed to be the one to take that first step. Which meant he was currently neck-deep in online advice telling him to send a message with everything from "Hey" to snapping a picture of his dick and texting it to her.

The first didn't seem like enough.

The last seemed like a surefire way to get blocked and ruin any chance of tasting those pretty red lips.

So, now he'd opened up the message center and was staring blankly at the box he should be filling with words, with a pithy joke or pickup line, and was back to contemplating deleting the app again, just to put himself out of his misery.

Then his phone pinged.

With a message from her. From Stef McKay.

Hey.

She got to just say *hey?*

Seriously?

What the fuck was that bullshit?

Well, two could play that game. His fingers worked on the phone screen, sent those same three letters back.

Hey.

Take that. Back in her court, Ms. Stef McKay.

Then he realized he was being an idiot and knew he should be saying something else. This was basically a business deal. A transaction that would get them both something mutually satisfactory.

If he looked at it that way, all would be good.

Nodding to himself, he took off his fucking horrible with women hat and put on his business one, and then typed out a message.

You have a nice smile.

Pedestrian.

But a compliment, especially one that wasn't about her tits

(which looked nice from the small glimpse of cleavage in her profile pic) or ass (which he hoped was lush, also based on the curves in her photo), so he figured it was a step up from *hey*.

A moment later, she replied.

You have nice eyes.

He grinned, the compliment flowing over him like warm water. Maybe this online dating thing wasn't so hard.

Except . . . what did he say now? Another compliment, but would that be trying too hard? Should he ask her about work? Or would that come off as creepy, trying to get too much information when they'd just matched on an app and didn't know each other?

Hobbies!

He should ask her about her hobbies.

Quickly, he navigated to her profile, saw a line in the description that said, *Science geek. Golden Retriever lover. Wars over Trek.*

The first and the last made him smile—the last especially—but he didn't know if it was one of those things that women just said, trying to be all nerdy cute. Her picture certainly didn't scream nerd in any way. But paired with the first, he felt a sliver of heat slide through him.

Damn. He needed to search up some science facts to impress her.

Except, what kind of science?

It was kind of a vast area of study, and . . . now he was overthinking this.

He'd stick with the dog. They at least had that in common, although he wouldn't go so far as to say that he was a Sweetheart Lover.

Okay. Dogs.

You like Golden Retrievers?

He sent after navigating back to their chat.
Barely a few seconds before she responded. With a picture.

My Fred.

A hairy face. Friendly eyes. A tongue hanging out that would probably drool all over Ben's expensive shoes. And the fucker was adorable. Not the evil and potential violence of Sweetheart, the I'm-gonna-cut-you-bitch gleaming black eyes.

He's cute. I wrote. *Why Fred?*

Another message came through.

Why not *Fred?*

There was that.

You make a good point.

Her reply came in just a few heartbeats.

Wow. A man who can admit that. Have I stumbled upon a Unicorn?

His brows were drawn together.

A unicorn?

A buzz.

No. Not a unicorn, *but rather a Unicorn. Capital U.*

Um. Okay . . .

Her next reply came, thankfully, before he'd been required to come up with a reply for that.

You like dogs.

Well, now, that wasn't phrased as a question, so he just let it lie there, not touching it, not revealing too much. He hadn't let himself think too much about the things he liked or didn't like, and he didn't think the red-lipped, curved beauty would think much of *him* if he admitted that his dog-liking capabilities fell more into the realm of dog-tolerating.

Instead, he sent,

What kind of science are you a geek about?

This pause was a bit longer.

Physics.

His brows lifted.

Physics? That's impressive. I nearly failed that class in college.

It was the single science class he'd been required to take for his business degree, and no joke, it had nearly killed him. He'd been thrilled to just pass with a C—the only C he'd received in all his advanced studies.

A bachelor's. Two master's.

School had been important to his parents and to him.

But thank fuck business administration and management hadn't required a second round of physics.

Too bad I wasn't around to tutor you. I wouldn't have let you fail, nearly or otherwise.

He knew he would have studied until he passed out if Stef had been his tutor and then probably died for another reason—if one could die of blue balls. Because if he found himself taciturn and withdrawn now, he'd been cripplingly shy in his younger years.

Nose in a book.

Gangly as fuck.

All the way up until his dad had died, and then the fury had taken over. He'd been pissed to lose him, pissed that his mom was devastated, pissed that the world had lost the one person he thought deserved to live over everyone else.

Ben's dad had been good.

So fucking good.

And he'd died for absolutely no reason. Same as his mom. Fucking cancer. Fucking people who just wanted something that didn't belong to him. Fucking . . .

World.

He'd hit the gym after his dad died. Hadn't stopped through his mom's illness, the cancer having been found just months after they had put his dad in the ground. And it had crept through her, taking her strength, her hair, her eyelashes, and finally, her life.

So, sometimes he wanted to go punish something, and he did that to a punching bag. Sometimes he wanted to punish himself, which he did running and lifting until he could barely move the next day.

Now, at least, he wasn't scrawny.

But he still hadn't mastered the art of talking to women.

Case in point, what happened next. Ben sent,

Do you want to grab a coffee?

Then waited for her to reply.

And waited a little longer.

Then still longer.

Or not, he typed. *If you're not comfortable.*

His pulse thrummed as he held his breath, waiting, but after long minutes without her responding, Ben knew he'd fucked up. Pressed too soon, asked her before she was ready. "Fuck," he muttered, tossing his cell on his nightstand and shoving himself out of bed.

Coffee had been the wrong move.

But seriously, this was why he stayed in his world. Because business negotiations were less complicated than women. Maybe he should have doled out another compliment, stuck with asking her something about herself, about fucking physics, rather than moving straight to asking her out.

She probably thought he just wanted to get laid.

Which, yes, that *was* his intention.

But he knew better—or at least he *should* know that this type of thing needed finesse.

He might as well have sent a dick pic.

Sighing, he cranked on the shower and set about getting ready for the day. He'd go into the office, get started on phase two for Hunt Inc. He wanted to go global, and in order to do that, he'd need to make sure all his plans for expansion were in place.

And to do that, he needed to focus on work.

So, he was done thinking about women with sexy red lips and a glimpse of curves he wanted to get his hands on.

Even if that glimpse had him wrapping his fingers around his cock and stroking as the water sluiced down his spine, as the release built up.

This was just as good as a woman.

He didn't need red lips.

Or breasts.

Or an ass to grab on to as he pumped into her pussy, deep and slow and steady. She'd be tight. She'd grind back against him, and—

"Fuck," he groaned, slamming his hand against the tile as he came.

Imagining red lips.

Imagining curves.

Imagining . . . Stef McKay.

And knowing his hand wouldn't be anything when compared to her.

SEVEN

STEF

Do you want to grab a coffee?

Such a simple question.

An easy yes or no . . . and in this case, it should most definitely be a yes. Because Ben Bradford was gorgeous, and he'd said he liked her smile, and he hadn't sent her a picture of his cock or asked her to meet up to fuck without any fluff.

He'd asked her to coffee.

And she'd launched her phone across the room in a fit of panic, startling Fred awake. Which had led to her pupper needing to get pottied and fed *right* then. Which was fine, because she couldn't look at that message and not start thinking about what in the fuck she had been doing to have swiped on the sexy Denzel in his younger days, cropped hair, stubbled jaw, deep, beautiful eyes man who'd come across her feed.

She was short and stout—

Like a fucking teapot.

Her hair was mud colored. Her eyes were fine, albeit a boring brown. Her skin was nice, if someone liked the nearly see-through version of white of someone who worked in a lab all day and rarely saw the sun—unless it was on beach day, and then that was as the sun was going down, so it didn't do much to add any color.

She didn't match with a man like Ben, even if an app had let her pretend that might be the case, just for a minute.

So, she'd left her cell in the corner of the room, had let Fred into the back yard for a few minutes so he could do his business, and then set about making his brekkie, with his vitamins and his shredded chicken and his super expensive kibble.

Then she fed her boy, showered, and she set about planning her meals for the week, just like she did every Saturday.

She went to the farmer's market, the grocery store. She chopped and threw chicken in the Crock-Pot and prepped her lunches for the week, using some of that chicken but saving most of it for Fred and his meals. While doing all that, she watched a couple of episodes of a promising new superhero show on Netflix, knowing she'd complete the eight-part binge that evening.

After beach time.

And beach time was glorious.

Beach time was beautiful, the perfect mix of late afternoon sunshine and early evening breeze, the stars just beginning to shine.

Fred was exhausted when they returned, having just barely summoned the energy to eat before putting himself in his crate, a rare occurrence that illustrated exactly how much fun her little man had had splashing in the waves.

So now, she was eating a salad and eyeing her phone.

Do you want to get a coffee?

She did. Stef wanted that. *Bad.* And that was what fucking terrified her. Because she'd barely recovered from Jeremy, and

Jeremy had been an asshole. Ben Bradford might turn out to be an asshole, too, but he'd complimented her smile, and Jeremy had never done that, never complimented much about her, and certainly not just out of the blue. To avoid a fight? Oh yeah. To get laid? Certainly. But just something nice without being prompted? No, not that she could think of. All of which said something sad about her, something that she didn't want to keep considering because it illustrated exactly how pathetic she'd been to waste her time with Jeremy.

Had he ever liked her?

Like at all?

Or had she been convenient and allowed herself to be a punching bag?

He must have been nice in the beginning. He had to have been. Right? Except . . . she couldn't think of any examples, and that just made her feel worse about herself.

Which . . . seriously, how was that possible?

More than six months of pretending to be fine about the breakup while knowing that she hadn't been fine before, hadn't been fine while they were together.

But she was going to be fine.

And she was also kidding herself if she thought that Ben didn't have an ulterior motive. He wasn't looking for love. Just like Jeremy, he wanted to bone and then go on with his life.

Tell me how you know that.

Why—seriously, fucking *why*—did every second guess she had of herself come in the form of her mom's voice? Always chastising and disapproving. Always making her second-guess what she was doing.

Fuck.

"Enough," she murmured. "Just enough."

That was a sufficient amount of self-reflection and pitying for the evening. She needed to go back to what she did best—looking forward, picking up, and moving on. She'd done it when her brother had been sick, so sick, so troubled, struggling so *fucking* much, that she'd basically been on her own. Alone, even amongst her family, she'd needed to live her own life. She'd done it when he'd taken his own life and her parents had needed someone to pick up the pieces and move everyone on.

But she'd spent too long picking up the pieces for everyone else.

Now, she needed to pick them up, only for herself this time.

That was why she left her phone in the corner of the room, the battery slowly draining, while she and Fred finished bingeing that superhero show.

EIGHT

BEN, THREE MONTHS LATER

He ran a hand over his head, feeling the bristles of his hair against his palm, knowing he needed a haircut, yet not wanting to take the time to bother.

Hunt Inc. was firmly in phase two.

He'd worked himself to exhaustion every night for the last few months. The company's stock was up. He'd never been more productive.

But he couldn't stop jacking off to red lips and deep brown eyes.

His cock twitched.

"Fuck," he muttered, tossing the file he'd been reading onto his desk, just as there was a perfunctory knock at the door and Claire stuck her head in the opening.

"Do I need to escort you down to your car?" she said, leaning a hip against the doorframe. "Or are you going to leave at a reasonable hour for the first time in an eternity?"

Ben sighed, considered telling her to piss off, or maybe

threatening to fire her again. But that never worked, and frankly, he didn't have the energy for it.

Not today.

Not on *this* day.

He'd put his mom in the ground exactly one year before.

"Ben?" Claire asked, the sass leaving her tone, worry taking its place. "You okay?"

He blinked, pushed to his feet, and reached into the top drawer of his desk to retrieve his wallet. "I'm out of here."

"You are?" she asked, shifting to the side when he approached the door. "Really?"

"It's Friday," he told her. "Why don't you take off early, too?"

Her brows lifted before she lifted her wrist and glanced at her watch. "Early meaning eight-thirty?"

Shit. Was it already eight-thirty?

He glanced out the windows, saw that it was dark. Ah. Yeah, it was.

"Okay," he amended. "Why don't you get out of here now?"

"That's the plan." She followed him toward the elevator after briefly asking, "You want to come out with us?"

He snorted. "You want to drink a beer with your boss?"

She glanced up at him as they stepped onto the elevator. "You realize we've been friends for near on a decade," she said. "Just because I'm your assistant—"

"Should I point out that you're my assistant because you refused my offer to be VP?"

She made a face. "I don't have the requisite fancy letters after my name to take that position," she muttered, hitting the button to take them down to the garage. "I didn't even finish high school, for God's sake."

Ben covered her hand with his. "You're the smartest person I know. Bar none."

A scoff, her fingers slipping from his. "So says the boy

genius."

He rolled his eyes. "So says your *boss*, who's not going to hire another VP because I expect your ass to be in that office come Monday morning."

"You won't be able to get through your day without me."

That was the worst part of offering Claire the position. He'd be out the best assistant in his crew. But also, he wouldn't be the person who was going to hold her back, and God knew he should have made this move for her years ago.

She knew every role in the company, had worked every job, had been his right hand from the moment he'd started the business. His first employee. His friend.

"You're right," he said. "But I'll have Spence and Baine and even though I won't have another Claire, I'll be happy because I know that you'll be where you should be."

"You'll be miserable."

"That, too." He shrugged, not bothering to hide his smile. "Except, I also know that you'll have a replacement ready for me on Monday, and you'll train him or her up so he or she will be a mini-Claire before long."

She made a face.

He shrugged again. "You're only mad because you know it's true."

The elevator doors opened with a ding, and they stepped off, this time with Claire glaring up at him. "Only because I don't want to hear you bitch about how incompetent your new assistant is, over and *over* again."

"I don't bitch about Spence and Baine."

"Not anymore." A beat. "And only because Baine is training Spence."

He rolled his eyes. "I'm not *that* bad."

She just looked at him.

"Okay, fine," Ben muttered. "But it's not a bad thing to like things the way I like them."

Claire smirked. "You're a boring stick in the mud."

Since that much was true, he didn't bother arguing.

"Stick. In. The. Mud."

He rolled his eyes. "*Claire.*"

"You deleted the app, didn't you?" she asked, as he walked her to her car. "Without even bothering to match with anyone."

No. He hadn't deleted the app.

He'd left it on his phone, buried in a folder, and occasionally opened the message chain and called himself a moron. And then he'd scroll to that profile, to that picture, to those red lips.

And he'd want to get *Moron* tattooed on his forehead.

"I don't have time to date."

"So, you're just going to work nonstop for another eight years, let the world pass you by, and not have anything on the other side of it?"

"Not nothing," he said, tugging open the door for her. "I have you."

Claire's lips pressed flat. "I'm dating someone."

This made his brows raise. "Is it serious?"

She grinned. "No."

He snorted. "Then I've still got my fabulous new VP."

Quiet, amusement drifting across her face. "That you do."

"Yeah?" he asked, fighting a smile at the first sign of her agreeing to take the positon.

Another grin. "Yeah."

Ben leaned down and kissed her cheek. "That's better than a match any day of the week."

Her expression went soft. "Ben—"

He straightened. "See you Monday."

Then he closed her door, moved to his own car, and drove home.

Because, between then and Monday, he'd do what he did best.

Work.

NINE

She was bordering on buzzed.

Margaritas for the win, but this time of the prickly pear variety.

They were eating at their favorite Mexican place, and while they usually met on Thursdays, this week Stef, Tammy, Cora, and the Couples, as they'd termed the other non-single women and their partners in their friend group, had gotten together on Friday.

They had chips and fajitas and prickly pear margaritas.

And fun.

Lots and lots of fun.

But even though it was tempting to dive into the newest pitcher of margaritas, she was tired. It had been a long week, and Fred had woken her up early that morning. She knew that if she had another glass, she was going to be straight buzzed, and then she wouldn't be driving home.

She'd need a ride to the restaurant in the morning, and her

chores and errands would start last. Which meant beach day would probably be delayed, and . . . Fred would unhappy.

Which meant *she* would be unhappy.

Because the little—big—fuzz bucket would probably take his unhappiness out on her sock drawer.

And she wasn't willing to give up a single pair of them.

So she had cut herself off, was eating her homemade tortillas like a champ, and going to make sure her buzz trickled away so she could drive safely home to her little Freddy-bear.

Grinning to herself, she scooped up an obscene amount of salsa onto a chip and crammed it into her mouth. Then another tortilla. Then more peppers and onions and steak and salsa and chips until she felt like she was bursting from all the food. Only then did she look up and see the entire table staring at her. "What?" she asked, and so yeah, maybe it was muffled from the remnants of a chip in her mouth.

Tanner's brows lifted, his gaze turning to Kelsey. "Should I check and see if the kitchen has any food left?"

Stef glared.

Kels popped him on the shoulder. "Rude much?"

"The girl just hoovered everything on the table," he said. "I don't think that I'm rude, so much as impressed. Where does she put it all?"

Now Stef rolled her eyes. "It's her fault," she mumbled after chewing and swallowing, pointing at Heidi. "She works me to the bone, night and day."

Heidi gasped. "How dare you?"

"How dare *I*?" Stef teased. "I'm not the one who ate *my* lunch."

Narrowed eyes, even as the table broke out into laughter mixed with admonishments. "That was one time," Heidi said. "And it was an accident."

Stef smirked. "An accident that you ate the whole thing?"

Heidi blushed.

"I'm just saying, I'm not the only one who can eat." She pointed at the table, where the rest of them had gone to town on their own plates. "And also, I like salsa too much to give a shit about the fact that I'm carrying a taco baby around."

Click.

She blinked at the flash, the sound of Tanner taking a photograph.

"Sorry," Tanner said, setting his camera on the table. "You're beautiful."

It wasn't a come-on, or weird—or not that much anyway. Tanner was a photographer. World-famous, supremely talented. People paid boatloads of money to get him to take their picture.

But he took a lot of photos of everyone when they were all together, and they were fabulous.

Including, she saw when she gestured for the camera and he handed it over, glancing at the screen on the back, the one he'd just taken of her.

If Stef hadn't been looking at herself, she would have agreed the woman in the photograph was beautiful. Fierce eyes, a flush on her cheeks, hair shining from the lights overhead. There was fire in her, even though she'd been yelling about food and taco babies.

It was . . . nice to see the fire again.

"Okay?" Tanner asked, squatting next to her and sliding the camera from her hands. He glanced at her face and winced. "Never mind, I'll delete it."

"No," she said, covering his fingers with her own. "It's . . . will you send it to me?"

His face gentled. "Of course." A beat. "And for the record, I wasn't trying to make fun of you, I *was* truly impressed." A grin. "From one Hoover to the next."

Laughing, she nudged his shoulder. "Speaking of which, you'd better go eat up before I take care of business for you."

A grin. "Noted."

She glanced up, saw Kels smiling apologetically, but Stef just shook her head, letting her friend know she was in on the joke and happy with the picture, even if it felt a bit like Tanner was their own paparazzo.

Still, it was nice to have the moments documented.

She didn't have many pictures of herself.

She wasn't really into selfies, and Jeremy certainly hadn't taken many of her, and her parents . . . well, sometimes things slipped through the cracks when a family was just trying to survive.

Tammy nudged her arm. "You okay, bugaboo?"

Stef's brows lifted. "Bugaboo?"

"Ignore me." Tammy's cheeks went a little pink. "As much as I want to not be like my mother, she still creeps in sometimes."

"That's not a bad thing," Stef told her. "I've met your mom, and she's great."

A sigh. "She *is* great," Tammy agreed, sadness flickering behind her pale brown eyes. "But try living in the shadow of all that greatness."

Stef knew something about shadows, something she'd shared the barest of details with her friends. *Something* that Tammy obviously remembered because she reached over and grabbed Stef's hand. "Shit," she said. "I'm sorry."

"Hey." Stef nudged her shoulder, squeezed back. "We're not in a one-upmanship trauma contest. If it hurt your heart, you don't get to discount it." She smiled. "You can move past it, but you don't get to discount it. It's part of you and important and—"

She broke off.

"Sorry," she murmured. "This is too serious of a conversation for prickly pear margaritas."

On that note, she decided to fuck it all, tugged her hand from Tammy's, and poured herself another margarita.

A Lyft it would be.

Fred would just have to deal.

Tammy's fingers brushed the back of Stef's. "You're an amazing woman," she said, and Stef forced herself to accept the compliment, to not snort and discount it like her first instinct pressed her to do.

"Thank you," Stef murmured. "You are, too."

Tammy grinned. "I wasn't done, you know?"

"Done with what?" Heidi asked, her focus drawn from across the table to their conversation.

"Done with complimenting Stef and watching her squirm because she doesn't believe them," Tammy said.

"Oh!" Heidi clapped her hands together. "I like this game."

Stef groaned, began sucking back her margarita.

"She's brilliant," Heidi said. "My lab wouldn't run nearly as efficiently without her."

Another groan, her head falling to the table.

Kate laughed, drawing Stef's focus. "I'd add kind to that list." A smile. "And a great baker." She rubbed her stomach. "Based on the dozen muffins I ate last time you brought them to our house."

"And didn't share," Jaime, her husband, added with a wink. Kate narrowed her eyes, but Jaime just smoothed her hair back, kissed her cheek, and then turned back to Stef. "My addition to the list is that she's a great dog mom."

Okay, now her heart was melting. Because Jaime was Jaime the Vet, and knowing that he approved of her dog mom skills meant a lot.

Her Fred was a special boy.

"Thanks, Jaime."

He winked, snagged a pepper from Kate's plate.

"Are we going around the table?" Brad asked, his eyes—a slightly deeper brown than his brother's—sparkling with humor.

"God, no," Stef muttered.

"Yes!" Cora said. "She has great taste in nerd. *Stargate-SG1* is the shit."

"Oh, Lord," Stef moaned, dropping her head to the table again. But only for a moment, because Cora tugged her up and shoved her glass in her hand.

"Drink and absorb," she ordered.

Drink. Oh, she'd *drink* all right. She glugged down that margarita, refilled her glass, and continued shoveling in chips and salsa.

"Great," Brad said. "I'll go next."

She clenched her teeth together, met his gaze when he waited for her to meet his eyes, all the aplomb of a magician gathering his audience's attention. "I'd second the good baker"—a pat to his belly—"and good dog mom."

Her cheeks blazed.

"That Fred, even with his obsession with squirrels, is a good boy."

"He is," she murmured.

He grinned. "But I'd say, more than that, you're a good friend, and we're all lucky to have you in our lives."

Not, the girls were lucky to have her.

But *all* of them.

She sniffed.

All the women sniffed.

"How the hell am I supposed to follow that?" Kels grumbled, even as Stef was thinking *how in the hell was she supposed to act like this was all normal when she felt like her heart was going to explode out of her chest?*

Meanwhile, Tanner said, "I'll just reiterate *beautiful.*"

Silence.

Then more sniffing.

Cora whispered, "All the good men." A beat. "The bitches have taken them all."

Stef sighed, even though they were both smiling. Because

fucking hell, she was right. "I know," she muttered and turned to Tammy. "How in the hell are you supposed to date someone and not compare them to those jokers?"

Tammy shook her head, ponytail fluttering behind her. "I don't date." A shrug. "So, the problem is solved." Her lips twitched. "No comparisons necessary."

"Probably for the best," Stef said, reaching for her glass again.

She held it up, touched it to Tammy's.

"To margaritas over men."

Tammy grinned, tapped back. "To margaritas over men."

TEN

BEN

His phone buzzed when he was debating getting up and going to bed.

He picked it up off the table, expecting to see a text but instead heat trailed down his spine and red lips flashed to the forefront of his mind.

Holding his breath, he opened the app.

I'm sorry I didn't reply.

Shock washed over him, and he found his fingers moving without thinking.

Why didn't you?

Silence.
No response for long minutes.
His gut sank, and he tossed his phone on the table. He needed to delete the fucking app and just be done with it.

Sweetheart snarled as he flopped back on the couch—well, more grumble than growl. Things between them had improved, mostly because he'd stopped trying to get pet sitters and had just been bringing the princess into the office with him every day.

He, apparently, was the least unpleasant scenario.

It might also be that him bringing her to his office every day meant that she could growl at him at will.

His phone buzzed again, surprising the hell out of him.

I was scared.

Ben read those three words and came to the obvious conclusion. He was a Black guy. She was a white girl. *Of course,* she was scared of him. It fucking sucked, but it wasn't the first time he'd gotten that reaction, and no doubt it wouldn't be the last. It just . . . hurt.

This time, he was the one who didn't respond.

He dropped his phone back on the table and went into the bathroom, brushing his teeth, washing his face, going to bed . . . except, he needed to charge his phone. And that was the only reason he went back to the family room and picked up his cell.

The *only* reason.

But when he happened to glance at the screen—happened to see the open app—he saw that it was filled with messages.

I was scared because you're beautiful. The most beautiful man I've ever seen. And I'm just me, whose boyfriend broke up with her because she was boring.

And also maybe because I loved my dog more than him.

You're mysterious and sexy and have amazing eyes and stubble and . . . I usually spend my nights watching Stargate while reading research papers.

You asked me to coffee and I panicked and I shouldn't be typing this.

But I'm drunk and waiting for my Lyft and . . . shit. I know I shouldn't be typing this.

So why can't I stop?

Right.

Because I'm drunk and my Lyft doesn't appear to be coming.

So I'm going to request another one, save you from my drunk ass, and go back to not messaging you.

Not that you'll do anything but block me after this.

Or not respond. Because I deserve that.

Anyway, goodbye, Ben. Sorry I ghosted you before.

He reached the end of that text diarrhea to find his heart pounding, hope he was trying to ignore blossoming inside him.

Because she was drunk and waiting for a ride, who knew where, and he shouldn't give a fuck, but his gut was twisting itself into knots thinking of red lips and curves being out there and drunk and . . . vulnerable.

Where are you?

He sent it and when she didn't immediately respond, he sent another message.

Stef, honey, where are you right now?

A few seconds, his stomach clenched tight, before she replied.

Bobby's Bar. My friends and I went for drinks after dinner.

Relief coursed through him.

You're not alone then? They'll get you home?

A long pause.

I put them in their Lyft. Waiting for mine.

"Fuck," he hissed, shoving his feet into his shoes and shrugging into his jacket.

How long?

He moved out his front door, down the elevator to the garage.

For what?

Clamping the phone into the holder perched in his air vent, he replied before backing out of the stall.

Until the Lyft comes.

He was already on the freeway when she replied.

Don't worry about it.

Fucking hell. He pulled over, typed a message, then continued driving.

How long?

A long pause, long enough that Ben's teeth felt as though they'd been ground down to their nubs. Then her response came through, and it made pain radiate down his jaw.

It's surging. Still trying to match.

He pulled in a breath through his nose, glad that he was only a few minutes out, and released it slowly as he exited the freeway and paused at the signal at the bottom of the off-ramp.

Risking a ticket, he speed-typed then continued driving.

I'll be there in five minutes.

Nothing.

Then a flurry of messages came through.

He caught one of them as he stopped at a stop sign, but then he was continuing to drive, nearing the entrance of Bobby's and slowing, looking for curves and red lips and . . .

There.

Shorter than he'd expected.

An ass that looked glorious in a pair of jeans. He'd known. He'd *known*.

Carefully, he pulled up to the curb and rolled down the window. "Stef."

Her eyes were wide, and when he said her name, she squeaked. Literally squeaked. Fuck, she was cute. He put on the flashers and got out, rounding the hood and stopping in front of her.

Freckles.

She had a swathe of freckles on her nose.

Her hair was pulled back into a low ponytail, a few whisps having escaped to frame her face. "Get in," he said. "I'll drive you home."

"You're here," she breathed, lifting her hand up as though she'd stroke his jaw. But her fingers halted, just before she touched him, near enough that he could actually feel the heat from them on his skin.

Then she skittered back a step.

"You're *here?*" Her mouth opened and closed a few times. "But why are you here?"

He glanced over his shoulder. "I need to move my car. You getting in, so I can drive you home?"

Her teeth nibbled on her bottom lip.

"Not a serial killer," he said. "I promise. You can call your friends and stay on the line with them on the way, if that makes you feel better."

She still nibbled.

He bit back a sigh. "I'll park and wait until your Lyft gets here." Ben turned back to his car and started to get in. He'd seen a spot just around the corner.

"Why are you here, Ben?"

The sound of his name in her voice, a little huskier than he'd expected, made a shiver skate down his spine. His nostrils flared. "You said you were drunk and without a ride. I needed . . ."

Her eyes widened, and she stepped closer. "Needed what?" she breathed.

"To make sure you got home safe," he snapped, glaring at the people gathered in front of the bar, coupled off and talking or kissing, the shadows where who knew what threat lurked.

"I'm perfectly capable of getting home."

"You *said* you were drunk." A beat. "And alone."

Her mouth hitched up. Then she patted his arm, brushed by him, and got into his car.

The slam of the door startled him out of his shock, and he spun, got into the driver's seat, and pulled down the street, navigating his way back to the freeway. "Where to?" he asked, when he realized he didn't know which direction to go.

She gave him directions, a far sight south of the bar, south of his place in the city.

"You don't seem very drunk," he said after a few moments.

Stef rolled her head on the seat, turning to look at him. He saw that her pupils were wide and dark pools in the moonlight before he forced his eyes back to the road. "It's just—" She broke off, was quiet for long enough that he wanted to press, but then she spoke again. "I'm really good at faking I'm okay." Then just as quickly as that admission came, she cleared her throat, looked back at the road, and her voice went chipper. "But I couldn't drive home, anyway. My car is at the restaurant we ate dinner at." She named a popular Mexican place in the area.

"I see."

He didn't see.

Not at all.

But her lips were painted red, her curves were in the seat next to him, and he had a long drive ahead of them.

All of a sudden, his night was looking up.

ELEVEN

STEF

S he still had a lovely floaty feeling, but she knew that her being in this car wasn't her drunk mind hallucinating.

Ben was here.

He'd come because he was worried she was sloppy and on the street without a safe way to get home.

Her heart was . . . vulnerable.

Oh boy, *was* it vulnerable.

Her kryptonite was someone taking care of her, looking out for her without her asking. Without her begging.

And even her margarita brain could recognize that it was a weakness, that it was stupid to have gotten in a car with a man she didn't know, to give him her address, to have drunk messaged him in the first place.

Stupid. So stupid.

Except . . . his eyes.

They were gentle, and then he'd told her to call a friend and stay on the line while he drove, and a muscle in his jaw had ticked, and she'd wanted to stroke the muscle twitching in that jaw, to feel the bristles on her fingertips.

And he'd gone out of his way to come help her.

So, here she was. In the passenger seat of a sleek sports car, its engine rumbling beneath her as he drove through the night. It was clear, the moon bright and gleaming, the fog having stayed curled over the ocean, not invading inland yet. That fog would probably creep inward at some point, but for right now, she was enjoying the gleam of the moon, casting everything in silver.

"Thank you," she murmured. "You didn't have to do this."

"It's nothing."

Not to her.

So she said, "Not to me." And then she said something that she certainly wouldn't have said if she'd been stone-cold sober, something she would have been too tongue-tied to say without alcohol. "I don't want to go home yet."

His gaze drifted to hers again. "Where do you want to go?"

She shrugged.

Quiet then, "I know a place."

She inhaled sharply. She should tell him to forget it, to take her home, to forget about this and her drunk message and her fantasies. Because her heart was vulnerable, and if he continued being nice, then she was going to fall for him.

Just like she'd fallen for Jeremy.

And look how that turned out.

But instead, she asked, "What kind of place?"

"A quiet one."

Her lips twitched. "Where you can pull out those serial killer skills?"

He chuckled, and the sound rolled over her, warm fingers trailing over her skin. "Quiet, but not private. Plenty of people around to keep those in check."

Stef's brows drew together, confusion and curiosity threading through her. "Is it an orgy?" she asked suspiciously, though not realizing until after it was out there that an orgy probably wouldn't be quiet.

Ben was, though.

Until he burst out laughing, and then *that* sound was warm, like rough palms on her naked skin, a hard cock between her thighs, sliding home. She shifted on her seat, legs pressing together, heat making her pussy slick.

"Not an orgy," he murmured.

But he wouldn't be opposed to it? her brain helpfully chimed in.

Or unhelpfully? Because Ben was wearing a tight navy T-shirt and gray sweats that clung to powerful thighs. His biceps were solid, his shoulders broad and something she could grab on to.

He might be the sexiest man she had ever seen.

No, he *was* the sexiest man she'd ever seen.

"And not a creepy basement?" she blurted.

His grin flashed in the moonlight. "Not a basement. But dark and quiet and talking is frowned upon." He slanted a glance in her direction. "You in?"

Her teeth found her bottom lip, nibbled lightly.

Then she inhaled, exhaled, and thought, *fuck it all*. Maybe it was the booze. Maybe it was Ben and his eyes, his smile, the fantasy of his stubble on her skin.

She met his eyes. "I'm in."

———

This was not what she'd expected.

Not at all.

She glanced up at the illuminated sign overhead, a vertical set of letters spelling out Cinema, at the white rectangle, black letters spelling out the title of the latest Sci-Fi flick, and felt her heart squeeze tight.

He remembered.

The movie theater was small, only one screen, an old-fashioned box office encased in glass, the smell of popcorn filling the air.

"Still in?" he asked, having returned from the box office with two tickets in hand. He held them up, tiny strips of white paper that were dwarfed by his large hands.

"That depends."

His head tilted to the side, the question written in his eyes.

"Will you let me buy you popcorn?"

His brows drew together. "You want to buy me popcorn?"

Her heart sank. "You don't like popcorn?"

"I love popcorn."

She frowned. "Then what's the problem?"

"You want to buy *me* popcorn?" he repeated.

Ah. She understood where this was going. "You got the tickets. You rescued me. You're driving me around on a whim. The least I can do is get some popcorn." She took his hand, fingers weaving together. There were hard callouses on his palms, and she wondered where he'd gotten them from, what kind of work he did. His profile had just said business owner.

But his hands seemed to scream something physical.

Suddenly, she was imagining him in flannel and a hard hat, or maybe flannel and an ax, all lumbersexual and yummy.

"Come on," she murmured, still filled with that fluffy, fuzzy margarita feeling, although the buzz was fading, and Stef couldn't help but wonder if it was more Ben Buzz and less anything to do with tequila.

"Come on," she said again, tugging him toward the doors. "I'll even spring for candy."

TWELVE

BEN

There was a giant tub of popcorn between them, two huge sodas settled in the cupholders on opposite armrests.

And candy.

A KitKat and licorice filled with something tart.

More sugar than he'd consumed in years, especially when considering the gallon of soda at his left arm.

But Stef was happily munching away, blasting through the popcorn, and he had to get in there or he might miss the buttery goodness. And then there was the fact that she'd lifted the armrest between them the moment they'd sat down, bringing her lush, gorgeous body close enough for him to smell the floral scent of her, to trace every glorious, curvy line with his eyes, to maybe even touch if he worked up the courage.

"You going to have some?" she asked through a mouthful of popcorn, holding up the bucket.

And fuck, she was cute.

Again.

He took a handful, shoved it in his mouth, and then, not so casually, slid his arm around her shoulders. She glanced up at him, the flicker of amusement telling him she was well-aware of what he was doing, but she didn't comment, just shifted a little closer, her shoulder tucking under his.

And his cock twitched.

No, not twitched.

It went hard.

And he was wearing fucking sweatpants.

Carefully, he took the bucket and shifted it over to his lap, covering his erection and knowing that he was a fucking pervert when the barest touch of her shoulder to his caused his dick to flare to attention.

"Thief," she accused lightly, but she didn't move or take the popcorn back.

Thank fuck.

Instead, she continued eating and then offered him a piece of KitKat.

He took it, nibbled as she devoured three-quarters of the pack. "You going to puke in my car later?"

Her head tilted against his arm, ponytail a silken sheet on his bare skin. Lips curving, she stared up at him. "I've been told I resemble a Hoover."

"As in the vacuum?"

Her mouth tipped up further. "Exactly."

"And no post-vacuuming puking?"

Her smile didn't fade. "None," she murmured, and then it did. "Ben?" she asked quietly as the lights had gone down.

"Yeah?"

"Thanks for this."

Now, he was the one who was smiling. "You're welcome," he said softly, brushing her hair off her face, tucking a strand behind her ear.

———

She'd been riveted.

Absolutely riveted by the movie, so focused on the story that *he'd* missed most of it. Because he'd been too absorbed with her. The soft gasps when the tension grew taut, the music building, some plot point blaring to life and making her jump in his arms. The way she cried when one of the main characters died. How she rested against him and sighed in happiness when the spaceship made it back to Earth, most of the crew intact.

Then the credits were rolling, and she was sitting up, and he hated that she'd left him, even though it was just to gather up her trash, even though she was still there, just two feet away. But not in his arms.

Because he liked her there.

"Have you sobered up?" he asked as the lights came back on and they began moving up the aisle.

Her ponytail fluttered behind her as she turned her head to look at him. "Yes." A frown. "Why?"

"If so, I can drive you back to your car," he offered. "That way, you don't have to get a ride in the morning."

Was that a flicker of disappointment over her face?

It was there and gone faster than he could process it, and then she was walking again. "Oh, okay," she whispered, and he barely heard her. But he *did* hear the sad creep into her tone, and yes, the disappointment that had his stomach clenching tight. "That would be great, actually."

One arm held the empty popcorn container, along with her nearly empty cup of soda, his nearly full one, and the candy wrappers.

But he had one arm free.

And *that* was the one he wrapped around Stef's waist, the one he used to draw her back against him, to turn her so every inch of those curves were pressed to him, her breath puffing against his lips.

"What are you doing?" she breathed.

"First date."

Her brows lifted, but she melted against him, and he was hard again, nearly shaking with the need to claim her mouth.

"What is?" she asked. "Do you want to go out—"

"Kiss," he managed, desire making it difficult to form words. But he'd managed that one, and it was a fucking relief.

"Kiss?"

"Yes. Kiss," he said, and through some herculean effort managed to add, "I'm going to kiss you." He slid his hand up, between her shoulder blades, and weaved it into her hair, probably screwing up her ponytail but unable to summon a care. Not when her lips were right there.

Not when she pressed closer.

Not when she took the bucket from him and dropped it to the floor.

"Okay then," she breathed, wrapping her arms around his neck and raising onto tiptoe. "Then kiss me."

Ben lowered his head, slanted his lips across hers, and felt . . .

Nothing.

Absolutely nothing.

No, not *nothing*. It was . . . peace and coming home and a dark, starlit sky on a summer evening. It was even and steady and balanced—

Stef moaned, her lips parting, her tongue darting out to touch the seam of his mouth.

And the world exploded—or at least *his* did. He was staring straight into the sun and the warmth was washing over him. He'd felt nothing and now he felt *everything*. His nerves were on fire, his dick was granite. She tasted sweet and salty with a floral note beneath. His hands roamed, taking in those curves as she thrust her tongue into his mouth and stroke it against his. The kiss—*she* was fucking glorious, and he was on fire and—

A throat cleared.

Loudly enough that it told him that it wasn't the first time the person had tried to get their attention.

Stef stiffened in his arms, her wide eyes coming to his.

He released her, bent to pick up the bucket, needing it because . . . fucking erections like he was twelve years old. Positioning it in front of him, he turned to face the person who interrupted them. The usher appeared all of eighteen, and though his cheeks were pink, he didn't look at them as he pushed the trash can by them.

"Did you want," Stef asked, her own color high, "to throw—"

Ben shook his head.

"You—"

He glanced down, back up, lifted a brow.

Her cheeks went pinker. "Ah."

Fucking cute.

Fucking not helping his situation.

"Did you want—"

His eyes shot to hers. So help him God, if she tried to get rid of the popcorn container, he was going to use *her* as a shield. Especially since it didn't seem like his erection was going to recede anytime soon.

Not with her swollen lips. Not with her fucking squeezable ass . . . *right there.*

So not helping.

"—to go back to my place?"

His cock surged again, and he almost felt dizzy from the amount of blood gathering in the southern portion of his body. As thus, it took him a moment to gather his thoughts, to be able to speak.

Enough for him to see that disappointment creep into her face.

"Or not—"

He took her hand, drew her against him, rocking his hips against her ass, knowing it was crude and not giving a shit since it felt so *fucking* good.

"My place is closer," he breathed into her ear.

She shivered, ass tilted back. "Okay then," she murmured.

Then she took his hand and led him from the theater.

Thirteen

Stef

He held her hand the entire way back to his condo, one rough finger stroking the inside of her wrist, shivers sliding up her arm, through her middle, and down between her thighs.

She was dripping wet.

She was aching.

Then he parked and opened her door, tugging her up and toward a bank of elevators. A swipe of a card. A code punched into the keypad.

The steel doors opened.

They stepped inside.

And then he was on her.

His body pinning her against one wall, his hands beneath her ass, lifting her so she was propped onto the railing, her legs wrapped around his hips, the fabric between them doing nothing to blunt the hard jut of his cock.

She rocked against it, and he hissed out a breath, the warm

puff of air hitting her lips just a heartbeat before he pressed his mouth to hers.

Another kiss, sinking deep into her, pulling her into another dimension where everything felt right and perfect and . . . as though she'd known this man for an eternity. As though she could continue kissing him forever.

The doors opened on an absurd *ping*, and they took a while to pull away from each other, Ben finally drawing back enough to clamp a hand around one of the metal panels when it began to close on them. Grinning, he tugged her off the bar, leading her out of the small metal death box and into the hall . . . or not the hall.

Into an . . . entryway.

Stumbling, she glanced around, brain trying to process mirrors and marble and a large thick white rug that had to be hell to keep clean. "This is your *place?*"

"Yup."

His fingers tight on hers, he drew her down the hall, past a huge kitchen with sleek white cabinets and gray countertops, past a sunken living room filled with a giant TV and a large gray sectional, past a—

Growling filled the air.

"Fuck," Ben hissed, yanking her behind him. "Careful," he said. "I'll grab her and—"

A tiny, fluffy white ball of adorableness sprinted down the hall, her growl far too fierce for her size, the sound of it echoing down all the marble.

He bent, but the pup dodged around him, fur ruffling under his fingers when he released her hand to snag the dog.

"It's okay," she said, kneeling down to meet the little pupper. "Hi, baby." She extended a hand—

"No, *don't.*"

A cold, wet nose grazed the back of hers.

"Stef," Ben ordered. "Stand up, slowly and carefully."

Her eyes found his. "Why—" The dog began licking her hand in earnest before burrowing close, nearly knocking Stef down when she all but crawled into her lap. Sinking back onto her ass, she began scratching and rubbing and found herself being kissed all over.

The last thought had her looking up at Ben, remembering how very close *he'd* been to kissing her all over.

His expression was a mixture of horror and shock.

Maybe he didn't want to kiss a woman all over who'd been on the receiving end of a dog's tongue?

She winced. Yeah, that was probably true.

"I'll . . . uh . . . wash my hands before we . . ." She trailed off, pointed her finger between them. "Continue with—"

Ben blinked and sank down next to her.

The adorable angel in her lap growled.

"She doesn't like me."

Now it was Stef's turn to blink, to wonder why a man who lived in a fucking penthouse with marble and mirrors and a white freaking rug in the entryway was living with a dog who couldn't stand him.

"She doesn't like *anyone.*"

Stef blinked again, glanced down at the white floof, trying to reconcile that fact with the sweetheart in her lap. "That's not true," she crooned, lifting her and nuzzling the pup's face. "She's a sweetheart."

"That's her name," Ben said. "But I've never seen her act like one."

"You're Sweetheart?" she asked the pup.

Who responded by kissing Stef's chin.

"Aw, baby," she said, cuddling the dog closer. She was a tiny thing, mostly fur and bones and when Stef stood, holding her against her chest, the pup snuggled against her, and it had to be the cutest thing she had ever seen.

"I'll put her in her crate," Ben murmured, reaching for her.

Sweetheart growled.

"Do we have to?" Steff asked, sending sad eyes in his direction.

His were filled with heat. "We don't," he murmured. "We can hang on the couch and watch *Dr. Pol*."

"I *love Dr. Pol!*" she exclaimed.

He groaned and let his head drop back. "Not you, too."

"I admit I cringe at the surgery parts—"

"I think that's the masochist's *favorite* part," he quipped, nodding toward the pooch. "She's particularly focused when the good doctor starts castrating."

Stef winced. "So, maybe not *Dr. Pol?*"

Big brown eyes on hers. "Whatever you want, baby."

Baby.

It slid down her nape, trailed across her breasts, tightening her nipples, curling in her abdomen, filling the space between her thighs.

She glanced from the pooch to the man.

Though one was cute, the other was responsible for the fact that her pussy was wet. "Where's her crate?" she asked. "I'll put her away."

The grin that Ben gave her had more moisture gathering between her legs, had desire flooding her senses. Her muscles were drawn tight over her skeleton. Her limbs trembled. Her nerves fired, sending sparks across the surface of her skin. Her lips—both sets of them—were tingling.

"This way," he said, leading her down the hall and into one of the bedrooms . . . that had been converted into a doggy playroom. Numerous beds and toys were scattered across a plush rug, a water fountain took up space in one corner, a crate with a pale pink cover in the other.

He held the kennel door wide for her and with a kiss to Sweetheart's head, she tucked the pup inside. Ben locked it in place, ignoring the rumble of displeasure from Sweetheart.

They both stood, and his mouth was still curved.

"You tame wild beasts in addition to Hoovering popcorn?"

Stef laughed as she stepped toward him. "Apparently, I have *two* superpowers."

Then she kissed him.

And found peace and heat, calm and tornado of desire, all at once, all in an instant. Her fingers dug into his shoulders, trying to get closer, even though every inch of her was pressed to every hard inch of him. His tongue didn't hesitate this time, just slid right into her mouth, coaxing hers into a rhythm that was as effortless as breathing.

She clung to him, held on as he transformed her.

Suddenly, she was lifted into his arms again as Ben spun them, pinning her against the wall. Her ankles clasped around his waist, his cock ground into her.

"Fuck," she whispered, her head falling back as his mouth trailed down her throat.

A nip to her collarbone had her bucking against him.

Another had her hands sliding beneath his shirt, feeling the smooth expanse of his skin, blazing hot and threatening to reduce her to ash.

But she walked right into that fire, drawing his mouth back to hers, clenching her legs tighter around him, bucking her hips against his and riding the rigid length of his cock.

So. Fucking. Good.

"Stef," he groaned, tearing his lips from hers again, this time trailing them over to her ear and lightly biting down on the lobe. She shivered and tilted her head to the side, giving him better access, falling into the fucking gloriousness of that hot mouth and silken tongue playing against her skin.

"God, Ben," she moaned. "That's—"

She groaned in protest when he unhitched her legs, set her feet on the floor. His fingers clasped hers, drew her from the room, pulled her farther down the hall to a set of double doors, kicking them open.

"Wow," she breathed.

But then she barely had time to suck in a breath before he was sweeping her back up into his arms, walking across the room. A gasp escaped her when she found herself falling onto a thick mattress, his body coming down onto hers. "This okay?" he asked huskily.

It was fucking perfect.

She didn't tell him that, though.

Instead, she wrapped her arms around him and tugged him down to her, said only, "More."

Another grin that set her insides on fire.

And then he gave her *more*.

FOURTEEN

BEN

More.

She wanted more.

She was going to get more, every fucking bit of him.

Dropping *more* of his weight into her, he took her mouth again, tasting that sweet and floral ambrosia on her lips, her tongue. Her nails bit into his scalp, pulling him even closer, until he was between her thighs, only the layers of their clothing between them.

He needed to do something about that.

But he couldn't tear himself away from her mouth, from her taste in order to do so. Her mouth was a drug, her body another. He needed to taste and touch and—

She shoved him back, rolling him over and yanking her shirt over her head.

Pale skin, a plain beige bra. Not lace, not particularly sexy, and yet it was still the best thing he'd ever seen. Her fingers went to the button on her jeans, and he moved, flipping them again and taking over the task, undoing the zipper, yanking them down her legs, chucking one shoe then the another.

They landed behind him with a *thunk*.

His eyes drifted down to her feet, clad in ankle socks that were printed with pink-haloed unicorns.

He grinned. "Unicorns?"

A shrug, her breasts jiggling in that bra, and his mouth watered. "I like fictional critters."

"Hmm." He bent, nibbled on her ankle. "They'll stay on."

She laughed, reached for her underwear. "But hopefully not these." Her fingers slipped beneath the waistband, began nudging them down. Then she paused. "Do you have a condom?" Her fingers slipped out, she turned for the door. "Because I can go get—"

A brush of his lips to hers.

Then he reached into the nightstand, pulled out a box of condoms.

One he'd bought after his message had gone unanswered, part of him hopeful, the other part resentful and thinking he might open that box with someone else. And one that had remained unopened since.

"Oh," she murmured.

"Oh," he agreed.

He was about to order her to get her hands back into her panties when she shifted her hips, pushed down the plain cotton then, just as he was reveling in the flash of cropped brown curls, her back arched and she reached behind her, unclipping her bra and tossing it to the side.

Ben had no fucking clue where it had landed.

He couldn't summon a fuck.

Not when Stef was naked and on his bed. Curves. Red lips. Fuck, he couldn't wait to taste every inch.

So he did—

Or at least, he intended to.

But then she placed a hand on his chest, stopping him. His heart sank, disappointment curling through him, certain she had changed her mind. "Off." She reached for the hem of his shirt, and only then did he relax enough to tear it over his head, to shove his sweats down and remove his shoes.

He kept his boxer briefs on because it would be far too easy, too tempting to slip back between her thighs, to slip *inside* her slick center. Even now, the moisture glistened on her thighs, making his mouth water, his desire the heavy strum of a bass guitar.

Take. Take. Take.

Patience.

"Okay?" he murmured when she abruptly sat up.

"You are the sexiest man I've ever seen," she said, her voice a rasp that slid over his skin, even before her fingers trailed it—caressing over his shoulders, down his arms, up over his abdomen before coming to a rest on his chest. They blazed, the heat sinking into him, scorching down his spine, his cock growing even harder.

His cheeks felt hot at the compliment, but thankfully he didn't have to worry about her seeing it. "You're beautiful." He moved so he was back over her, bracing himself on one hand, using the other to smooth back her hair. "I've dreamed about kissing these lips."

"And getting my lipstick all over you," she said, smiling up at him, her thumb running along his bottom lip. "All because I'm vain."

"Vain?" he asked, smoothing his palm up her side.

Her skin was silk beneath him. "I can't live without my lipstick." A shrug, her ribs moving beneath his palm. "So, yes, vain."

"Should I tell you that I've been dreaming of red lips for months now?"

Her mouth curved. "So, at least vain has a purpose?"

"Yes," he said, leaning down and dragging his mouth along her jaw, pausing at her earlobe. "But only if I get to taste them again."

She smiled and tilted her chin up.

And then there were no more words.

His tongue was in her mouth, his lips on hers then, when his lungs protested, trailing them down, stopping to pay homage to her breasts, suckling and nipping and deducing what she liked best—hard, steady pulls on her nipples. Then he was moving down again, across the soft curve of her belly, allowing his tongue to drift along her hips . . . and still down.

Nudging her thighs apart.

Moving in between.

Kissing up one thigh and skipping the part he was desperate to taste, wanting her writhing beneath him. He might not have had a hundred women, might have been a late bloomer and be uneasy with words, but he paid attention. He knew people, could read them.

Could read *her*.

How her legs trembled when he nipped, how her hands found their way into his hair and tugged when he brought the flat of his tongue up, when he slid it along the outside of her labia, darted it out to taste the sweetly tart folds.

"Fuck," he groaned. That was good.

Her lips parted on a moan, and she drew him closer, her legs wrapping tight, moisture flooding his mouth. Ben didn't stop, just continued to figure out all the things she liked—how much pressure, the way he circled his tongue, how he used the flat of it to press against the bundle of nerves. But when he slid a finger inside her damp tightness, she arched beneath him, and when he slid another in, she bucked, his name tumbling from her tongue.

He sucked her clit deep, curved his fingers, and his name became a chant.

"Ben, Ben, Ben—"

The best sound on the planet.

No.

He was wrong. The best sound on the planet happened next. When her body bowed on the mattress, when she ground her pussy against his mouth, when every muscle in her body was tight, straining.

And then she exploded.

A gasp. A long, trailing moan.

She went limp, her pussy clenching around his fingers.

She was beautiful, her color high, her lips swollen, sweat glimmering on her brow, and then those red lips tugged up into a smile, and she crooked a finger at him. "Come inside me."

He wasn't done. Not nearly.

He'd had months to plan this. Months to think about everything he wanted to do to her.

But when she smiled at him like that, when she crooked her finger, he knew he couldn't deny her anything. Reaching for the box of condoms as he slid up her body, Ben tore open the top and took her mouth at the same time. His hands were busy—one on the bed next to her side to not crush her, one on the box—so he couldn't fend off hers.

Not that he tried very hard, if he was being honest.

Because her hands had slid down his abdomen, slipped beneath the waistband of his underwear, and grasped him tight.

Groaning, he thrust into her hand, into those firm fingers.

"You're hard," she whispered. Though the statement was nonsensical—because *of course* he was hard, he was harder than he'd ever been in his life—the statement sent fire to his cock. He knew it was weeping, that he was seconds away from exploding.

After yanking a condom out of the box, he jerked her hands off him then tore open the packet with his teeth, rolled it down, chucked his underwear to the side, and . . .

Inhaled.

Because he knew that once he was inside that tight, wet heat, he wouldn't be able to stop, wouldn't last long.

So, he clenched his jaw, sucked in one more breath, and then set about turning her into an absolute frenzy of need. He took her mouth, returned to her breasts. Not gently. None of it was gentle. He suckled her breasts, drove his fingers in between her legs, his thumb on her clit, his finger inside.

She gasped and moaned and clung to him, and then he heard the hitch in her breathing again, knew that she was close.

Thank fuck.

He prowled down her body, positioned himself, and . . . glanced up at curves, at red lips, at pretty brown eyes.

Her pupils were huge. Her mouth tempted him.

"Now, Ben." Her smile was almost feral as she moved before he could, gripping his ass with one hand, wrapping a leg around his hip, and finally . . . finally drawing him inside.

They both moaned.

She clenched around him—her leg, her pussy, her arms.

He'd been right.

He wasn't going to be able to last long. But thankfully, she wasn't going to either.

Her hips met his, her fingers clenched on his ass, his shoulder, and they *moved*. A rhythm that was instinctual, that didn't take any effort to stumble into. They were two sides of the same coin, knowing each other without struggle.

And it was good.

And it . . . wasn't going to last long.

He slid a hand up, cupped Stef's breast, running his finger back and forth across the hard bud of her nipple. She clenched tighter, arched further, her head falling back onto the pillow, her lips parted on a moan.

She went over the edge, and not a moment too soon. His orgasm was coiling in the base of his spine, threatening to explode out through his cock.

One stroke.

Another.

He toppled, pleasure dousing him from head to toe, a steaming bucket of water dumped over his head. It soaked into his skin, settled into his very bones, so much fucking bliss washing over him that it took every bit of effort to not collapse on top of her.

But then Stef made a mewl of complaint, tugged him down, and he lowered himself to the mattress, barely summoning the energy to roll to his side and gather her close.

Their breaths came in rapid gusts.

He'd been cracked open, reformed, every past experience erased from his mind until the only thing that remained was Stef —beautiful, intoxicating, Stef.

She nuzzled into his neck, and then she laughed.

"What?" he asked, smoothing a hand down her back.

"That was—" She laughed again. "That was fucking incredible."

Ben froze, his arms tightly around her, his lungs still straining, the sweat not yet dry on his body, and . . . he laughed, too.

FIFTEEN

STEF

E ventually, Ben slid out of bed to take care of the condom, and Stef knew that she should get dressed, should either take him up on the ride or see if the surge in demand had eased so she could get back to her car.

It was late, they'd gone to the midnight showing, so it must be nearing four. God, she hadn't been up this late in years. Not since her college years—and her all-nighters hadn't ever included great sex. Great *studying* maybe, but not sex. Oh, the sex itself had been good, definitely satisfying. Her partners had always been fun, and she wasn't shy between the sheets. So she had enjoyed herself and especially enjoyed the orgasms that weren't courtesy of her own fingers, but it had never been like this.

Never been this . . . incredible.

She could easily get addicted.

She could easily end up wanting something that would wind up with her brokenhearted.

That happy thought killed her post-orgasm glow, and Stef pushed out of bed. She should go before this got weird. Maybe set up another time for some incredible sex. It was late. She was tired. Plus, Fred would be missing her.

He'd need to go out to the bathroom in a couple of hours, would be wondering where she was.

She didn't leave him, except for doggy day care, and he would worry.

So she searched for her panties, yanked them up her legs, and was just reaching for her bra when Ben walked back into the room.

"What are you doing?" he asked, prowling over to her, his delicious body on display.

"I need to get home," she said. "Fred will be waiting for me."

His brows drew together, the light from the hallway enough that she didn't miss the blast of fury in his eyes. Then they cleared. "Your dog."

"Yup." She pulled on her bra.

He frowned. "Why don't you stay for a couple of hours? Get some sleep, and I'll drive you to your car in the morning."

She yawned. "It *is* morning," she said. "And Fred will be worried."

Something else in his eyes, but he merely nodded then moved around the room, gathering up the remainder of her clothing and handing it to her. Then he went through a door, and flicked on a light, illuminating a closet.

He came back out as she was stepping into her shoes, fully dressed, a hoodie in his hands, thrusting it at her. "It'll be cold."

There went her heart again.

It was dangerous how vulnerable the sliver of kindness made her. The care that he presented was nothing. She'd seen inside his closet, saw the racks of clothes. Surely, he wouldn't miss one sweatshirt.

But it still meant a lot.

Because he'd thought about it.

About her.

"Thanks," she whispered, tugging it over her head and slipping into the bathroom to use the facilities and to wash her hands.

He wasn't in the bedroom when she came out, and she strolled down the hall, popping in to say goodbye to Sweetheart on her way out. The little pup was curled up in the back of her crate, her eyes closed, but she gave Stef a tail wag and lick on her hand when she reached in and scratched Sweetheart between her ears.

"Bye, baby," Stef crooned, locking up and turning off the light in the dog room, her lips twitching when she saw that Ben had rigged up several nightlights that left the space in a comforting glow.

Ben was standing across the hall, so handsome that she felt her heart lurch.

"I can't believe you tamed the beast," he said, his voice roughened velvet that slipped between her legs. Combined with that and the spicy scent of his sweatshirt surrounding her, and she thought she might already be addicted.

One hit and she'd gone down the rabbit hole.

"She's not so bad," Stef said, walking past him. He held her purse, apparently having retrieved it from wherever she'd dropped it.

Maybe the white rug.

Maybe the hall.

Honestly, she couldn't remember.

"Tell that to the dozens of pet sitters and everyone in my office who have either quit or are terrified of her."

Stef took the purse when he held it out. "I'm hoping the quitting is related to the pet sitters and not your employees?"

A grin that sunk like an arrow into her heart.

If an arrow was good.

Okay, that was a horrible analogy, but still she felt the impact of his grin like it was something physical.

"The quitters were the dog sitters," he said, inclining his head to the front door. "The terrified are my employees."

"Poor things."

"When you have a snarling beast chasing you, tell me how you'd react."

Stef snorted. "What is she? All of four pounds?"

"Four-point-*six* frightening pounds."

Laughter bubbled in her chest. "That point-six makes a difference."

"Damn right, it does."

He held the door open—or rather, pushed the button to call the elevator—and after a few moments the panel slid open, the silver doors parting behind it, and they stepped on.

"A private elevator is pretty fancy."

His eyes slid to hers. "Perk of owning the building."

Her brows lifted. "That's fancy, too," she said. "And here I was proud of paying off my Prius."

He went quiet, very quiet, and she almost felt him spooling back into himself, locking down the outer layers and locking them down tightly.

"I'm kidding." She touched his arm. "My friend's mom owns one of the big cosmetics businesses, so I know that money can make some people feel awkward." A wince. "Sorry if my lame attempt at fishing for a joke did the same. She prefers directness, and I shouldn't have assumed you are the same."

Still quiet.

The doors opened and she stepped off, immediately seeing the exit of the underground garage and turning toward it.

Ben caught her arm. "My car's that way."

She shrugged him off. "I know." She moved to the exit.

Suddenly, his broad, hard body was an inch from her nose, and she was reminded how she hadn't had enough time to explore it. She wanted her mouth on every centimeter, wanted to tease out every single sensitive nook and cranny.

"What the fuck are you doing?" he snapped.

"I'm just going to get a Lyft," she said. "You've done more than your due diligence and—"

She yelped in surprise when he suddenly had her pinned against the wall.

He didn't hurt her, quite the opposite, actually. He'd weaved his arms around her, his hands a barrier between the wall and her body. "What the fuck are you doing?" he snapped again.

"I'm going home," she said into those eyes of deep, deep russet. Beautiful eyes. His picture on the app hadn't done them justice. "Go to bed, Ben. You've done more than your fair share tonight."

His brows dragged together.

Sparks flashed in those beautiful eyes.

And then he didn't say anything, just wrapped his fingers around her arm, and said, "I'm driving you home."

Stef knew she could argue, knew she probably should. The need to give in and let him take care of her was certainly the biggest reason for it. The fact that she'd made him uncomfortable in the elevator was another. Her addiction, still one more. But . . . she just wanted a little more time.

Because, who knew if she'd see him again?

Because she'd been groomed over and over again to expect that any good times would invariably come to an end.

So probably, she should retreat, protect herself.

Instead, she did what she always did. The stupid, idiotic thing. She reached out and grasped on.

"Okay," she said.

She'd barely gotten the agreement out before he was guiding her over to the car. Her purse slipped down her arm, and he snagged it for her, opening her door and waiting for her to sit down before buckling her in. The metal panel shut, and he walked around the car, opening his own door and dropping into his seat. Gently, he set the purse down at her feet, started up the engine, and backed out of the stall.

Through the city streets . . . in silence.

To the freeway . . . in silence.

South toward her house . . . in silence.

She thought of a dozen things to say and just as quickly dismissed them. Too tired. Too vulnerable. Too—

His hand rested on her knee, and she jumped, jarred out of her thoughts.

Immediately, he withdrew, and she opened her mouth to tell him that she hadn't jumped because of him, had rather just been so locked into her thoughts that she'd forgotten she wasn't alone.

For God's sake! Get out of your head, Stef.

And while it was always a shitty time to hear Jeremy's voice, it was especially a shitty time when it was—her eyes flicked to the dash to see the time—4:36 in the morning.

God, she could fuck the man, but she couldn't talk to him?

Say something. *Anything.*

Thanks for the orgasms and the movie, let's do it again.

You're sexy and I want to give you my number.

Please, don't ghost me like I ghosted you.

Thank you for the ride and the—

But the words stayed locked on her tongue, in her mind, in her throat, and then she looked out the window and realized where she was.

Nearly at her condo.

Well, she supposed with a yawn, that she'd just get her car after she slept. She was probably too tired to drive anyway.

"What number?" Ben asked, both hands now clenched tight on the steering wheel. Strong hands, strong fingers, fingers that had been inside her.

His eyes came to hers, and she blinked. "On the end. White mailbox."

He nodded, navigated to her driveway and pulled the car to a stop.

Her throat was still tight, the words still stoppered up. "Thanks," she managed to squeeze out. "For the—"

Ben opened his door and got out so quickly that she was still talking when the door shut, still blinking at his movements when hers opened. He reached in, unbuckled her seat belt, and snagged her purse, waiting for her to get out before trailing her to the door.

She unlocked the door, stepped inside.

Ben waited on the porch, and she was summoning more words when Fred came bounding down the hall, a soft "woof" in the air that had her ordering, "Wait."

Her good boy waited.

Her . . . complicated, confusing man *also* waited.

Although Ben wasn't hers.

They'd watched a movie. They'd fucked. They'd talked a bit. He wasn't *her* anything.

Fred crept forward, his feet not crossing that invisible barrier of the threshold, even though his nose crept over it, smelling Ben's hand when he held it out. Tentatively. Fred sniffed and then licked and then, as per his usual, his tail went propellor.

"Wait," she reminded him.

He plunked his butt on the floor and looked up adoringly at Ben, who carefully and slowly set her purse on the porch before bringing his other hand down and beginning to scratch the sides of Fred's head, his ears, his neck.

Fred practically turned into a puddle.

"You're a good boy, aren't you, buddy?" Ben murmured, and his rough, sexy voice had *her* melting into a puddle, desperate for him to call her a good *girl*.

"Thank you," she blurted.

Ben had crouched as he scratched Fred, and now he glanced up at her, those eyes deep, unreadable pools of brown.

He still didn't say anything.

"And I'm sorry about the elevator and that you had to drive out to pick me up—"

"I'm not."

But the words that had been smothered in her voice box were now out in full force, a different kind of smothering, a blurt that filled the air with unnecessary words. "And I know it was an inconvenience for you to come get me and to bring me home and probably the movie, too, since you hadn't planned on going out. And then I made it weird in the elevator, and I like your rug in the entryway, but how doesn't it get dirty? And—"

He cupped her cheek. "Goodnight, Stef." He brushed his lips over hers, released her. And as she was still catching her breath, he bent again, snagged her purse, and put it over the threshold, then reached for the handle.

The door *snicked* closed.

She stared at that closed panel of wood and knew that she'd had her fun.

And now it would be done.

"Goodbye, Ben," she whispered.

————

In the morning—or rather, well in the *afternoon*—Stef managed to peel herself out of bed and shower.

Her body was deliciously sore, long unused muscles tense from their exertions.

But the shower went a long way to making her human, along with a bagel absolutely slathered with her cinnamon cream cheese. And coffee. Couldn't forget regenerating herself with the hearty, black brew.

By the time she was human again, she retrieved her purse and her phone and started to call up the app to get a ride to the restaurant.

Then she happened to walk by her family room.

Or rather, by the large window in the family room, her gaze catching on . . . her car in the driveway. That couldn't be.

Mouth falling open, she lurched for the door and yanked it open.

A blue Prius. The right passenger's side rim a little damaged since she sucked at parallel parking. A golden retriever shaped air freshener hanging from the rearview. She couldn't check the license plate, because she never remembered the combination of numbers and letters—though she *could* recall it having a seven, which this Prius also had.

Except . . . she'd left her car at the bar.

Frowning, she moved closer to it, glancing inside to see the collection of trash on the floor (since she was one of those messy car people), along with several empty disposable coffee cups crammed into the cupholders.

Her cell buzzed in her hand, and she stared down at it in confusion.

Part because it was a text message, and one that appeared to be from Ben.

Part because her car had mysteriously appeared in her driveway.

The text only said.

Mailbox.

Another blink.

More confusion.

But she made her way to her mailbox, tugged open the little door, and saw the envelope inside. "Um, okay," she muttered, snagging it and tearing open the top, even though she'd already suspected and could feel what was inside.

Her car keys.

She blipped the locks, just to make sure, and predictably, the lights flashed, the locks clicking open.

Her heart seized, squeezing hard enough to take her breath away.

How he'd done it, she didn't know. Well, she supposed she knew how he'd done it, snagging her keys from her purse at some point—her car fob was separate from her set for the house, since she had all of her work keys on that same ring and hated the noise of them rattling when they hung from the ignition.

Still, she didn't know *how*.

Or maybe the more important question was that she didn't know *why*.

She'd gone to bed thinking she would never hear from him again, thinking that all his quiet meant that he was done with her.

And then he'd fetched her car.

Or had someone do it for him, considering he owned that penthouse with the private elevator—considering he owned that entire building. San Francisco real estate prices were insane. That told her enough about his financial status. The man probably had underlings for days.

Retrieving a car was nothing more than a nice man doing a nice thing.

And washing his hands of her.

She frowned.

Hating that thought.

Hating that it chased her all the way inside.

Sixteen

BEN

He didn't turn on his car until after Stef went inside, even though exhaustion was pulling at his eyelids.

He'd kept up his vigil from the moment he'd dropped Stef off. Staying until it was a semi-reasonable hour and he'd called Baine and Spence to come and retrieve the keys. Waiting as they'd gone and returned with the car, parking it in Stef's driveway. Baine had come to Ben's window after stashing the keys in the mailbox as ordered, grinning like a lunatic and asking, "Anything you want to tell me?"

"F.I.R.E.D," he'd responded.

To which Baine had just grinned and shaken his head. "Car needs a wash."

Maybe he'd arrange that next.

"Go home," he said. "And take Monday off. I know it's not your favorite waking up at dawn to work on a Saturday."

Baine stared at him, shook his head, and started walking over to Spence's car. "I'll see you Monday," he called over his shoulder.

"Baine—"

His assistant spun back. "I didn't do it because you're my boss," he said, closing the distance between them. "Spence did," he added with a jerk of his chin, "because he hasn't been around long enough to know that you fucking bend over backward for us every chance you get."

Ben sucked in a breath.

"You know how many times you've ever asked me for a favor?" Baine demanded. "On a Saturday or otherwise?"

Ben shook his head.

"Never." Baine's jaw clenched and then relaxed. "You've done me a shit-ton of them, starting with giving me the job even though my dumbass lied on the application, letting me have time off to be with my daughter anytime I needed it, giving me raises I didn't deserve when her mom disappeared—"

"You deserved them."

Baine just continued talking. "I didn't," he said, "I was barely around for those six months, and then when I finally got my shit together and was able to focus on work, when Beth"— his baby mama—"showed back up, fucked up out of her mind, you hooked me up with that lawyer. She helped me get full custody, even though I knew that it wasn't an easy fight. Who helped me get her into that good preschool? Who set me up with the nanny?"

Ben's hands clenched into fists, the words rolling over him.

It was nothing.

All of that was hardly anything.

"You're a good dad," he told Baine, "and Lei deserves to have you in her life all the time. She deserves a good school and you work better for me if you know she's secure."

Baine tapped the frame of the car. "I know," he said. "She deserves the fucking world." His pale blue eyes locked on Ben's. "And you gave it to her. So, don't you ever act like you asking me for one thing outside of work is an inconvenience. You haven't

ELISE FABER

been just my boss for years. You're my friend, and I have your back."

Ben sucked in a breath, wanting to disagree, to tell him not to bother.

But Baine probably recognized that opposition rolling up his throat, dancing on the tip of his tongue. "See you Monday," he said.

"Spence—"

"Will be there, too."

"Fuck," Ben muttered, rolling up his window and preparing to drive away. He needed to get home, needed to see what kind of trouble Sweetheart had gotten into. Claire—another favor he owed—had let her out of the kennel earlier that morning, had fed her.

And though she'd texted and said that Sweetheart had been markedly . . . sweet—or at least sweet for her (meaning she hadn't attempted to bite ankles, instead just grumbling her way to her food dish), he knew he couldn't ignore his responsibilities. Even if he was tempted to walk right up to Stef's door and take credit for returning her car.

And take something else.

"Fuck," he muttered again, hitting the ignition and reaching for the gear shift.

His phone buzzed.

He started to ignore it, thinking that Baine was going to give him more shit, but when his eyes caught on the contact's name, his heart thudded. Once and very hard against his ribs.

Red Lips.

Stef.

His cock went hard.

How'd you get my number?

His fingers were typing before he fully processed picking up his cell.

I have my ways.

A beat then,

Like the ways you managed to get my car mysteriously back in my driveway?

His lips twitched.

Yep.

Another buzz.

I thought you'd forgotten. I was just going to get it today.

He replied.

I know. But you were tired, and it wasn't any trouble.

Not for him, anyway. Baine, who'd had to call in his nanny, and Spence, who'd had to get his and Baine's asses to the restaurant at the butt crack of the morning, they might say differently.

Even though they specifically *hadn't* said differently.

Even though he was ignoring that part.

A heartbeat passed.

I keep having to thank you.

He sent back,

You don't, you know.

The "..." appeared. Then,

I do. But not because I feel obligated. Because I am thankful. Those were really kind things you did and—

Ben waited for her to finish the rest of the text. When she didn't, he typed out a reply.

And what?

Long moments passed.

And I just wanted to say thank you because that was kind, even though I know I made things weird. That's my superpower, making things weird.

He smiled.

I thought your superpowers were Hoovering and taming beasts.

Only a couple of seconds before she replied.

You've discovered my evil secret. I, in fact, have three superpowers.

Ben chuckled.

I'm a lucky, lucky man.

He pressed send, and a full minute passed before she replied.

Will you tell me something?

Anything.

That was what he wanted to send. Instead he typed out something else.

Does it involve my superpowers?

She did that react thing with the message, a little "ha-ha" icon appearing by his text before the "..." went again.

I didn't think I'd hear from you again.

His heart thudded.

He clenched his jaw, forced it to relax. For a moment, in the elevator, he'd thought the same. Thought it would be smarter to let her go. It was never a good sign for someone to talk about his money. He'd been convinced in a couple of sentences that she'd fooled him, that she was after something, after a meal ticket or maybe a funny story to sell the tabloids—*Billionaire has Viscous Dog. Hunt CEO is Too Good to Ride with the Common Folk.*

But then she'd started babbling, explaining about her friend's mom and apologizing, and even then he'd still thought it was a line, a way of trying to get back on his good side, so she could get that meal ticket.

Until she'd headed for the exit.

Until she'd been shocked he had stopped her.

Until he remembered the look on her face when he'd pulled up outside the bar, when he'd offered to drive her to her car, when he'd passed her the sweatshirt.

As though she'd been lacking in receiving kindness.

And the urge to give it to her was instinctual.

He couldn't let her go.

He'd seen her phone flashing inside her purse as he'd tucked her into her seat, had noticed it didn't have a passcode (something he was going to talk to her about soon), and hadn't been able to stop himself from programming in his number, from using it to call his cell so he had hers.

Then as he'd driven, listening to her yawn, her half-lidded stare out the windshield, he'd ignored his previous promise of picking up her car.

He'd programmed her street into his GPS without the number, not wanting to disturb her thoughts, to jar her out of her sleepy state, at least until he'd gotten as far as he was able. Then he'd touched her.

And she'd jumped.

He hated that jump, despised that reaction. He wanted her to be comfortable with him. But he wasn't good with people, at least not outside of the business world. He didn't do soft words, for one, sucked at explanations for his defensive behaviors, for another. So, he was struggling to come up with a way to put her at ease, to let her know that the thing in the elevator wasn't a big deal after all when he'd pulled into the driveway.

Then had still wrestled with it as he'd walked her up to her house.

Had actually considered taking the coward's way out and letting her go in that instant.

Until Fred.

Fucking cute ass dog, and well-behaved, and sweet, and nothing like Sweetheart and all her snarling. He'd actually listened. Then had relaxed into Ben's scratching.

So he'd swooped back into Stef's purse, knowing he was an asshole for invading her privacy like that a second time. But he'd convinced himself it was for a good cause, so he'd swiped the key fob.

He'd retrieved her car.

He wanted to hold on to Stef.

Ben?

Muttering a curse, he yanked himself out of his brain and typed.

That wasn't a question.

A beat.

Oh.

His fingers worked on the screen.

For the record, that wasn't either.

He could almost picture her nibbling at her bottom lip.

Can I take you to dinner? As a thanks?

That had him straightening in surprise. She wanted to take him to dinner. As a thanks? After the orgasm she'd given him?

His shock had him taking too long to reply because his cell vibrated again.

Never mind. That's okay. Thanks again. Have a nice life.

Have a nice life.

The words ricocheted through his insides, startling him into motion, his fingers flying on the screen . . . but not to text Stef.

Instead, they pulled up Claire's contact and hit call.

"I've got the beast," Claire said. "I took her back to my place, and for some reason, she didn't even try to bite me in the process."

Not for some reason.

But for the sunshine inside that house, blasting through the darkness they'd both lived with for too long.

"Gonna tell me why that is?" she pressed.

"No."

A chuckle. "Figured it was worth an ask."

He snorted.

"Figured you'd respond like that, too." A beat. "Which is why I'm telling you, as your new VP, to go . . . play."

Then she hung up, the pain in his ass.

But he didn't ignore her order.

Instead, he got out of his car, walked up the driveway, and knocked on the front door.

SEVENTEEN

STEF

She was gathering her stuff for the beach, intending to make it a longer outing than usual to make up to Fred for her absence the previous night, when there was a knock on the door.

Freezing, remembering what the last knock had brought her to her doorstep, she sucked in a shoring breath and hoped like hell who was on the other side would go away.

The knock came again.

"Fuck," she muttered, rotating from the small wall unit in the entryway where she kept all of Fred's various accoutrements, she leaned to the side and peered through the small window on the side of the door.

Like she probably *shouldn't* have done in that moment.

Because Ben must have seen the flicker of movement, and his deep brown eyes came down onto hers, and heat boiled in her belly.

He didn't knock again, just waited and watched as . . . she flicked open the lock.

He turned the handle, slowly pushed the door back so she had enough time to get out of the way, and she did, stumbling back a step as the panel swung wide, landing with a soft *smack* against the doorstop.

"Going somewhere?"

Fred skidded around the corner, crashing into the wall and running toward them—or rather, toward their new visitor. Stef opened her mouth—

"Wait."

It hadn't come from her. Instead, it slid through the air on Ben's soft but firm baritone, the same voice that had ordered her to "Come" at some point hours before.

She shivered.

Fred plunked his ass on the floor.

They both looked at Ben.

"Going somewhere?" he asked, bending to scratch Fred, whose tail immediately began dusting the floor.

"The beach," she breathed.

He glanced from the bag on her shoulder to Fred. Then back to her.

She shivered again.

"Okay if I come in?"

Was it?

He hadn't replied to her asking him for dinner. Maybe he'd been driving and couldn't? But then he'd been texting fast and furious before, so perhaps he'd . . . gotten a ride with whoever picked up her car, so hadn't seen it?

Or maybe she wouldn't have any of these answers unless she let him in.

Nodding, Stef stepped back, turning and catching the bag on the corner of the door, nearly sending it toppling off her shoulder.

Warm fingers caught it, slid it down her arm.

Another shiver.

And she was bustled backward, the door closing, Ben taking the bag and setting it on the ground before he snagged a hoodie off the hook and thrust it at her. Then when she just stared blankly at it, he stepped behind her, tucked it over her shoulders, and moved her limp arms into the sleeves.

"Better?" he asked, when he'd zipped it for her.

No.

Because now she was both burning up with desire and at risk of plunking her ass on the floor like Fred and begging Ben to deliver some of his touches that had made her melt only hours before.

He touched her cheek. "You want to buy me dinner?"

Her heart squeezed. "Seemed like a fair trade."

"You want to see me again?"

Stef lifted her chin. "You tell me. You're the one who got all quiet last night."

"I tend to . . ." He shook his head. "I'm not great with people outside of a business setting. I can make a deal and charm and schmooze, but talking to a beautiful, smart, funny woman is . . . less comfortable."

Brows lifting, she blurted, "You think it's hard to talk to *me*?"

A small smile. "I'm not exactly a Lothario."

"But . . . you're the sexiest man I've ever seen and—"

His jaw fell open and then he started laughing, bending over at the waist, laughing and shaking his head, and when he glanced back up at her, his lips were curved into a grin that had her heart thumping. "That's the second time you've said that, and now I know you need to get your eyes checked, baby."

Clearly, *he* was the one who needed an optometrist, but she liked his smile so much that she didn't point that out.

And anyway, she knew something of what it was like to look in the mirror and judge oneself. That was part of being a normal human with insecurities, and just because she thought he was beautiful didn't mean that he saw the same in himself. Hell, she'd argue that the dent in confidence was something most people—including her—had.

Funnily enough, that unstuck her enough to cup his cheeks, to step closer.

Too close for hardly knowing him.

Not nearly close enough after the intimacy of last night.

"Thank you for getting me my car."

His eyes flared, one hand covered hers. "You're welcome."

Thud-thud went her heart.

"Dinner?" she asked.

He hesitated, just for the barest moment before he nodded.

Her heart did a happy dance.

"Unless you'd rather come to the beach with us first?"

Another nod, the corners of his mouth turning up.

Not a happy dance this time. No, her heart was cracked open, laid bare, exposed and vulnerable . . . and she fell for him, just a little bit, right then and there.

———

"You do this every Saturday?" Ben asked, his hands in his pockets, his bare feet mixing with the sand below.

They'd both left their shoes and socks in the car—or in her case, her flip-flops—because she'd gotten one of the primo spots right near the steps that led down to the beach and had backed in.

Fred hadn't even needed the leash she'd now clipped around her shoulders.

She'd just opened the back door, undid his seat belt, and he'd hit the waves.

Even as she'd winced, knowing how cold the ocean was in this part of California.

Not the warm waves of SoCal.

But the biting surf of the Bay Area. Good for swimming only on the rare days it was above ninety here on the coast, when the cold was actually a relief from the blazing heat that reflected off the sand.

She nodded, shifted carefully over a piece of seaweed and felt her ankle clench. "Every Saturday," she agreed. "If only for a short walk. Fred loves the ocean."

Ben turned to stare down at her. "You love it, too."

Stef found her lips curving when Fred turned and barked at a wave that had dared sneak up on him, dousing his tail. "I like to see him like this." She nodded in his direction. "But yes, I like it here, too. Even if it isn't a warm Caribbean beach with clear blue waters, even if there are Great Whites prowling just off the coast, I do love to watch the sun set over waves."

He turned, and she followed his gaze.

The sun was a while away from setting.

"Usually, we go later in the day," she told him, just as Fred came back with a stick and dropped it at her feet. She launched it out into the surf, and he took off for it as she grinned up at Ben. "Otherwise my arm gives out."

Laughter in his eyes as they both watched Fred retrieve the stick and then return it.

She threw.

He ran.

They repeated the pattern until he got distracted by a seagull and dropped it at Ben's feet.

"Oh, you don't have—"

Ben launched the stick much more effortlessly than she had.

And further.

"Is that too far?" he asked, shooting a concerned look in her direction.

She shook her head. "He'd swim forever," she said. "But I usually just make sure to not throw it much farther than the first break."

A quiet gaze studying the surf.

Then he nodded.

"Do you want to sit?"

His eyes came to hers. "Do you?"

She nodded, shifted her weight, and his stare flicked down, that careful, quiet studying now coming to her, to her ankle.

"What happened?" he asked, sitting down.

Following suit, she arranged her legs in front of her, knowing the scar from the surgery was easily spotted, bright pink against the white of her skin. "You didn't notice it last night."

"I didn't say that."

Her eyes darted to his.

"I . . . was more focused on other things."

A bolt of heat slid through her. Indeed, he had been. "Surgery," she offered when that now intense stare, probably remembering what she did—the heat, the pleasure, the *fun*— met hers. They were at a beach with her dog, and she wanted to strip him naked. That, too, was probably obviously displayed in her eyes. "Fred is a good boy"—he dropped the stick; Ben threw it again—"but his fatal flaw is squirrels. The turkey is obsessed with them, and it's the only thing he'll pull at, albeit rarely. I was on call for the lab, and my phone buzzed. I answered it, thinking it was work, when really it was my ex—"

He winced.

She nodded, wondering why she was telling him this part when she hadn't told anyone else about Jeremy calling, about him yelling at her and distracting her, and . . . no, about her stupid self picking up the phone, *allowing* herself to be distracted.

"Fred saw the squirrel. Fred decided that this was his one opportunity out of ten to lunge for the squirrel that had come into his orbit—"

Another wince.

"Yup," she said. "The leash wrapped around my legs and

took me down. I fell awkwardly, dropped my purse, my cell, and landed wrong. *Really* wrong. And I remember just lying there, trying to summon the strength to push myself up, to reach for my phone that was just out of reach." She sighed. "And when I grabbed it, I could still hear my ex being an asshole, yelling about *me* yelling into the speaker when I'd fallen and then continuing on with some grievance about a sweatshirt."

"A sweatshirt."

"I may or may not have decided to keep his comfy sweatshirt after that," she admitted, not really feeling guilty about it, even though she probably should, considering it was stealing. "Because he was a total dick about it, and then I had to have the surgery so it wasn't exactly at the top of my priority list. The worst part is that he didn't even ask if I was okay when I told him I thought I'd broken my ankle." She wrinkled her nose. "He just told me that I'd better drop it by his place and . . ."

She trailed off at the expression on Ben's face.

Thunderous was the mildest description she could come up with.

"He didn't ask if you were okay?"

A deadly question.

"I—"

"You told him you thought you'd broken your ankle, that you'd fallen, and he was worried about a fucking sweatshirt?"

Stef winced. "Um. Yes?"

The only sounds were those of the waves breaking against the shore.

Then Ben asked, "What's his name?"

Now, he looked downright scary, and she knew it must be the ruthless business side of him coming out, the part that made it possible for him to own that building in the city, to make whatever deals were necessary in order to achieve his ends.

Heat curled between her thighs.

Probably, it shouldn't. But the fury had her shifting on the sand, clenching her legs together, wondering what it might be like to unleash that ferocity in bed.

"Stef."

A slightly sharp command, not fierce enough to make her bristle, but enough to make her wet, to make her want to argue with him, just to see where it would get her.

What was *wrong* with her?

But nearly the same moment, a thought grasped onto the coattails of the first, one that was opposite and important and—

Because what was finally going *right* with her?

She felt blazingly alive. She wanted things, and yeah, so maybe wanting Ben wasn't the same as wanting *things,* as in plural. Though she supposed it was plural in the sense that she wanted to do multiple things *with* him.

"It doesn't matter," she said. "*He* doesn't matter. We've been broken up for almost a year now. My ankle was . . . *God* . . . six? Seven? No, it must have been nine months ago. He's ancient history." A shrug, deliberately ignoring the fact that it hadn't been *that* long since he'd showed up on her porch demanding that stupid vase. She hadn't heard from him since; that was all that mattered. "I've moved on."

"It still hurts you."

Stef shrugged. "It was a bad break. It probably always will ache a bit."

His palm came to her cheek. "And he yelled at you about a fucking sweatshirt instead of helping you."

That was what people did.

People who weren't Ben with his picking up at bars, his returning of cars. He was an anomaly. People weren't good, not like him. Unless you really meant something to them, they didn't go out of their way for others.

And she'd never fallen into the category of meaning enough.

She *wanted* that.

She'd seen what her friends had with their significant others.

She'd even been lucky enough to feel the care they gave her as friends. So, she wasn't so cynical as to think that it didn't exist, that she was ultimately unworthy of it.

Stef was a good person. She had some great qualities.

But she was realistic enough to understand that if it came down to it, her friends would choose their spouses, choose each other. She was the newest addition. Well, Tammy had come after, but she was Kate's sister-in-law, Brad and Jaime's sister. Stef was aware of where she'd fall on the hierarchy.

And look, she knew how that sounded.

Like she'd signed up for a pity party for one.

She hadn't.

She worked in numbers and formulas, within the rules of science. Cause and effect, correlations, associations . . .

They all pointed to the same thing.

She just didn't matter that much to the people in her life, wouldn't matter enough for them to choose her if the world were ending and they could only cling to one person.

Which was morose and dramatic and . . . fine.

Ben's fingers flexed on her cheek, and she forced a smile. "I was fine."

Something flashed through his eyes, telling her he knew that she wasn't going to tell him Jeremy's name—even if it was tempting to allow Ben to unleash whatever businessman badassness he possessed on her ex.

She didn't want to go backward.

She wanted to hold on to this feeling, to enjoy her time with Ben, for however long it lasted.

His thumb brushed over her cheek. "Stubborn."

"Now you know one of my many faults, right along with my superpowers."

"I don't consider being stubborn a fault."

"Liar."

His lips twitched. "Okay, maybe in this instance, I would

like you to be a little *less* stubborn, but I know when I've been beaten."

She jumped when a cold, wet nose nudged against her foot.

Ben barely spared a glance, scooping up the stick and launching it away, Fred chasing after it.

His thumb continued stroking, his palm shifting, dragging down her throat, making her shiver. "Will he really play fetch all night?"

Her lips curved. "Until he passes out on the sand." She lifted and dropped her arm. "Until my arm gives out."

"So, if I kept throwing the"—Fred dumped the stick on Ben's lap, right on cue—"stick," he said, scooping it up and tossing it again. "If I save your arm . . . then what will you give me?"

His hand drifted down beneath the neckline of her sweatshirt, traced across her collarbone. Another quiver, goose bumps rising on her skin.

She shifted closer, her thigh pressing to his, her hand lifting to rest on his chest.

"I'll give you—"

The stick landed on her shins and . . . Fred decided to shake, splashing them both with icy cold ocean water.

She shrieked. *"Fred!"*

Ben froze.

She expected him to curse, to back away, or jerk up to his feet, wiping away the water and glaring at her. It's what Jeremy would have done, if she'd twisted his arm and somehow had managed to get him out here at all. But Ben didn't do that, didn't move at all actually, as water dripped down his cheek.

Stef reached up and wiped the drops away.

The touch had him shifting closer, his words brushing hers on a hot rush of air. "You'll give me . . . what?"

It took her a minute to focus, to remember what she'd been saying before the dousing.

Then she *did* remember.

Her hand slid down his cheek, cupping his jaw, feeling the bristles there against her palm. "A kiss," she murmured. "I'll give you a—"

"Thank fuck," he muttered.

His mouth slammed down onto hers.

Eighteen

The dog was trying to kill him.

He'd just slanted his lips across hers, and Fred was back, wanting to fetch, and Ben swore to fuck that he'd *just* thrown the damned stick.

He launched it again, a little farther this time, hoping it wasn't too far.

Then Stef's tongue touched the seam of his lips, and he stopped worrying about the dog and started worrying about whether or not he'd be able to stop himself from stripping her naked on the beach and fucking her right there.

Not only would that be uncomfortable—sand, so much sand in all the wrong places—but he didn't want to get either of them arrested.

Plus, naked sand fucking in the middle of the day would certainly hit the gossip sheets.

And he didn't want his bare ass on any blog.

Just as that thought trickled through his mind, Fred

dropped the stick on his lap and shook again, and Stef tore her lips away, shrieking again.

"Come on, Fred!" she snapped.

Her pooch just nudged the stick closer and wagged his tail.

Ben captured a drop of water where it trailed down her throat, scooping it up with his thumb, and she shivered again. Though he was finally getting it through his thick skull that it was less from cold and more from him.

Which he was just enough of a posturing alpha to appreciate.

Especially when she leaned close and buried her face in his throat, her lips grazing his skin, her soft exclamation of "Kryptonite" reaching his ears.

Ben laughed. "I was thinking the same thing." A beat. "Well, that and along with needing a third person to chuck the stick so I could kiss you properly." She giggled, and he found his fingers in her hair again, the soft locks dancing along the back of his hand. "You okay?"

She nodded. "Though I could do without another Fred dousing."

Speaking of which, the pooch came back with the stick and Ben scooped it up, throwing it before he had the chance to stop and shake.

"Smart man," Stef teased.

He laughed. "I occasionally can be," he said, slipping his hand from her hair and wrapping it around her shoulders when she wiggled closer. "But usually, I just get lucky."

"What do you do, anyway?"

This was the part that always got dicey and uncomfortable and . . . people just got weird when they found out that he ran Hunt Inc. It was too big, too often in the news, too strange knowing he was the brains of the giant conglomeration, that it—and he—was worth that much.

She sensed his hesitation. "Never mind," she told him. "You don't have to tell me if it makes things awkward."

Except, it was one of the most innocuous questions she could ask him, wasn't it?

It was also an important one.

Something he needed to share if he wanted to have her in his life. Because that was what this came down to, wasn't it? She'd sent that text, giving him the way out, and he had known in an instant he hadn't wanted that. He wanted her, *had* wanted her from the moment he'd spied those red lips, from the short conversation, hadn't been able to stop thinking about her, in all honesty.

He hadn't even stopped to think when she'd said she couldn't get a ride.

He'd just known it had to be him.

Same as the movies, the food, those moments with Sweetheart . . . the sex. The *car*.

Him. Him. *Him.*

"I work at the lab"—she named one of the big biotech firms in the area—"with my friend, Heidi. Well, really, she's my boss, but she kind of bullied me into being her friend when she realized that I was alone here and things with Jeremy—"

He stiffened.

She glanced up at him, her eyes going wide. Then they narrowed. "Forget you heard that."

Not a chance in hell.

But he didn't comment as her coffee-colored eyes remained on his, continued *glaring* at him.

"You're not going to forget that, are you?"

He just lifted his brows.

"You're not," she muttered. "Well, anyway, Heidi took me under her wing, and then it wasn't just Fred and me any longer. We had Kate, Cora, and Kelsey—they'd all been friends since college. We also got Tammy, who's Kate's sister-in-law who moved to town not long ago. And Kels's fiancé, Tanner, Kate's husband, Jaime, and Heidi's husband, Brad. Brad and Jaime are brothers and Tammy is their sister, and they're just all really nice people. Kate's mom, Marabelle, is the one who owns the cosmetics company . . ."

Ben could admit this was the point that he began tuning out, just began watching those lush lips move, throwing the stick when Fred came back, and wondering how long it would be until he could kiss her again.

Stef realized that. Or at least she realized that she'd lost him in the sea of names. Probably, she wasn't all that aware of the need burning through him, not his shirt conveniently placed over one bent leg.

Sweats would be dangerous around this one.

"Sorry," she said, so softly he could barely hear her over the crash of the waves. "That was a lot to throw at you."

He tugged her a little closer, smothering a groan when her palm brushed his thigh. "I'm probably not going to remember all of those names," he admitted, "but I like hearing you talk."

Her brows shot up. "You like . . . hearing *me*"—her voice squeaked here—"talk?"

Ben couldn't resist brushing a kiss over her forehead. "Yes."

"Just to clarify," she said. "Me?"

Laughter bubbled up in his chest, burst out of him. So fucking cute. "Yes," he said again, bopping her lightly on the nose. "Squeak aside, you have a pleasant voice, and I'm glad your boss bullied you into friendship."

Stef's eyes went wide, concern drifting into those coffee-colored depths. "I was kidding about the bullying part. She's not like that."

"I know."

A slow blink. "*How* do you know?"

"Because of the way your face looks when you talk about her, about them."

Another blink, surprise weaving its way through her expression. "What do I look like?"

"Your face gentles and light comes into your eyes."

"Oh."

It was a whisper, her gaze going out to the horizon and no stranger to needing a few quiet moments, he let her have this one. Just picked up the stick and threw it several more times, his stare alternating from the setting sun, to Stef, to Fred.

"I love them," she said, turning back toward him when the sun had turned into a half circle, the rest of it slipping beyond the skyline. "I didn't realize how much I did until you said that." She glanced at him, then away again, her voice nearly inaudible. "I didn't realize how much I'm going miss them when it's over."

He straightened. "Why would it be over?"

Was she moving? Fuck, was she *dying?*

His mind immediately went worst-case scenario, picturing his mom wasting away, the cancer taking her piece by piece.

She just shook her head, not looking at him.

"Stef?" he asked. "Are you sick?"

Something in his tone—probably the panic—had her glancing back. "No," she said. "I'm fine. My friends are fine."

"Are you moving?"

"No."

Then what the fuck are you talking about? he wanted to yell.

But there was something fragile about her in that moment, something even Fred, as though sensing her disquiet, seemed to recognize, sprawling on the sand next to her, the stick forgotten, his side pressed to her leg. She didn't protest against Fred's wet fur soaking through her jeans, just stroked her fingers through it and silently watched the sun go down.

So, he did the same.

Even though he had a million questions running through his mind.

NINETEEN

STEF

B en took the towel from her hands, efficiently rubbing the worst of the sand and water from Fred's fur.

She knew it wouldn't all get out.

Sundays were Fred's bath day.

He lifted Fred into the car, buckled his seat belt, leaving her to stand uselessly to the side of the car, watching the strong lines of his body do something that was often a struggle for her.

Fred, as previously established, was a good boy. He, however, wasn't graceful while navigating hallways or chasing squirrels or jumping into cars. Most of the time he jumped and missed, crashing his face into the seat, so mom guilt had her lifting all eighty-plus pounds of him, front legs first, then followed by back legs. Not the easiest thing, especially when Fred was slippery from dancing in the waves.

The belt *clicked*. The door closed.

Ben turned to face her.

She'd expected questions about why she'd gone quiet.

Instead, he'd just sat next to her, no pressure, no stress, and watched the sunset with her and Fred.

God, she liked him too freaking much.

She was firmly in cling mode—as in, wanting to cling to him forever.

His fingers brushed her cheek, and she realized she'd been staring. "Did you want me to drive?" he asked.

"No," she said. "I'm fine. I've got it."

Deep brown eyes on hers. "That's not what I asked."

She replayed her answer, his question, then bit back a smile. "You remember."

She'd complained about hating to drive on the way to the beach, lamenting the traffic on her circuit of doggy day care, lab, back to doggy day care, and finally back home, and how with Bay Area traffic, it took longer than a reasonable human being should have to deal with.

His eyes flared, but he didn't say anything other than, "I remember."

"Do you mind?"

Another flash. "I wouldn't have offered if I did."

This man . . . was confusing and wonderful and . . . confusing. "Do you really mean it?"

"Stef." His hands cupped her cheeks. "*I wouldn't have offered if I minded.*"

Thud.

Thud.

"Okay."

"That you understand I wouldn't have offered if I minded, or that you want me to drive?"

After considering that for a moment, she said, "Both."

A flash of bright white teeth. He plucked the keys from her fingers, threaded his arm through hers, and led her around the hood of the car, opening the passenger's side door, then waiting for her to sit before buckling her in.

"Thank you," she whispered.

He cupped her cheek, held her gaze. "You're welcome."

Then he got into the driver's seat, having to wrestle with the controls for a few minutes to try and fit his long legs in her tiny Prius. But then he was in, and the car was on, and he drove her home.

———

"This isn't what I had in mind when I told you I'd buy you dinner," she said, setting the paper plates and napkins on the coffee table alongside the pizza that had just been delivered.

She'd been thinking fancy restaurant, candles and table-cloths, and soft music in the background.

Not necessarily because she liked those things.

But because he lived in a penthouse and owned a building in SF. He was probably used to fancy shit. Hell, he had that white rug where anyone might just stain it.

Then again, he'd gone to the small theater, walked on that sticky floor, and shared popcorn and a KitKat.

That wasn't exactly fancy.

Neither was eating pizza and drinking beers.

But that's what he'd suggested when his stomach had rumbled on the drive home, and she'd ordered the food on the app, so it had arrived almost when they did.

Ben opened the lid, inhaled deeply. "Fuck, that smells good."

Her pussy clenched.

As though he felt it, Ben glanced over at her, and she got lost in the heat in his eyes. He closed the pizza box, prowling over to her. Her nostrils flared, and she didn't back up when he stepped right into her space, sharing her air. "You have condoms?" he asked.

So not the most romantic of statements.

But also the same question she'd been asking herself.

The answer to which had her cursing internally.

"No," she breathed.

His eyes slid to half-mast, and though she detected the disappointment there, the same that she was feeling (why, seriously, didn't she have an emergency condom? Also, why didn't *he* have one?) He didn't say anything, just trailed his knuckles down her throat, halting at the neckline of the sweatshirt.

Then he took her hand and tugged her over to the couch, a plate laden with pizza plunked into her lap a moment later.

He was beside her in the next, pizza on his plate.

But neither of them ate.

Fingers on her throat again, another shiver wracking her frame. "Stop looking at me like that," he rasped.

Her lips parted, a shuddering breath escaping. "I can't help it."

His plate hit the table.

His hands slid into her hair. His lips came down—

Fred launched himself onto the couch . . . and snatched a slice of pizza off her plate.

She was so in Ben's thrall that it took her a moment to realize what Fred had done. Gasping, she jumped to her feet, Ben somehow managing to snag her plate before she dumped it on the ground.

"Fred!" she snapped, taking a step after her pooch, but the little asshole had already eaten the slice.

Stef couldn't believe he'd done that.

She'd already fed him, and she'd broken him of the counter-surfing for food habit when he was a puppy, and he'd never been much of a food-snatcher, least of all right off her lap.

And the turd didn't even have the common courtesy to look guilty.

He just licked his lips.

"I—I—"

Ben started laughing, setting her plate on the table, before crossing the room to crouch in front of Fred.

Everything inside her went tense for one moment.

She didn't know this man, and if he did something to Fred . . .

He reached a hand out to her dog, stroked his fingers over fluffy, golden ears. "That was naughty," Ben murmured in a voice that made her want to be naughty herself. "Pizza will make you sick."

Fred had stilled, staring up at him.

"You can't do that again, got it?" Ben ordered, firmer now. "No stealing food. No pizza."

Fred whined and sank down onto his belly.

Apparently satisfied, Ben stood up, crossed back to the table, put another slice onto her plate, then came to her and tugged her down next to him on the couch. "Now then," he said. "No more looking at me. Just eat."

She opened her mouth.

"*Eat,*" he ordered.

She took the plate he shoved at her but didn't pick up her pizza. Instead, she grabbed the remote, shoved it at *him*, then snagged her cell.

"Stef." Another order.

Well, good thing she knew how to give orders herself . . . or at least with Ben she found that she could.

"You find something to watch," she told him. "And I'm using Instacart to *order*"—heh—"us some condoms."

His gaze shot to hers.

A grin, wicked and so different from what he'd given to her before. Different in a good way, in the *best* way.

She folded his fingers over the remote. "Put something on."

Another hot look, but then he turned on the TV, she got busy on the app, and by the time their delivery showed up, the pizza was gone, a nerdy Sci-Fi horror flick was watched, and . . . then Ben put something *else* on.

And it was glorious.

TWENTY

BEN

She was asleep next to him, her breathing slow and steady. Lips reddened from his kisses, her lipstick long since rubbed off. Beautiful and cute and sweet and . . . funny.

That had surprised him as she'd watched the movie, droll commentary interjecting their viewing. She'd been quiet in the theater, and when he'd asked her why, she'd only said that she could talk over previews but never over the sacredness of a movie in a theater.

Either way—*both* ways—he liked her.

A lot.

He liked her body just as much, her personality to equal measure. Hell, he'd burst out laughing when she'd looked up from her phone as he'd paused his scrolling through the selections on the streaming platform, bent to look over her shoulder, and pointed to the screen, lips curving in a self-deprecating smile, joking, "Magnum. Definitely get magnum."

"Boys and their penises," she'd teased, rolling her eyes, and running with the joke.

Because he wasn't magnum, not that he gave a shit, and when the condoms had arrived, they weren't either. But he just liked making her smile, even if the joke was at his expense.

Plus, he'd still made good use of the condoms, no matter the size.

After chuckling his ass off when she'd smirked and said, "Big hands. Big . . . Sci-Fi nerd."

Laughter, so much of it over the last two days, and he knew that his decision to pursue this was the right one.

She was the right one.

He smoothed her hair off her face, smiling as she nuzzled closer, her arms tightening around him. Even sweet in her sleep.

Ben let his eyes slide close, pondered his next move, determined to negotiate the weeks and months and hopefully *years* ahead with Stef like a business deal and not like he'd normally handle a relationship with a woman.

He wasn't going to be tentative.

He was playing to win.

———

He'd just drifted off to sleep when Stef jerked up in his arms.

"Sweetheart!"

"What?" he asked, sitting up next to her. "What's the matter?"

"Sweetheart," she said again, spinning in his arms to stare up at him. "We forgot about Sweetheart, and she's probably hungry and has to go to the bathroom." Guilt slid across her face. "She's probably terrified and—"

"Baby," he said, cupping her jaw, feeling a piece of his heart break off, drift through the air, and float to her. It was hers. And probably not just that one part of it. "She's fine."

Stef's hand clamped over his. "You haven't been back—"

"My assistant came and picked her up this morning." He

smiled gently. "She's fine. I need to get her tomorrow"—his eyes flicked to the clock on the nightstand—"or later today, actually. But they're getting along fine. Claire even said that she hasn't tried to bite anyone."

Stef relaxed. "Your assistant is watching your dog?"

A nod as he coaxed her down to the mattress. "Well, technically, she'll be my newest VP on Monday—tomorrow, that is. The important thing is that she's fine, Sweetheart is fine, and you can go back to sleep."

A few blinks, her sleep-hazed and half-panicked mind processing his words.

"Your VP has your dog?"

He nodded, biting back a grin as he smoothed back her hair again.

"Okay," she murmured, nuzzling close, and it wasn't three more heartbeats before she was out again.

So fucking cute.

———

She was less cute in the morning.

Mostly because they were in an argument.

Okay, who was he kidding? She was fucking adorable, dwarfed in his shirt, her arms crossed over her breasts, as one bare foot stomped on the floor.

Fred whined, his food in his dish.

"I'm not bringing Sweetheart here," he said, for what must have been the fifth time since he'd told Stef he needed to retrieve Sweetheart soon.

"You are." There that foot went again.

"Sweetheart isn't good with other dogs."

"You said she wasn't good with people," she pointed out. "But she was good with me, and Fred is the therapy dog at doggy day care. If a pup is having a bad day, they put it with Fred, and he gets them through the nerves."

"Sweetheart doesn't have nerves."

Her nostrils flared. Her lips pressed flat. "Ben," she said. "I'd like to spend more time with you. That would be easier if our dogs got along. It's not like you can ask . . ." Her eyes slid to the side then back to his as she remembered Claire's name. "*Claire* to dog sit all the time."

"It's not—" He broke off when a flash of pain slid through her eyes, and he was struggling to process it when she spoke again.

"I'll go change." A smile that was *not* normal, even based on the limited time he'd known her. "Let you get your shirt, so you can get out of here."

If the smile wasn't normal, then her tone was . . . peculiar.

Off.

Shut down.

And then she was gone, spinning and striding down the hall. The door to the bedroom *clicked* closed.

He looked at Fred. "What was that?"

The pooch just lay down by his food dish, head resting on his paws.

Ben didn't have time to process the tone and smile any further because the bedroom door opened, and Stef came out in a pair of black leggings and a loose sweatshirt. Her eyes met his, and that smile made another appearance.

Silently, she handed him his shirt.

But she was obvious about not letting her fingers brush his, and as soon as she passed it to him, she turned away and went to the sink, starting to wash the dishes from the simple breakfast she'd made them.

A bagel.

Enough cream cheese to clog his arteries.

Delicious with a bit of spice, and he'd eaten the entire thing, along with two cups of coffee.

None of that, however, explained the change in Stef.

Still, he knew there weren't that many dishes, so instead of storming over and demanding that she talk to him, he did what he might do if someone was trying to negotiate him out of a deal.

He waited.

Silently.

And eventually, she ran out of things to clean. Though, he had to give her credit; once the dishes ran out, she moved to wiping down the counter, the table, the sink, even the fridge, and inside its glass shelves.

She closed the fridge, turned around, and froze.

As though having expected him to be out the door.

"What's going on?" he asked.

Another flash in her eyes before they flicked over his shoulder. "I'll help you get your stuff together so you can go. Do you need a ride?"

"My car's here," he said, taking a step to the right to block her path when she would have slid by him.

"Okay, good. I'll just get your keys."

Wrong. *Wrong.*

This was so wrong.

He snagged her arm before she could disappear down that hall. "What is it?"

She tugged her arm free.

Fuck that. He scooped her up in his arms, carried her to the couch, and sat down with her in his lap.

"What are you doing?" she asked, squirming in his hold.

"What are *you* doing?" he retorted, tightening it. "Why are you freezing me out? Are you that mad about the dogs?"

"No, of course not," she said, and her tone told him that was the truth.

But there was something else he'd missed, something he was going to get to the bottom of. So, while he wouldn't hold a business rival on his lap, he *would* hold them accountable, at least until he understood the motivations that went into the process.

And that was the part he was severely missing.

The motivation for Stef shutting down.

Not the dogs. Not the argument. She seemed to be having as much fun bickering as he had . . . until he'd said . . . *what?*

He couldn't pinpoint it.

She'd stopped squirming, going still on his lap, and Ben scrambled to tease out the answer to what he'd done.

He was no closer to the answer when she gave him a clue.

"Just go," she whispered.

And he remembered her talking about her friends, the light and happiness . . . and the way she'd said, *"How much I'm going to miss them when it's over."*

Over.

When it's over.

Not if it would end someday, but as though her friendships ending with them was a forgone conclusion.

And she'd come to the conclusion that he wanted things to be over.

Which couldn't be further from the truth.

But they'd known each other for no time at all. How could he possibly convince her that he wanted to see where this went?

That he wanted her, hopefully forever.

"Stef," he said. "I want to get to know you better, too."

"Right." A nod, her eyes meeting his just for a moment, but then they darted away again, drifted back down to her hands.

"You going anywhere today?"

Silence.

Then her lips pressed flat.

"Stef?"

"No," she whispered.

"I'll go take care of Sweetheart, drop her at my place, but I'm coming back."

"Right," she whispered again.

And he knew in that moment that words wouldn't mean much to her.

That was okay. He would just have to show it to her.

Carefully, he set her on the couch, patted Fred on his head, and gathered his things.

"I'll see you soon," he said, and kissed her forehead.

Another of those wrecked smiles, one that almost had him staying, but he knew that wouldn't show her anything, wouldn't prove anything. She needed to understand that he was going to come back. "Okay."

He'd show her that.

Because not once did he think she wouldn't be worth fighting for.

Twenty-One

STEF

He left, the door clicking closed behind him.

Why had she ruined the loveliness, the good time they'd been having?

She'd pushed, and he'd left.

Oh, she knew that he'd promised to come back, but he wouldn't. She'd seen that look on his face, and it was familiar. It was something she'd seen over and over again. Plus, who would return to a woman who argued with him about something at hour . . . what? Thirty-six or so? Two dates in and already making demands. Waking him up in the middle of the night with her anxiety. Making him the only breakfast she could— both because she sucked at cooking and because all she'd had to offer were bagels and her cinnamon cream cheese and coffee. If she'd had time to shop, she could have made him muffins, but . .

.

She sighed.

Add in a dog tagging along on dates, anxiety nightmares, picking a fight before nine in the morning.

The ideal woman she was.

"Okay, Yoda," she muttered, forcing herself to get up and lock the door, her heart squeezing when she saw that he'd turned the bolt on the knob, so it was already locked.

Dammit.

She should have hung on a little longer.

But all she could think was that it was better now than when she was even more involved.

When it would hurt more.

So maybe she *did* know why she'd taken the first opportunity to push him away, to pull back and protect herself. For all her talk of clinging to him, to absorbing as much of him as she possibly could, in the end, she'd chosen self-preservation.

Close down.

Protect whatever shred of herself that was left.

Probably the smartest thing she'd ever done, even if she hated the idea of never seeing Ben again.

Losing Chance had broken something in her. Her parents trying to cope with his suicide, his mental illness, and distancing themselves from her had broken something else. And then Jeremy. Who she'd thought was a fucking savior, that white knight on the horse sweeping in to save her.

She didn't have it in her.

She'd wanted to be brave and soak in every moment.

But when Ben had gotten that familiar look on his face, she'd known she couldn't.

Stef had snapped so quickly back into herself, a tape measure whirling back into its case, the metal ricocheting and biting at her fingers just before fully closing. It hurt, but it belonged there, just like her.

She'd had her fun, and it was done.

Fuck, that hurt.

But she only had herself to blame.

"Enough," she whispered, going to the fridge and getting on

her meal prep for the week. She could slow cook chicken—plunk some olive oil, salt, and pepper into the Crock-Pot, throw in the chicken, and forget about it for eight hours.

Then shred it, throw it into some bagged salad, and be done with it.

Not a gourmet cook, but she could make a few edible things, and luckily, she didn't mind eating the same thing day in and out.

She went through the motions of meal prepping for the week, of cleaning her house and giving Fred a bath—well, Fred got cleaned up first and was turned out into the back yard to run off his after-bath zoomies, and *then* she cleaned the house, including the trail of wet pawprints and hair that stretched from the bathroom to the slider.

What she didn't do was allow her mind to wander back to Ben.

Which meant she thought about him every minute.

And as the hours went by, the small tendril of hope she'd been holding on to, even knowing it was stupid as hell, faded.

"It's okay," she whispered.

She'd forget about Ben and move on, and all would be good.

"Right," she muttered, not believing herself, not even for a moment.

But she'd be okay, eventually.

Sighing, knowing it was the truth, she walked to the slider, intending to let Fred back in. It was getting late, and she needed to make dinner, get ready for work the next day, to figure out some way to not be sad.

Because she wasn't really ready for Heidi to see that she was pining for a man she couldn't have—

A knock at the front door pulled her from the slider.

She didn't even get halfway to it when she saw Ben's face appear in the sidelight, big brown eyes on hers.

Her feet slid to a stop, and she swallowed hard.

He held her gaze as he knocked again.

"Right," she whispered, moving to the door. Nothing had changed, even if he'd come back this time. There would be a time when he wouldn't return or would tell her to go and . . .

She wasn't going to open that door.

She'd drawn her line in the sand.

He held up something in the window.

No, not *something*, but a fur baby. Sweetheart and her cute little black eyes peered through the glass, her white body looking so tiny in Ben's large hands.

And she knew she was fucked.

Her feet began moving, and she reached the door, hesitating again until there was another knock, Ben's voice saying, "It's cold out here."

"Right," she muttered, unlocking the door, knowing that she should just walk away and make him go back to his car.

But . . . Sweetheart.

But . . . Ben.

Her vulnerable, desperate heart wanted him for just a little longer.

She unlocked the door. Ben pushed it open.

Sweetheart wriggled her way out of his arms and into hers and began licking Stef's chin with enthusiasm. Not sleepy this time, not calmly cuddling after a burst of protectiveness. She was a writhing ball of fluff, and Stef found her heart squeezing, her lips turning up into a smile.

"Hi, baby," she murmured, stroking a hand down her back.

Her fur was so soft, and she couldn't help but cuddle her closer. Ben slipped by them when she was distracted, and it took her a moment to realize he'd made more than one trip.

A backpack. A crate. A tote bag printed with Sweetheart's face.

A paper bag with grease stains on the side.

The air filled with a delicious scent that went along with that paper bag, something fried, something that made her stomach, that had a week's worth of boring salads ahead of it, rumble.

She needed.

"Dinner," Ben said, unnecessarily.

"Right," she whispered.

He closed the door, locked it, and ran his knuckles down her throat. "How do we do this?"

For a moment, she thought he meant her and him.

Then she realized he meant how did they introduce the dogs to each other. "Let me grab Fred's leash." Just in case her boy got a little rambunctious. She shoved Sweetheart at Ben, reached into her wall organizer for Fred's leash, and then moved to the slider, opening it a fraction so that she could clip it to Fred's collar.

"Okay," she said. "You can let her down."

Ben's face was a study in concern, but he merely held her eyes for a second, as though reading her resolve, and then he nodded and put Sweetheart on the floor.

Please, let this go okay.

Sweetheart glanced around then her gaze came to her, to Fred.

And . . . it went horribly.

She sprinted over toward Fred, barking and snarling and becoming the beast Ben had accused her of being. But this wasn't Stef's first rodeo. She held tight to Fred's leash, positioned herself between them, and waited for Sweetheart to reach them.

She'd already slowed by the time she came within five feet.

Then stopped at three feet away, her body quivering in fear this time.

Fred didn't pull at the leash, just slumped to the floor in a movement that made Sweetheart jump and growl.

Silence filled the room, Sweetheart eyeing Fred like he was evil incarnate.

Then she tentatively took a step forward.

Fred didn't move, merely opened one eye as she took another, and then another until they were nose-to-nose and Sweetheart was sniffing delicately. Fred huffed out a breath, flopping to the side and making her jump again, minus the growl this time. He held perfectly still as Sweetheart made her way around him, sniffing every blade of hair, it seemed.

Her eyes came to Stef's, and Stef slowly reached a hand down to scratch Fred then her little head.

Sweetheart rumbled in contentment this time.

For just a moment before she surprised everyone but seemingly herself, and curled up between Fred's outstretched legs, a tiny white ball amongst golden fur. Another contented hum, her eyes closing. Fred glanced at Stef, who gave him and Sweetheart another scratch. Then, he too, shut his lids.

"I'll be damned," Ben murmured.

Stef set down his leash, making sure to stay within reach, just in case there was an issue, but her gut told her there wouldn't be.

Not with how relaxed Fred was.

"He shares your superpower?"

A little smug crept into her expression, and she didn't bother to stifle it, "Told you."

He smiled. "And rightly so, apparently." A beat. "Remind me to never doubt you again." He held up the bag of food. "Can I make it up to you with dinner?"

She stared at the bag, at the items in the hall.

Ben shifted a little closer. "I told you I was going to come back."

"But for how long?"

He went so still that it only took her a second to realize that she hadn't said that in her head as she'd intended. Oh no, she'd said it out loud. God, she'd said it *out loud,* revealing too much.

Ben set the bag on the table.

Her heart thudded, and she took a step backward, but he was already there, snagging her hand, drawing her over to the couch, turning her so that the backs of her legs hit the couch, pressing down on her shoulder until she sat.

"I'm going to tell you a story," he said.

She inhaled.

"It's not a happy story, and it's not the kind of thing I share with anyone." Her fingertips tingled, pulse pounding in her veins. "And I want you to know that I've never told anyone all of it."

Trust.

He was trusting her with something that made him vulnerable.

The magnitude of that sat heavy on her chest, her tongue, her throat.

"Okay?"

She nodded, managed to force out "Okay" back.

"In all my enjoyment of hearing you talk yesterday, I didn't get around to telling you what I do," he said. "I'm the CEO of Hunt Inc. I started the business, grew it, still chair the board, and am now the majority shareholder."

Her eyes went wide.

Hunt was . . . big.

Like owning the most popular social media apps and search engines and delving into video and TV and movies big. They'd been fairly small until the previous year, and now they were on the stock exchange and had gone global.

Last she'd heard, Hunt owned the most downloaded app in the U.S., U.K., India, and was expanding to Europe and China.

From blowing up the stock market to dominating world-wide in just three months.

Their independent movies had been popular for years, had won all those fancy awards, but the movie he'd taken her to see in the theater on Friday, *that* was their first big blockbuster, a film that was threatening to break opening weekend records—at least for a film that wasn't a superhero flick.

"Most of Hunt's success has come from the people below me who are smart and talented and have built it with me brick by brick," he said, his hands resting on his thighs. "But the rest has come from me both being open to new ventures and also from me being a stubborn ass by refusing to jump into some when I didn't feel like they were worth the risk."

Her lips opened, closed, not sure what to say.

"I love the company," he went on. "I've literally bled for it, but in the eight years I've been building it, I have always followed my instincts—even when people said I was a dumbass to do so."

"Ben," she began, still not sure what to say.

"And then three months ago, I got to where I wanted, and I felt . . . empty. My parents are gone, and I'd built Hunt for them, to show them I could be something, could make them proud." He laughed humorlessly. "But I didn't have anyone to share it with. Then Claire downloaded Tinder." His lips twitched. "Maybe I need to get Hunt into singles apps?"

She found herself chuckling. "Maybe."

"So, she downloaded it onto my phone without me knowing, set up a profile, and . . . then you swiped."

Her throat went tight. "I told you that I thought you were the most beautiful man I'd ever seen," she whispered. "But I had to get good and drunk to get up the courage to swipe."

"Well," he said. "I'm glad you were drinking that night."

Stef nibbled on her bottom lip. "What did you think when you saw the notification?"

"That I wanted to kiss that sexy mouth of yours."

"Oh."

He lightly bopped her nose. "Yeah. *Oh.*" A grin. "Then I was furious with Claire for doing it. She was the only one at the time with access to my phone," he added. "That has now changed—my password and passcode, that is—so there won't be any more downloads. Speaking of which, you need to set one up on your phone."

Her nose wrinkled under his finger. "Not you, too. I hate having to type in my code every time I want to use my phone."

"We'll talk about that later," he said with just enough pushiness that she frowned. But then he began talking again, distracting her. "My instincts said you were different, that there was something special about you."

Special?

Um . . .

"I—"

"But I'm not great with women. I'm a geek who loves fantasy and Sci-Fi. I was a skinny geek until a few years ago when I started working out because I . . ." His lips pressed flat. "I didn't have anything better to do. I spent my life being gangly and thin and not fitting my body. I'm not used to women giving me a second glance—or at least one that was due to the way I looked and not because they want a slice of Hunt."

She reached for him, covered his hand, realized the callouses on them were from the hard work he put into the gym. "I'm not . . . I'm not like that—" Not special. Not after his money.

"I know." A beat. "Why do you think I didn't delete the app?"

"I . . ." She shook her head. "I don't know. It just seems like we don't fit. You're gorgeous and successful, and . . . I'm me. I work at a lab. I live in a condo, not a penthouse. We don't make sense." Another shake. "Hell, my longest relationship with a male is with Fred."

His eyes flicked over to Fred and Sweetheart, now both soundly sleeping, and his mouth curved up.

"I don't care about your past relationships or where you work or that you don't think you're absolutely the sexiest woman I've ever had the privilege of touching." His hand found hers. "I don't care that you live in a condo or that you like a God-awful amount of cream cheese on your bagels." A squeeze. "I care that you love Fred and have weekly beach days with him.

I care that you liked the movie on Friday and were fine just staying in, cuddling on the couch, and watching a show last night. I care that you kiss me like you mean it and that you worried about Sweetheart."

He came a little closer, and her heart thumped at the intensity in his gaze. "I like you, Stef. For real. More than I should, considering the amount of time we've spent together, but I'm not backing off. I thought I'd messed up my chance with you three months ago, so to have this with you, now . . . I'm not just going to walk away."

God, how she'd dreamed of such words.

God, how she wished she could believe them now.

Ben, apparently, could see that.

He touched her cheek. "I know that words are hard to trust," he said. "Trust me, I've been around enough people to understand that. So"—his lips brushed hers—"I'm just going to show you that I'm not going anywhere." Another brush. "Unless you want me to go."

She'd spent the day building up armor around her heart, trying to ignore the pain of Ben leaving, of not being able to explore this thing between them, attempting to pretend it was for the best.

And after all that angst, one thing was critically clear.

She didn't want him to go.

The part of her that still had hope, held tight to his words, his promise of showing her he'd stick around.

Maybe it was stupid.

But he was here and so earnest and . . . she wanted him, wanted this man.

"So, can you do something for me?"

Her stomach clenched, waiting for the other shoe to drop.

"Can you just give me a chance to prove I'm going to stick around?"

God, she liked this man *so* much.

So much that she felt her heart grow lighter, felt as though she could actually do this, and . . . she found herself teasing.

"That depends."

His eyes warmed. "On what?"

"On two things, actually."

He just lifted his brows and waited for her to speak.

"First, on what's in the bag?"

Wordlessly, he snagged it, opened it to show her two delicious-smelling cheeseburgers and an obscene amount of French fries.

Okay, that passed.

The cocky grin Ben shot her confirmed that he knew she was thinking that.

"What's the second?" he asked.

"You let me pick what we watch."

His smile now was soft, his fingers on her cheek gentle. "Done," he murmured.

And Stef had the feeling that she was *done,* too.

Done for *him*.

TWENTY-TWO

BEN

The dogs slept curled together on the bed in the front room.

Stef had dozed off a couple of minutes ago in his arms.

The show blared on TV.

Stargate.

He nearly laughed at remembering her quoting all those lines, her sighing obsession with the colonel who'd eventually become a general obvious.

But Ben hadn't minded, not in the least, not when she was cuddled up next to him, her steady breath on his neck, her arms wrapped tightly around him. She stirred, and he knew he should tuck her into bed, take himself and Sweetheart home, but he'd brought all the gear hoping to get the invite to stay the night.

The thought of going back to his place, to his empty bed and that cold, large space wasn't appealing.

"Ben?" she murmured, running her nose across his throat.

"Hmm?" he murmured back, sliding his hand gently up and

down her back. She shivered, and fuck, he loved when she did that.

"Will you stay?"

He felt like fist-pumping, had to physically lock down the *whoop* inside him. "Of course," he said once he could manage not sounding too much like an idiot.

"Mmm," was her only response.

Smiling, he kept his hand moving, settling her further, waiting until her breathing had gone deep and slow again before carefully sitting up and carrying her into the bedroom.

The pups got up and followed him, Sweetheart trailing Fred, and he half-expected Fred to jump into bed ahead of him. Stef had teased him earlier about him having spent the previous evening sleeping in Fred's spot, and that Fred wouldn't stand for it. But the pooch barely even glanced at him as he went to the corner of the room and lay down on the cushy bed in the corner, Sweetheart right behind him.

After tucking Stef into bed, he moved to his bag in the front room, retrieving his phone and charger, finding a spare plug back in the bedroom to set it charging.

She was out, burrowed into the blankets, and he crawled into bed behind her, feeling another piece of his heart flow to her when she immediately rolled and burrowed into his embrace.

He wasn't a man who liked cuddling.

But he didn't think he'd be able to sleep without Stef in his arms.

————

Coffee roused him.

Along with Stef crawling back into bed on top of him.

Her hands slid along his bare skin, pulling him out of the fog of sleep, doing the remainder of the job that the coffee hadn't. He was hard already, not an uncommon morning occurrence, except *this* morning Stef's hands were on his body, and he was granite, a throbbing pulse of need.

"Morning," she whispered, her mouth pressing to his jaw, drifting down his throat, along his abdomen, tiny torturing presses of her mouth slowly moving down toward the waistband of his boxer briefs.

She tugged the material out of the way, and without warning, sucked his cock into her mouth.

Deeply.

His curse was garbled, his voice barely recognizable to his own ears, and then he cursed again when her hand joined the party, stroking as she sucked, and fuck . . . just that quickly he was seconds away from exploding.

Reaching under her armpits, he yanked her up his body, stealing her mouth in a scorching kiss as he wrestled the blankets to the side and flipped them so she was beneath him. Her eyes blazed and she'd changed, was wearing just a soft, fuzzy robe that had parted from his movements, revealing so much pale skin that his mouth watered with the need to taste.

"Are you wearing anything underneath this?" he asked roughly, trailing a hand up her side.

Her teeth nibbled at her bottom lip, a wicked gleam in her eyes. "Why don't you find out?"

That was a request he wouldn't deny.

His fingers shook as he undid the robe.

Spoiler alert: she wasn't wearing anything.

"Fuck," he groaned, his gaze tracing over her body, cock twitching when her stare drifted down, too, and he wondered if the sight had her on the razor's edge of control, like it had his—catching on the tips of her breasts, hardened and desperate for his mouth, then lower over the curve of her stomach he wanted to kiss his way across, then down to the flare of her hips. He wondered if the sight of his hand as it slipped between her thighs fractured her control to wisps like his.

"Fuck," she echoed, legs spreading wider.

She was wet. He'd known that even before he touched her, could see it gathering on her skin, coating the insides of her thighs, allowing his fingers to slide through the hot, silken folds of her labia easily.

Her face was stark with desire, jaw clenching, eyes flared bright.

He slipped one thick finger inside her.

Gasping, Stef threw her head back on the pillows, her hips bucked against his hand, bucking again when he dragged his thumb over her clit.

"That's it," he murmured, bending and sucking her nipple.

Deeply and without warning.

Partly because he couldn't stop himself. Partly because she liked it a little rough.

Drawing deeply, he let her cries wash over him, didn't gentle, didn't yield, not even when her back arched up off the mattress, legs going even wider. He needed more. He needed her—to be in her and on top of her, pressed to her soft body, her curves soft to his hard. He needed to be fucking her fast and furious and—

Her hips arched up, and he felt all that silken heat against the tip of his cock.

His control withered away.

Her hips tilted a second time, brushing against him, calling for him to thrust, to plant himself deep.

He pulled away.

Stef cursed, reached for him.

But he was already stretching for the nightstand, for the box of condoms, grabbing one and tearing it open with his teeth, rolling it down his cock. Then he was stroking deep.

This wasn't slow or controlled.

It was fast and frenzied, a frantic race to the end, a baton pass, him trying to get her there before he exploded. Stef doing the same for him. Her hands didn't stop moving on him, gripping tight to his shoulders, his ass, gripping him tight inside, too. Over and over he plunged into the tight, wet heat of her pussy, riding that razor's edge, so damned close to exploding—

And then her breathing hitched.

Her neck arched.

She clenched around him as she came.

One more thrust and Ben was done, his orgasm barreling up and down his spine, sending heat and pleasure to his fingers, down to his toes.

He collapsed, barely able to prop himself on his elbows, chest heaving, sweat dripping down his spine. "Fuck, you're beautiful," he murmured, summoning enough energy to roll to the side, to keep her close as he stroked a hand up and down her side.

Her lips curved, but thankfully, she didn't argue with him over the compliment, just kept her eyes closed and snuggled into him.

Fuck, he loved when she did that.

He held her closer, enjoyed the feel of her slowing breathing on his throat before he managed to roll away from her, to pull up his boxer briefs, to move to the bathroom and take care of the condom then make his way to the kitchen.

To the coffee pot.

He filled two mugs, added cream and sugar to Stef's—his, he took black—and then made his way to the bedroom.

But not before he saw Fred and Sweetheart standing outside in the back yard, staring at him through the glass, sad puppy eyes on full display. "I'll be right there," he said before walking down the hall, knowing that Stef must have let them out before she'd come and attacked him.

In the best way possible.

He handed Stef the mug, turned back for the kitchen, and started taking care of the dogs' food. He'd seen Fred's intricate food prep the day before and had done his best to replicate it when Stef came out of the bedroom, her sexy robe pulled around her again, though now that he knew she didn't wear anything beneath it, she was even more of a temptation.

Ben wanted her.

He'd just had her.

But he wanted to be buried balls deep in her again.

"You're making Fred's breakfast?" she murmured, coming close and glancing over his shoulder, her breasts pressing into his arm.

"Trying to," he said. "Did I do it right?"

Her gaze flicked over the bowl and then she smiled. "Yup," she said, breaking up a piece of chicken he hadn't apparently shredded small enough, sprinkling it over the kibble. "Thank you." She rose on tiptoe, pressed a kiss to his cheek. "You didn't have to do that, or bring me the coffee."

God, had that asshole who she'd dated not taken care of her at all?

But all he said was, "I wanted to."

Her mouth curved, and she squeezed his arm before going to the slider and letting in Fred, bending as though to scoop up Sweetheart.

But Sweetheart dodged away.

"Hang on," Stef said. "We should be careful with—"

He'd already set the food dish down and didn't process what she'd said until her voice went a little panicked. Then he realized there were two dogs heading for Fred's bowl, and Sweetheart wasn't good at sharing.

Shit.

He tried to scoop the bowl up, but he didn't beat the dogs to it, and then there were two heads in the stainless-steel container.

Gut clenching, he turned to snatch up Sweetheart—

"Wait," Stef said, coming over.

Ben froze, blinking at the sight. Sweetheart took a handful of bites and then laid down next to the bowl, letting Fred finish the rest.

Letting Fred.

What the hell had the witch done to his dog?

Sweetheart was practically civilized now.

Stef put a few more kibbles in, since Sweetheart had apparently found her breakfast in Fred's, and then Fred ate until the bowl was empty before flopping down next to Sweetheart, alternating between licking the container and his pup-friend's ear.

"You're amazing," Ben told her as she came to his side.

"No," she whispered. "That's Fred. All Fred."

He thought she was wrong. That it was her—all her.

And he looked forward to proving it.

TWENTY-THREE

"Oh. My. God." A beat. "You got laid."

Despite herself, she felt her cheeks heat, knowing that Heidi was clearly able to see that Stef had, in fact, gotten laid.

Multiple times.

With multiple glorious orgasms.

So glorious that she was a little sore as she meandered her way into the lab. Meandered because Heidi was there, and Stef knew her friend would notice the difference. Hell, when she'd looked in the mirror that morning, she'd hardly recognized her own face.

Happy.

She'd looked utterly happy.

And had decided it was a good look on her.

That had been after her momentary panic with the food dish and the two pups, of course. She hadn't thought Fred would get possessive, but he was so much bigger than Sweetheart, could easily hurt her, so she'd worried.

But then, like two peas in a pod, it hadn't been an issue in the least.

Then Ben had made her a bagel, with loads of cream cheese, had downed a second cup of coffee, and disappeared into the bathroom to shower and change, coming out in a suit that had taken her breath away.

"I thought you tech guys didn't wear suits."

He'd merely grinned, kissed the top of her head. "I'm glad you like it." Then he'd told her he had a meeting with the board that day, so he had dressed up for the occasion. Though from the glimpse she'd gotten of his closet Friday night, she knew that he was no stranger to a suit.

The entire back wall of his wardrobe had been filled with suits.

Now, Heidi squealed and clapped her hands together. "Yes! You got the best kind of laid."

Stef bit her lip. She had.

"Who is he? What does he look like? Where did you meet him? What did you do? How many times did you—"

Stef held up her hand. Not only to thwart the pure onslaught of questions but also in order to cut off Heidi. They were at work, for God's sake, and she wasn't going to spill her guts when an intern could come in at any point. "We're not talking about this right now."

Heidi started to protest.

The lab door opened.

Stef lifted her brows, silently telling her friend, "See?"

Heidi just lifted her hands in surrender as their newest intern walked in then issued some instructions to Stef and Aarav, before strolling over to her computer.

Aarav, quiet, shy—and did she mention quiet?—merely said, "Good morning."

Then they all got to work.

Stef on going over some data from the weekend, mostly

seeing if their equipment was functioning properly, but also prepping some things for an experiment that Heidi wanted to conduct later in the week.

Her job probably wasn't exciting from the outside—spending her time going over spreadsheets and spectrometer readings—but she enjoyed the challenge of working with atoms, with trying to discover their secrets, trying to study something that couldn't be seen with the naked eye, with a normal microscope . . . hell, with *any* microscope.

It was all theory and testing and studying the blank spaces left behind. Atoms were too small to be able to see, so they studied the reactions between molecules more than the small, basic units of life themselves.

The ultimate puzzle.

And she was thrilled that she got to work on it, even her small part of it.

Her cell buzzed, and she glanced down at the screen quickly, knowing that she needed to turn it off and unable to believe she'd left it on. It could mess with the equipment, for one, and was a general distraction, for another.

But it wasn't Ben texting, as she'd hoped.

It was from . . . Heidi.

On a scale of one to a million, how good was it?

Stef glared.

Deliberately held up her cell, the screen facing her boss as she turned it off. But then because she was so fucking happy, she found herself mouthing, "A million and one."

Heidi grinned.

Stef slid her cell back into her pocket.

Then she let her life happy bleed into her work happy . . . and found herself *happy* happy for the first time in a long time.

She was driving to doggy day care when Ben called her.

"Hello?" she answered via her car's Bluetooth.

"You done with work?"

"Just finished." She glanced over her shoulder, checked for traffic as she changed lanes.

"Come to my place."

Four husky words and her legs pressed together, her brain struggled to focus on the traffic clogging the freeway. "I have to go get Fred."

"Get Fred. Then come to my place."

Signaling again, she forced her way into the next lane, one step closer to the exit. "You have a white rug."

Silence.

Then, "Yes, I do."

"Right," she said, half-distracted as she crammed her car into a tiny opening and managed to navigate onto the off-ramp. Fucking California traffic was the worst.

"I'm not understanding your obsession with my white rug."

She thought it was rather obvious. "It can get dirty."

Another pause, shorter this time. "Isn't that what rugs do?"

Okay, he had her there. But still, it was a white rug and Fred was Fred. He'd get into something, and the white rug wouldn't be white and—

"Stef?"

She turned right at the signal. "Yeah?"

"It's just a rug."

He also had her there. Except, "It's probably an expensive rug, and you haven't seen what kind of damage a golden retriever can do to expensive *and* white household objects. He'll ruin it, and it's probably not washable, and I certainly can't afford to buy you a new one and—"

"Baby?"

The endearment had her heart fluttering up into her throat. "Yeah?" she managed to push out for a second time.

"Come to my place. Bring Fred."

Her protests welled again, but he just hung up.

Well, that was one way to end a conversation, and she found that she wasn't even mad that he'd just disconnected. It was bossy and a little annoying but also a whole lot sexy, and . . . he wanted her to bring Fred.

That had her smiling and staring out the windshield.

A knock on the window had her jumping, clamping her hand to her chest. She hadn't realized that she'd made it into the drive-through pickup for day care, and Fred was there, a handler holding his leash.

She scrambled to unlock the doors, made small talk as Fred was buckled into his seat belt.

Just before she was going to pull away from the curb, her phone buzzed.

With a text from Ben.

Then again with another.

The first was a pin for her to navigate to the proper entrance of the parking garage. The second was a QR code for her to show the security office.

A final buzz told her to park in spot PH-3.

Stef stared blankly at her screen for a few minutes before Fred whined. That snapped her out of it, and she drove forward, pulling out of the lot and heading back for the freeway. She'd still need to stop at her place to feed Fred. He might be happy to see Sweetheart, but he wouldn't be thrilled for his dinner to be late—meaning arriving later than five minutes after she walked through the door at home.

Her phone rang again.

"Yes?" she said, seeing that it was Ben.

"I have food for Fred."

The signal turned red, and she slid to a stop, struggling to find the words. The directions. The gate pass. The parking spot. Food for Fred. It was too much. She didn't know what to say.

And Ben seemed to understand that.

"Hope you had a good day, baby," he said, right as the light turned green.

She waited as the cars in front of her moved then slowly accelerated, heading north on 101 to make her way into the city. But even though she drove carefully, checked traffic, and made her way through the on-ramp and merging, her heart was pounding. Why was he doing all of this?

I'm just going to show you that I'm not going anywhere.

Remembering his words didn't slow her pulse. They only made her grip the steering wheel a little tighter.

"Stef?"

She swallowed hard, cleared her throat. "Yeah?"

"Did you have a good day?"

She was a smart woman. Some might even say smarter than average, but it took her much longer than average to process those words. But as though he'd sensed that, Ben waited patiently for her to answer. "I did." She cleared her throat again when it came out raspy. "Did you?"

"I did, baby. Thanks for asking."

"I—"

He waited.

She had too many thoughts and emotions roiling within her to give voice to them all, to give voice to even one of them. Her mind was a whirling dervish—Fred, directions, pass, dinner last night, Sweetheart, coffee, kisses, and—

"I'll see you soon," she eventually murmured.

"Okay, Stef. Drive safe."

They hung up, and she crawled her way through the traffic.

Toward Ben.

And for the first time in her life, she had to wonder if she'd finally found herself moving in the right direction.

Twenty-Four

BEN

The security office had called up the moment Stef drove through the gate, giving him time to take the elevator down to the garage.

She parked next to his SUV and his sedan, her tiny little hybrid's back seat full to the brim of Fred's fuzzy, golden body.

He waited until she opened the driver's side door then stepped close.

"Ben," she whispered.

"Hi," he said, brushing back her hair. "Want me to get Fred?"

A nod. "O-okay."

He wrangled the pooch while she reached in for her purse, and by the time both doors were shut, Stef seemed a little more relaxed. Enough, at least, to lean close and kiss him on the cheek. "Hi."

"You good?"

Her eyes were soft. "Yeah."

"Good," he said, slipping his arm around her and leading her toward the elevators.

"How did your meeting go?"

His heart squeezed that she'd remembered, that she'd asked. "Typical bullshit. No big problems, but endless droning on."

"Meetings," she said on a sigh.

"You have your fair share?"

"Unfortunately." A smile. "Though, Heidi has more of them than me, much to her chagrin."

Heidi her boss. Heidi her friend.

"When am I going to meet your friends?"

Her steps hitched, and she glanced up at him. "You want to meet my friends?"

Again. He wanted to murder that fucker, Jeremy. To have deposited the insecurity so deeply into her, who'd had her doubting that he wanted to do something as simple as meeting her friends, who'd had her shocked that Ben remembered how she took her coffee or would make breakfast for her and her dog.

At first, he'd looked at Stef and had seen red lips and curves.

Then he chatted online with her and thought she was funny and smart, someone he wanted to know better.

So getting to meet her in person, seeing how sweet and lovely she was, then knowing that someone had dimmed that, made her doubt herself, absolutely killed him. Especially when he got those glimpses of her humor, of the fire that was often banked inside her, and he knew that if she hadn't been smothered, they would be there all the time.

That she wouldn't still be carrying all those shadows in her eyes.

The elevator doors opened, and he ushered her onto the cart, punching in the code that would take the car up to his floor, asking, "Are they important to you?"

"My friends?"

He nodded.

Her teeth pressed into her bottom lip, a flash of white digging into red. "Yes, of course they are."

"Then I want to meet them."

Her throat worked, and she released her bottom lip. "I . . ."

He shifted Fred's leash to the other hand so he could cup her cheek. "I want to meet them, but only if you're okay with it."

A pause, her eyes searching his until the elevator opened up into his entryway. He held the door as they stepped off, and then her gaze came back to his, studying until Sweetheart heard them and came running.

Fred wiggled like he was full of jelly, and Ben bent, undoing Fred's leash, biting back a smile when Stef winced as he traipsed across the white rug.

Sweetheart jumped up to kiss Fred's face, the pair of them circling each other before taking off, nails clicking on the floor.

Stef winced again.

"What?" he asked.

"He'll scratch your floor."

He snagged her purse from her, dropping it onto the table where he left his keys. Then he wove an arm around her waist and tugged her close, his other hand slipping into her hair, tilting her head back. "Baby," he said, "I'm only going to tell you this once." Her throat worked, and he ignored the temptation of that creamy skin, continuing, "Fred could chew up the couch cushions, could shit on this white rug. He could scratch the floor and dump over the garbage, and *I wouldn't care.*"

A breath shuddered out of her, coating his lips.

"Everything here is replaceable. It's all just stuff. He and you are more important."

A slow blink, her brown eyes chock full of emotions. "But you don't know me."

He trailed his fingers along that throat. "I know enough," he said. "And I know enough to know that what I'll learn won't change that fact."

She swallowed.

"Okay?"

Her nostrils flared on an inhale. Then they relaxed, her mouth curving into a small smile. "Okay."

"Friends, too?"

Her lips tipped up further. "We all usually have dinner on Thursday. If we're all in town," she added.

"Are you having dinner *this* Thursday?"

A nod.

"I'm coming."

"Okay," she said again.

"Okay." He brought her a little closer. "And now, I'm going to kiss you."

"It's about time."

Sweet and soft, a flash of fire and spice . . . and red, *red* lips. *God,* he liked this woman.

He dropped his head, took her mouth in a kiss that he felt to his toes, that rebuilt him from the bottom up to the top, cell by cell by cell.

Now, he just needed to do the same for her.

———

Nails clicking on the floor had broken their kiss.

Or rather, their make out session, as their kiss had transitioned from standing in the middle of that rug to the table where he dropped his keys. He'd set her on top, stepped between her thighs, and let their tongues dance together, all while mentally making a note to fuck her here as soon as possible.

Preferably without two dogs nudging at his knees.

Stef was out of breath and looking deliciously rumpled, her lips swollen, and her fingers clenched into the fabric of his shirt.

He wanted to kiss her again.

To not stop.

But Fred—now nudging harder at the back of his knee—was apparently hungry.

Reluctantly, he pulled his mouth away from Stef's and glanced down at the cute, fluffy cock-blocker. "You hungry?"

Fred's tongue lolled out of his mouth in a way that seemed to signal the affirmative. Smothering a smile, he helped Stef down from the table, made sure she was steady on her feet. Then he took her hand and led her into the kitchen.

"Come on, pups"—he slanted a glance to his red-lipped, curvy woman—"and Stef. It's time for dinner."

This time, her smile wasn't filled with any uncertainty.

This time, her smile didn't come after a moment of hesitation.

This time, she just met his eyes, gave him her unhindered smile, and asked, "What'd you cook me?"

TWENTY-FIVE

STEF

She was waiting outside the restaurant, trying not to shiver against the chilly air, nerves bubbling up in her throat.

It was Thursday.

She and Ben hadn't spent a night apart since the previous Friday.

Tuesday he'd come to her place.

Wednesday she'd gone to his again.

Tonight she was going back to his place, had actually boarded Fred for the evening, not that he was sad about getting extra doggy day care time, and Ben had asked his assistant—no VP—Claire to watch Sweetheart for the night.

Because he wanted to take her somewhere after dinner.

Somewhere he wouldn't divulge.

But somewhere he'd said wasn't time dependent when she'd worried about the dinner running long and ruining his plans.

He'd merely nuzzled her throat, fingers threading through

her hair, and had told her, "It'll hold if you're too tired or it gets late. Just have fun with your friends, and we'll see how it goes."

And her heart, already vulnerable from that first night nearly a week ago, from the dinner he'd cooked on Monday and brought for her on the other days, from the coffee and bagel and food for Fred, from the other small things he'd paid attention to, had firmly cracked open.

She was exposed.

She was gone for him.

As she'd known she would be three months before, when she'd avoided that coffee date.

As she'd known when he'd left on Sunday, and she'd convinced herself he wouldn't come back.

And Stef was scared.

So fucking happy and sexually sated and enjoying the hell out of Ben, but she was also scared of what would happen to her when it ended. Still *when*, no matter if he'd said he'd stick around. Because a week wasn't enough time for him to find what everyone else had, to know her, *all* of her, including the parts that made people leave.

So, she was scared for a lot of reasons—because he might—probably would—leave and then she would be broken, because he might not show up that evening or her friends might hate him or—

Knuckles down her cheek.

A soft kiss to her forehead. "I'm going to show you," he murmured against her skin, slipping an arm around her shoulders and tugging her close.

And that right there was another reason she was freaking terrified.

Because she wanted to believe him.

Was quite desperate to.

Was quite desperate to kiss him, since it had been nearly twelve hours since she'd last had her mouth to his and when he was kissing her, she could pretend that everything was fine and her world hadn't been tilted on an axis it might eventually topple off, all in a little less than a week.

He brushed his thumb over her bottom lip, and she shuddered, lifting on tiptoe, her hand on his chest and able to feel the thundering of his heart beneath.

His arm around her shoulders tightened. His mouth came close.

Her tongue darted out, wet her bottom lip, and—

"*Ahem.*"

Stef startled, nearly flying out of Ben's arms, but he merely tightened his grip, brushed his thumb over her mouth once more.

An impatient tap of a foot. "Well, are you going to introduce us?"

She stifled a groan, ignoring Ben as he chuckled before releasing her, turning them to face Heidi, who was standing hand in hand with Brad, the former's tone sharp, though seriously tempered by the utter delight and mischief on her face. Brad, on the other hand, was staring at them with curiosity.

"Heidi, meet Ben."

Heidi's eyes narrowed, and Stef couldn't resist interjecting a little bit of teasing. God knew she'd be getting plenty of it inside the restaurant and for the foreseeable future. It was the way of her friends, to give as good as they got, and since this was the first time Stef had dated anyone since Jeremy, she knew there was to be no little amount of playful banter. Most of it at her expense. "Ben, this is my boss and bully of a friend, Heidi, and her lovely husband, Brad."

Heidi gasped.

Cora, who was just walking up behind their friend, cackled, her brown curls bouncing. And God, she seriously had the *best* hair. "Hi, lovely Brad," she said, kissing him on his cheek. "And bullying Heidi." She came over to Stef and Ben, narrowing her eyes at the latter. "You will treat my girl like the queen she is."

Stef winced, opened her mouth to . . . say something.

But Ben merely nodded. "Yes, I will."

"Good."

A beat as he extended a hand, his other arm still around Stef's shoulders as he lightly rubbed his palm up and down her arm, knowing she was nervous and soothing her; be still her heart. "I'm Ben."

Her friend studied his arm then Stef's face, but after a moment, she shook Ben's hand. "Cora."

A breeze kicked up, and Stef shivered, burrowing into his warmth. He nudged her toward the door. "Why don't you head inside? I can wait here for everyone else."

It was silly, but they always waited outside for everyone before they sat down at their table. She didn't know who had started the tradition, but it was kind of nice, all walking in as a big group together. They always made a reservation, usually sat at the same table, but it was different chatting with everyone outside—no interruptions from the waiter taking orders or food or drinks being delivered. Just them and their little circle of small talk before everyone came and voices started getting lost, conversations flowing over one another.

"You don't know everyone else," she pointed out.

"I'm sure I can figure it out," he began, right as Jaime, Tammy, and Kate, along with Kels and Tanner walked up.

Introductions were made, small talk commenced, and though she was shivering through her hoodie, she was loving the anecdote Jaime was telling about a kitten he'd taken care of that day. Ben shifted, slipping his arm away, but a moment later, his jacket was around her shoulders, his arm on top, and she was wonderfully warm.

And surrounded in the masculine spice of him.

She glanced up at him, but his gaze was on Jaime, lips turned up.

As though sensing her look, he glanced down, brushed his mouth over her forehead, and then returned his focus to Jaime, who was getting to the punch line of the little mischief maker clawing her way up his arm to perch on his head . . . and then launch herself on top of the cabinets in the back of the office.

It had taken them nearly thirty minutes to get her down, mostly because she was yowling over her predicament, and all the staff couldn't stop laughing.

And neither could they, because Jaime was damned good at telling stories.

But eventually they got it together and moved into the restaurant, Ben holding the door for them as they moved inside.

Cora lingered at the tail-end of the group, pausing and studying Ben once more. Only this time, her eyes relaxed, and she rose on tiptoe to press a kiss to his cheek. "Thank you," she said softly before she moved inside.

Stef, trailing her friend, did the same, adding after her thanks, "She likes you."

Ben winked, ushered her inside.

And then they went to dinner.

———

"What do you do?" Kate asked, as they sat around the table, beers and prickly pear margaritas in hand.

Stef's gut seized, remembering the way he'd reacted that first night.

But tonight, Ben was relaxed, his mouth soft and curved when he shrugged. "I'm the CEO at Hunt Inc."

There were raised brows all around, but Kate just smiled. "I loved the new movie. Did you have any part in that?"

He shook his head. "No. I just helped negotiate some of the

distribution deal. Though I can't even take credit for that. I'm just lucky to have great people working for me."

"That's why you looked familiar," Kels said. "I read an article about you a couple of years ago. Didn't you build the initial streaming platform yourself?"

Ben nodded. "As clunky as it was, I did. Luckily, I was able to bring on some engineers much better than I to perfect it, and they did such a great job that we were able to transition into creating our own content." He chuckled. "I'm much better with contracts and ideas than the nitty-gritty of actual programming."

Kels turned to Tanner. "He's being modest. He actually revolutionized the delivery system. That's why Hunt Inc. got so many users. Instead of the menus being so clunky, he stream-lined it and made it very user-friendly—"

"We know it's user-friendly," Cora drawled. "That's why we all use it."

Stef bit back a smile as she studied Ben's face, and she had the feeling that he was blushing. She squeezed his hand, opened her mouth to change the subject, but Kels kept talking.

"But how did you come up with that algorithm to suggest recommended content? It's a freaking stroke of genius."

"Um," Ben said.

Kels kept going. "No, really. You've got to tell me how you came up with the idea for the source code. It's so much better than—"

Tanner covered her mouth with his hand. "Nice to have you here, Ben."

Kels's eyes narrowed.

"Why don't we let the poor man off the hot seat?"

"Yes, please," Ben muttered.

"Seriously," Cora said. "My brain is bleeding."

Kate, nice as always, tried to turn the conversation to something else. "Tell me about work, Kels. Did you finish your project?"

Kels, the smartest one of them, was thankfully as excited enough about her latest project—something about improving the delivery system for one of RoboTech's newest drone systems —to get off the topic of Ben's algorithm she was lusting over.

Unfortunately, her project and subsequent explanation was just as dry.

Which meant that Heidi and Cora listened for about three seconds before pouncing on Stef.

"You owe me details," Heidi said. "You've been avoiding telling me how you met Ben all week."

She felt Ben look down at her, but she didn't glance up.

She *had* been avoiding telling the story.

Not because she was embarrassed, but because having a *How We Met* story felt like they had a relationship, and then having a relationship—or the possibility of one—had her heart clenching and worry creeping in and—

Ben squeezed her hand.

"I met her outside of Bobby's. We saw a movie and hit it off, and I've been trying to tempt her into spending as much time with me as possible."

Cora grinned.

Heidi studied him closely. "Why do I feel like there's more to the story?"

Because there was.

But she wasn't going to share her breakdown three months before, nor the fact that she'd drunk messaged him on Tinder, nor that they'd only been seeing each other for a week.

It felt longer, and she supposed it was in a way.

In the past, when she had gone on a date with someone, she'd seen them once a week, maybe a couple times a month. Then they parted ways or moved up to twice a week.

She and Ben were on date . . . seven? Maybe eight or nine if she counted the full day on Saturday and Sunday as separate from the evenings.

Yes, she was grasping at straws.

Yes, it made her feel better to think that their time together was equivalent to two months of dating.

"Whatcha thinking?" Ben murmured.

She blinked, realized that Heidi had gotten pulled into conversation with Kate, Cora with Tammy, and Ben was staring down at her quizzically.

And his eyes were so pretty that she found herself blurting, "I was adding up our dates."

He lifted a brow.

"We've had two months' worth, in case you were wondering."

His lips quirked. "Yeah?"

She nodded, grinning at her own silliness. "Yeah."

He lifted her hand, pressed a kiss to the back of it. "Well, that sounds like a good start."

The server came with their food then, but the words were pinging around her brain. Simple words, but they unlocked something inside her. Because it *was* a start, and even if it would have an end, if she spent all her time being focused on it, then she was missing out on the now.

Missing out on the good times they were having.

Not that she was doing it every moment, but she was spending enough time worrying about it to pull her away from Ben, from her friends, from the fun and loveliness of *now*.

She dropped her hand to his thigh, leaned up to kiss his cheek.

He turned his head, eyes blazing.

"A good start," she agreed.

Those knuckles found her throat, brushing lightly over her skin. "Eat, honey. Put those Hoovering skills to work."

Her heart kicked against her ribs, love blossomed somewhere deep inside her.

But she didn't panic.

Instead, she embraced the feeling . . . and got down to eating her fajitas.

Twenty-Six

BEN

Stef smelled like heaven as she leaned against him, riding the elevator all the way to the top of the Hunt Inc. building.

The reason he hadn't been worried about how long dinner would take.

He'd just wanted to bring her here.

To show her this.

The elevator doors opened into a dim hallway, and she slowed, lifting an eyebrow. "Um, so you don't have a creepy serial killer basement, but you have a creepy, dark hallway instead?"

He tugged a lock of her hair. "Just a short one."

"That's what she said."

He burst out laughing, shook his head, and stepped ahead of her to push open the door at the end of it.

"Oh," she murmured.

And he knew the feeling. It was the same one that he'd had when he'd first come up here after he'd bought the building.

Now it had been spruced up.

A safety railing added, several couches on one side, a table between them. Even an outdoor heater.

But the suave furnishings weren't what he wanted to show her.

Instead, it was the view.

"Wow," she said, when he'd taken her hand and coaxed her out. She still wore his jacket, hadn't taken it off since he'd settled it on her shoulders. "This is amazing."

He brought her to the railing, to the view that had taken his breath from the first moment he'd seen it. The lights of San Francisco glowed in the distance, some twinkling and bright, others more muted by the curls of fog coming in from the ocean. The Golden Gate was to the north, the lights of the East Bay visible on the other side of the inlet of water.

"I grew up there," he said softly.

Stef turned from where she'd been looking at the Golden Gate and curled into his side. "Across the Bay?"

He nodded. "In Hayward."

"I haven't heard of it."

He tugged a lock of her hair. "I forget that you didn't grow up here. It's a smaller city between San Jose and Oakland. Great place when I was a kid, but it changed when I got older."

"In what way?"

"Got bigger, felt less like that small town, and . . ." The words got stuck in his throat, but she just waited for him to find his voice again. "It was still home. I loved the hills and the downtown. We had a special curb."

Her head tilted to the side as she glanced up at him with questions in her eyes. "A curb?"

He flashed a smile. "Yup."

"C-u-r-b? As in one you stepped off." Her brows drew together. "I'm struggling to understand the significance."

Laughter flowed up his throat, filled the air around them. "It was built on a fault line, so every year it moved, separating from the sidewalk, jutting out a little more." He shrugged. "It was always cool to go see it and measure it, to see how many millimeters it moved from one year to the next. A stupid thing, but my mom and I would keep track of our measurements in a notebook. We'd be so freaking careful to make sure we took them in the same exact spot. And my dad would be sitting on a bench across the street, a stack of books from the library in his arms, reading through one as we fussed."

"That sounds really nice."

"It was." A beat. "Until they fixed the curb, and we couldn't measure anymore."

Stef gasped. "They didn't."

"Unfortunately, they did. I guess the city thought it was getting dangerous." Another shrug. "And I supposed that I thought I was getting too old to enjoy doing it anyway. A teenager who was too cool to hang with his parents."

"I'm sorry."

"Because I was a pain in the ass teenager?"

She pinched his hip. "No," she said. "But because you lost that part of your past."

He'd never thought about it that way.

But he supposed he'd been mourning for it in some small way since his mom had passed, missing all the easy times of the traditions they'd had, the chance to make new memories with her.

"What happened to your parents?" she asked gently. "You said they were gone, but . . ."

He blinked, and for a moment, grief threatened to swell up over him, but he battled it back, kept this woman who had become intrinsic to his life in such a short time close. "My mom died a year ago, my dad five years before that."

"I'm sorry."

"What about yours?" He slid his hand up and down her arm.

"They still live in the town I grew up in." There was a note of sadness in her tone, and he wondered if he should ask about it, but then she kept talking. "Still the same house, actually. Hell, they drove the same station wagon from my teenage years until two years ago when it broke down and the mechanic couldn't find parts to repair it." The words came fast and furious. "So, they were stuck buying a new car and hated every minute of it." Her voice had been overcome with sadness, the words finally coming to a halt.

"You want to talk about it?" he asked after she'd gone quiet and stayed that way for several moments.

She cleared her throat. "No," she whispered. "I'm sorry I hijacked your story."

He frowned. "I asked you about your family."

"Right." Another whisper, something fragile in her tone.

"I want to know all the things that make you tick."

A shudder wracked her frame, and this time it wasn't from the cold or the way he was holding her, touching her. This was a pain remembered, slices of agony that ran deep inside a person's soul. He knew because like recognized like, because he'd so often felt those same cuts after his father had been murdered, after cancer had stolen his mother. Two good people taken, leaving him behind with just memories. So, he stayed quiet, held her close, and waited.

"You don't."

He opened his mouth to argue, but then she was pulling out of his hold and moving over to the railing, hands gripping on the metal bar. He might have let her have the moment, allowed the quiet to grow and stay that way if not for her wiping away a tear.

Just a sly small motion, fingers darting up for her eye.

But he *did* see it.

And he was moving toward her before he even registered that his feet were in motion.

"Hey," he said softly. "What is it?"

She shook her head, wouldn't look at him. "I'm sorry."

Another apology.

"Stef." He turned her to him, hooked a finger under her chin. "Honey, *what is it?*"

She stepped away from him, tears glistening on her cheeks. "I'm so—"

"Don't apologize," he snapped, not as gently as it should have been, worry having crept in as the tears started to come in full force. "Tell me what's wrong."

But she either couldn't or wouldn't, and when she stumbled back a pace and bent at the waist, a sob hiccupping out of her lungs, he closed the distance between them, scooped her up and carried her to the couch.

And all the while she kept apologizing.

And all the while he kept telling her to *stop* apologizing.

But eventually, he realized that his orders weren't helping anything and just shut up and held her as she cried, as she repeated, "I'm sorry. I'm sorry," over and over again.

It killed him, that painful nonstop rhetoric, as though by saying it repeatedly she was atoning for something.

What could she possibly have to atone for?

He knew he needed to find out, that it was locked up with whatever he'd seen the previous Sunday, what had occasionally crept into her eyes throughout the week—the expectation that he would look too close and then leave.

This was the puzzle piece to the distance she held.

The wall she'd erected, the barb that was shoving them apart.

When all he wanted was to get closer.

Finally, she grew quiet and limp in his arms, and he was almost afraid to speak, afraid that if he gave voice to any of the thoughts in his head, she would retreat. So he held his tongue, stared out at the lights, and just stroked a hand up and down her spine.

The words, when they eventually came, surprised him.

Because he didn't talk about it.

Hadn't *ever* talked about it.

Not with his mother. Not with Claire or Baine, who'd been with him when he'd received the phone call.

He'd buried it down. Deep down. Perhaps as deeply as this pain of Stef's was buried.

"My father isn't just gone," he said. "He was murdered."

Stef's breathing had slowed, but when he spoke, it picked up again.

"He was just driving home from work," Ben said. "Stopped at a signal, and someone shot him through the window, yanked him out of his car with a bullet wound to the chest, and drove off." Ben's gaze turned to the Bay Bridge, to the steady stream of red and white lights from cars that made their way back and forth across the bottom and top decks—away from the city on the bottom, to it on the top. "They left him to die in the middle of the street and then took his car."

"Oh, Ben," she whispered. "I'm so sorry."

"The police found it three blocks away, parked half up on the curb, the door wide open. They took it and just *left* it there, discarded it like they had no use for it, for him—" His voice cracked.

She shifted in his arms, her hand lifting to rest on his jaw. "I'm sorry," she said again.

He covered the back of her palm with his own. "I miss him. Every day, I miss him."

Another tear slid down her cheek. "I know, baby."

He lifted his hand to wipe it away, and she shifted, wrapped her arms around his waist, nuzzling into his throat.

"I miss him, too," she said, so softly that he could hardly discern the words. "I shouldn't miss him so much. I'm not worthy of that grief, not when part of me hated him so much when he was alive."

Ben's heart ached at the agony of her words, but part of him also hoped.

Hoped so fucking much that she would share her hurt with him, allow him to take some of it away.

Instead, she held on tight to him, and he stayed quiet.

For minutes.

For hours.

Until the moon began to set, and Stef's breathing went slow and steady, and he knew she'd fallen asleep in his arms.

Not tonight then.

Ben grasped on to his patience, held it firm, and carried her downstairs to his car, drove her back to his place.

Soon. He had to hope that soon she would give him the rest.

Because he'd take it, would wrap it up carefully inside him, remove the hurt, the agony, and he would give her back happy.

He would do anything to give her back happy.

Twenty-Seven

STEF

S tef woke up and instantly knew where she was.

In Ben's arms.

In Ben's bed.

And even though exhaustion still tugged at her, she smiled. Because she really liked waking up with him.

As though sensing that she was awake, his eyes opened and his face gentled. "Morning, baby."

"Morning," she whispered, wanting to brush her fingers over his jaw.

As though sensing *that*, he tipped his head down, close enough so that his forehead rested against hers, so that she could easily touch him.

"You okay?" His eyes were on hers.

She nodded.

Then noticed the time on the clock on his nightstand. "Shit! I'm late." She started to toss the blankets back, to slide out of bed, but Ben merely clamped a hand around her arm and tugged her back against him, rolling to pin her between him and the mattress.

Hard lines. Hard muscles. Hard . . . cock.

She shivered.

He grinned.

And suddenly, work became the last thing on her mind.

"I called Heidi last night," he murmured. "Told her you wouldn't be in today." Her mouth dropped open. "Same as I called Claire and told her to forget my phone number for the day."

Stef's eyes widened.

"And she's going to keep Sweetheart. And doggy day care is going to keep Fred for one more night."

"I—"

His hips dropped down onto hers. "Is that okay?"

Her lips parted, her breathing shaky as pleasure began coiling itself like a snake in her abdomen. Always like this. Always needing him so fiercely.

"Baby?"

Heidi was probably going to interrogate her to no end, and she'd be hopelessly behind on Monday, but, "Yes, it's okay." It was wonderful actually. She hadn't taken a day off in ages, not one during the week anyway, ignoring her responsibilities for the day. She didn't think that she'd ever played hooky, nor had anyone she'd dated gone so far for her.

To call in to her boss.

To take care of her dog.

To think about the details so she didn't have to.

Falling. Falling. So fucking deep, and . . . she couldn't bring herself to care, couldn't do anything except push back against his chest.

He moved instantly, giving her distance.

But it wasn't distance that she wanted. Instead, she kept pushing, rolling him onto his back, clambering on top of him.

Hands perched on his pecs, massaging the muscles that overfilled her hands, dragging her nails over his nipples, loving the hiss of his breath escaping the mouth she was suddenly quite desperate to kiss.

So, she did.

And had the lovely side benefit of being pressed to every inch of him, of tasting him, of his slightly roughened fingers coming to her ass.

She'd made a tactical error in not getting naked first.

Otherwise, she would have those hands on her bare skin.

Ben's moan rumbled up his throat, filling her mouth, drifting down along her spine, winding its way between her legs. Her underwear was sopping wet, the T-shirt—Ben's, she now realized—a cumbersome hindrance when she wanted her skin against his.

Forcing herself to break the kiss, she reared back and yanked off the material, thankful that Ben was reaching for her hips, shoving her panties down her thighs, not bothering to propel them farther than her knees. Which was fine with her because then his fingers slid back up and in between, stroking through the evidence of her desire. So wet. Always so wet for him.

She went to work on his boxer briefs, pushing the material out of her way, revealing the hard cock encased within.

"Yes," she breathed, wrapping her hand around him and pumping.

Velvet over scorching steel.

He circled her clit, dipped a finger down and in, making her arch back against him, riding his hand as pleasure rocketed through her.

So quickly, she was close already.

But she didn't want to come.

Or at least, she didn't want to come *yet*.

She wanted him *in* and deep and thrusting hard and fast.

Shifting, she dislodged his fingers, started to ease down on him, the broad, bare head of his cock stretching her wide.

"Wait," he murmured, reaching a hand overhead for the nightstand. "Condom."

All the movement did was push him deeper inside her, making them both groan. "I have an IUD. Are you clean?"

"Yes." He groaned. "Just had a physical last week."

"Thank God," she said. "I'm clean, too. Was tested after my ex and I . . ." Her hips weren't in her control, not in the least, rocking and shifting, bringing him deeper and deeper, and though it felt so fucking good, she paused, met his gaze. "I haven't been with anyone else. I want you without—" She broke off, nibbled at her bottom lip.

"Yes," he panted, his fingers clutching her hips.

"Yes," she repeated. Then, "Come inside me?"

He bucked, impaling himself deep, and they both groaned again, louder this time, and hers might have been a scream, but she didn't care. Not when his hands were gripping her tightly, bringing her down on top of him, over and over again.

Not when his abs flexed, curling his shoulders up, changing the angles of their bodies so he could hit just the right spot.

"Fuck," he growled. "You are so fucking beautiful."

He was the beautiful one, or the things they were doing, building were beautiful, or . . . maybe she was beautiful. At least, the person she could dream about becoming. That confident, gorgeous woman was there, just within reach if only—

Ben's thumb moved between them, pressing against her clit, just the way she liked.

Thoughts of beauty faded into thoughts of need, of desperation.

She moved faster, driving herself down onto his cock, her orgasm barreling toward her with the force of a hurricane, swirling and whipping her around and around, bearing down on her, and—

Boom.

The force of it rattled her to her core, pleasure condensing and then flaring out, forcing her to move faster and faster and *faster* until the waves of that bliss eddied, until Ben was gripping her tight and pouring himself inside her as he came.

She collapsed.

His arms wrapped around her.

She buried her face in his throat, inhaled the scent of him deep inside her.

And because they were playing hooky, she let sleep drag her back under.

———

Four weeks later, she was still in the same blissful cloud.

She and Ben had spent that day playing hooky in bed together, making love until they were too exhausted to do anything but order in food and sleep and watch old Sci-Fi shows on TV.

They'd laughed and cuddled before doing it all again.

Sex. Talk about work. About movies and TV and pop culture.

Ben had told her about his parents, about building his company, and how he'd started developing the idea for Hunt Inc., how it had started as something small that could be an alternative to the big streaming networks, then had developed into something much bigger than he could have anticipated.

And now was their major competitor.

He was busy, very busy with meetings all day.

They didn't talk or text during those hours, which was just as well, since her phone needed to remain off most of the time, but he had recently introduced a hard stop at six, no matter what was happening, and he expected it to be the same for everyone beneath him. No emails. No calls.

Just people able to go about their lives without work's shadow constantly intruding. Easier to see how important that was now that he actually *had* a life.

Untraditional, same as the remote work he allowed his staff to do without question or clearance.

But it made for happy employees.

Plus, she got him all evening with no interruptions. Which was more than she could say for herself. Sometimes she had to be on call for the lab, if an experiment was running overnight or throughout a weekend, and if there was an issue, she had to go in.

They'd gone out every Thursday with her friends, and tonight—*tonight!*—she was meeting his friends.

Claire, Baine, and Spence. Oh, along with CJ, because Ben's newest assistant, was coming along, too. Apparently, Spence was a little quiet but a nice guy, and they were trying to get him to hang out more. CJ would likely be freaked out and silent, but Ben was convinced it was important for them all to hang out. And Stef agreed. A work environment where everyone was comfortable with each other was better for everyone.

Claire and Baine, on the other hand, had been with him from nearly the beginning and were chomping at the bit—Claire, especially, according to Ben—to meet her. *Meet* might be code for interrogating her, but he'd been interrogated plenty by her friends, so she figured he was due.

But, as she surveyed her closet, what did one wear to a future interrogation?

A dress? Jeans and a T-shirt?

Something in between?

In the end, she decided on jeans, a blouse, and knee-high boots, a simple infinity scarf around her neck to ward off the night air.

So, maybe she was a basic bitch.

And she didn't give a damn. They would pry her skinny jeans and scarves off her cold, dead body.

"Exactly," she muttered as she finished slicking on her lipstick, of which she'd had to buy extra tubes because Ben kissed it off her so often. Not that he seemed to mind his own lips getting stained from her, and she loved the gleam that came into his eyes when he wiped his mouth of the lipstick.

The wicked glint.

The promise of more.

More.

She was starting to believe that *more* was a possibility. She'd certainly had more with Ben than she'd ever had with anyone else. They fit, and she liked the person she was with him, especially since she'd stopped doubting every gesture and promise.

He showed up when he said he would. He called or texted to check in with her during the rare times they were apart, and he wasn't passive-aggressive. He meant what he said, and there was no hidden message she needed to untangle. And beyond that, he was . . . nice and patient. He made her smile.

She was happier than she'd been in ages. Maybe ever.

Five weeks they'd had.

And he hadn't turned away from her, hadn't pushed her to share things that made her sad, not because he didn't notice when something made her sad, but because he did. He'd ask if she wanted to share, and when she'd found the words stoppered up, unable to admit that final piece of her that she held back, he'd just held or kissed her, murmured again that he would show her.

Five times seven was thirty-five. Plus eight for the four weekends together. Forty-three days. How many months of dating was that?

Six? Seven?

Enough that she was thinking about it.

Enough that she *wanted* to tell him, because he'd shown her repeatedly that he was patient and kind.

Enough that she desired to let go of the burden.

This weekend.

She'd do it this weekend.

TWENTY-EIGHT

Claire leaned back in her chair, hazel eyes sparkling, curly brown hair shining under the lights as Stef burst into laughter.

He wanted to close the distance between them, to kiss the woman he was utterly in love with—Stef, not Claire—though he loved the latter, too, albeit in a sisterly fashion, and despite her efforts to embarrass him.

"And then he came to that first production meeting with his hair all messed up, his shirt half-unbuttoned, and smelling like booze."

Baine gave him a wolfish smile. Spence looked vaguely uncomfortable, having said only a handful of words. CJ had been still and silent as a statue.

"In fairness for my idiocy," Ben said. "I'd never been to a strip club, and that one"—he pointed at Baine—"decided that I *needed* to have the full experience."

"You were twenty-seven and hadn't had a lap dance. That needed to be remedied."

Stef's grin stayed in place, but Ben saw a glimmer of insecurity dancing on the edges of her expression.

Baine got that, too, and he didn't lie to her, just said the words that would put her at ease. "This one hated it. Sat there like a statue when I brought the girls over, no matter how many drinks I bought him."

The insecurity faded. "Not your thing?"

Ben shook his head, but Baine answered for him. "Definitely not his thing. No matter how much I coaxed, I couldn't get him back there."

"It was too much for this nerd," Ben said lightly. "Plus, I had enough people trying to get close to me because of Hunt. I didn't need an entire club's worth doing that."

Baine shrugged. "At least you knew what they were after the moment you walked through the door."

He considered that, nodded. "That's true," he agreed.

"But still not your thing," Stef murmured.

Lacing his fingers with hers, he brought them up to his mouth and kissed them lightly. "For the scrawny kid who didn't even have a date to prom . . . it was less a fantasy and more a nightmare."

Claire tsked. "Oh poor, poor CEO. Everyone wants a piece of him."

Baine snorted.

Ben rolled his eyes.

Spence's cheeks went a little pink. CJ still played statue.

Stef bristled, turning to Claire, her delicate features pulled into a scowl. "He's allowed to feel the way he feels," she ground out, adding when Claire scoffed, "And those feelings are valid, whether or not you think they are."

A glimpse of the fire beneath the sweet.

Hidden steel wielded for him.

Claire leaned forward. "You have a defender."

Stef narrowed her eyes. "Ben is a good man, and he deserves your respect. He's done so much for me and—"

Silence.

Then Claire's voice took on a note of cold, one that drew Ben's sharp glare. "And what has he done, exactly?"

He could read the undertones in the question, same as Stef could, if her going stiff as a board beside him was any indication. "Claire," he began, warning lacing his tone.

Stef talked over him. "He's given me hope."

More silence.

She spoke softly but fiercely, each word carefully clipped out. "And shown me that I can trust people again. Not because I was dragged along by someone else, included because someone took pity on me and brought me along. Not even because he's stuck with me due to us working together, like . . ." Her lips pressed flat then relaxed, voice even softer, and he realized she was talking about her friends, about Heidi. "Ben chose me, and I know what a gift that is."

His heart thudded, twisting the words over in his mind.

She thought her friends only liked her because of some bizarre obligation?

That drove a blade right through his insides. He wanted to yank her out of this restaurant, find some quiet place, and yell at her until she realized that she was loveable and worthy of her friends. Then he wanted to track down Jeremy Whatever-His-Name was and hurt him for hurting her. *Then* he wanted to find out who else had hurt her because he understood now that her wounds weren't from one man. They ran deeper than that, ingrained so deeply that they'd been imprinted on her soul.

"And you've known him how long? A month—"

Ben jerked his gaze to Claire. "That's—"

"Yes," Stef snapped. "A month. Or five weeks, if we're not counting that we first talked four months ago and that I chickened out and ended it." She rolled her shoulders, and he hated the glimmer of disgust on her face, but she kept talking before he could take her to task for it. "Try as I might, I couldn't get him out of my mind, and found that I had to talk to him, so I reached out, and we've been together since. So yeah, maybe we've been dating for barely more than a month, and maybe that's not a long time, but maybe it *doesn't* always take a long time." She inhaled, released it slowly, her tone gentling. "Life can change in a minute, an hour. Life can change the moment that you meet someone. Life doesn't follow a set of rules, and when you find someone who's worth you taking a fucking risk, you grab on tight."

Ben was too stunned, too touched by her words to manage to do anything other than just stare at her in awe.

Her color was high.

Her eyes flashed with temper.

But her grip on his hand was gentle.

"For the record," she continued, Claire having fallen silent, Baine, CJ, and Spence no doubt gaping very much like he was.

She had a heart of fire, a spine of steel, and had unleashed that for him.

For *him*.

"Ben was that for me."

She turned, her gaze alighting on his, something warring within her gaze, as though she were trying to come to terms with a decision. Then she seemed to come to it, straightening her shoulders and saying softly, "I love you."

Electricity shot down his spine.

But before he could recover, she stood. "Excuse me. I need to use the restroom."

Then she took off across the restaurant, disappearing down the hall, and moving out of sight.

"I like her," Claire breathed.

Baine grunted in agreement.

CJ and Spence didn't say anything.

But Ben barely noticed. He was already on his feet, following her.

———

But she wasn't in the bathroom.

Wasn't in either of the two single stalls—a fact he knew because he'd actually checked in both, barging in front of a couple of people waiting and peering inside.

She definitely hadn't come out of the hall, so the only logical place she could have disappeared through was the back door. He moved swiftly to it, pushing the steel panel wide and searching the dimly lit alley behind the restaurant.

Nothing.

Nothing.

There.

He moved to her. "Stef."

She turned, blinked up at him, tears clinging to her lashes. "I'm sorry," she said. "Your friends—"

"Are as in love with you as I am," he interrupted swiftly. "Claire, especially, as it takes a rare person to both laugh at her stories and to shut her down when she goes too far."

"I'm—"

"Stef, baby," he said, tugging her against him. "I love you, but I swear to God, if you apologize one more time, I will not be held accountable for my actions."

A chuckle bubbled up in the space between them. "Are those supposed to be sweet words?"

"No," he said, and was relieved to see light enter her eyes. "But these are." Lightly, he brushed back her hair, brushed a kiss over her forehead. "I look at your face and I'm stunned by your beauty, but the way you look here"—he ran a finger over her lips, her jaw, one eyebrow and then the other—"is nothing compared to the woman in *here.*" He placed a hand over her heart. "I've spent every night with you because I can't stay away, because the moment I began talking to you, I felt like I was home again, like the sun was shining down on me, the clouds having finally, *finally* cleared."

"Ben," she whispered.

"I saw red lips and curves, was desperate to taste them both, but when I talked to you, when I held you, I knew a taste would never be enough. I want to spend an eternity with you, every night from now until they put me in the ground."

A tear slid from her eye, and he brushed it away. "Ben," she whispered again.

He loved the sound of his name on her tongue, hated the sight of her tears, even though these were of happiness. "Should I keep going?"

She laughed as he brushed more tears away, the joy in her stare taking his breath away. "God no, I can't take it without turning into a complete watering pot."

"All right," he teased. "I'll save them for when we're in bed together."

Her red lips twitched. "Okay."

"Okay," he repeated, sliding his hand up and down her back, not wanting to let her go, but knowing they couldn't stand in this alley all night.

Stef seemed equally as reluctant, her arms wrapping around his waist, her breathing slow and deep. But eventually, she must have realized the same thing as him, "We should go inside," she said. "We're probably messing up their dinner."

Honestly, he didn't give a shit about Claire, Spence, CJ, and Baine's dinners.

He had the woman he loved in his arms, and she'd taken a huge step today. She'd been vulnerable and still let him in, trusted her with his heart. Ben knew exactly how big of a gift that was.

Because of that he didn't release her, not yet anyway. Instead, he wove his fingers into her hair and tilted her head back so that he could see her face. "Only if you do one thing for me."

She lifted her brows.

"No more apologies."

Those brows dragged together.

"You apologize too much for things that aren't your fault."

"I'm—"

"Uh-uh," he said, bopping her on the nose. "No sorries."

"I wasn't going to apologize," she huffed. "I was just going to say that I'm so glad you came back that day. That you're here in my life and—"

They needed to go inside.

But fuck if he could stop himself from kissing her again.

TWENTY-NINE

STEF

Come Monday, she still hadn't told Ben about Chance, about her parents and the twisted turn her childhood had taken.

Not because she was avoiding it.

But because Ben had kept her so busy in bed and at the beach and then watching an early release for a new movie Hunt was releasing. It was top secret, but he'd told her about it the week before. It featured a couple of Hollywood A-listers Stef loved, and he'd told her he'd had to beg, borrow, and practically steal the copy, just so he could bring the DVD home so she could see it. Despite the challenge, he'd brought it all the same, and she'd coaxed him into watching it twice (and crying both times).

And did she mention he'd kept her busy in bed? Because he'd been absolutely ravenous. Not that she hadn't been—*wasn't* —the same, needing him with an intensity that was all-consuming.

She was.

She looked at him, saw his smile, and she was wet.

Desire and orgasms aside, she'd decided that today would be the day. Her past was heavy. It was stifling. Not the topic for normal dinner time conversation. But she found that she needed to let that burden go.

Finally, she needed to be done with it.

So, she'd explain, tell him about her parents and Chance, about how she'd searched for her worth and value in other places.

And how she had finally begun to accept that her value came first from her.

Because Ben had given her the patience and kindness to understand that. By him seeing her value, loving her for being herself and not the over-the-top caregiver she'd been with Jeremy; nor the small, quiet, trying to never step a toe out of line girl she'd been with her parents; not even the everything was fine young woman she'd been with her college boyfriends and afterward, she found that worth.

She was done with always doing things for everyone but herself.

Done with thinking that doing something for herself, or wanting something, or saying no would be selfish when everyone else needed it more.

Because it was different with Ben.

He took care of her, making sure to give back what she offered freely . . . and that had opened doors inside her heart she had never risked cracking before, doors that had been slammed and locked for many years. He made her understand that a relationship could be different, that they could have give and take. It wasn't always perfectly equal, sometimes one person gave or took more, but when everything was averaged, their relationship wasn't lopsided.

Because he never took more than his fair share. In fact, if she were being truthful, she would say that he'd given more.

Tonight, however, would be different.

It was her turn to give more.

Smiling, she took the exit. She was heading back to her place after work, Fred in the back seat. She'd filled the Crock-Pot that morning with the one recipe for dinner that she couldn't fuck up, and she was going to feed the man, give him a glorious orgasm, and then pass over the final pieces of her, offer them up on a silver platter.

And she was going to hope that he didn't dump them on the floor.

Her stomach twisted, worry sliding through her.

"No," she gritted, gripping the steering wheel. "He's not going to do that. He's a good man and—*Ugh*, Fred!"

Her pup had licked her ear and she cringed, trying to drive as she wiped it on her shoulder, and not having much success. Luckily, she was almost home, just turning onto her street, so she just waited until she was in her driveway and parked to get the doggy saliva out of her ear.

"Thanks a lot, Fred," she muttered, shuddering as she dried her ear then reached for her purse. She got out, let Fred out, not bothering with the leash since he was sure to be focused on dinner and not on any rogue squirrels who might be lurking. He barked, and she kept muttering, grabbing a grocery bag with some prepacked salad and store-bought chocolate cake, "Hold your horses, bud. I'll be right . . . there?"

Finishing on a question came from the fact that the front door was open, and Fred had let himself inside.

She smiled, hurrying to the porch, thinking that Ben had beaten her here, and since she'd given him a key a couple of weeks before, he'd let himself in, too. Fred was probably excited to see him, and—

Another bark.

This one deeper. Not a friendly one.

Her eyes flicked to the driveway, to the street, across it, realizing that she didn't see Ben's car anywhere.

Fred barked again and then she heard a sharp, "Shut up!"

And then . . . a yelp.

She ran inside.

As stupid as it was, she ran inside her house. Because Fred had yelped, and she couldn't leave him to be hurt and . . .

She dropped her purse on the entryway floor when she saw who was there.

Jeremy. Rifling through the drawers in her kitchen.

Fred had backed himself into the corner, his teeth bared, and he seemed to be favoring one leg awkwardly.

And Stef saw red.

"What in the absolute fuck are you doing here?"

Jeremy stopped, turned to face her. "Where is it?"

She stifled a sigh. Were they really on this merry-go-round again?

"How did you get into my house?" she asked, carefully moving so that she put herself between Jeremy and Fred.

"*Where is it?!*" Jeremy screamed.

He looked unhinged, dark circles beneath his eyes, his cheekbones sharply pushing against pale, clammy skin, the stubble on his jaw patchy and overgrown.

Fear clamped a heavy hand on her shoulder.

He might hurt her, she suddenly realized. He might actually be capable of physically *hurting* her.

She'd never seriously considered that possibility before.

The truth had her pulse speeding until it was a rapid drum against her veins, her vision hazed and narrowed to the man who returned to searching through drawers, yanking one open and then the next, rifling through them, dropping the contents on the floor. She reached in her pocket for her cell, unlocked it as she asked, "Where is what, Jeremy?"

Another drawer's contents hit the floor, this one with silverware. It clattered deafeningly, forks and knives and spoons scattering in all directions. "You know," he muttered, moving to the next, dumping her towels out of it and yanking another open, nearly ripping it from its slides. "You damn well know."

Something snapped inside her. *"I don't know what the fuck you're talking about!"*

It was a mistake, that.

She'd snagged her phone, but hadn't unlocked it, hadn't dialed 9-1-1, or just grabbed Fred and got out. Then she'd yelled, loud enough to gain Jeremy's unhinged focus.

His *deadly* focus, if the gleam in his eyes was any indication.

He moved toward her, kicking his way across her belongings —a spatula going one way, several forks another, her turkey baster bouncing off the toe kick of the cabinets and skittering across the floor.

And he didn't stop moving, not even as he closed the distance between them, as Fred growled, as he grabbed her arm, yanked her to the side, and pinned her against the wall so quickly that her ankle exploded with pain. "Where." His fingers dug in hard enough to make her cry out in pain, her hand spasming, and her cell phone falling to the floor. "Is *it?*"

"I don't know—"

She didn't finish the rest of the statement because as suddenly as he'd cornered her, he was gone.

Just ripped away like the wind stealing a hat on a gusty day.

Ben gripped Jeremy by the throat, his face in a rage that was far scarier than Jeremy's, something that any sane person would see.

But Jeremy wasn't in his right mind.

He was gone to the anger, struggling against Ben's hold, even as Ben leveled a left hook at his face.

The sound was . . . gross. A crunching noise, blood immediately bursting from Jeremy's nose. It dripped down his chin, stained the front of his shirt, then more blood as Ben wound up and punched him again.

And again.

And again.

Until Jeremy was limp in his hold, his legs barely holding him up, Ben's hand around his throat the single thing keeping him up.

"Get the fuck out of this house," Ben growled, propelling him to the front door, as though he weighed nothing. "And if I ever see you within fifty feet of Stef, I will cheerfully murder you and then pay someone to make sure your body is never found."

Jeremy sneered, his eyes rolling around in his head. "I—"

Ben shook him. "Am not going to say another word." A beat. "Because that would be the first good decision you've made since you decided to break up with Stef."

"She—"

Ben shook him again. "Is a fucking goddess who is too good for me and you?" A feral smile curved his lips. "You're right. She is. But your idiotic loss is my gain, and I will protect what is mine. So heed my words, *do not come back here.*"

Then he threw him out the front door, slammed it shut, and locked it.

Stef's knees gave way, and she found herself sliding down the wall, collapsing onto the floor. Tears leaked from her eyes, but she angrily brushed them away, turning her focus to Fred, even as her ankle screamed out in pain as she crawled toward him. Fred whined, his tail thwapping once on the floor. He tried to get up, but one of his back legs wouldn't work, so she held him in place. "No, buddy," she said through her tears, "just stay down."

She kept her hands on his side, scrabbled for her cell.

"Here," Ben said, handing it to her. "Are you all—"

Banging began on the front door, the wood panel rattling on its hinges, Jeremy screaming and ranting. Ben cursed, rising to his feet, at the same time sirens sounded, came close, and tires screeching somewhere close.

Perhaps her driveway.

Voices rose and fell, Jeremy's and several unfamiliar ones shouting orders. Jeremy refusing them.

Then a scuffling, a crash, more scuffling, and . . . finally, all went quiet.

Ben crossed to the door, but before he got there, a knock sounded through the panel.

She turned her head, watched as Ben carefully opened the door, keeping his hands open and wide at his side as police officers stood in the opening. "Thank you for coming," he said.

They studied him then her on the floor, Fred trying to get up.

"Are you okay, ma'am?"

She nodded. "Ben"—she pointed, wanting to be sure that they knew exactly who the good guy was—"is my boyfriend. He saved me from"—she nodded to the porch where her ex was trussed up like a turkey—"Jeremy. My ex who broke in and assaulted me. H-he—"

Then Ben was there at her side, pulling her into his arms. "It's okay. I'm here, baby. I'm here."

She clung to him. "Fred's hurt."

"I know." He pulled out his phone, spoke quickly into it. "Claire and Baine are coming. They'll get him to the vet."

"O-okay," she whispered, slipping out of his arms and turning back to her dog.

"Sir?" one of the officers asked. "Can we have a word?"

Ben gently cupped her cheek. "You okay for a minute?"

She nodded.

"Tell me what happened," she heard the officer said. "And start from the beginning."

"I pulled up and saw the front door was open," Ben began.

Fred whined, and she knew she should splint his leg, should do something useful, do something to make him more comfortable. Maybe get a towel under him so he would be easier to carry.

She pushed her hands beneath herself, started to push to her feet.

She cried out and collapsed before she got there.

Instantly, Ben was there, two police officers flanking him. "What is it, honey?" he asked.

"My ankle," she groaned. "I'm fine—"

He gently lifted the hem of her pantleg, and cursed. "It's not fine."

His tone had her glancing down. Fuck. It wasn't fine. It was swollen already, and she could hardly feel her toes. "I'm going with Fred to the vet first," she said.

"No."

Two letters, one word, said so fiercely that she blinked.

"Claire will take Sweetheart, who's in my car, home. Baine will take Fred to your vet. Who you'll call right now, and if they're closed or can't take him, then he will take him to the emergency vet." She opened her mouth to protest. "Then as soon as these officers will allow us out of here, I'm taking you to the hospital."

"But—"

"Plus, Spence will be backup if either Claire or Baine need him," he said. "They have it, okay? Let me take care of you. Let me get you to the hospital."

The shorter officer with red hair nodded at her ankle. "Which should be right now." He passed Ben a card. "Call me when she's up to talking."

Ben nodded, shook his hand. "Thank you."

"Oh, my God!"

They all looked, saw Claire, her hair flowing behind her as she rushed into the room.

"Stef!" She dropped to her knees beside her. "Shit. Are you okay?"

Stef felt her eyes well. They hardly knew each other, and yet Claire was here, worry on her face, and her hand gripping Stef's tightly. "I'm fine," she said, but her voice broke, and a tear slipped out.

"Can you stay with Fred until Baine gets here?" Ben asked.

"Of course."

"I—"

Claire squeezed her hand, wincing and glancing down. Stef followed her gaze, saw that dark bruises were already appearing on her wrists. "Let us do this for you, okay? I'll text you updates for Fred every step of the way."

"But . . . why?"

"Because you're Ben's." A gentle smile. "And you're you."

THIRTY

BEN

Claire was true to her word.

After Stef had called her vet, she and Baine, who'd arrived by then, got Fred to the vet, Sweetheart tagging along in her carrier.

Luckily for Fred, nothing was broken, and he would recover from his sprained foot and bruised ribs in another week or so.

Stef hadn't been so lucky.

Jeremy had fractured one of the small bones in her foot, and because of her past injury, she'd needed surgery to reset it.

Stef had just made it back to her room, after the hour-long surgery and then two hours in the recovery suite, but she was still groggy and sleeping off the aftereffects of the anesthesia, though she had asked for a Fred update the moment she realized Ben was in the room.

He was able to give her one—a good one—showing her the picture Claire had sent of Sweetheart and Fred curled up on a bed in the living room of his place.

"Tomorrow, we'll go back to my place," he said, brushing

back her hair. "Stay there until I can get an alarm system installed at yours. Then we can go to yours—"

Her eyes had closed. Her mouth gone slack.

But just before she'd drifted off again, she'd reached for his hand, lacing their fingers together, and he kept his vigil, his grip tight, as she slept through the night.

———

The detectives left on the same elevator that had brought Stef's gaggle of friends up.

Stef's face was drawn, but her eyes were happy.

Claire sat by her side, folded into the group whether because she was female or just had the right attitude or because that was the way they were, accepting whoever came into their periphery.

And they were all fussing, Heidi adjusting the pillow beneath Stef's ankle. Tammy bringing her a cup of hot chocolate, Kels searching through the guide for something that Stef would want to watch. Cora was making everyone laugh, and Kate had been gently brushing her hair, was now braiding the silken locks into a crown across her head.

"You look like shit," Baine said.

"I haven't had a chance to thank you," Ben said by way of answer.

Baine shook his head. "You know there's no thanks needed, not between us."

Ben *hadn't* known it, not really. He still wasn't used to reaching out for help. It had been easier to take care of everything for everyone else, rather than making himself vulnerable by asking for it.

But he wouldn't forget it now. Wouldn't *ever* forget it.

Red lips had shattered the wall around him, and he couldn't stop himself from caring . . . about Stef, about Baine and Claire, about Stef's friends. Because he'd watched her constantly finding herself unworthy of their affection, terrified they would take it away and leave her, and despite that, still finding the strength to give it, to care, to love.

He wasn't going to let that go.

"Thank you anyway," he said.

Baine rolled his eyes but nodded, turning for the elevator, just as cackling broke out in the living room, Claire no doubt telling more embarrassing stories about him. She and Baine had been staying at his place, managing the dogs and the business so that Ben could focus solely on Stef. Friends, not employees, and he was ashamed to think that it had taken him so long to realize that fact.

More cackling.

Baine winced as he stepped onto the elevator. "I'm going to rescue my ears from the noise." A smirk. "Good luck with yours."

"Fucker." But it was said without heat, his gaze on Stef, on the fading bruises on her wrists, the foot propped on the pillow, guilt eating at him.

Baine caught the elevator door, holding it open. "Hey," he said, eyes concerned. "You okay?"

He was a long shot away from okay—the sight of Stef pinned against the wall, her fucking ex with his hands on her, had brought back the nightmares he'd thought long gone. He'd hardly slept, dreaming of his father being dragged out of the car, blood soaking the street, of his mother taking her final rattling breath, of what might have happened to Stef if he'd been delayed, if he hadn't left work early because he was so anxious to see her.

Broken and bleeding, a final rattling breath.

He shuddered. Not okay.

Definitely not okay.

But he'd eventually be, if only for the woman who held his

heart in her palm. Effortlessly caught and grasped tight, and he didn't give a shit that he'd been snared.

"No," he said, when Baine made to step off the elevator, despite the cackling rising in volume behind them. "I'm not okay," he admitted. "But I'll get there."

Baine studied him closely, his hand still on the elevator door.

"Ben? Are you all right?" Stef's soft voice trailed through the air, and Ben watched Baine's face gentle, even as he was already turning to face her.

A clap on his shoulder had him glancing back.

Baine nodded, stepped back and released him. "Yes," he said. "You will."

———

It was much later that the apartment was empty of everyone save the dogs, Fred curled up next to the couch, Sweetheart on Stef's lap, her fingers running through the soft, white fur.

Still, he couldn't imagine how the fuck she'd tamed the beast that Sweetheart had been—except that she'd tamed him, too . . . or perhaps, she'd soothed him.

Just like she'd soothed the jagged edges of Sweetheart missing his mom.

He sat on one end of the couch, Stef's head on his thigh.

And just as she ran her fingers through Sweetheart's fur, he stroked lightly through the locks of her hair, slowly undoing the braid she'd said was hurting her scalp.

"Is your ankle bothering you? Do you need your pain medicine?" he asked once it was out and the tangles were loosened, his voice soft, not wanting to break her relaxed state.

"No," she murmured.

He went back to stroking, memorizing the lines of her face, and for long minutes, neither of them spoke.

"I was going to cook for you," she whispered, and he

blinked, pulling himself from the very quiet place he'd drifted into, calmed by her presence, thankful and happy to just be here, that she was safe and happy.

"What were you going to cook?" he asked.

"The one thing I can make that isn't breakfast. It's nothing fancy, a chicken and rice soup with vegetables. I'd just . . ." She swallowed. "I'd just needed to put the rice in it when I got there and . . ."

Quiet again.

He continued moving his fingers through her hair, not changing the rhythm, soothing her until she found her words again.

"Anyway, I'd wanted to cook for you because I'd finally realized you weren't like them—no, I'd always known you weren't like them. I was just too scared to let you in because . . ."

He'd gone stiff, fingers stilling, but forced himself to relax, to breathe, to resume his stroking.

"Because no one around me has ever really cared about me. Not my parents. Not my brother. Not anyone I dated." Her tongue darted out, danced across her bottom lip. "Not until I met Heidi, and she introduced me to the girls and . . . even then, I didn't believe it."

He inhaled.

She sat up carefully, putting Sweetheart on the floor. The dog grumbled at being displaced but curled up next to Fred and closed her eyes. Stef's face was soft as she shifted and studied Ben's face. "And then you came into my life, rather auspiciously." She smiled and touched his cheek, so gently, her brown eyes blazing with love. For *him*. "You showed me what it was like to have someone care for me. Showed and *showed* me until I actually started to believe it. Until it propelled me to look into myself and realize that I *was* worth someone's love."

"Stef," he whispered, his heart breaking for her, breaking and reforming. For her.

"You didn't press me to tell you why I held back," she said. "You just showed me that you'd take me as I was, that every day you would be there when you promised you would." Her voice dropped until it was barely audible. "And I've never had that. Or at least, not that I could remember."

She winced, trying to turn to face him, so he carefully tucked a pillow behind her back and shifted around, moving to the other end of the couch, easing next to her propped-up foot and sitting so he could see her more easily.

"You told me a story once," she said. "So, I'm going to tell you one now."

He nodded.

"My brother was born just a year after me." Her throat worked. "Chance and I were Irish twins, but in reality, we were more like real twins. Babies at the same time, and once we were both walking and running, we hit most of those kid milestones at the same time—learning to read, playing catch, silly things like singing songs and dancing. He was ahead, I was behind. Always. He rode his bike first, tackled the scary obstacles at the park, the mean kids at school. He was . . . larger than life, and really, *really* good at everything. It was easy to get lost in his shadow, easy to disappear." Her eyes met his and drifted away. "My parents didn't notice when I scored a goal in soccer because he scored three, or scraped my knee learning to ride my bike because he was launching himself down steps or curbs or finding some new obstacle to tackle."

Ben reached over and grasped her hand, ran his finger over the back of it.

"And I probably should have been jealous of him, but Chance was . . . wonderful and I loved him. He had this spirit that surrounded him, a cloud that attracted people to him like flies. He was confident, bordering on cocky, but he was also kind. He didn't pick on people, even if they were . . . pale shadows of him."

Ben squeezed.

"Then he got sick," she whispered. "Or maybe he was always on the edge of that. He lived a big life, but he also lived big downs. *Always*. And when we were ten—well, he was ten and I was almost eleven—things turned darker. Those lows grew until there were hardly any highs, until he couldn't get out of bed, until he'd lost joy in everything. Wouldn't go to school, wouldn't *live*. And my parents started bringing him to doctors, rightfully so. Therapists and medical doctors, so many specialists that it almost became an obsession."

She stared at the TV, blank as it was. "There wasn't a day he didn't spend with the doctors, or that my parents weren't researching, or on the phone searching for a way to make him better. Therapy didn't help, not for long anyway. He'd dive again, and they'd start over, but they couldn't get the medication right. He'd seem fine for a few days and then suffer."

A deep breath released slowly. "For ten years we lived and breathed that, everything on hold, all of us just barely existed. I didn't do anything but go to school and come home, and even at school, I existed as a buffer between Chance and anything that might knock him off track. If he couldn't go one day, I didn't go. If he needed to leave and go home, I brought him home or drove him when I was old enough."

A tear trailed down her cheek, and he longed to wipe it away, to take her in his arms, but he didn't want to stop her from telling her story.

So, he just clung to her hand and offered the only thing he could.

He listened.

"But eventually, I just couldn't do it anymore. I'd already delayed going to college, had stayed and gone to the community one in our hometown because I couldn't leave him, not when leaving might unbalance him, not when I wouldn't be there to protect him." She shook her head. "Then I couldn't breathe, found myself not wanting to. Instead, I was willing to let myself slip down and not exist and . . . that finally snapped me out of it."

"You left."

She nodded. "I had to."

He squeezed her hand again. "Yes, you did."

"I went off. I had two great months. It was amazing living in the dorms, surrounded by people who didn't want anything of me. And then . . ." Ben's throat seized, but he didn't press, just held her hand as she gathered her strength. "He killed himself."

His breath hissed out of him. "Oh, baby," he whispered. "I'm so sorry."

"My parents . . . they didn't explicitly blame me, but I saw the accusations in their eyes, in their sharp words when I returned for the funeral. Why hadn't I been able to give everything when they could?" Her eyes were unfocused, drawn back to that time. "I couldn't stand it, so the moment he was in the ground, I went back to school. Stayed there. Got my first boyfriend, lost my virginity, lost myself in trying to make people love me as much as my parents had loved Chance. But . . . college boys are, as you might remember, not inclined to love truly. They want to party and be free but . . . at the time, it seemed like further proof that I was unlovable, unworthy."

He couldn't stand this, but he had to, not only because she'd endured it, but because she needed him to shoulder this burden, to aid her in letting it go. Slowly, he tugged his hand free, leaned in carefully to cup her cheek, to brush the tears that continued to fall.

"Then I met Jeremy, and he was wonderful. At first. Or I thought he was, anyway, until I met you." She gave him a ghost of the smile. "I get now that our relationship was unbalanced. I gave. He didn't. Not in graduate school, when we met. Not after I moved here, and we were supposed to be building our future." Her hand covered his on her cheek. "I don't know why he broke up with me, why he pushed me away. Maybe part of him sensed that I was too desperate for him, too willing to do anything, he knew it would destroy me, so he turned me loose—"

Ben snorted.

She smiled sadly again. "You're probably right. I doubt it was anything altruistic. But he broke up with me brutally enough that I knew I wouldn't ever go back to him. Even though I was still desperate to feel loved, I couldn't forgive what he did and said and how he left me alone in a new state without a place to live and a broken heart."

"I want to kill him."

A chuckle slid from her lips. "After today, I don't think I would have minded. Especially after what he did to Fred." She shook her head, and he shook his. This woman and her dog, worrying over him rather than herself. "But it's better that he's gone, out of our lives forever."

"Our," Ben said, shifting closer to brush a kiss to her forehead. "I have to admit I like the sound of that."

Her lips turned up. "I do, too."

"Almost as much as I like the sound of *forever*."

Laughter on the air. "I like that, too." She covered his hand with her own. "You gave me that. Gave me a reason to hope, the strength to throw open the door and realize that I deserve more, not the crumbs that someone is inclined to toss my way. I deserve *everything*."

"Baby," he whispered.

"You, Ben," she added softly. "*You* gave that to me."

"I love you." His fingers slid over her cheek, into her hair. She sniffed, and he felt near enough to tears himself to ask lightly, "Do you think I could kiss you, if I'm very gentle?"

More laughter, this time in his ear, her smile beatific. "I really wish you would."

So he did.

THIRTY-ONE

STEF

It was Tammy's turn.

To keep her busy, or really, to keep her from going insane from being locked up in Ben's apartment.

Three weeks since Jeremy had broken into her place.

And somehow, she'd been coaxed into moving in with Ben.

Her condo was on the market, her things packed and moved to his place. The only thing that was missing was a back yard for Fred, not that her condo's had been anything to celebrate. A tiny postage stamp had nothing on it. Plus, Ben had already had grass installed on one of the patios for Sweetheart, and he'd had some workers expand it, so the pups would have more space to run.

It had worked out perfectly, and she was done with being scared and living in the past. She'd told him the dark secrets in her heart, the things that made her ashamed, that had her parents looking at her with disdain.

And he hadn't run.

He stayed.

He'd remained the Ben she knew and loved, and . . .

In the meantime, she convalesced, worked as much as she was able to from home, and Ben still had his hard stop at six, though oftentimes he was home much earlier, working beside her on the couch.

Yesterday, he'd brought home the news that Jeremy had pleaded guilty to his charges and would face both jail time and mandatory rehab.

Because what he'd been looking for that day when he'd broken in was oxycontin, leftover from her first surgery. She didn't know whether that was what he'd been looking for the first time he'd come earlier in the year, but she suspected it, suspected that the vase had just been an excuse to get into her house, one she'd unwittingly thwarted.

Temporarily, at least.

Because then he'd come back . . . and ruined her dinner plans.

She snorted, felt Tammy glance over at her. "What is it?" her friend asked, glancing up from her book.

She'd been reading while Stef watched, as she called it, another "boring pointy-ear show." But there was little to do besides read and watch TV, especially when she wasn't allowed to bear any weight on her ankle.

Tomorrow, though, she'd go back to the doctor, and if all looked good, then she'd be in a walking boot.

Woo-hoo.

The world would open up again.

"I'm just antsy," Stef said. "I need to get off my ass and *do* something."

Tammy laughed. "When's that supposed to happen?"

"Tomorrow. If I don't fuck it up."

"What could fuck it up?"

Stef rolled her eyes. "Nothing, according to Ben, so long as I keep my ass on this couch." She groaned. "Give me something. Distract me."

"How?" Tammy asked. "I'm boring and single and have absolutely no life outside of work."

"Tell me about work."

"You cannot possibly want to hear about that."

Okay, so maybe she didn't. "Tell me about your love life."

"I just told you I was single."

Stef groaned again. "Give me *something*. You're beautiful. Isn't there a guy or girl you're interested in?"

Tammy's voice was pained. "Now you sound like my mother. When are you going to get married, Tammy? You're the only one left, and you shouldn't work all the time. A man or a woman would settle you and—"

She broke off on a fake gag.

"No dating?" Stef asked.

"I'm not interested in turning into one of those sappy, love-struck idiots"—a grin—"no offense."

Stef *was* sappy, love-struck. The idiot part was questionable, she supposed, but she didn't take offense. Not when she supposed that everyone was a bit of an idiot when they were in love, especially when they were in love with a man like Ben.

"Ugh."

Stef blinked. "What?"

Tammy waved a hand. "*That.* You've got Ben-fog going on, dreaming about the man who holds your heart and all the rest of that barf-worthy nonsense." She slanted a look in Stef's direction, contrition in her gaze. "Not that I begrudge you your happiness. It's just . . ." Her lips pressed flat as she trailed off.

"You don't want that."

"No," Tammy agreed. "I don't. I just want to build my career and find success and . . . I guess, I just want to be me before I become an us." She sighed. "I don't know why everyone thinks that's so unreasonable."

She reached out and squeezed Tammy's hand. The other woman was a few years younger, just in her mid-twenties, as opposed to Stef's thirty-five. She had time to find herself. "I don't think it's unreasonable," she said. "Not at all." Another squeeze. "I think it's admirable. You have plenty of time to find someone, or not. And either way, you have time to make that decision."

Tammy smiled. "For a love-struck sap, you're not too bad."

Stef laughed. "Thanks for the vote of confidence."

A buzz had Tammy glancing down at her phone. "Oh, shoot that's the office. I need to take this."

"Go on," Stef told her. "And why don't you take off? Free yourself from my pointy-eared torture. Ben should be home soon, and I wouldn't want to subject you to more sappy lovey-dovey torture either."

Dancing brown eyes. "You sure?"

Stef nodded.

Tammy grinned, gathered up her book and her purse, said a quick goodbye, then answered the call as she disappeared into the elevator.

Stef was grinning as she turned her attention back to her show.

———

A crash woke her up with a start.

She blinked, saw the penthouse was dark, the sun having gone down beyond the windows.

Clearly, she'd fallen asleep. Had Ben come home and let her rest?

Her lips turned up at the corners, of course he had. He'd been nagging her about getting enough sleep so her body could heal properly. She didn't doubt he would have tiptoed by and taken care of the dogs and dinner.

Pushing her elbows beneath her, she sat up and glanced around.

Then nearly fell off the couch.

Ben was standing in the entryway, face hidden in the shadows, a bag at his feet, but there was something about the way he stood that had fear shivering down her spine.

"Why?" he asked, voice chilled as it slid along the air to her ears.

"Why what?"

He strode over, and she saw that his expression was furious and cold and completely unrecognizable.

This wasn't *her* Ben.

She knew that in an instant.

"I could have forgiven the movie being leaked. Thought it was just a mistake, that you loaned it to someone you shouldn't have." His jaw clenched as he crouched in front of her. "But then it was the details about the contract with Talbot Green, the confidential information of my deal to stream to Europe, the specifics about the new algorithm."

His fist banged down on the table.

"Was it worth it?" he asked. "What they paid you? Was it worth hurting me?"

"Ben," she breathed, swinging her leg down and sitting up fully. "I don't know what you think, but I didn't do anything—"

"You used my laptop," he interrupted. "When you came home from the hospital but hadn't gotten one from work yet. You went into my email and shared—"

This was madness.

"I didn't share or steal anything," she said. "This is all some stupid misunderstanding and—"

His voice was deadly soft. "Why did you do it?"

She pushed off the couch, squatted before him, ankle protesting the movement. She ignored the pain, both striking through her heart and shooting through the joint. "I didn't do anything. I promise you. I would never—"

"Except, you *did*."

She grasped his cheeks. "I *didn't*."

"Four isn't a coincidence, Stef," he said, not moving, his deep brown eyes boring into hers. "And you were the *only* one with the movie. The *only* one with access to my email and the other details. I didn't want to believe it—"

"Then don't," she begged. "Because. I. Didn't. Do. It."

Ben went still beneath her. Just stopped breathing, every muscle in his body going rock-hard. But there wasn't any heat in him, in his eyes.

No.

It was ice—pure and simple and biting, almost burning her with the intensity of the frost.

He jerked himself out of her grip.

"Get up."

Stef blinked. "What?"

"*Get up.*"

This time she didn't get a chance to even blink. Ben grasped her arm, yanked her up to her feet, and not all that gently either. Not like the tender, lovely man she'd grown to love.

The man who stood in front of her was a stranger.

He strode to where the bag sat, sitting on that white rug. "Get. Out."

"Ben," she began, wanting to beg, wanting to get him to see reason.

"I'll have your stuff sent back to your place, the realtor take your condo off the market."

Something cracked wide open in her chest. Her trust, her love, that all drifted away like clouds floating across the sky.

She tried one last time.

Because he was Ben. He'd shown that he was different. She wouldn't cower. She would fight for what they'd built, fight to hold on to all that was special between them.

"Don't do this," she whispered.

He bent, grabbed the bag, and strode to the elevator, waiting until the doors opened before he launched it onto the car. "Go," he snapped. "And feel privileged that I won't be suing you." He made a sound of disgust. "I can't believe that I ever thought you were different from *her*. From all those people who just wanted to get close to me, just wanted a piece of me. But you're not, are you? You're just like her. Probably laughing at my idiocy."

"I've never thought you were an idiot," she said. "I love you, so fucking much."

He scoffed.

And lips parting, a shaking sigh emerging, she stifled any further thoughts of begging, of trying to understand, trying to get him to believe her.

Because *fuck him*.

Because he'd given her the strength to do it, but she was the one who'd actually looked into herself and found worth and value, found a woman who could be loved.

Who *deserved* to be loved.

"Get the fuck out," he said in that icy tone of his.

"I'm gone," she said, limping toward the elevator, stopping only to grab her purse off that table in the entry, to pick up Fred's leash and snap it to his collar. He was excited for a moment, probably thinking it was walk time despite the dark skies outside. But when she didn't bring Sweetheart along, when she merely stroked that soft, white head and whispered, "Be good, Sweetie Pie," he slowed, glancing over his shoulder and giving a quiet whine.

Stef felt a sharp crack in her heart, pain radiating through her, but she pushed it down.

"Stay, Sweetheart," she said firmly when the dog started to rise.

Sweetheart plunked back down onto the fluffy bed.

Fred whined again.

That pain pulsed.

But she straightened and made her way to the elevator,

proud her voice was completely neutral when she spoke. "I can't believe that I ever thought you were different," she said, anger drifting in, taking the place of all that hurt. She stopped in front of him, as he still held the elevator doors, despite the warning buzzer inside the cart, telling him to close them. His eyes were chips of ice, but she felt frosted over herself, and merely lifted her chin as she added, "I gave you pieces of myself that I've never given anyone. I *trusted* you. I—"

She broke off, shook her head.

"I loved you," she said and released a long, slow breath.

Then she pushed back his hand, tugged Fred forward, and they both stepped onto the elevator.

Ben stood there. No. Not Ben. Some stranger who she realized she didn't know at all.

The doors began to slide closed.

"And if you thought for one second, I could share with you what I shared," she said, stretching a hand out and stopping them once more. "If you thought I could conquer the demons I held tightly for so long to be with you, then could have turned around and sold your company's secrets for a quick buck, then you never knew me at all."

She let go.

The metal panels shut with a soft *snick*.

The elevator descended.

And then she left.

The first thing she did when she and Fred got into the Lyft she called was delete his texts and messages, block Ben's number, and set about erasing everything of him from her phone. Until she could almost pretend he didn't exist.

The next thing she did was wipe her eyes.

Because she was not going to cry.

Not over a man. Not ever again.

THIRTY-TWO

BEN

He wasn't a man who drank himself into oblivion.
Or he hadn't been.
But he'd changed.
Or at least, Stef had changed him.

Guzzling directly from the bottle of whiskey, he shoved himself into the corner between the TV stand and the windows, staring out at the city lights and ignoring Sweetheart when she nosed his side, probably wondering where Fred was. Well, she'd have to get used to being without him. Fred wouldn't be back, and neither would his owner. Not now. Not *ever*. He'd trusted Stef, given her everything he had, opened his heart and home and—

You never knew me at all.

Her words had echoed in his ear for the last hours, along with her smell filling his nose, her belongings in his sight.

This dark corner was the only place he'd found peace. Where he couldn't see her, scent her, *remember* her.

Except, he had the feeling he would *always* remember her.

"Fuck," he whispered, taking another guzzle.

It would be dawn soon, and he wanted to be black out drunk, to not remember, to—

"What the fuck are you doing?"

His head snapped back, cracking against the TV stand, the bottle slipping from his grasp, pouring all over the floor.

But he couldn't be bothered to pick it up, couldn't be bothered to do much of anything except ignore Claire as she strode toward him, her footsteps loud on the tile floor.

"Did you bathe in that on purpose?"

He flipped her off but didn't otherwise answer.

"Where's Stef?" she asked.

He kept his gaze determinedly on the buildings in the distance.

"Where is Stef?" she repeated stubbornly.

Well, he could be just as stubborn. Doubly so, if necessary. He clenched his teeth together and stared unseeing through the glass.

"What did you do?" She kicked his foot, jarring him away from the window, causing him to jerk his gaze to his. "What the fuck did you do?" she snapped.

"What I had to." His voice was raspy, hardly distinguishable from a growl.

"What does that mean?"

"Stef sold me out." He picked up the bottle. "So, I told her to go. I won't sue her for damages. I can't stomach that, not when—" He lifted it, sucked down some dredges. "I just can't."

"You told her to go?" Claire asked icily. "I thought we'd all decided to wait and see what the investigation yielded."

He sniffed. "I knew how it would go." Maybe if he got a straw, he could get the last little bit. "Knew it was the same as before."

Claire was suddenly in his face, knocking the bottle to the side. "It is *nothing* like before."

Something in her tone had the fog clearing slightly.

"What are you talking about?"

She gripped his shoulders. "It wasn't Stef who sold you out. It was *Spence*. The audit team discovered that about two hours ago." She shook him. "We said that we weren't going to do anything until we knew. You fucking promised and—"

"It was Spence?"

Her nails dug into his shoulders. "Yes."

"Not Stef?"

The pain from her grip focused him. "No. Not Stef."

Fuck. *Fuck!*

It wasn't Stef, and he'd said . . . *oh fuck*, he'd sent her away. He'd told her to go, and hadn't been there like he'd promised, and—

He stumbled to his feet.

He needed to go find her, to apologize, to—

Claire shoved him down. "Do you know what I received the moment I was out of that meeting? The moment I finally had a chance to breathe after spending the last sixteen hours working my ass off for you, for our company?" She didn't wait for him to respond. "I got a message from Stef saying that she didn't steal from Hunt, and that she wanted me to know that, and that she would be sorry to lose my friendship, because even though she was just getting to know me, she liked me a lot."

She heaved him back against the wall. "So you, motherfucker, are not going anywhere. You are going to sit there, sober the fuck up, and figure out how to beg her for forgiveness." A short, sharp breath. "And then you are going to come with me to the office so that we can be there when the lawyers and HR confront Spence."

He reached up, gripped his hair. "I fucked up."

"Yes, you did."

Scrambling to the coffee table, he grabbed his phone off it, dialed Stef's number. It rang and rang and rang, but she didn't pick up. He called again. It did the same thing. And the same on a third time. "Shit. *Shit.*"

"Shut up," Claire snapped, snatching the phone from his hand. "Just shut the fuck up, get in the shower, deal with this shit at work, and start thinking."

"About what?"

"Finding some way to make this up to Stef, even if she doesn't take your sorry ass back," she said. "Because she deserves peace and a fucking apology."

She slammed the phone down on the table and walked to the elevator.

"Eight. Fucking. O'clock."

She jabbed the button to call the metal car.

"Don't be late."

———

He was sober but felt like hell, even more so by the time he'd made it out of the meeting, his lawyers and HR department doing the heavy lifting.

Spence had confessed.

He might face criminal charges.

He'd called and texted Stef dozens of times from the moment he'd realized the truth.

But she hadn't picked up, hadn't called back.

Not that he blamed her.

He'd been . . . awful, worse than those who had hurt her.

"Fuck," he breathed, shoving out of the building and striding across the parking lot. He didn't know what to do, how to get through to her. He just knew that he had to talk to her, to apologize, to try and make things right.

He drove to her place, parked in the driveway, and got out of his car . . . just as she was limping up to her front door.

In a walking boot.

Shit. He'd forgotten that she had the appointment today.

Hurrying out of the car, he moved up the path and got to her porch the same time that she did, taking the purse from her hands.

She didn't fight him, just let him unlock the door and hold it wide for her, as she moved inside. Didn't say a word when he followed her in, when he closed the wooden panel behind himself.

Didn't say a word as Fred bounded over, just scratched his head and disappeared down the hall, the bedroom door clicking closed behind her.

He didn't know what to do, didn't know how to make this right.

So he waited in the hall, silently standing there and feeling like an intruder, and maybe he was.

The door opened, Stef now in pajamas, and she slowed, as though surprised he was still there. But she still didn't speak, only hesitated for a moment then moved into the kitchen.

"How did you get to your appointment?"

It was her right foot that was broken.

"A Lyft."

Fuck.

She turned away.

"It was Spence," he said.

A flash of brown eyes before she looked away. "I'm sorry," she murmured but didn't say anything further as she reached into the fridge and pulled out a carton of milk, grabbing a bar of chocolate and a cup from a bag on the counter. She had gone out and bought groceries, a mug, because her belongings were at his house.

And she was apologizing.

He moved, trapping her between his body and the counter. She didn't react, just broke off pieces of chocolate and placed them one by one into the mug. "I'm the one who should be saying sorry," he told her. "I—I didn't tell you all of my story before. I was engaged right when the company was taking off. She stole from me, from us, and . . ."

"I see."

She poured milk into the mug, pushed against his arm, and placed the cup into the microwave.

Still with her back to him, still hardly acknowledging his presence.

"I assumed wrong, and I treated you . . ." He blew out a breath, stared down at his feet, wondering how he could make this right. "*I* was wrong."

"I forgive you."

Surprise had his eyes flying up. "You forgive me?"

"I do."

But there was something off with her voice, with her expression.

"I forgive, but I want you to leave. To not come back. To—"

"Stef, no."

Her throat worked. "I can't hate you because you showed me what I deserve from a relationship, and I forgive you because we all make mistakes. But I can't have you in my life. You need to go."

"Stef," he said, getting onto his knees, grasping onto her thighs. "I'm literally begging you to give me another chance. To let me be the man you deserve."

Silence as she studied his face closely.

"No."

His heart sank.

"Leave, Ben. And don't come back."

He didn't know what to say. He didn't know how to make this right, couldn't treat this like a business deal that had gone this wrong, couldn't salvage something this fucked, and he certainly didn't have the words to ensure she gave him another chance.

So, he did the only thing he could.

He walked out the front door and left Stef to her life.

THIRTY-THREE

STEF

T he letter arrived the next morning, left on her front
porch.
        But she didn't open it.

Just set it on the counter, met her Lyft out front, and went
to work, her first day back in weeks.

Heidi took one look at her and opened her mouth, but Stef
merely lifted a hand and begged to give her an explanation
another time. Preferably never, but she knew she wouldn't be so
lucky, so she just had to hope that it would hurt a little less by
the time she was interrogated by her friend.

Then she'd worked.

Straight through breaks and lunch and all the way until it
was time to leave. Heidi had only spoken to her about non-work
stuff once, asking softly, "Are you okay?"

To which she'd answered, "No, but I will be."

And when she got back home that evening, saw the letter on
the counter, she read it . . . and it didn't change anything. He'd
explained more in depth about his former fiancée, who betrayed

him and hurt his business right when it was just getting underway, but . . . it didn't make one fucking bit of difference.

Not when he'd thought she was capable of that.

Not when she'd thought he was different, and he'd broken that trust.

Not when . . . she had loved him and—

So she forgave him because she understood how the past might hurt someone, might make it so damned difficult to live in the present . . . but she'd given him every part of her, and he'd thrown it back into her face.

She wasn't a punching bag. She deserved respect.

One apology and a letter didn't erase that.

———

Flowers arrived the next day. Sunflowers, in fact, which were her favorite, of course. She'd expect nothing else of Ben, the sweet Ben, trying to win her over.

She wanted to throw them in the trash.

Because when would he become angry Ben again?

Despite that, the cheerful yellow blooms stayed on her counter, and every time she looked at them, her heart melted a little bit.

She hadn't told him her favorite, but he'd found out.

Stupid? Yes.

But just because she kept the flowers didn't mean she was going to let Ben back into her life.

———

There was a car in her driveway.

She wanted to ignore it, but the driver exited it the moment she stood on the porch, pausing to lock her door.

"Ms. McKay?"

BAD SWIPE 649

Stef glanced up.

"I'm to drive you to work."

She sighed, thought about arguing, but instead just canceled the Lyft she'd ordered, allowed the driver to assist her into the car, and accepted the ride.

She didn't want to be late.

———

Chocolates and a fridge full of groceries.

A new leash and collar for Fred.

A *Stargate* script signed by the whole cast.

The car at her disposal, every single day.

And more flowers, so many sunflowers that her condo threatened to explode with them.

But not her promised belongings.

She only had the bag he'd packed, the minimal clothes, and when she had unblocked his number to ask him for the rest of her things, he'd said she was welcome to get them herself.

She was welcome to go to his place and pack them up.

Seriously?

The balls on the man.

She hadn't responded.

But he had.

I love you.

He'd sent that multiple times per day.

Along with,

I'm sorry. Please give me another chance.

And both were punctuated with pictures of Sweetheart.

She should have blocked his number again, but those pictures had her hesitating, and she didn't reply to any of the messages, nor pick up the phone calls he made morning and night.

Though she listened to the voicemails he left.

Over and over again.

Sick. She was absolutely sick.

But she didn't block him.

Or throw out the sunflowers, the script. She ate the chocolates, used the leash, and when she came home from work to find the box on her porch, she nearly began crying.

Because inside was a hoodie.

One of Ben's, the spiced scent in her nose, the worn material like velvet on her skin. She'd put it on, and hadn't taken it off, hadn't turned away the food he'd had delivered, nor the custom walking boot adorned with her name in pink glitter that arrived the next day.

"Fuck," she whispered, holding it close to her chest.

Fred had jumped on the couch and cuddled close, and she knew that it was the hoodie. He'd gone crazy looking for Ben the night before, when she'd come in with the sweatshirt.

She knew the feeling.

"Oh, Ben," she whispered, running her fingers over the boot. "What are you doing?"

What was *she* doing? She was miserable without him, missed spending time with him, sitting on the couch, watching TV, eating together, making love, and staying up all hours of the night talking.

But if she went back to him, accepted his groveling and apologies, what did that make her?

She'd fought to be strong, fought to finally find her worth, and if she accepted back a man who'd talked to her like that, who'd kicked her out of his place without cause, without talking it through with her, then how could she say she was whole, that she was valuable and worthwhile?

She couldn't.

She just . . . couldn't.

Sighing, she set the boot on the floor, curled up with Fred, and lost herself in the world of fantasy.

It was so much better than real life.

———

"All right," Heidi snapped, tossing down her notebook. "We're done for today. Everyone out."

They all froze and looked at each other, weighing her seriousness and judging it to be fierce. They'd had a shit day, experiments going wrong, data going missing.

Because of Stef.

Because she'd been up half the night trying to figure out if she could call Ben and thank him for the boot.

Stupid, huh?

Heidi cleared her throat, and she along with the interns, rose and move toward the door.

"Not you."

Stef glanced up, saw her boss's eyes fixed on hers.

Fuck.

The girls had come over a couple of days before, and she'd told them everything. They'd been suitably upset for her and absolutely furious at Ben. Including Claire, who'd surprised Stef by showing up at all, and who'd chimed in additional details as they'd all cursed all of Ben's bad character traits.

That had felt good—that they all were on her side.

But it had also felt bad.

Because she'd realized that for all the bad in that one moment in the penthouse, she'd missed their time together, missed . . .

Ben.

She missed him.

There. She admitted it.

Was that such a terrible thing?

She kind of thought it was.

"What are you doing?" Heidi asked, once everyone else had gone.

Stef blinked, glanced up. "What do you mean?"

"I mean, you're absolutely miserable, but you haven't even talked to him," Heidi snapped, tossing up her hands as she moved around the lab table. "I *mean,* you're in love with the man and he fucked up, but he's spent the better part of the last two weeks trying to make it up to you."

"That—"

"Doesn't mean what he did was right," Heidi said. "Of course, it doesn't. But you're miserable and he fucked up and he's apologized. I want to flay him open for hurting you, but, babe, he's *trying to make it right.*"

Stef swallowed hard.

"He's going to mess up," Heidi said. "That's part of being a fucking human. But part of being a good person, a good man, is what he does in the wake of that."

Stef's heart pounded, her pulse shuddering through her veins. She closed her eyes, letting Heidi's words wash over her, remembering all the things Ben had done, both before and after that one horrific moment in the penthouse, remembering that moment, too.

And how she hadn't broken.

How she'd stood up for herself.

She could have done better, too, could have refused to leave, shouted and fought until he heard her.

She'd left.

But she also hadn't withered and made herself small.

Stef sank onto her stool as the realization struck home, echoing through every part of her—she wasn't going to be that person again, the girl used by everyone.

"No matter what," she whispered. "I won't be her again."

"No, you won't," Heidi said.

Her eyes met her friend's. "He messed up."

Heidi nodded. "He was an asshole," she agreed. "Just like we all are sometimes, but you didn't let him walk all over you."

"I didn't," Stef said. "And he's trying to make it right."

"Plus, he's doing it in glorious fashion," Heidi said, her voice lightening. "He apologized with style, held nothing back, and he's not giving up."

"He's a good man," she whispered, and knew it to be the truth.

"Yes."

"And now I have to decide what to do, because we can't go on like this forever."

A smile. "Also, yes."

Stef fell silent.

"For the record," Heidi said. "I think you should keep him."

THIRTY-FOUR

BEN

The elevator doors opened on a ding, but he'd long ago stopped hoping it would be Stef.

He had so much to make up for.

So much to prove.

It might take forever for her to accept him back into her life.

And rightfully so.

He'd been . . . well, words couldn't describe how much of an asshole he'd been.

Pathetic. Angry. Stupid. Horrible. Oh, and he might as well throw undeserving in there as well.

Just for good measure.

He had the TV on in the background, the show a painful reminder, and yet he felt the need to keep punishing himself. Because it was part of her. Part of Stef. And he'd take any piece he could get.

"Stargate?"

He jumped, launching himself off the couch, dislodging a very unhappy Sweetheart.

Stef was here.

Here.

A kernel of hope gathered in his chest, he started to round the couch, wanting to take her in his arms, but she put her hand up, and he stopped in his tracks.

"I missed you," he said. "And I'm so sorry and I love you and I'll make it up—"

Her hand lifted higher.

He shut up.

"You will never, *ever* talk to me like that again."

That kernel grew, spreading outward from his chest. "I promise you, I won't."

"And you won't order me to leave or shut me down." Her shoulders rose and fell on a breath. "You will talk to me. We will work out our problems. Together."

"Yes, honey. I swear to you that we will be in this together."

"And you will also understand that it will take me time to trust you again."

That dimmed the kernel, but he knew it wasn't anything less than he deserved. "I understand. I . . ." He hesitated. "Can I show you something?"

She nodded.

He brought her the stack of paper he'd intended on having delivered in the morning, pressed them into her hands.

She flipped through them, her mouth gaping open.

"I—" Her eyes shot to his. "I . . . you're giving me a *building?*"

"I don't want you to ever think that you don't have a place here," he said, daring to brush his knuckles over her cheek. "So, it's yours. This floor, the rest of the building. It's all yours. You have the leverage, the right to kick *me* out if you want. You *belong* here."

A single tear slid down her cheek. "Ben," she whispered.

"I know you said you forgave me, but I haven't begun to

forgive myself. I'm so sorry. You told me all your weak spots, you found courage to plaster them up and move forward, and I—I broke—"

His voice cracked, tears blurred his eyes.

Soft fingers on his cheek. "You didn't break me."

He sucked in a breath. "I'm—"

"No more apologies, baby. No more looking back." Her lips curved. "You were an asshole. But I should have fought to make you see—"

"I wouldn't have let you."

She stepped close enough that her breath brushed his lips. "Let's call it that we both fucked up—you significantly more than me, of course—" Her mouth curved. "And move on, okay?"

"I feel like I should be groveling more."

"You gave me a *building*." She held up the papers. "And a signed script and chocolate and sunflowers and a glittery boot with my name on it . . . and I'm never giving you that sweatshirt back, not for as long as you live."

"You can have every single one in my closet, all that I haven't bought yet. They're all yours."

"Such romantic words." A grin. "If only we weren't talking about hoodies."

"Would you rather me talk about you?"

Humor in her eyes. "Yes."

"Okay then, let's start with these beautiful, gorgeous brown eyes. I can stare at them for hours and still not discern all the secrets."

"Ben."

"And these lips." He ran his thumb along the bottom one. "I could taste them for days and—"

"*Ben.*"

"—and still never be satisfied." She moaned, but he kept going. "And this heart." He stroked his fingers along her chest, just over where it pounded against her rib cage. "It's huge and brave, and I am utterly amazed at its strength."

"Ben!"

"What?"

"Just shut up already and kiss me."

"I love you, and I just have to tell you one more thing."

"Ben," she groaned. "What is it?"

"I'm going to kiss you now."

She burst out laughing.

And when he finally got to slant his mouth across hers, her laughter slid across his tongue, filled his heart and soul to over-flowing.

It was the best thing he'd ever tasted.

EPILOGUE

STEF, ONE YEAR LATER

She smiled when she woke up.

But she did that a lot now.

In fact, she did it every day, but most especially on mornings like this. Saturday sleep in days and beach days and work days and . . . his arm tightened around her waist, his lips pressing to her nape.

Every day.

She woke up happy every single day.

Because she had Ben.

And herself. That was just as important.

"Morning," Ben murmured, his voice husky as his hand slid down between her thighs. The man had skills like that, could easily arrow right to the spot that would bring her the most pleasure.

Not just in bed, either.

Her whole life was happier.

And not just because she lived in a penthouse, either.

Though she couldn't lie that the view was good. Maybe even incredible, if one considered the naked man in bed next to her.

Okay, not maybe.

It *was* incredible.

Ben's fingers brushed over her clit, and she moaned, shifting her thighs apart so he could reach better—

Right as two furry bodies launched themselves onto their bed.

Ben groaned, not in pleasure this time.

But Stef just laughed. "They know it's beach day."

Ben groaned again, but it was good-natured this time. "I'm up," he groused as Fred climbed on top of him, licking his face. "I'm up."

Except he didn't get up.

Instead, he rolled to the side, retrieved something, and said to Fred, "Give this to your mom, would you?"

And like the good boy he was, Fred turned and deposited whatever it was onto her lap. It took her a minute to fish the drool-covered box out of the blankets, then another to push Fred and Sweetheart back enough for her to sit up.

"What's this?" she asked breathlessly.

Even though she already had a good idea of what it was.

Ben just smirked. "You'd find out if you opened it."

"Or you could tell me."

"Or"—he pressed her fingers to the lid—"you could just open it and find out."

"Or—"

"Stef." He leaned up, kissed her until her lungs threatened to explode. "Open the damned box."

She started to, stopped. "It better not be another building."

"*Stef.*"

She opened the box, gasped, even though she'd already known what was inside. Because the ring was beautiful and exquisite and too much and . . . she loved it. Loved *him*.

So freaking much.

"Will you—"

"Yes!"

She launched herself into his arms, kissing him with every bit of love and joy and affection she possessed for this man. But she only got to kiss him for a few heartbeats before two furry beasts joined in on the party.

Four tongues in the mix wasn't ideal.

But those other three tongues were also her family.

Which, she got, sounded gross and weird and wholly unappetizing.

Still, they were her family, even with the dual doggy breath, even with Sweetheart wriggling between them, licking her chin and Fred knocking the air out of her as he climbed on top of her to settle on her chest.

Even with Ben—

No, *especially* with Ben, smiling down at her as he dodged paws—and tongues—to slide the ring on her finger, proving to her day in and out that he was a good man.

The perfect man for her.

"I love you," she whispered.

"I—"

There was a clamoring in the hall, and they froze.

"Did you ask her yet?" Claire.

"Did she say yes?" Heidi.

"I brought breakfast!" Kate.

"I don't think we should be here." Kels.

"We should definitely be here, if only to get a shot at seeing Ben naked." Tammy.

A cackle. Cora. "I think you're my favorite friend."

The dogs jumped off the mattress and sprinted from the bedroom, as though finally realizing people who would love on them were just mere feet away.

"Sweet Christ," Ben muttered.

Stef tugged the covers up. "What are they doing here?"

Ben winced. "I might have accidentally mentioned that I was going to propose this morning."

She glared.

Another wince. "Does that yes still stand?"

God, she loved him. "Yes," she whispered, rolling so she was on top of him. "It's still a yes. Because my friends are punishment enough—"

"Hey!"

She darted a glance to the entrance to the bedroom, saw her friends crammed into the door. "I said, yes, now go," she ordered. "And shut the door behind you."

They went.

But not before Cora whined, "But we didn't get to see—"

They closed the door.

Stef was left alone with her man.

And *she* was the lucky one to see him naked.

———

Thank you for reading! I hope you loved diving into Ben and Stef's happily ever after! The next book in the Billionaire's Club series is BAD GIRLFRIEND. Find out how Kels for fell for her brothers' best friend...and what her protective brothers do when they find out.

CLICK HERE TO READ BAD GIRLFRIEND NOW >

And if you enjoyed BAD SWIPE, you'll love the small town of Stoneybrooke, its swoony heroes, and the klutzy, lovable heroines who steal their hearts. The first book in the series, TRAIN WRECK, is free to download!

"I laughed out loud all the way through the book, except perhaps

during the sexy scenes. I'm not telling you what I did during those." —Amazon reviewer

The more she falls for Stefan, the more she risks her career... Don't miss the Gold Hockey series. It begins with the over 400 five-star-reviewed BLOCKED!

"Off-the-charts hot, smexy scenes with one of the best book boyfriends I have come across!" —Amazon reviewer

DOWNLOAD BLOCKED FOR FREE >

I so appreciate your help in spreading the word about my books, including sharing with friends! Please leave a review on your favorite book site!
You can also join my Facebook group, the Fabinators, for exclusive giveaways and sneak peeks of future books.

SIGN UP FOR ELISE FABER'S NEWSLETTER HERE: https://www.elisefaber.com/newsletter

———

Excerpt From BAD BOYFRIEND

TAMMY

Are you really breaking up with me via text?

Tammy winced as she read the text message and started to set down her cell.
But it vibrated again.

While I'm in your bathroom?

Yeah, so her timing wasn't ideal.

Sighing, she tugged the covers back and pulled on her robe. Her frumpy, holey, old flannel robe that absolutely dwarfed her and was so unappealing that it had run off more than her fair share of men.

Which was why she only pulled it out for very special occasions.

Her period when she felt horrible and crampy and exhausted and just wanted to veg on the couch and pretend that her uterus wasn't shredding itself to pieces.

The other very special occasion?

This.

The bathroom door cracked open as she was belting it, and a very pretty, probably too pretty for her man walked out. Naked. She picked up his clothes, turned them right side out, and handed them to him.

"This is me breaking up with you. Not in the bathroom," she added when he opened his mouth to say something she didn't want him to say. "Not that we were together in the first place."

"We've been sleeping together for three months."

She lifted a brow. "We've been fucking together. That's it. That's what I made clear from the moment I brought you home from Bobby's."

"That's not—"

He broke off, and she pointed to the clothes. "Get dressed," she ordered, moving to the bedroom door. "I'll clue you in. You're upset because you're usually the one who ends things, and you're used to women fawning all over you because you're pretty." A beat. "And you are. You're gorgeous."

His face went soft, and Tammy remembered why she'd brought him home in the first place.

But the man was getting too attached.

It would be much less messy to end things now.

"But I'm done."

"But—"

"Done," she repeated, having done this too many times to do anything but end it here and now. Adam was a nice guy, and she'd kept him around for so long because he'd seemed on board to be a fuck buddy, but tonight . . . tonight he'd been different.

Tonight he'd made love to her.

Tonight hadn't been about mutual attraction.

He had feelings for her, and she couldn't let that stand. Better to cut ties now before he grew even more attached, before things got messier.

"Get dressed," she said again, exiting the bedroom and walking down the hall, moving to the front door.

It was better to be by an exit.

That made things less complicated . . . and easier to slam and lock the door.

A minute later, Adam emerged from the bedroom, shoving his cell and wallet into his pocket, his eyes blazing, his lips parting as he lifted his arms, preparing to take her in his arms.

Fuck.

She sidestepped, gripped the doorknob, and opened the door.

"Bye, Adam," she murmured.

"We'd be good together."

"No," she said. "We wouldn't."

"You like me."

She clenched her jaw. "Look, you're a nice guy, but—"

He came close, lowered his head.

She put up her hand, pushed him back. "No."

"Tammy—"

"It's not you. It's me."

That finally seemed to penetrate, probably since it was such a shitty line, a crappy thing to say. But Adam at least backed away, his eyes furious. "Seriously?"

Tammy just lifted her brows.

He made a disgusted sound, but she was far too well-versed in this to feel guilty.

"Goodbye, Adam."

A shake of his head, but he didn't say anything further, just walked down the steps.

She watched him get into his car, screech out of her driveway.

Sigh.

Now she'd need to find a new source of orgasms.

Rolling her shoulders, she started to turn to go back inside.

"It's not you, it's me?"

That voice was silk brushing along her thighs, dipping up to test the moisture between them. It was heat in her abdomen, fingers grazing her nipples.

It was . . . instant sexual attraction, the same heady feeling she'd experienced the moment she'd laid eyes on Fletcher King. Eyes catching as she'd strode to her office, blazing blue irises and dark brown hair, so dark that it was nearly black. She'd clocked sexy stubble, a built body, and a great smile.

But he wanted *it.*

It being a real relationship, a girlfriend, a wife and the picket fence. *It* being everything she couldn't give, because she wasn't a relationship, girlfriend, or wife and picket fence kind of woman.

She wanted free . . . and freedom.

More than she wanted the gorgeous man in front of her.

"What are you doing here, Fletcher?"

"I need a favor."

The refusal was already on her lips. A favor that brought her sexy co-worker to her house on a weekend certainly didn't bode well for her.

But then he smiled, and she actually had to force her knees

to lock so she didn't melt into a puddle and . . . *that* right there illustrated just how much she didn't want to be in a relationship.

Because she'd been resisting this attraction with Fletch for an entire year.

Locking her knees, ignoring the melting, denying the temptation of him.

But that sexy smile, highlighted by the setting sun, the warm lights of her porch . . . undid her.

That sexy smile had her refusal staying lodged in her throat.

That smile had her saying . . . *yes*.

———

Want a free bonus story? Hate missing Elise's new releases? Love contests, exclusive excerpts and giveaways?
Then signup for Elise's newsletter here!
https://www.elisefaber.com/newsletter

———

And join Elise's fan group, the Fabinators https://www.facebook.com/groups/fabinators for insider information, sneak peaks at new releases, and fun freebies! Hope to see you there!

BILLIONAIRE'S CLUB

Also by Elise Faber

Breakout

Checked

Coasting

Centered

Charging

Caged

Crashed

A Gold Christmas

Cycled

Caught

Breakers Hockey (all stand alone)

Broken

Boldly

Breathless

Ballsy (April 26,2022)

Love, Action, Camera (all stand alone)

Dotted Line

Action Shot

Close-Up

End Scene

Meet Cute

Love After Midnight (all stand alone)

Rum And Notes

Virgin Daiquiri

On The Rocks

Sex On The Seats

Life Sucks Series (all stand alone)

Train Wreck

Hot Mess

Dumpster Fire

Clusterf*@k

FUBAR (March 29,2022)

Roosevelt Ranch Series (all stand alone, series complete)

Disaster at Roosevelt Ranch

Heartbreak at Roosevelt Ranch

Collision at Roosevelt Ranch

Regret at Roosevelt Ranch

Desire at Roosevelt Ranch

Phoenix Series (read in order)

Phoenix Rising

Dark Phoenix

Phoenix Freed

Phoenix: Lex Tal Chronicles (rereleasing soon, stand alone, Phoenix world)

From Ashes

In Flames

To Smoke

KTS Series

Riding The Edge

Crossing The Line

Leveling The Field

Scorching The Earth

Cocky Heroes World

Tattooed Troublemaker

ABOUT THE AUTHOR

USA Today bestselling author, Elise Faber, loves chocolate, Star Wars, Harry Potter, and hockey (the order depending on the day and how well her team -- the Sharks! -- are playing). She and her husband also play as much hockey as they can squeeze into their schedules, so much so that their typical date night is spent on the ice. Elise changes her hair color more often than some people change their socks, loves sparkly things, and is the mom to two exuberant boys. She lives in Northern California. Connect with her in her Facebook group, the Fabinators or find more information about her books at www.elisefaber.com.

facebook.com/elisefaberauthor

amazon.com/author/elisefaber

bookbub.com/profile/elise-faber

instagram.com/elisefaber

goodreads.com/elisefaber

pinterest.com/elisefaberwrite

www.ingramcontent.com/pod-product-compliance
Lightning Source LLC
Chambersburg PA
CBHW060208030726
47499CB00004B/966